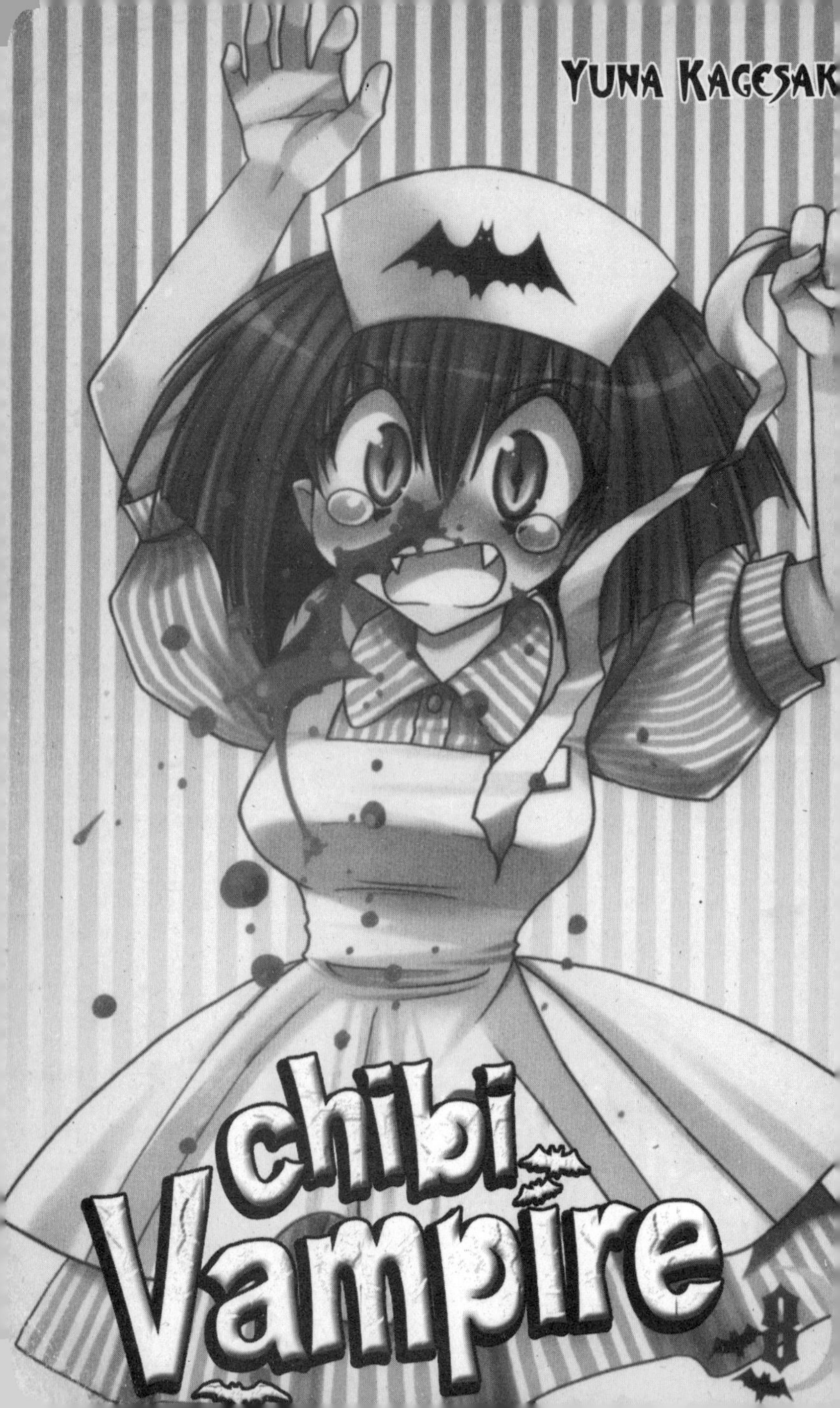
YUNA KAGESAK
chibi
Vampire
8

Chibi Vampire Volume 8
Created by Yuna Kagesaki

Translation - Alexis Kirsch
English Adaptation - Christine Boylan
Copy Editor - Jessica Chavez
Retouch and Lettering - Star Print Brokers
Production Artist - Lauren O'Connell
Graphic Designer - Colin Graham

Editor - Nikhil Burman
Digital Imaging Manager - Chris Buford
Pre-Production Supervisor - Lucas Rivera
Production Manager - Elisabeth Brizzi
Managing Editor - Vy Nguyen
Creative Director - Anne Marie Horne
Editor-in-Chief - Rob Tokar
Publisher - Mike Kiley
President and C.O.O. - John Parker
C.E.O. and Chief Creative Officer - Stu Levy

A **TOKYOPOP** Manga

TOKYOPOP Inc.
5900 Wilshire Blvd. Suite 2000
Los Angeles, CA 90036

E-mail: info@TOKYOPOP.com
Come visit us online at www.TOKYOPOP.com

KARIN Volume 8 © 2006 YUNA KAGESAKI
st published in Japan in 2006 by FUJIMISHOBO CO., LTD.,
kyo. English translation rights arranged with KADOKAWA
TEN PUBLISHING CO., LTD., Tokyo through TUTTLE-MORI
AGENCY, INC., Tokyo.
English text copyright © 2008 TOKYOPOP Inc.

ISBN: 978-1-4278-0113-5

First TOKYOPOP printing: May 2008
10 9 8 7 6 5 4 3
Printed in the USA

Chibi Vampire

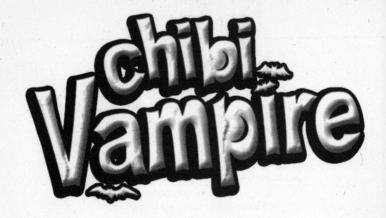

Volume 8

Created by

Yuna Kagesaki

TOKYOPOP®

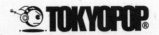

HAMBURG // LONDON // LOS ANGELES // TOKYO

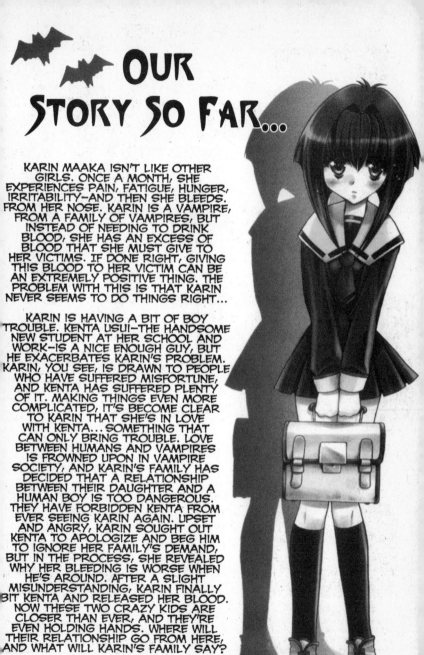

OUR STORY SO FAR...

KARIN MAAKA ISN'T LIKE OTHER GIRLS. ONCE A MONTH, SHE EXPERIENCES PAIN, FATIGUE, HUNGER, IRRITABILITY—AND THEN SHE BLEEDS. FROM HER NOSE. KARIN IS A VAMPIRE, FROM A FAMILY OF VAMPIRES, BUT INSTEAD OF NEEDING TO DRINK BLOOD, SHE HAS AN EXCESS OF BLOOD THAT SHE MUST GIVE TO HER VICTIMS. IF DONE RIGHT, GIVING THIS BLOOD TO HER VICTIM CAN BE AN EXTREMELY POSITIVE THING. THE PROBLEM WITH THIS IS THAT KARIN NEVER SEEMS TO DO THINGS RIGHT...

KARIN IS HAVING A BIT OF BOY TROUBLE. KENTA USUI—THE HANDSOME NEW STUDENT AT HER SCHOOL AND WORK—IS A NICE ENOUGH GUY, BUT HE EXACERBATES KARIN'S PROBLEM. KARIN, YOU SEE, IS DRAWN TO PEOPLE WHO HAVE SUFFERED MISFORTUNE, AND KENTA HAS SUFFERED PLENTY OF IT. MAKING THINGS EVEN MORE COMPLICATED, IT'S BECOME CLEAR TO KARIN THAT SHE'S IN LOVE WITH KENTA... SOMETHING THAT CAN ONLY BRING TROUBLE. LOVE BETWEEN HUMANS AND VAMPIRES IS FROWNED UPON IN VAMPIRE SOCIETY, AND KARIN'S FAMILY HAS DECIDED THAT A RELATIONSHIP BETWEEN THEIR DAUGHTER AND A HUMAN BOY IS TOO DANGEROUS. THEY HAVE FORBIDDEN KENTA FROM EVER SEEING KARIN AGAIN. UPSET AND ANGRY, KARIN SOUGHT OUT KENTA TO APOLOGIZE AND BEG HIM TO IGNORE HER FAMILY'S DEMAND, BUT IN THE PROCESS, SHE REVEALED WHY HER BLEEDING IS WORSE WHEN HE'S AROUND. AFTER A SLIGHT MISUNDERSTANDING, KARIN FINALLY BIT KENTA AND RELEASED HER BLOOD. NOW THESE TWO CRAZY KIDS ARE CLOSER THAN EVER, AND THEY'RE EVEN HOLDING HANDS. WHERE WILL THEIR RELATIONSHIP GO FROM HERE, AND WHAT WILL KARIN'S FAMILY SAY?

THE MAAKA FAMILY

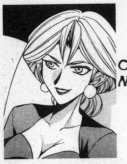

CALERA MARKER

Karin's overbearing mother. While Calera resents that Karin wasn't born a normal vampire, she does love her daughter in her own obnoxious way. Calera has chosen to keep her European last name.

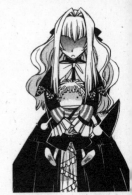

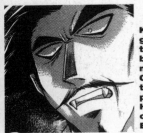

HENRY MARKER

Karin's father. In general, Henry treats Karin a lot better than her mother does, but Calera wears the pants in this particular family. Henry has also chosen to keep his European last name.

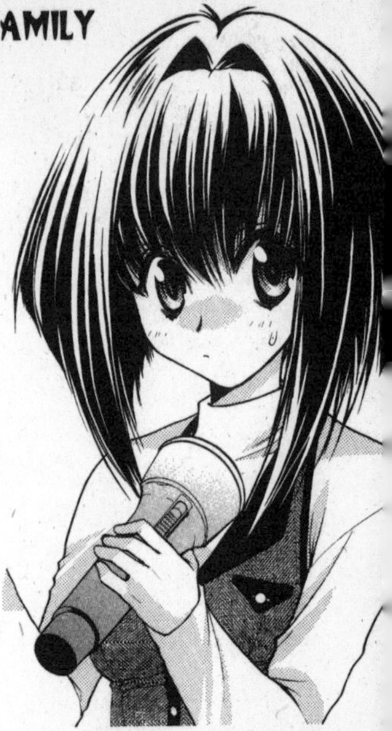

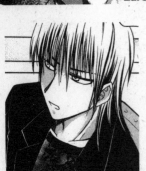

REN MAAKA

Karin's older brother. Ren milks the "sexy creature of the night" thing for all it's worth and spends his nights in the arms (and beds) of attractive young women.

KARIN MAAKA

Our little heroine. Karin is a vampire living in Japan, bu instead of sucking blood fron her victims, she actually GIVES them some of her blood She's a vampire in reverse

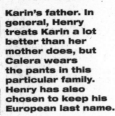

ANJU MAAKA

Karin's little sister. Anju has not yet awoken as a full vampire, but she can control bats and is usually the one who cleans up after Karin's messes. Rarely seen without her "talking" doll, Boogie.

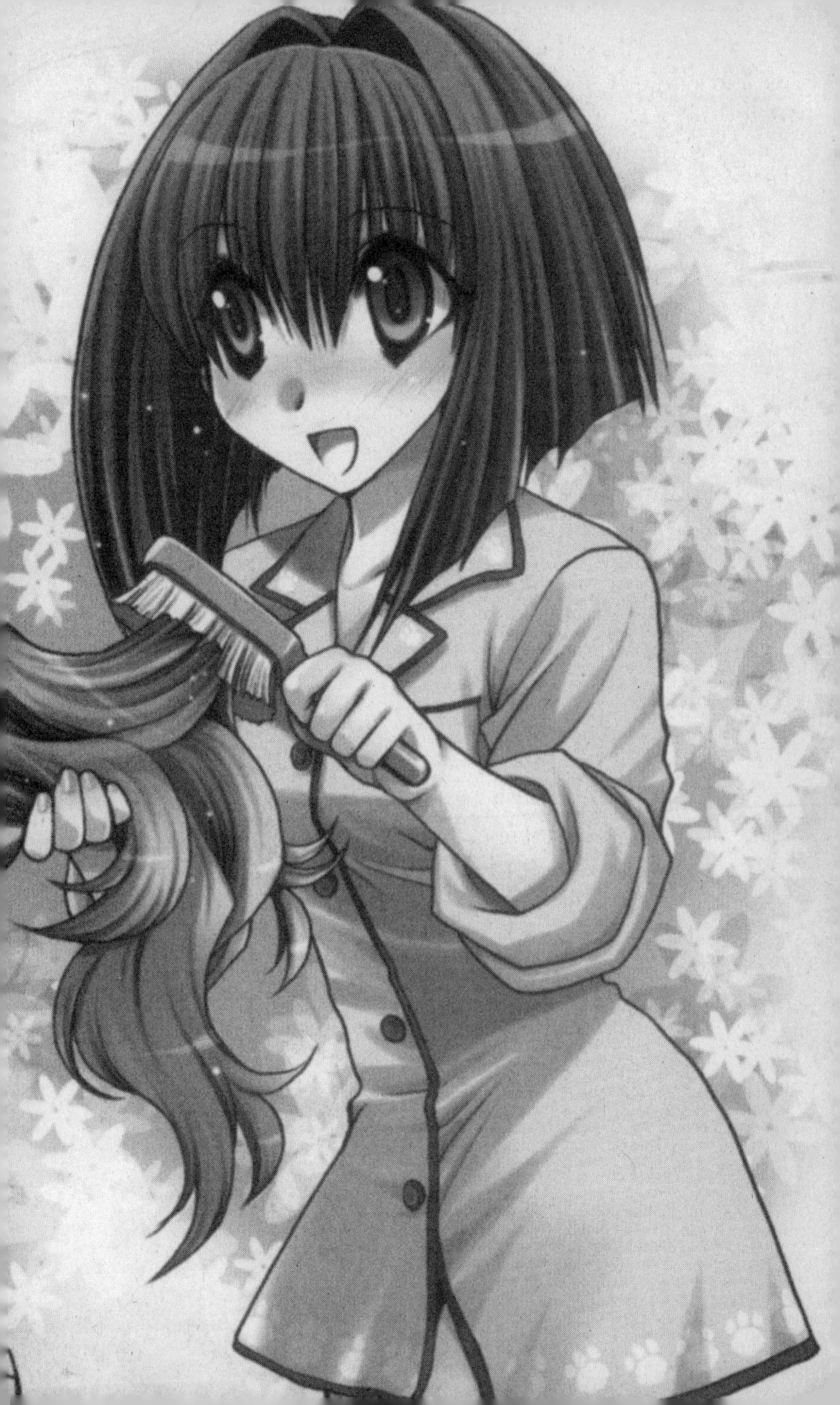

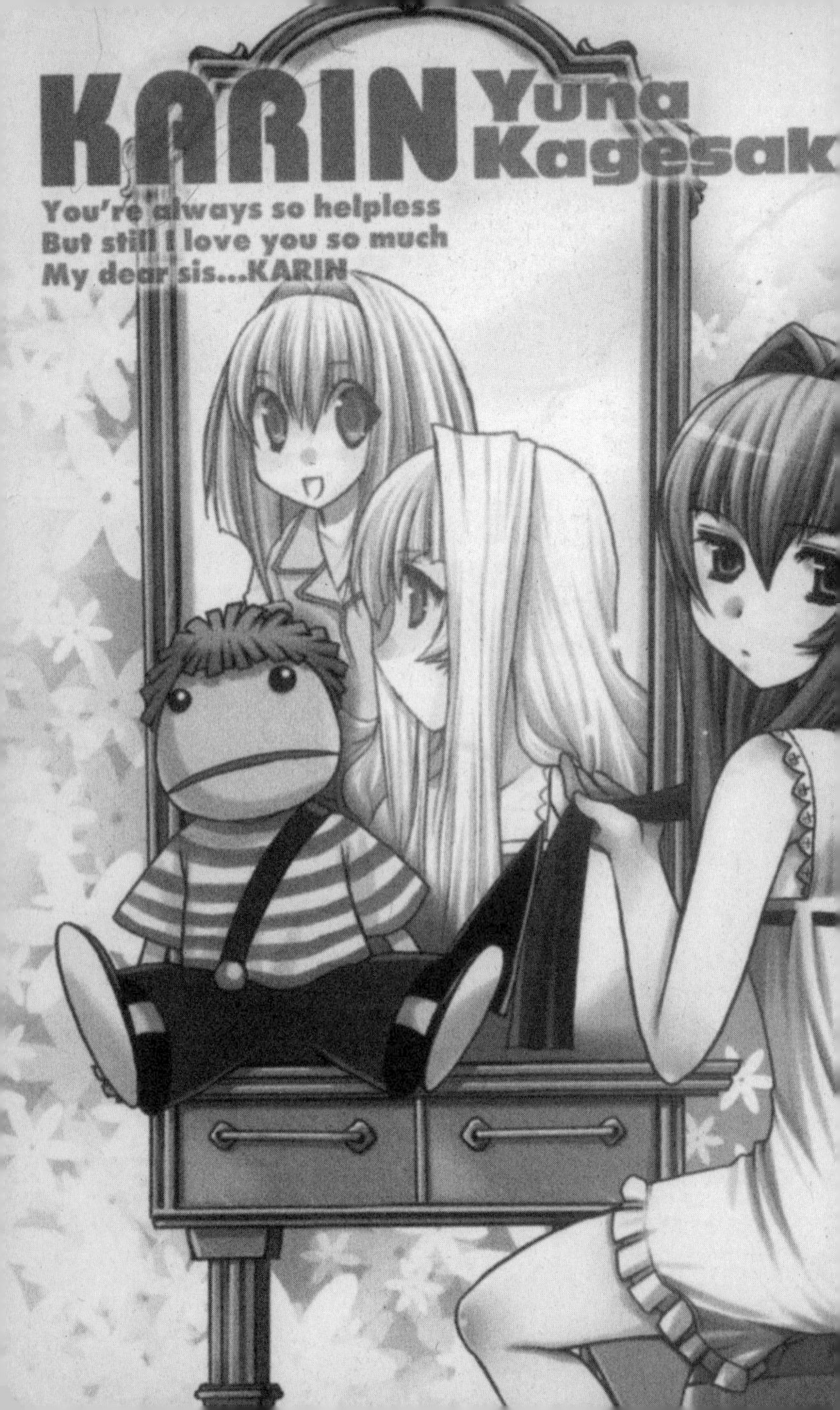

KARIN
Yuna Kagesak
You're always so helpless
But still I love you so much
My dear sis...KARIN

VOL. 8

CONTENTS

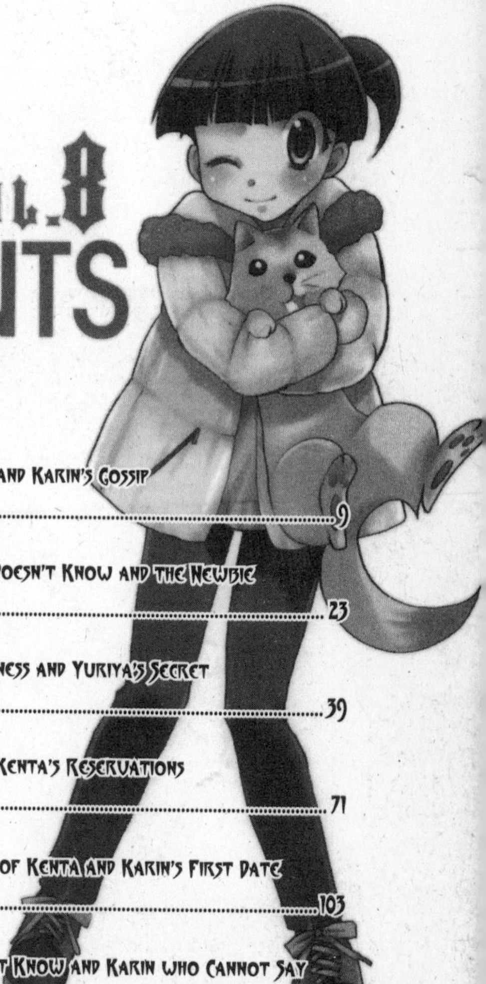

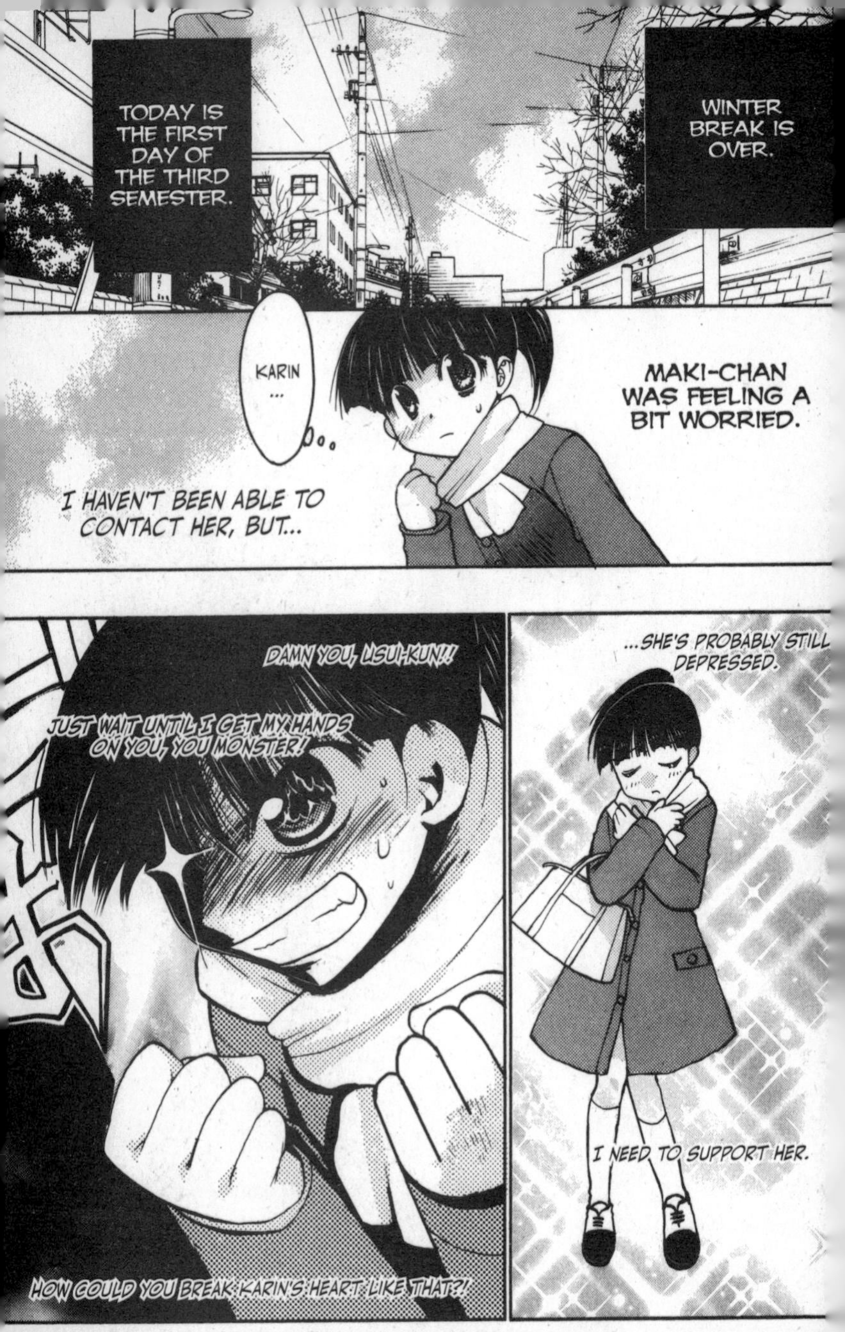
WINTER BREAK IS OVER.
TODAY IS THE FIRST DAY OF THE THIRD SEMESTER.
MAKI-CHAN WAS FEELING A BIT WORRIED.
KARIN ...
I HAVEN'T BEEN ABLE TO CONTACT HER, BUT...
...SHE'S PROBABLY STILL DEPRESSED.
I NEED TO SUPPORT HER.
DAMN YOU, USUI-KUN!!
JUST WAIT UNTIL I GET MY HANDS ON YOU, YOU MONSTER!
HOW COULD YOU BREAK KARIN'S HEART LIKE THAT?!

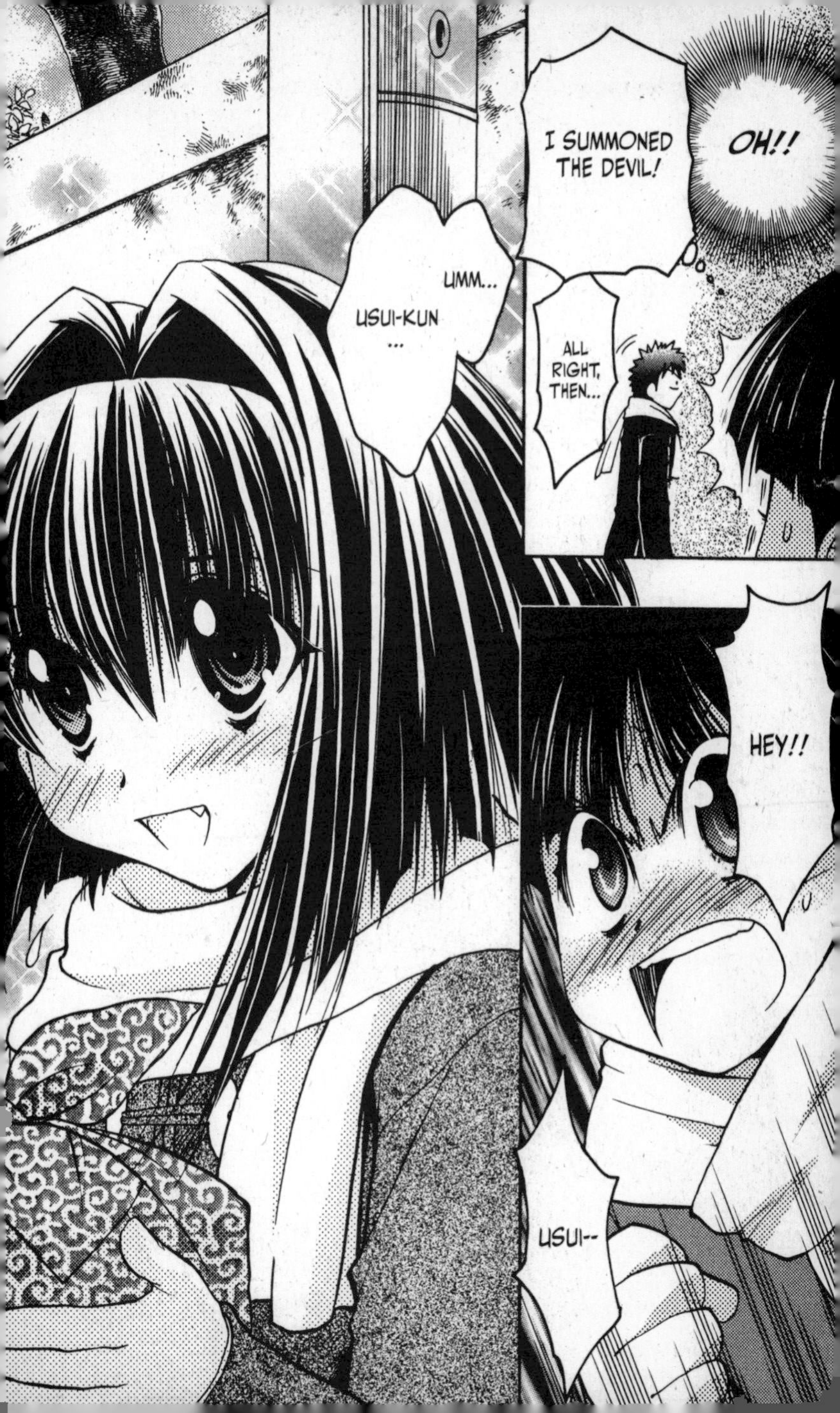
OH!!
I SUMMONED THE DEVIL!
ALL RIGHT, THEN...
HEY!!
USUI--
UMM...
USUI-KUN ...

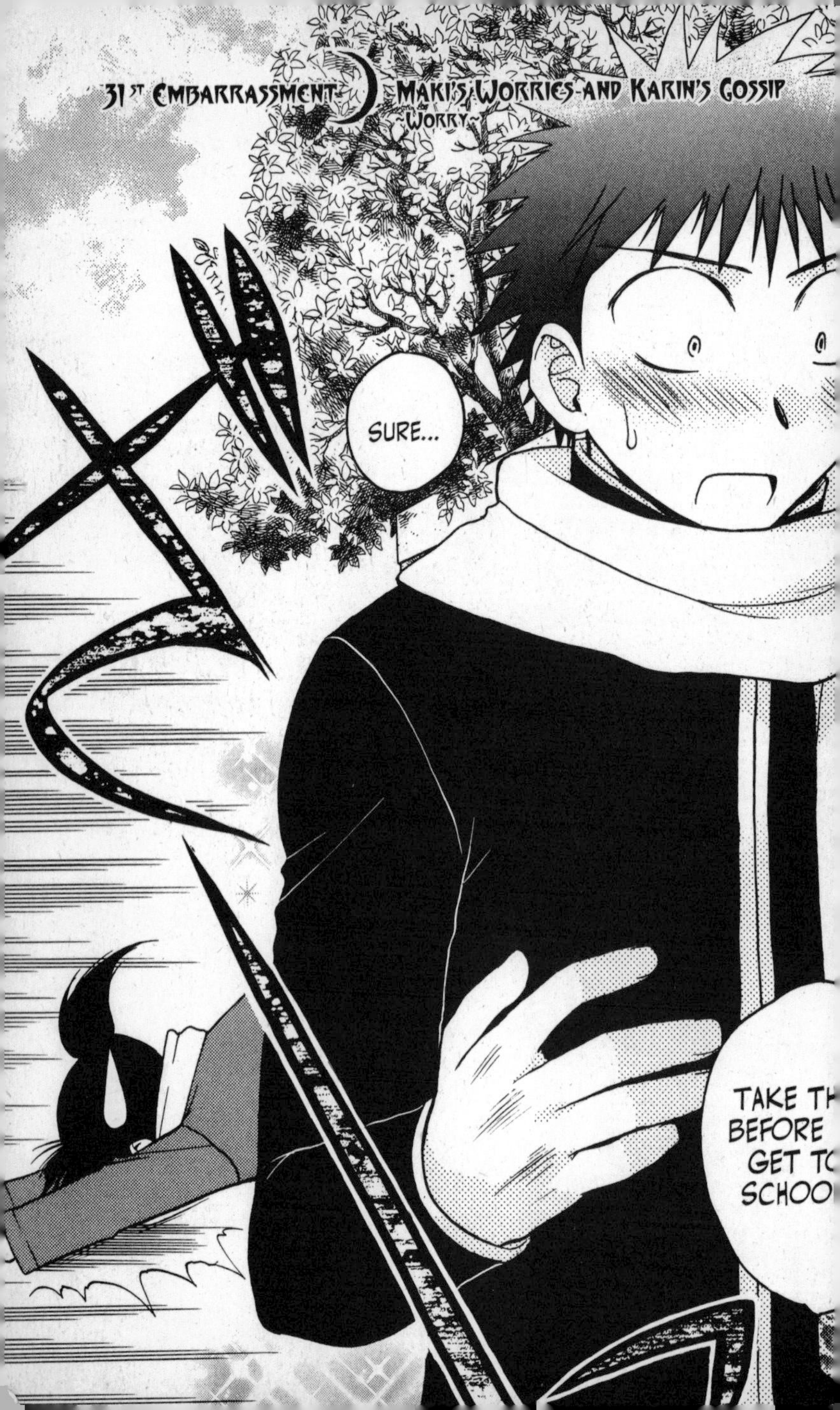
31st Embarrassment Maki's Worries and Karin's Gossip
~Worry~
SURE...
TAKE TH
BEFORE
GET TO
SCHOO

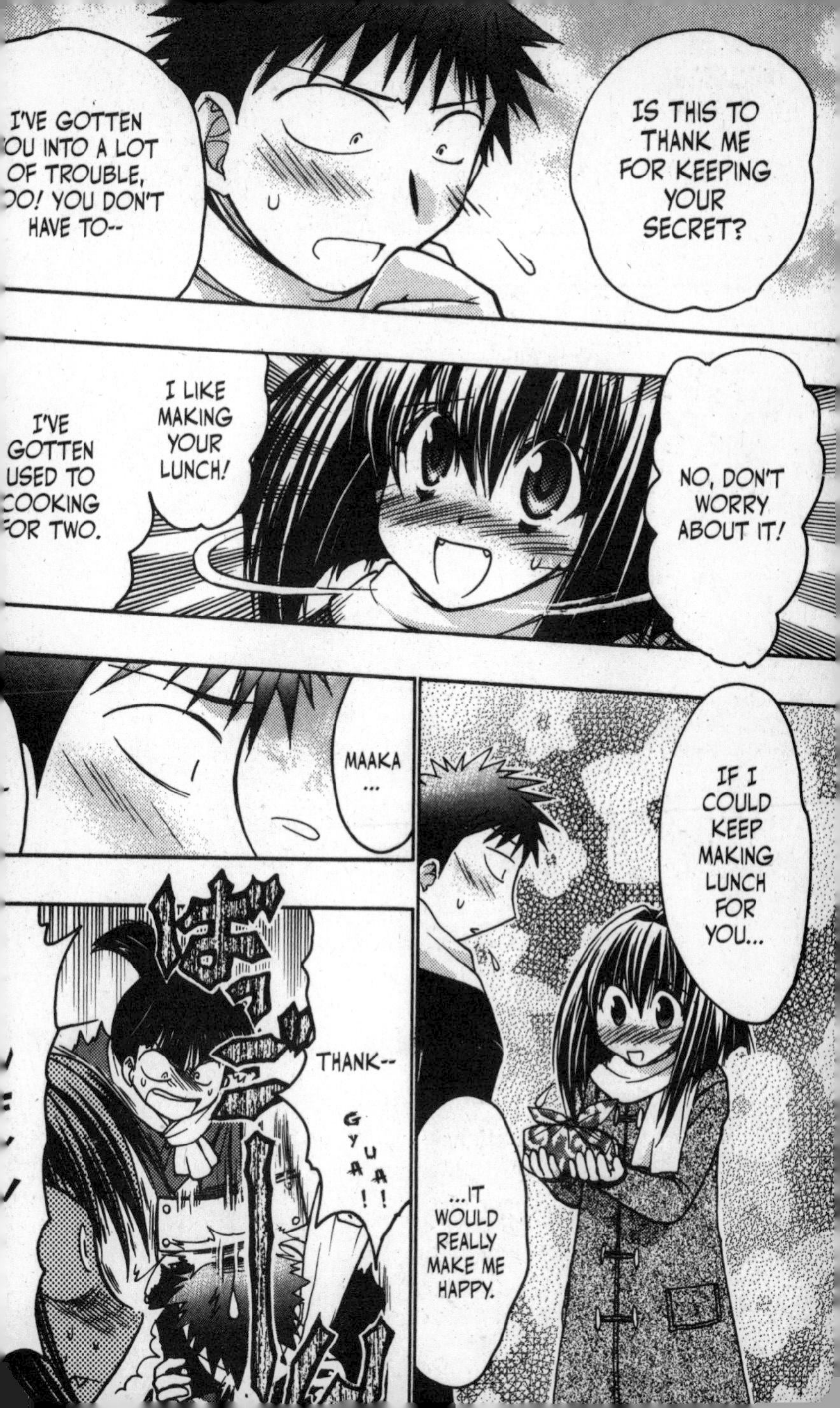
IS THIS TO THANK ME FOR KEEPING YOUR SECRET?
I'VE GOTTEN OU INTO A LOT OF TROUBLE, OO! YOU DON'T HAVE TO--
NO, DON'T WORRY ABOUT IT!
I LIKE MAKING YOUR LUNCH!
I'VE GOTTEN USED TO OOKING OR TWO.
IF I COULD KEEP MAKING LUNCH FOR YOU...
...IT WOULD REALLY MAKE ME HAPPY.
MAAKA...
THANK--
GYAA!
UAA!

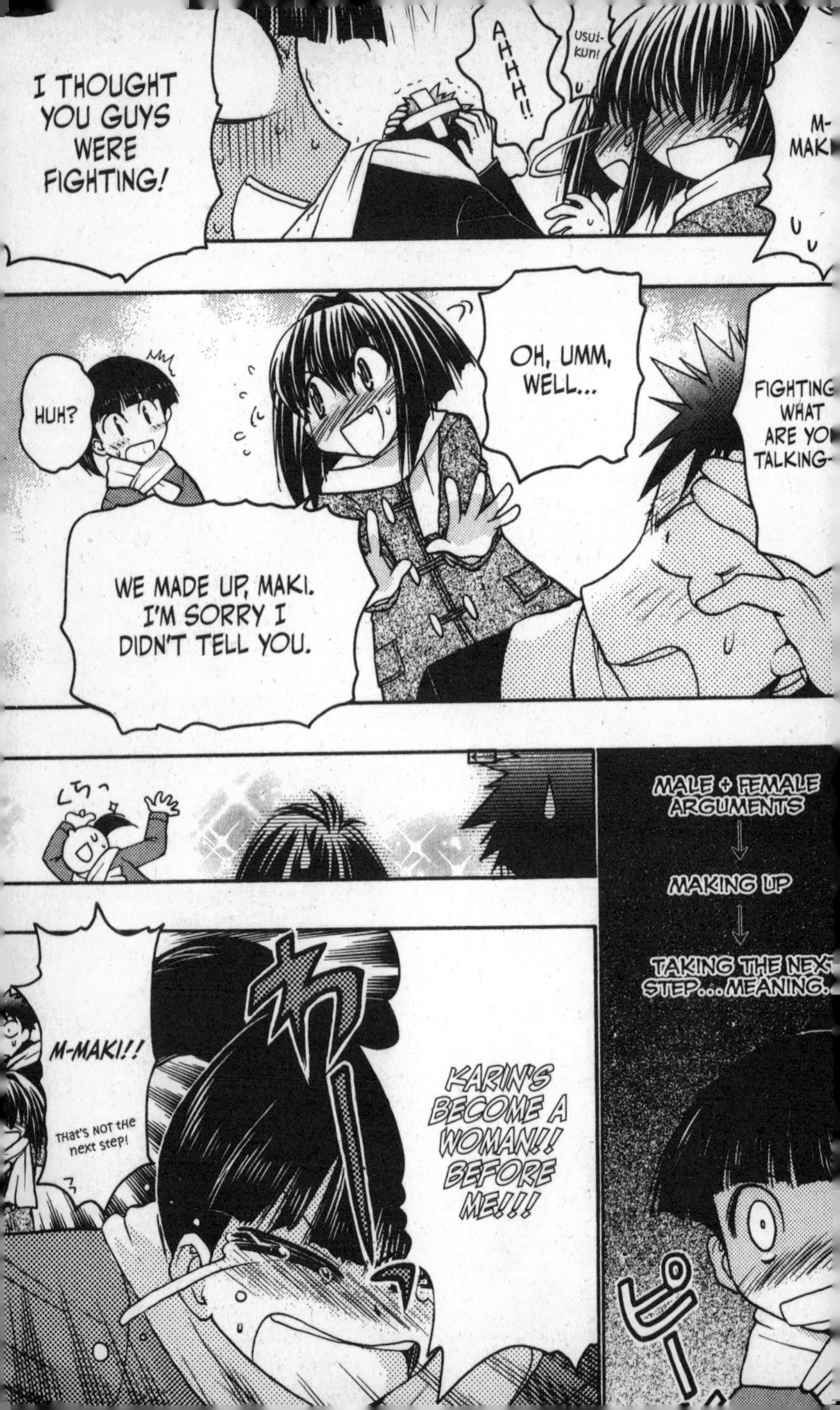
M-MAKI
Usui-kun!
AHHHH!!
I THOUGHT YOU GUYS WERE FIGHTING!
FIGHTING WHAT ARE YO TALKING-
OH, UMM, WELL...
HUH?
WE MADE UP, MAKI. I'M SORRY I DIDN'T TELL YOU.
MALE + FEMALE ARGUMENTS
MAKING UP
TAKING THE NEXT STEP... MEANING..
KARIN'S BECOME A WOMAN!! BEFORE ME!!!
M-MAKI!!
That's NOT the next step!

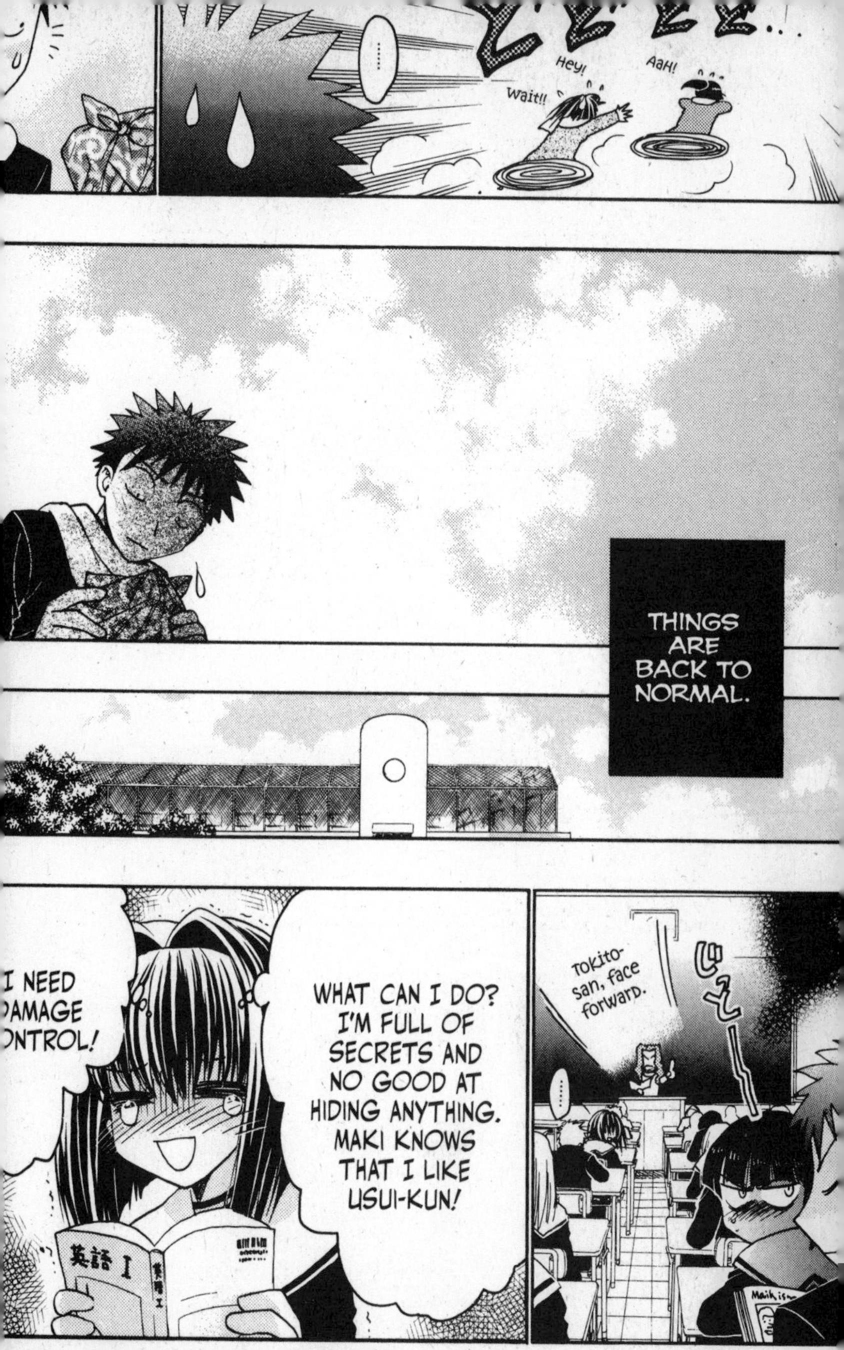
どどどど…!
AaH!
Hey!
Wait!!
……
THINGS ARE BACK TO NORMAL.
Tokito-san, face forward.
じ〜
……
WHAT CAN I DO? I'M FULL OF SECRETS AND NO GOOD AT HIDING ANYTHING. MAKI KNOWS THAT I LIKE USUI-KUN!
I NEED AMAGE ONTROL!
英語 I

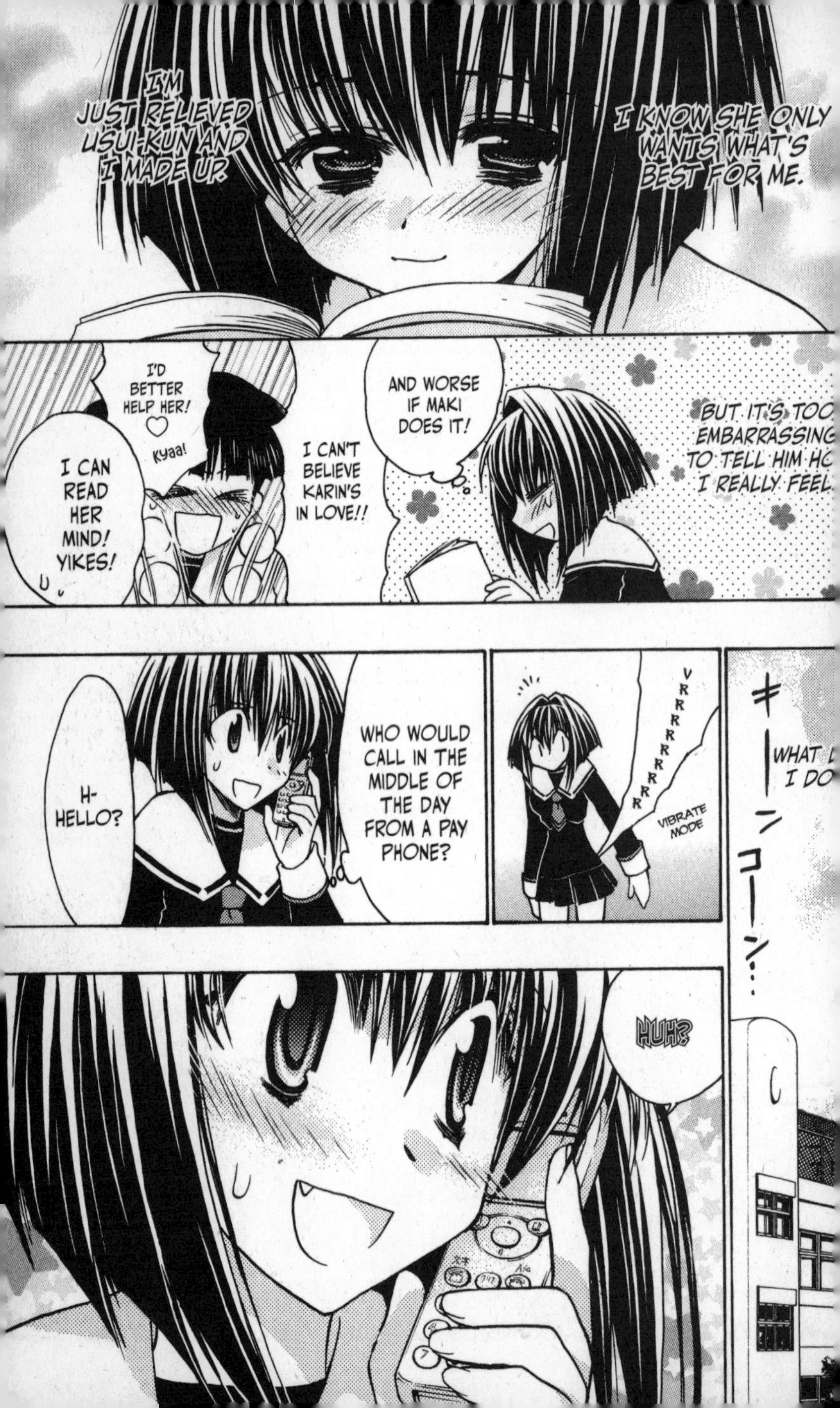
I KNOW SHE ONLY WANTS WHAT'S BEST FOR ME.
I'M JUST RELIEVED USUI-KUN AND I MADE UP.
BUT IT'S TOO EMBARRASSING TO TELL HIM HO I REALLY FEEL.
AND WORSE IF MAKI DOES IT!
I CAN'T BELIEVE KARIN'S IN LOVE!!
I'D BETTER HELP HER! ♡
KYAA!
I CAN READ HER MIND! YIKES!
キーンコーン…
WHAT I DO
VRRRRRRRRRRR
VIBRATE MODE
WHO WOULD CALL IN THE MIDDLE OF THE DAY FROM A PAY PHONE?
H-HELLO?
HUH?

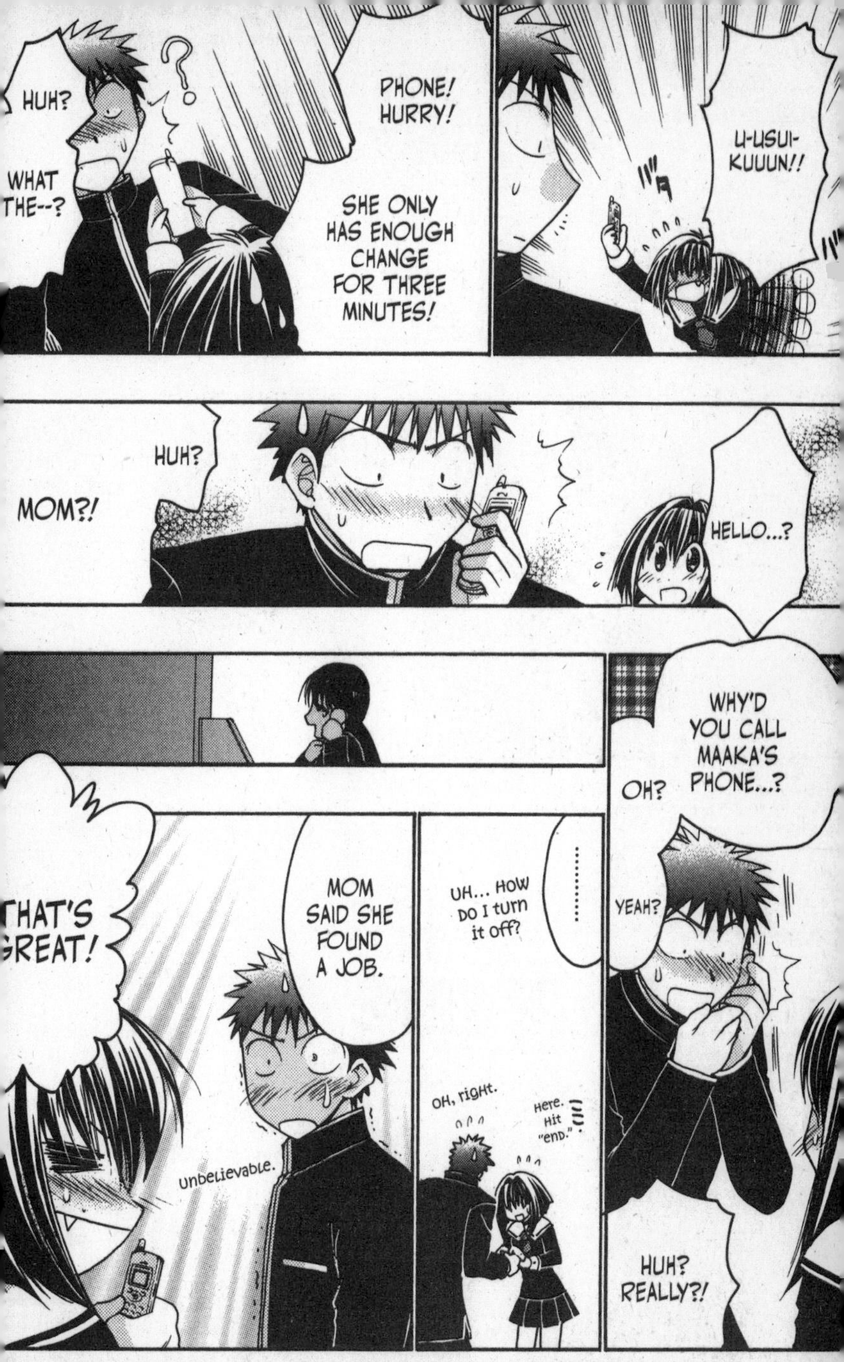
U-USUI-KUUUN!!
PHONE! HURRY!
SHE ONLY HAS ENOUGH CHANGE FOR THREE MINUTES!
HUH?
WHAT THE--?
HELLO...?
HUH?
MOM?!
WHY'D YOU CALL MAAKA'S PHONE...?
OH?
YEAH?
HUH? REALLY?!
....
UH... HOW DO I turn it off?
OH, right.
Here. Hit "end."
MOM SAID SHE FOUND A JOB.
THAT'S GREAT!
unbelievable.

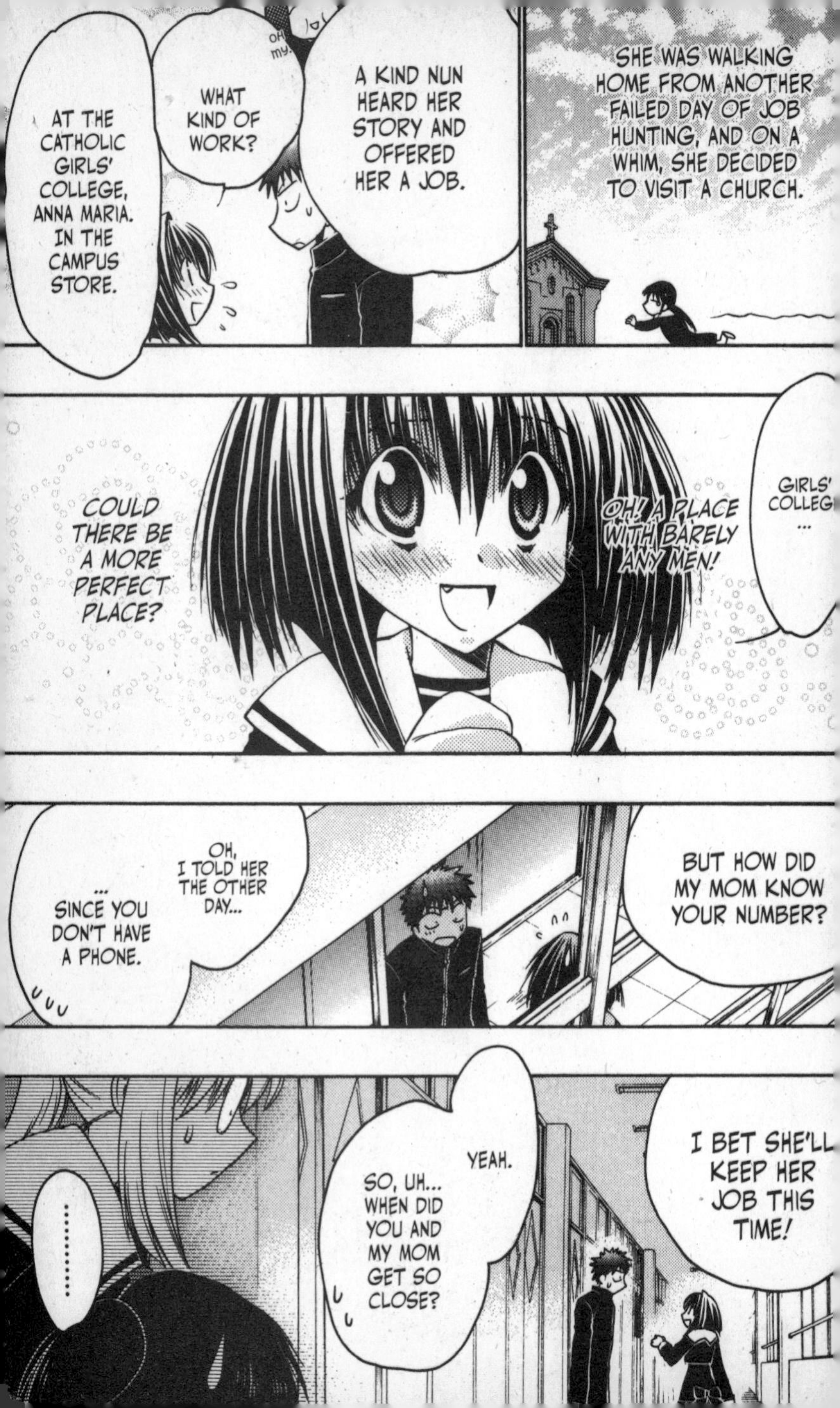
SHE WAS WALKING HOME FROM ANOTHER FAILED DAY OF JOB HUNTING, AND ON A WHIM, SHE DECIDED TO VISIT A CHURCH.
A KIND NUN HEARD HER STORY AND OFFERED HER A JOB.
OH my.
WHAT KIND OF WORK?
AT THE CATHOLIC GIRLS' COLLEGE, ANNA MARIA. IN THE CAMPUS STORE.
GIRLS' COLLEG ...
OH! A PLACE WITH BARELY ANY MEN!
COULD THERE BE A MORE PERFECT PLACE?
BUT HOW DID MY MOM KNOW YOUR NUMBER?
OH, I TOLD HER THE OTHER DAY...
... SINCE YOU DON'T HAVE A PHONE.
I BET SHE'LL KEEP HER JOB THIS TIME!
YEAH.
SO, UH... WHEN DID YOU AND MY MOM GET SO CLOSE?
....

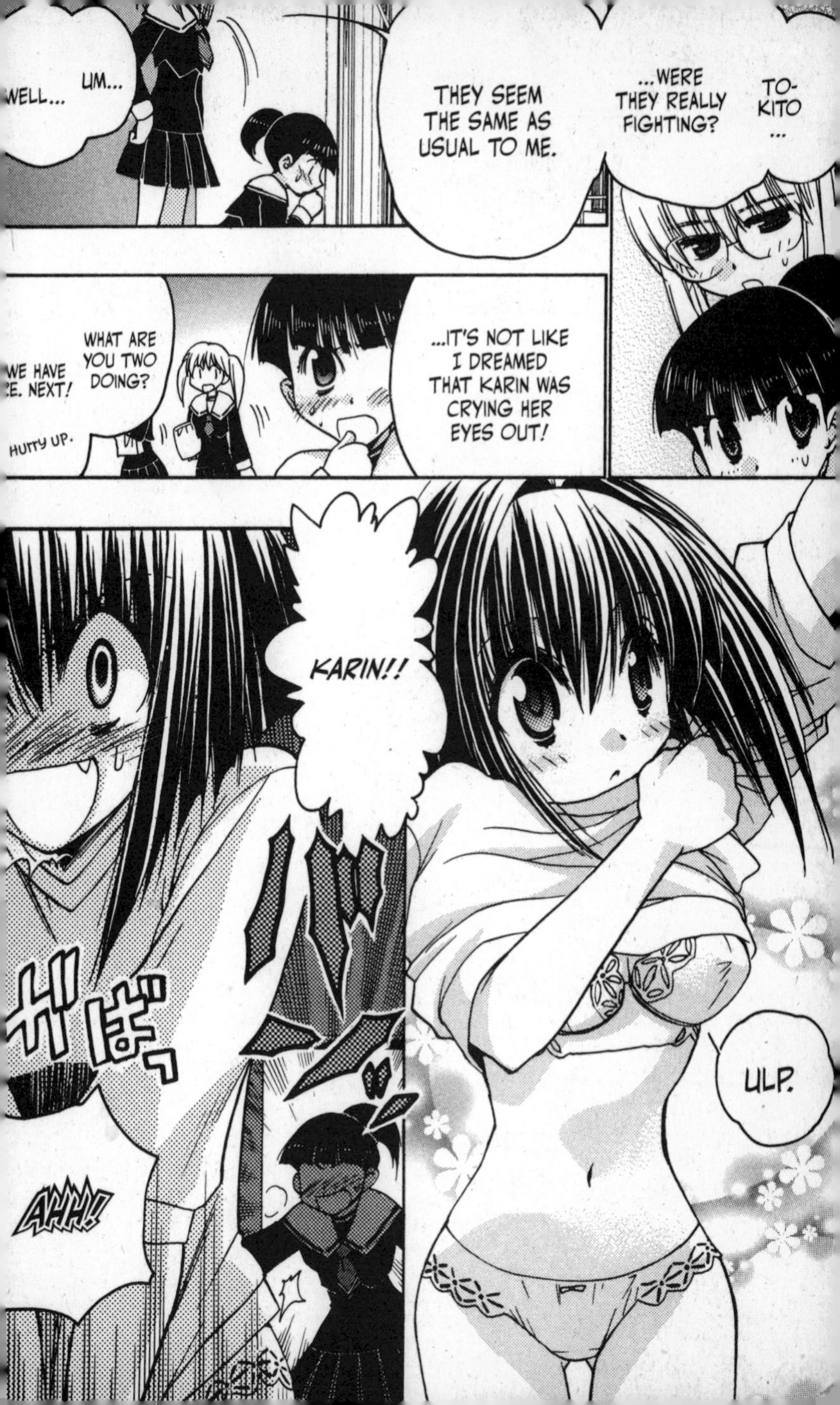
TO-KITO ...
...WERE THEY REALLY FIGHTING?
THEY SEEM THE SAME AS USUAL TO ME.
UM...
WELL...
...IT'S NOT LIKE I DREAMED THAT KARIN WAS CRYING HER EYES OUT!
WHAT ARE YOU TWO DOING?
WE HAVE
E. NEXT!
HUrry UP.
KARIN!!
ULP.
ガばっ
AHH!

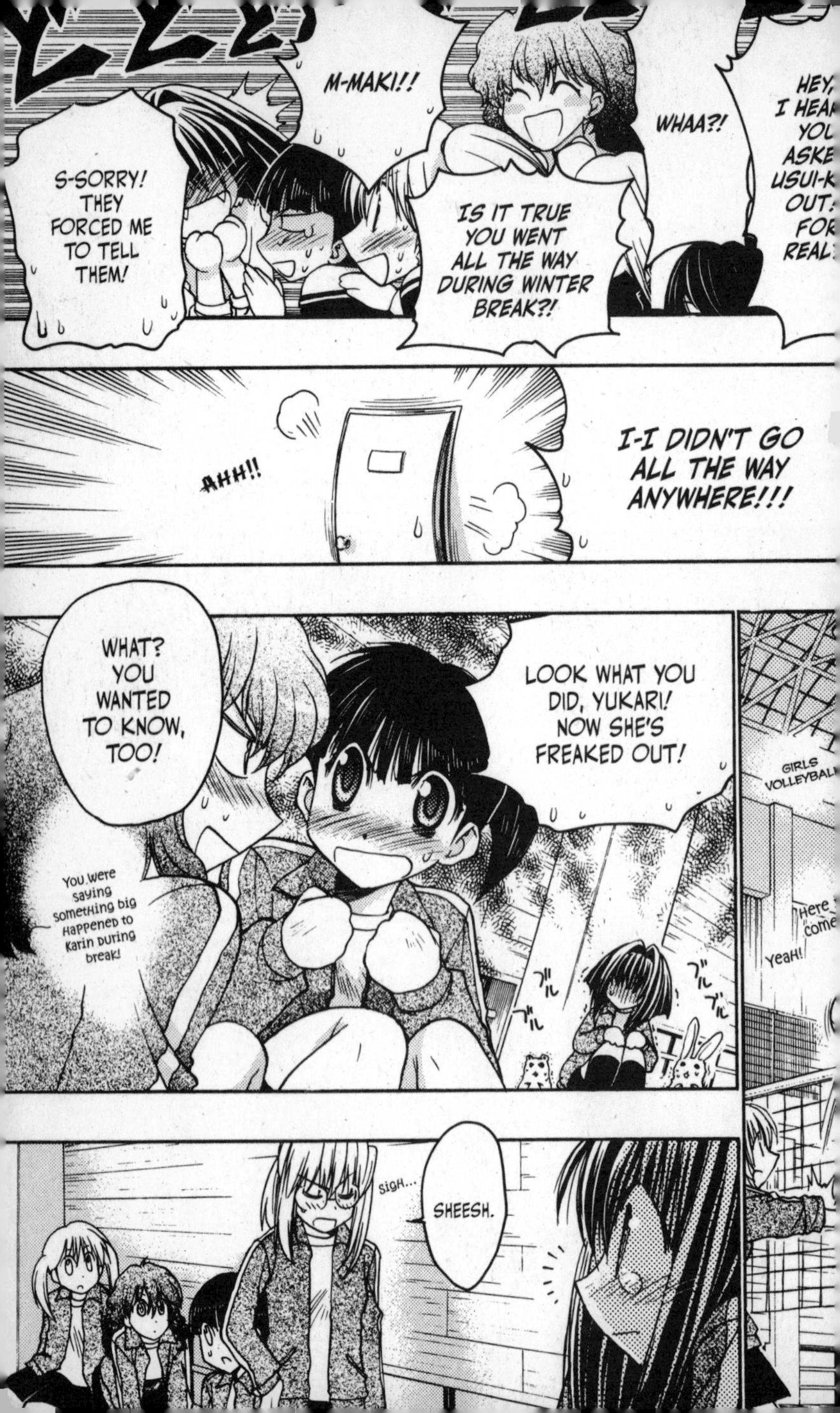
HEY, I HEA YOU ASKE USUI-K OUT. FOR REAL
WHAA?!
IS IT TRUE YOU WENT ALL THE WAY DURING WINTER BREAK?!
M-MAKI!!
S-SORRY! THEY FORCED ME TO TELL THEM!
I-I DIDN'T GO ALL THE WAY ANYWHERE!!!
AHH!!
GIRLS VOLLEYBAL
Here come
Yeah!
LOOK WHAT YOU DID, YUKARI! NOW SHE'S FREAKED OUT!
WHAT? YOU WANTED TO KNOW, TOO!
You were saying something big happened to Karin during break!
SHEESH.
Sigh...

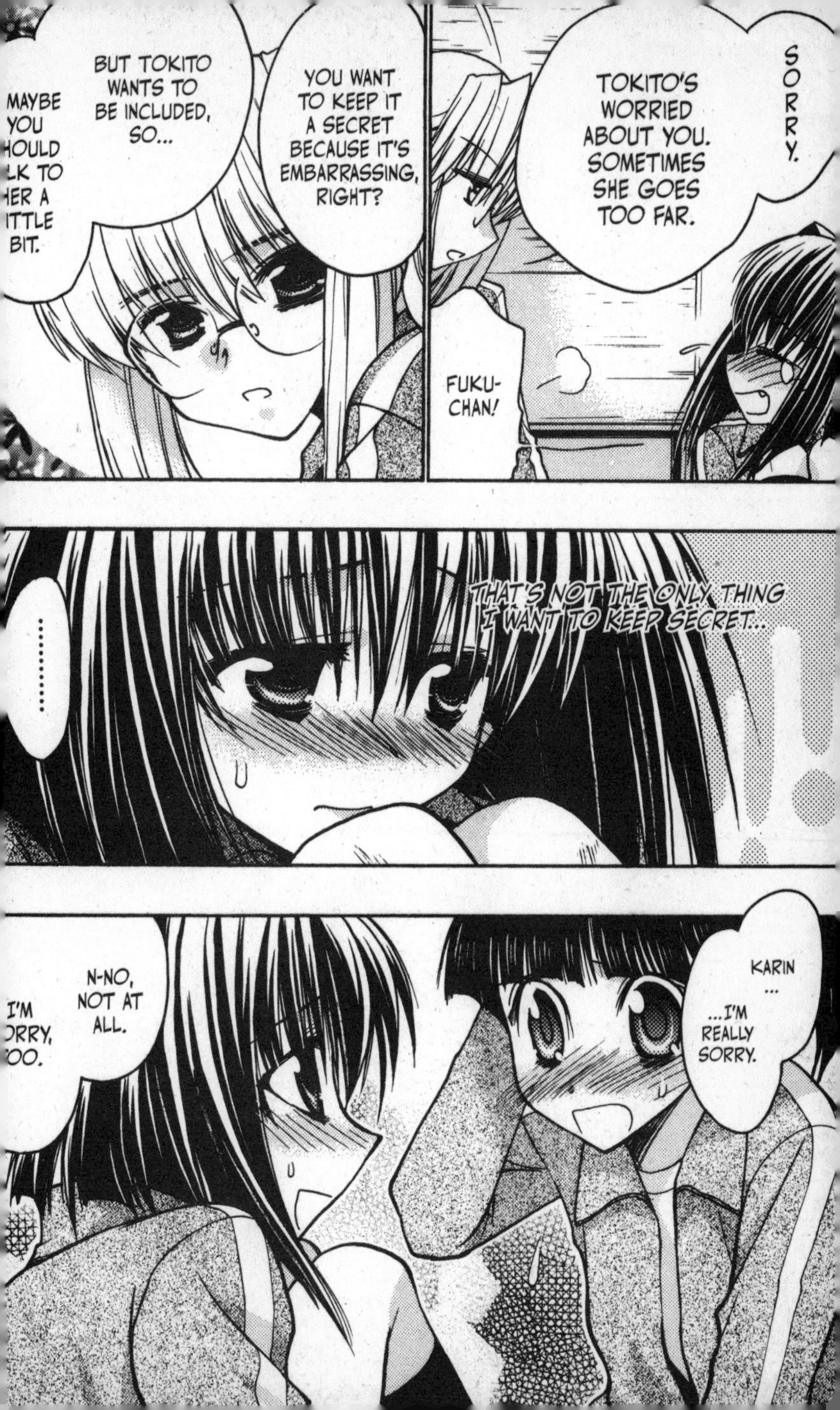
SORRY.
TOKITO'S WORRIED ABOUT YOU. SOMETIMES SHE GOES TOO FAR.
FUKU-CHAN!
YOU WANT TO KEEP IT A SECRET BECAUSE IT'S EMBARRASSING, RIGHT?
BUT TOKITO WANTS TO BE INCLUDED, SO...
MAYBE YOU HOULD LK TO HER A ITTLE BIT.
THAT'S NOT THE ONLY THING I WANT TO KEEP SECRET...
......
KARIN ... ...I'M REALLY SORRY.
N-NO, NOT AT ALL.
I'M ORRY, OO.

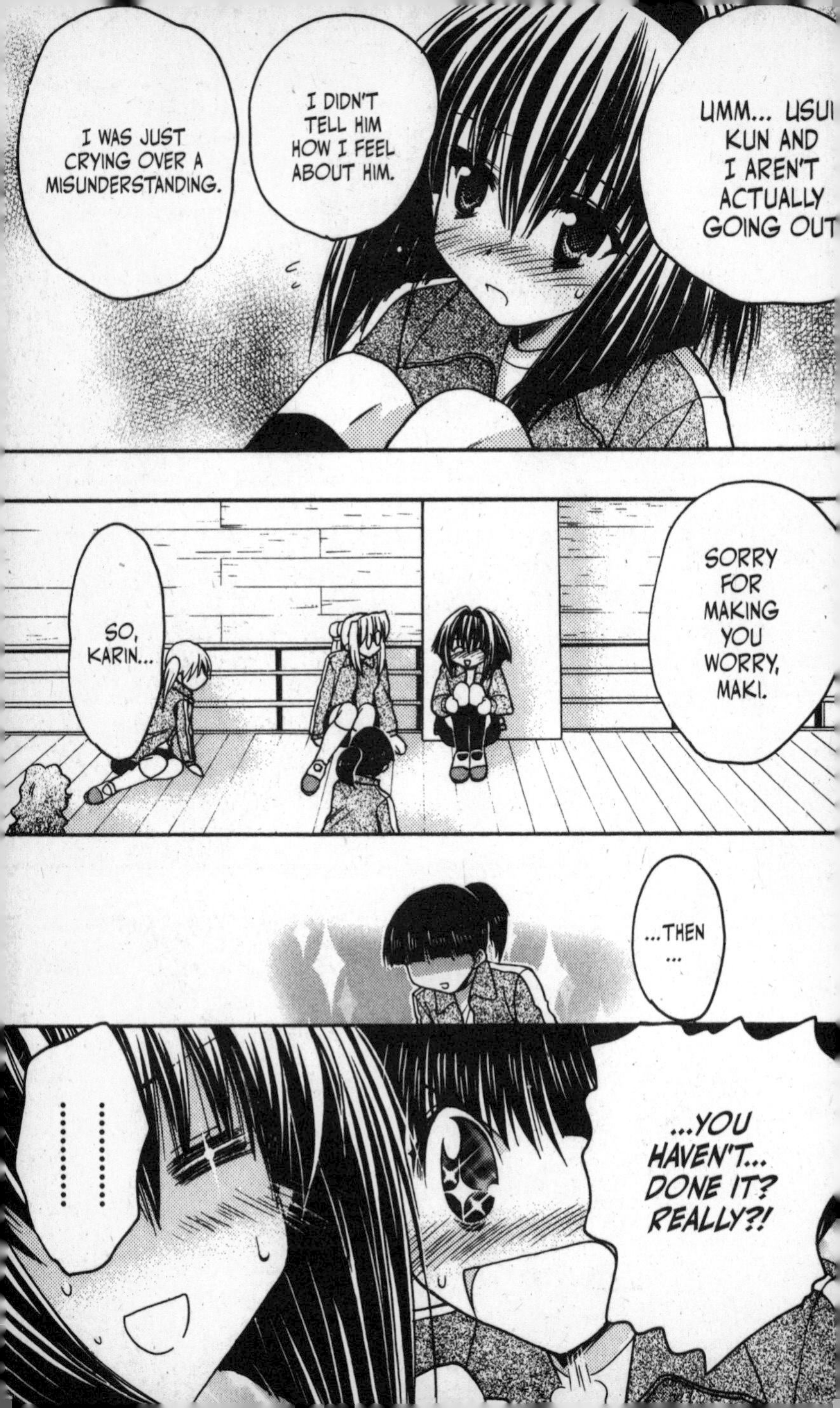
UMM... USUI KUN AND I AREN'T ACTUALLY GOING OUT
I DIDN'T TELL HIM HOW I FEEL ABOUT HIM.
I WAS JUST CRYING OVER A MISUNDERSTANDING.
SORRY FOR MAKING YOU WORRY, MAKI.
SO, KARIN...
...THEN ...
...YOU HAVEN'T... DONE IT? REALLY?!
......

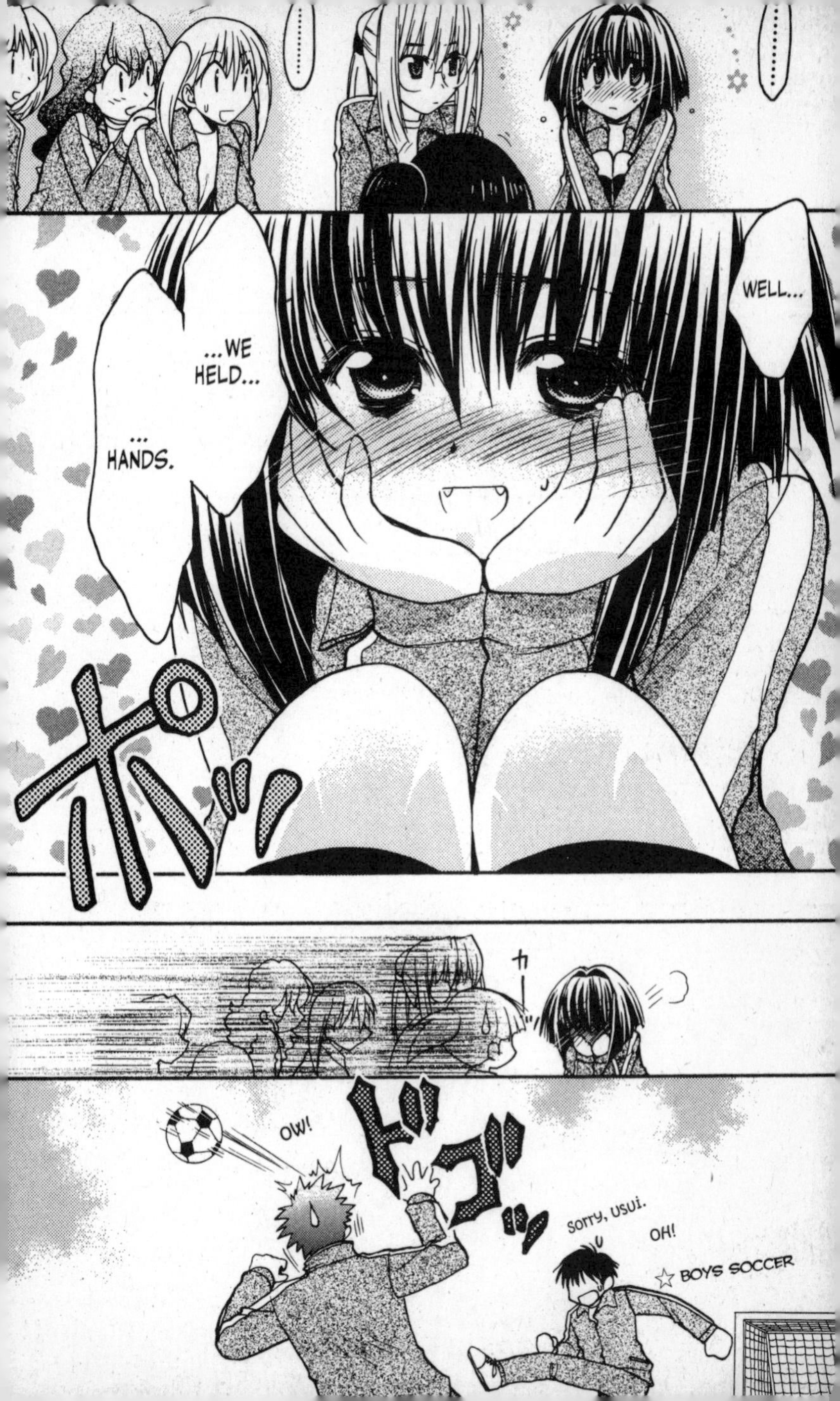
......
......
WELL...
...WE HELD...
... HANDS.
ポッ
カー
OW!
ドゴッ
OH!
Sorry, Usui.
☆ BOYS SOCCER

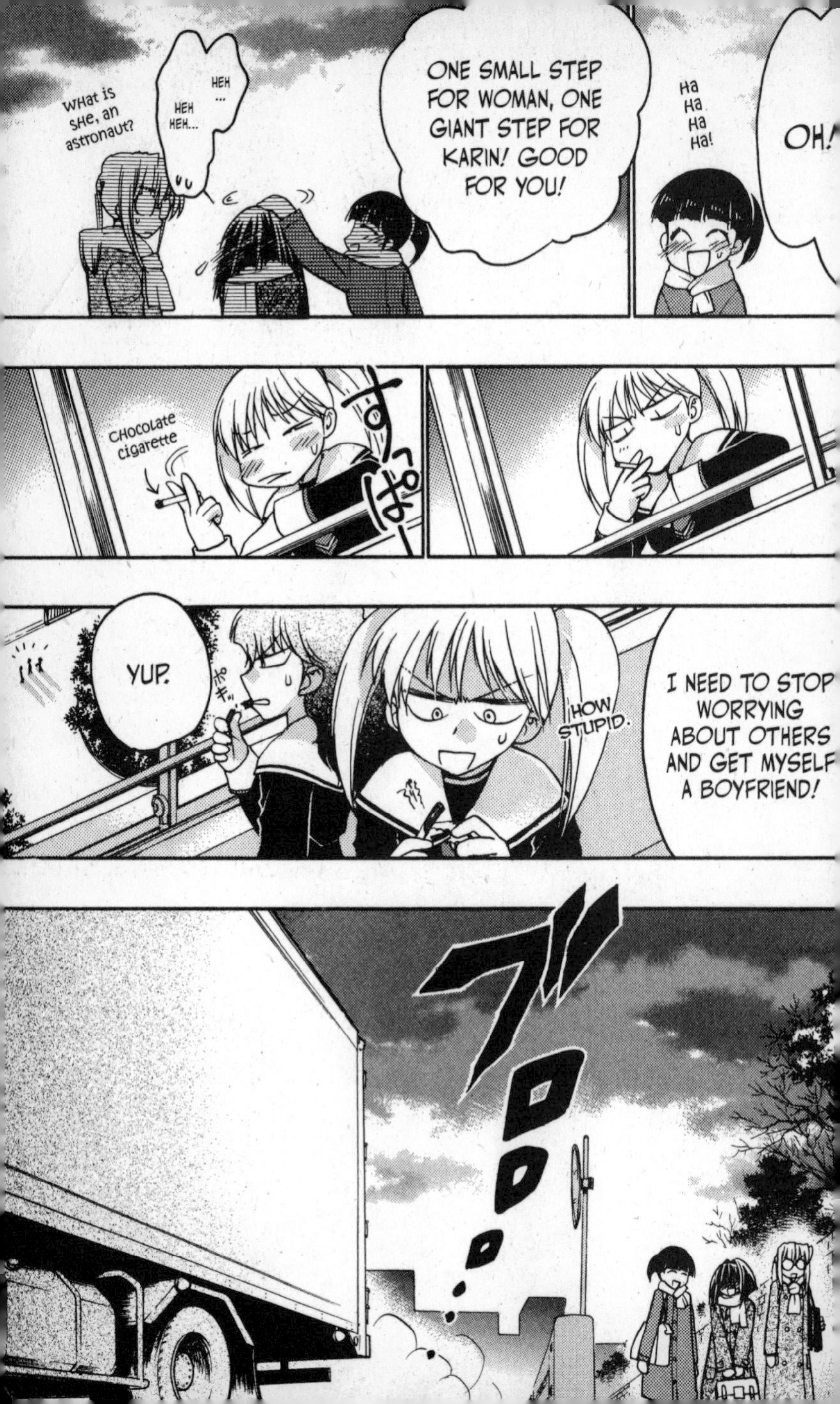
OH!
Ha Ha Ha Ha!
ONE SMALL STEP FOR WOMAN, ONE GIANT STEP FOR KARIN! GOOD FOR YOU!
HEH ...
HEH HEH...
What is she, an astronaut?
すっぱー
Chocolate cigarette
I NEED TO STOP WORRYING ABOUT OTHERS AND GET MYSELF A BOYFRIEND!
HOW STUPID.
ポキ
YUP.
ブロロ

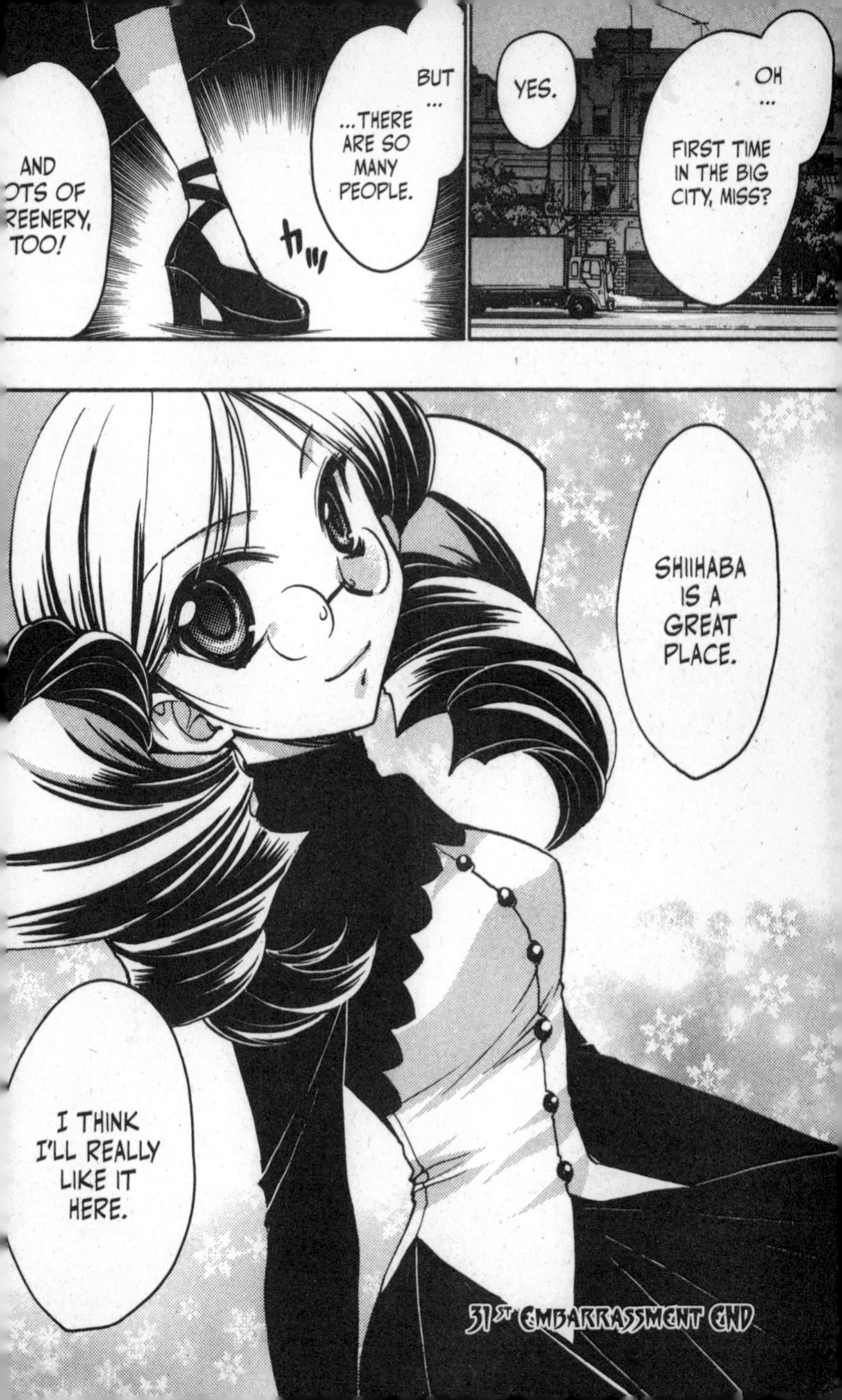
OH ... FIRST TIME IN THE BIG CITY, MISS?
YES.
BUT ...
...THERE ARE SO MANY PEOPLE.
カッ
AND
OTS OF
REENERY,
TOO!
SHIIHABA IS A GREAT PLACE.
I THINK I'LL REALLY LIKE IT HERE.
31ST EMBARRASSMENT END

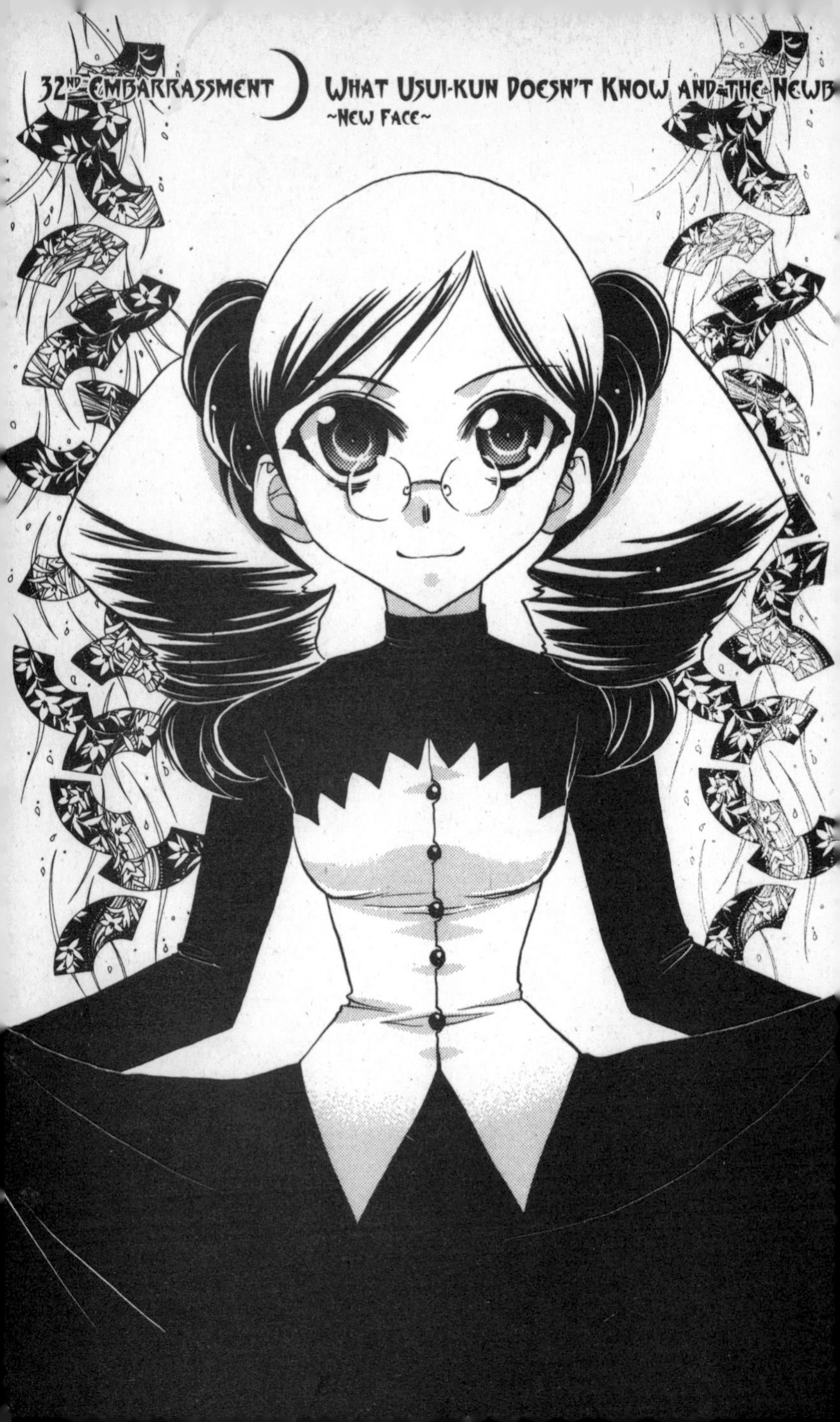
32ND EMBARRASSMENT
WHAT USUI-KUN DOESN'T KNOW AND THE NEWB
~NEW FACE~

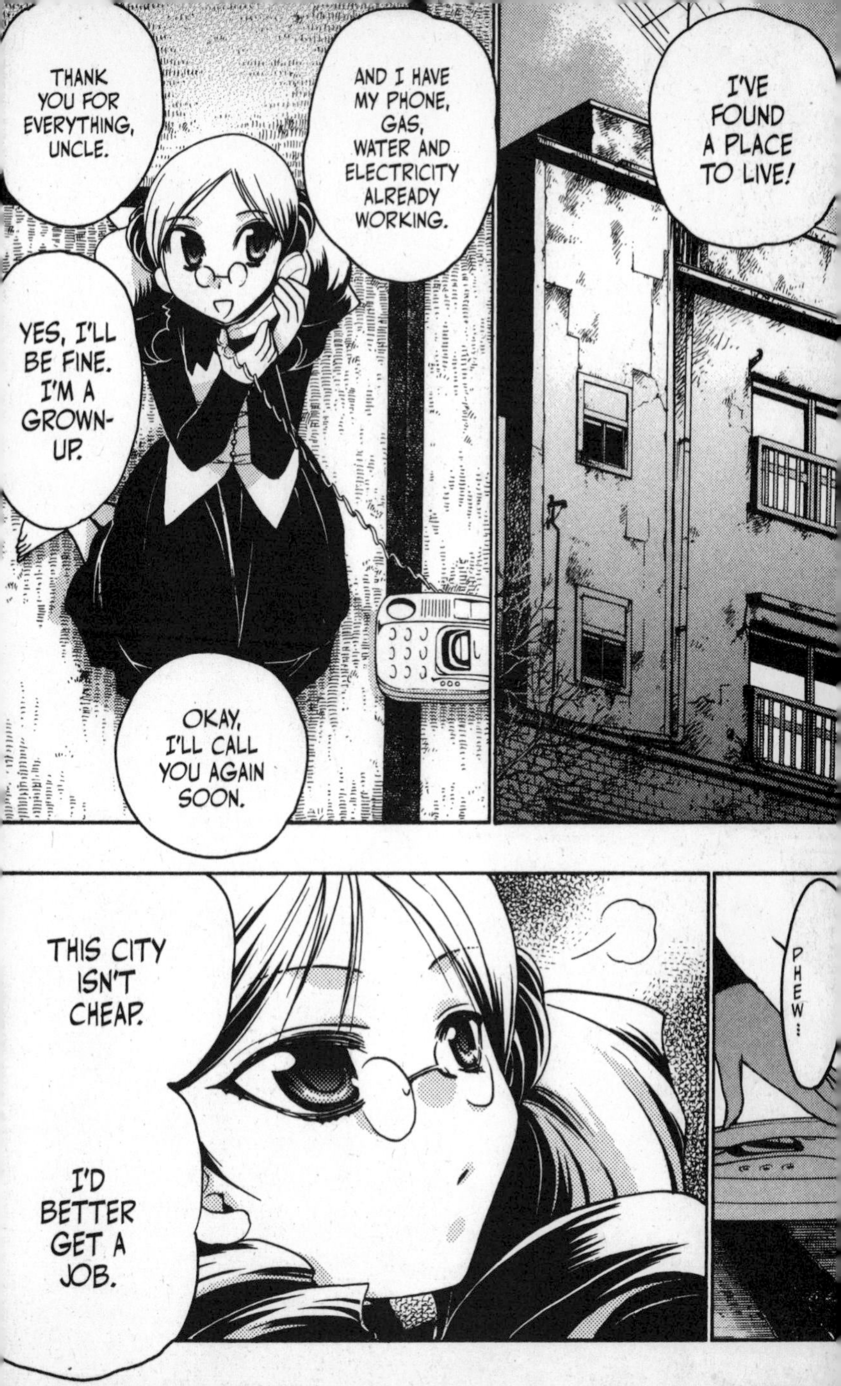
I'VE FOUND A PLACE TO LIVE!
AND I HAVE MY PHONE, GAS, WATER AND ELECTRICITY ALREADY WORKING.
THANK YOU FOR EVERYTHING, UNCLE.
YES, I'LL BE FINE. I'M A GROWN-UP.
OKAY, I'LL CALL YOU AGAIN SOON.
PHEW...
THIS CITY ISN'T CHEAP.
I'D BETTER GET A JOB.

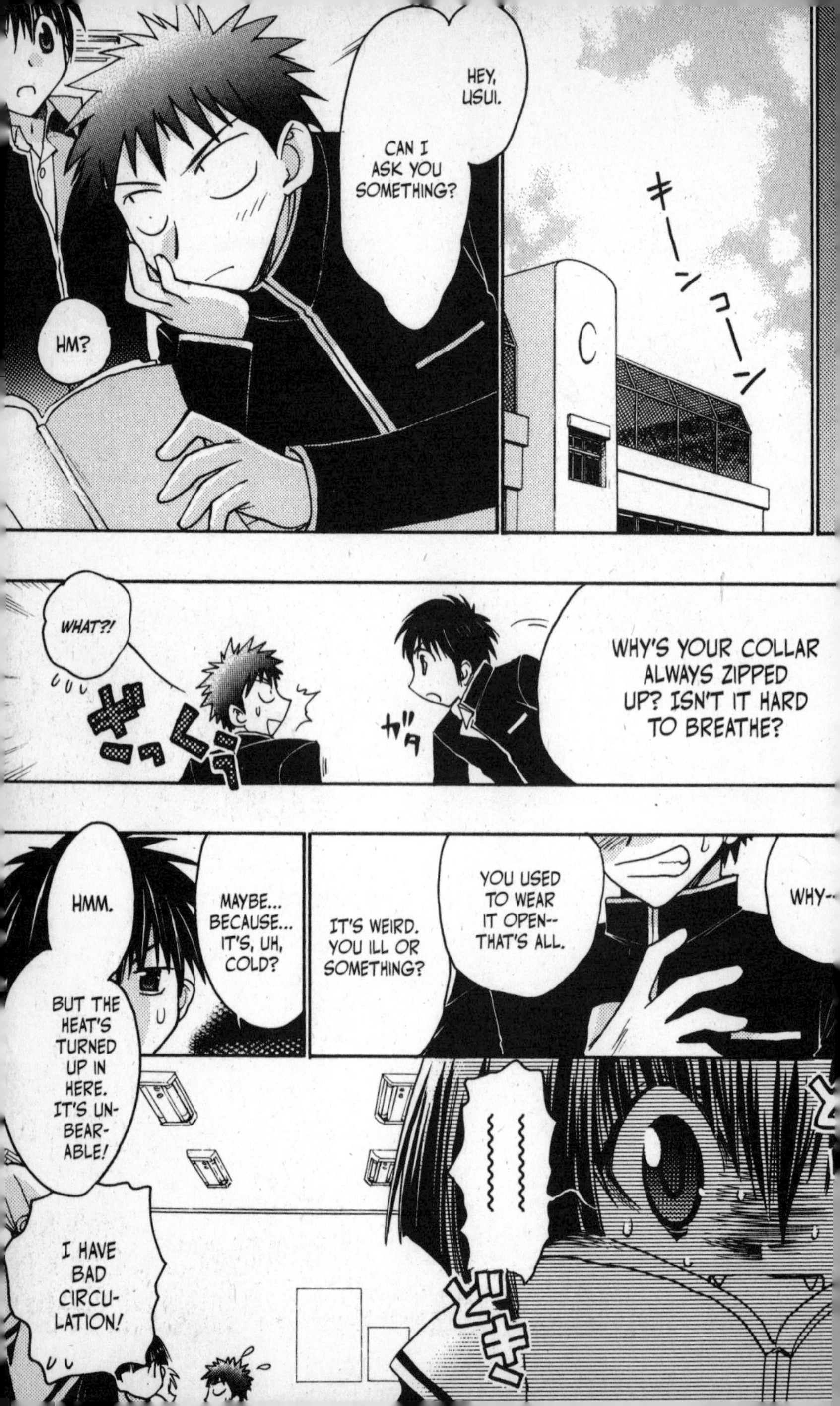
キーンコーン
HEY, USUI.
CAN I ASK YOU SOMETHING?
HM?
WHY'S YOUR COLLAR ALWAYS ZIPPED UP? ISN'T IT HARD TO BREATHE?
ガタ
WHAT?!
WHY--
YOU USED TO WEAR IT OPEN-- THAT'S ALL.
IT'S WEIRD. YOU ILL OR SOMETHING?
MAYBE... BECAUSE... IT'S, UH, COLD?
HMM.
BUT THE HEAT'S TURNED UP IN HERE. IT'S UN-BEAR-ABLE!
I HAVE BAD CIRCU-LATION!

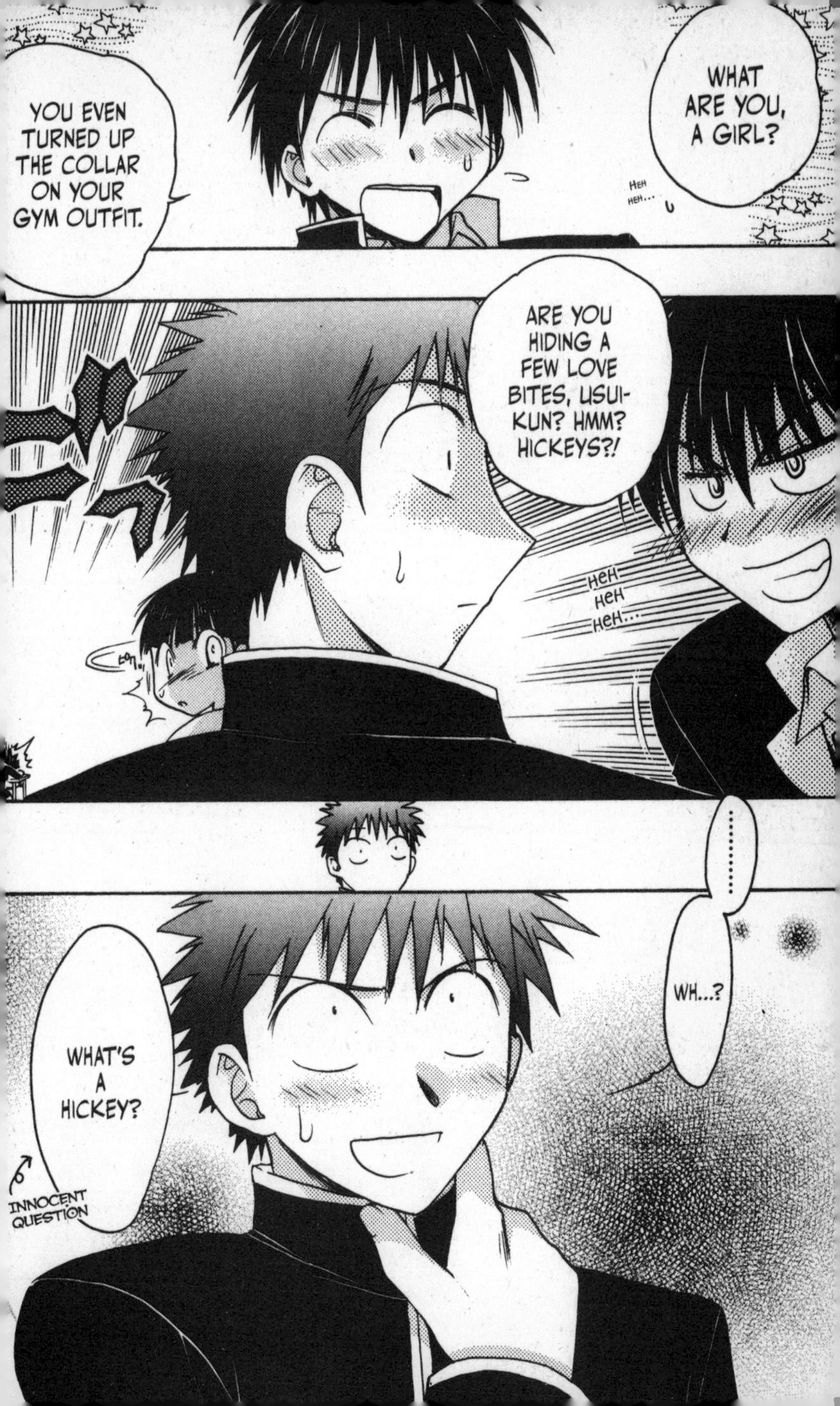
WHAT ARE YOU, A GIRL?
HEH HEH...
YOU EVEN TURNED UP THE COLLAR ON YOUR GYM OUTFIT.
ARE YOU HIDING A FEW LOVE BITES, USUI-KUN? HMM? HICKEYS?!
HEH HEH HEH...
....
WH...?
WHAT'S A HICKEY?
INNOCENT QUESTION

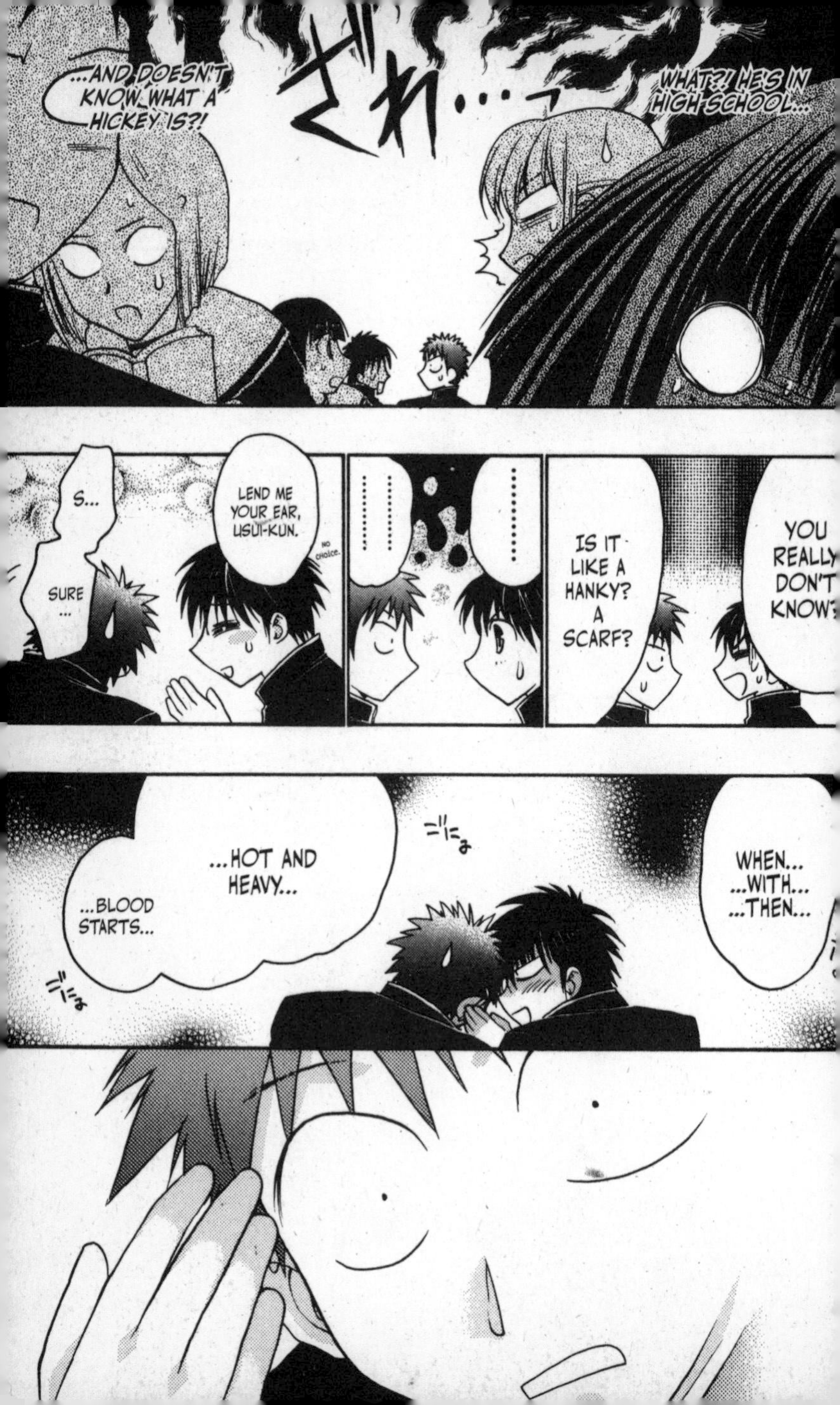
WHAT?! HE'S IN HIGH SCHOOL...
ざわ…っ
...AND DOESN'T KNOW WHAT A HICKEY IS?!
YOU REALLY DON'T KNOW?
IS IT LIKE A HANKY? A SCARF?
......
......
LEND ME YOUR EAR, USUI-KUN.
NO CHOICE.
S... SURE...
WHEN... ...WITH... ...THEN...
ごにょ
...HOT AND HEAVY...
...BLOOD STARTS...
ごにょ

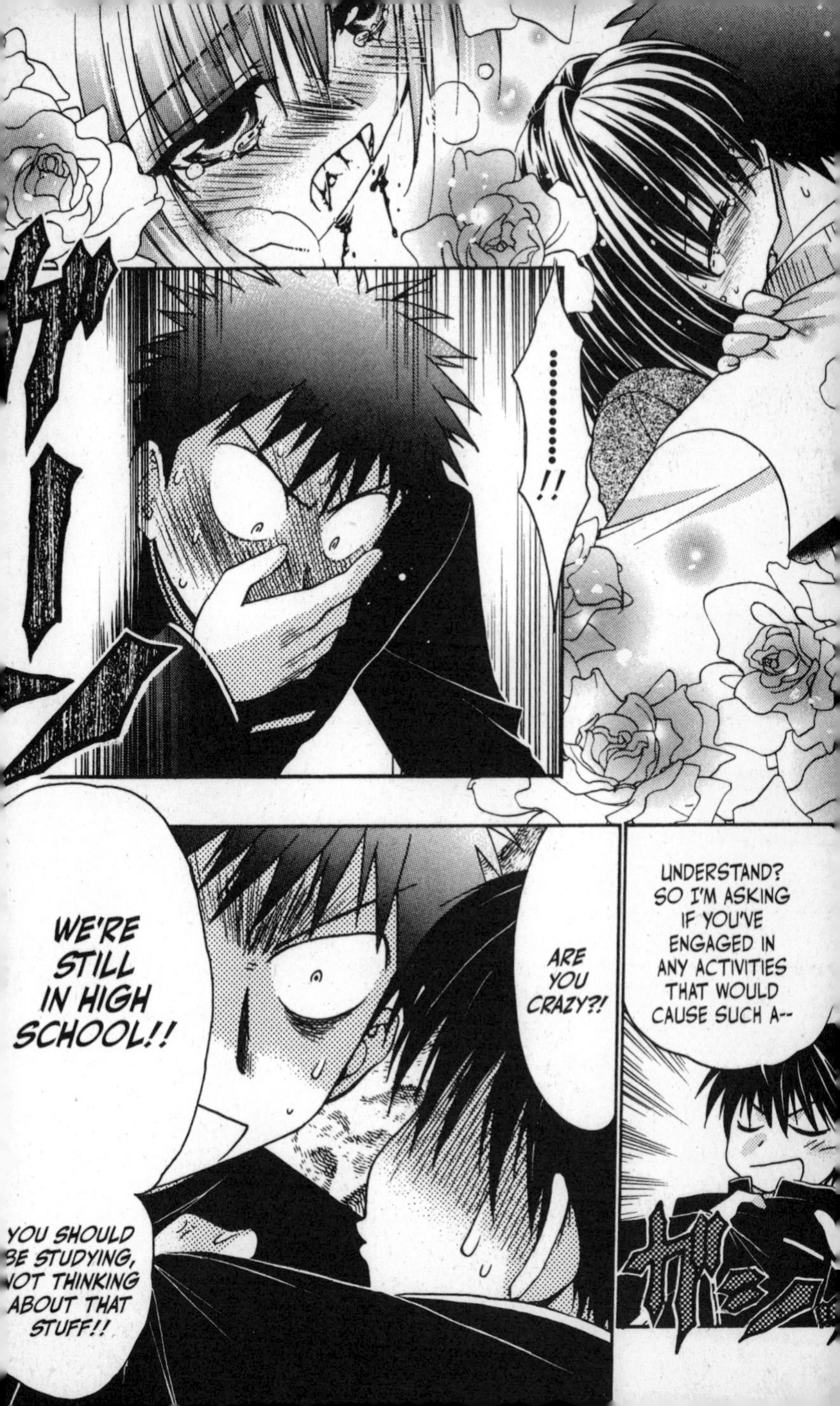
......!!
UNDERSTAND? SO I'M ASKING IF YOU'VE ENGAGED IN ANY ACTIVITIES THAT WOULD CAUSE SUCH A--
ARE YOU CRAZY?!
WE'RE STILL IN HIGH SCHOOL!!
YOU SHOULD BE STUDYING, NOT THINKING ABOUT THAT STUFF!!

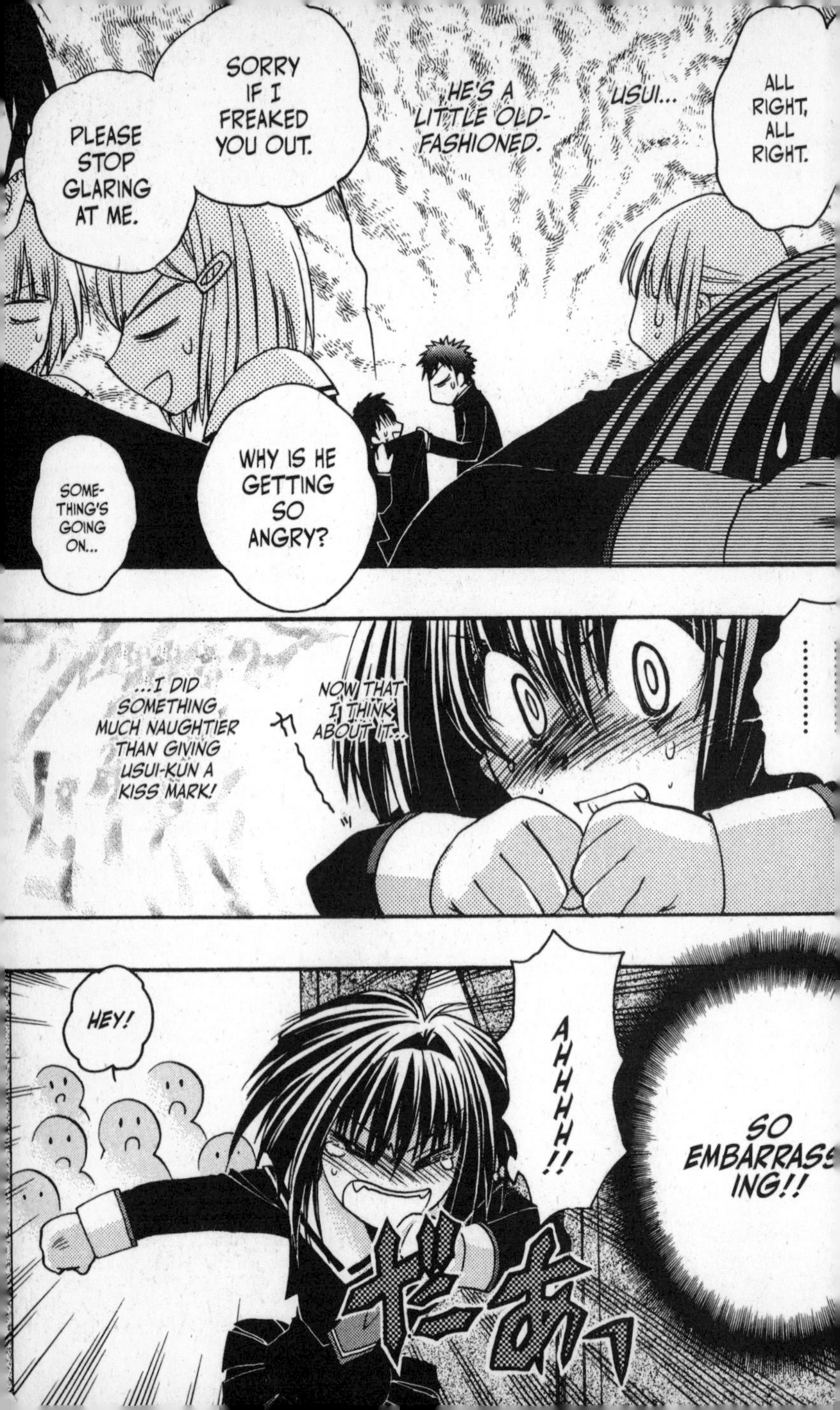
ALL RIGHT, ALL RIGHT.
USUI...
HE'S A LITTLE OLD-FASHIONED.
SORRY IF I FREAKED YOU OUT.
PLEASE STOP GLARING AT ME.
WHY IS HE GETTING SO ANGRY?
SOME-THING'S GOING ON...
......
NOW THAT I THINK ABOUT IT...
...I DID SOMETHING MUCH NAUGHTIER THAN GIVING USUI-KUN A KISS MARK!
SO EMBARRASSING!!
AHHHHH!!
HEY!

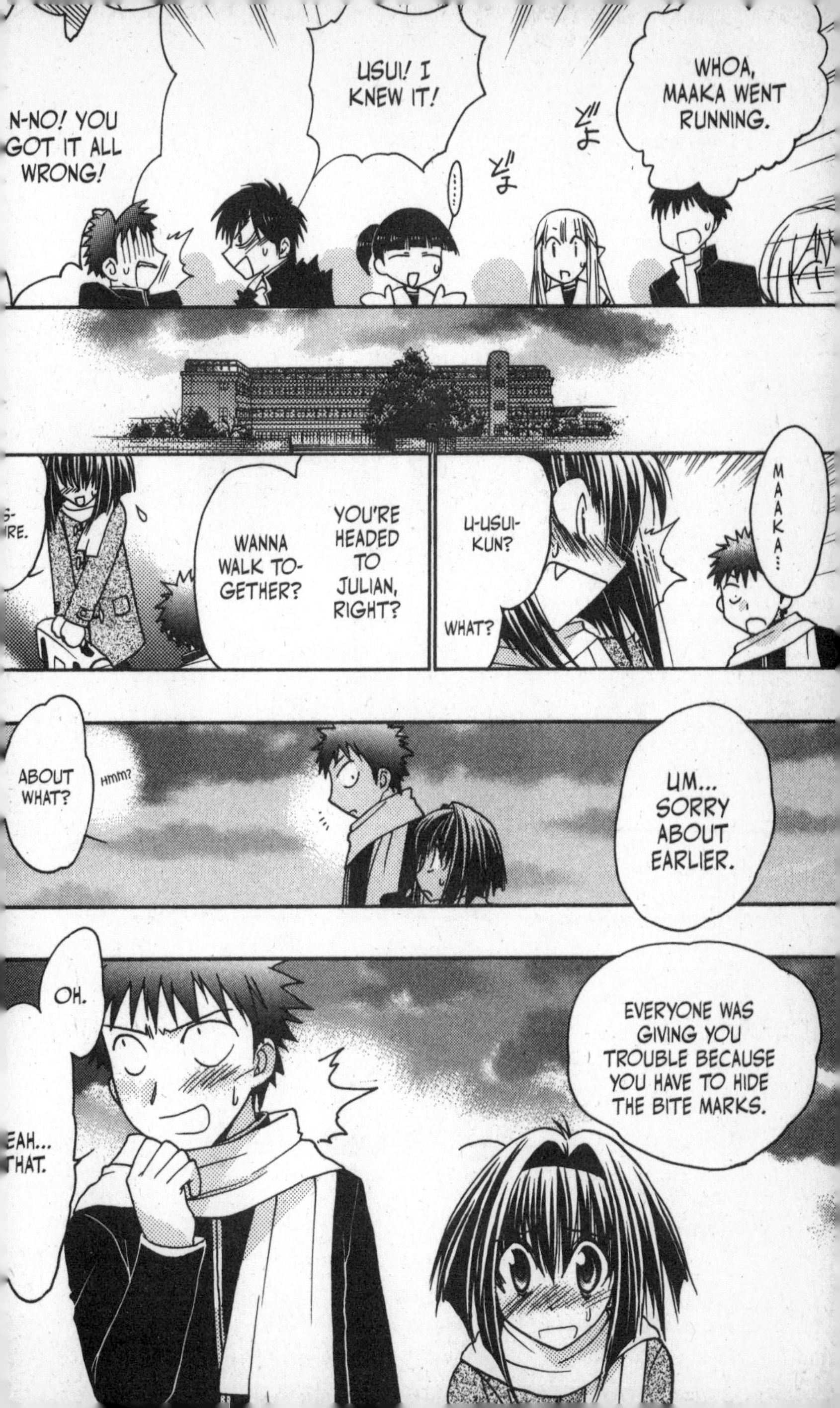
WHOA, MAAKA WENT RUNNING.
ぞよ
ぞよ
......
USUI! I KNEW IT!
N-NO! YOU GOT IT ALL WRONG!
MAAKA...
U-USUI-KUN?
WHAT?
YOU'RE HEADED TO JULIAN, RIGHT?
WANNA WALK TO-GETHER?
UM... SORRY ABOUT EARLIER.
HMM?
ABOUT WHAT?
EVERYONE WAS GIVING YOU TROUBLE BECAUSE YOU HAVE TO HIDE THE BITE MARKS.
OH.
EAH... THAT.

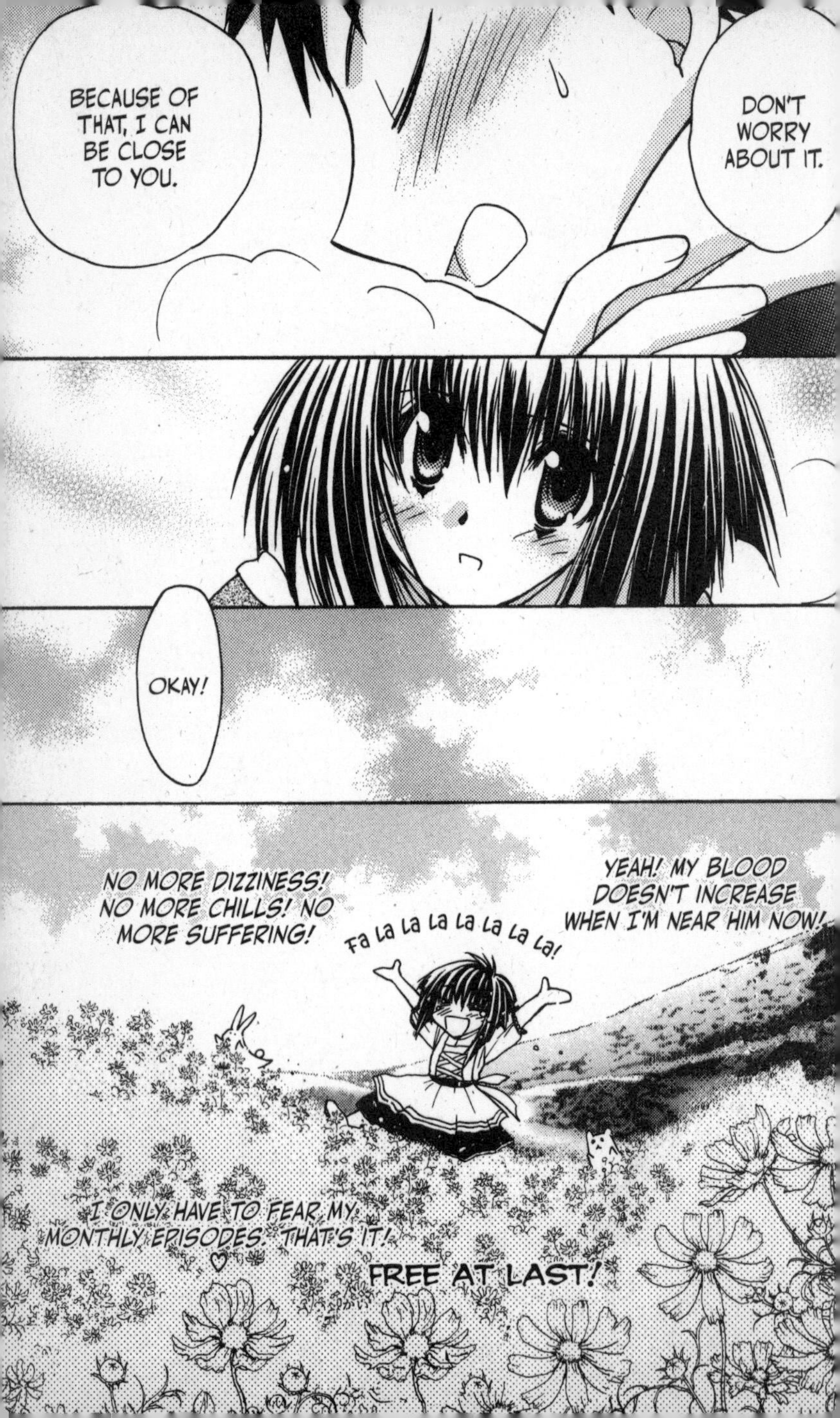
DON'T WORRY ABOUT IT.
BECAUSE OF THAT, I CAN BE CLOSE TO YOU.
OKAY!
YEAH! MY BLOOD DOESN'T INCREASE WHEN I'M NEAR HIM NOW!
Fa La La La La La La La!
NO MORE DIZZINESS! NO MORE CHILLS! NO MORE SUFFERING!
I ONLY HAVE TO FEAR MY MONTHLY EPISODES. THAT'S IT! ♡
FREE AT LAST!

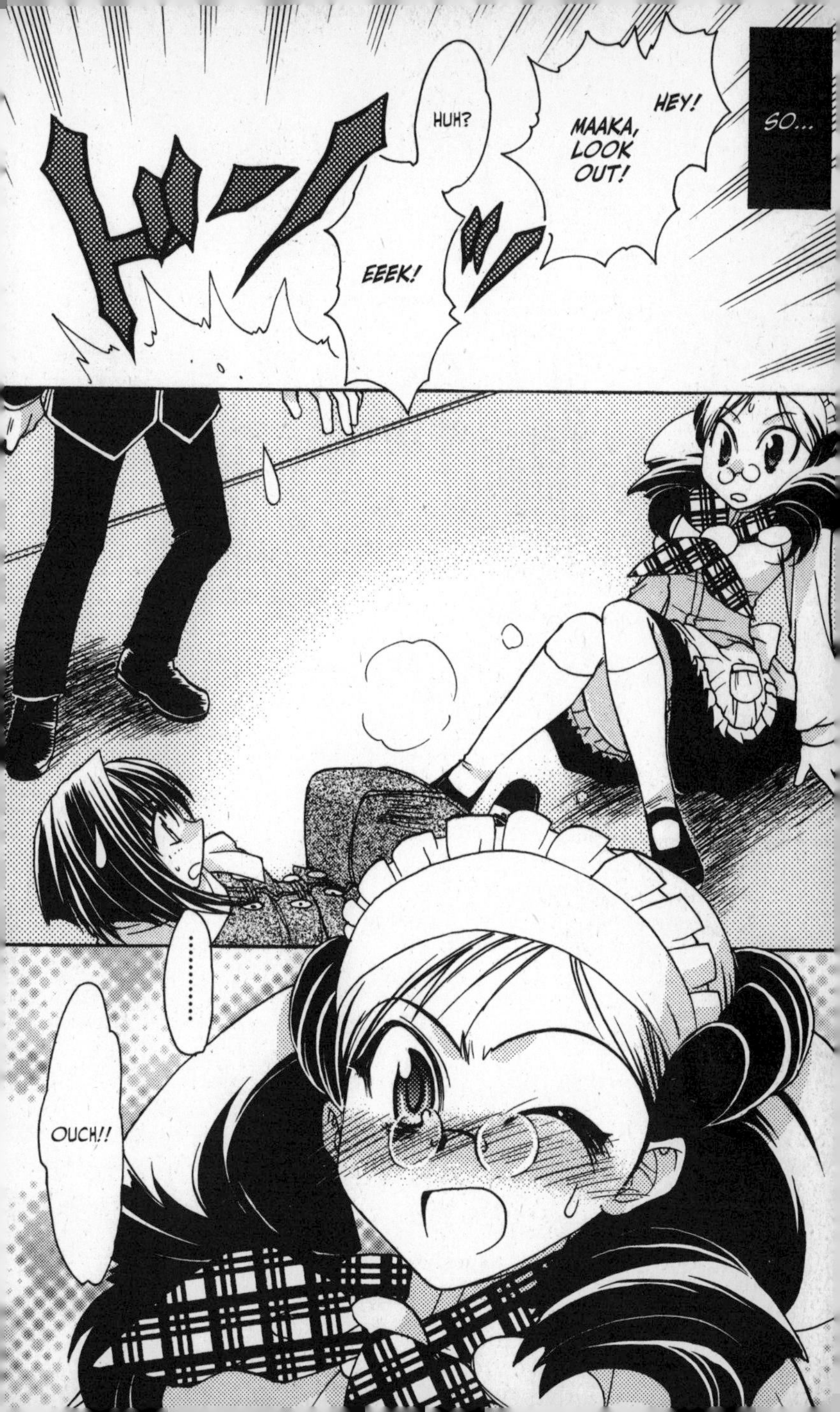
SO...
HEY! MAAKA, LOOK OUT!
HUH?
EEEK!
....
OUCH!!

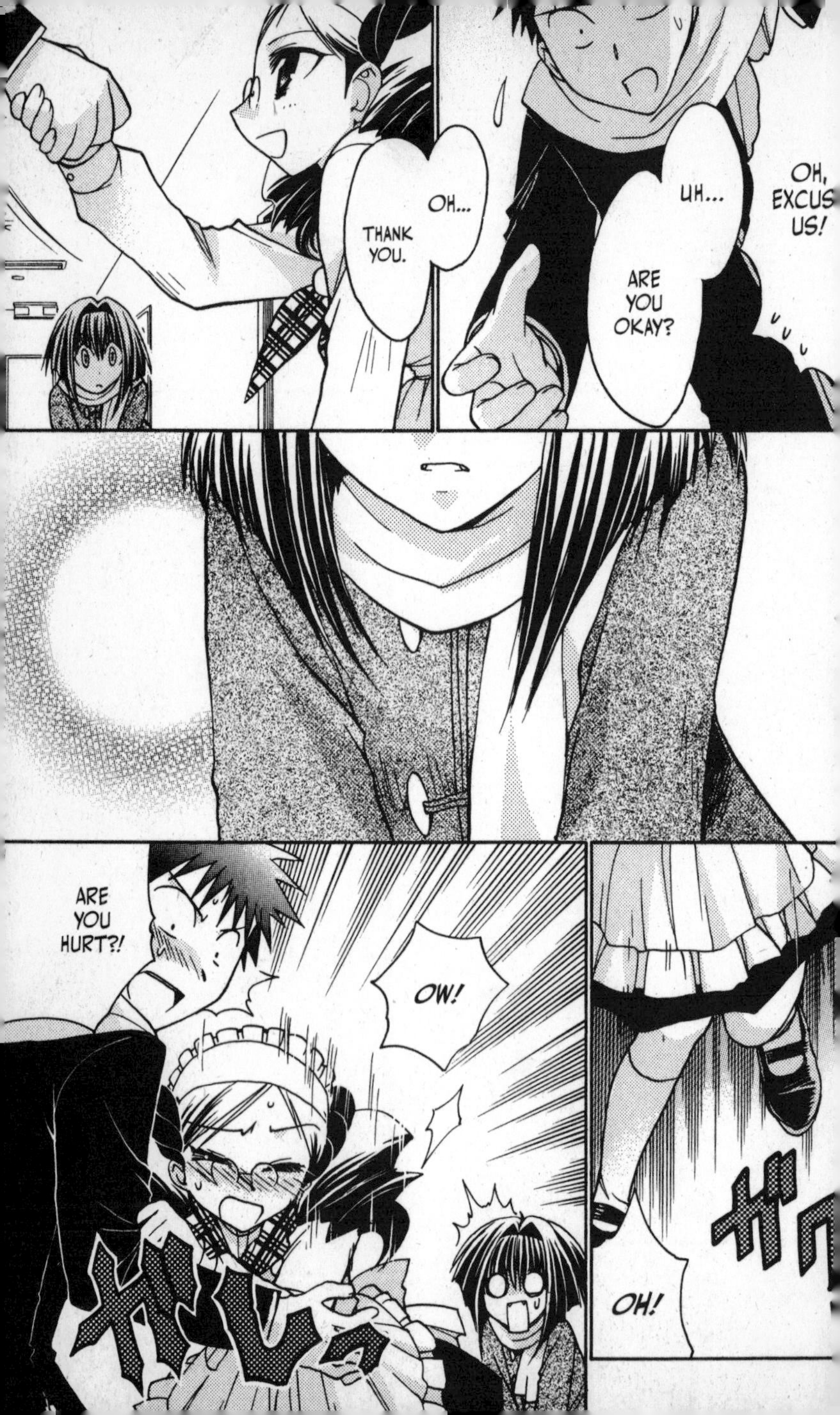
OH, EXCUS US!
UH... ARE YOU OKAY?
OH... THANK YOU.
OH!
OW!
ARE YOU HURT?!

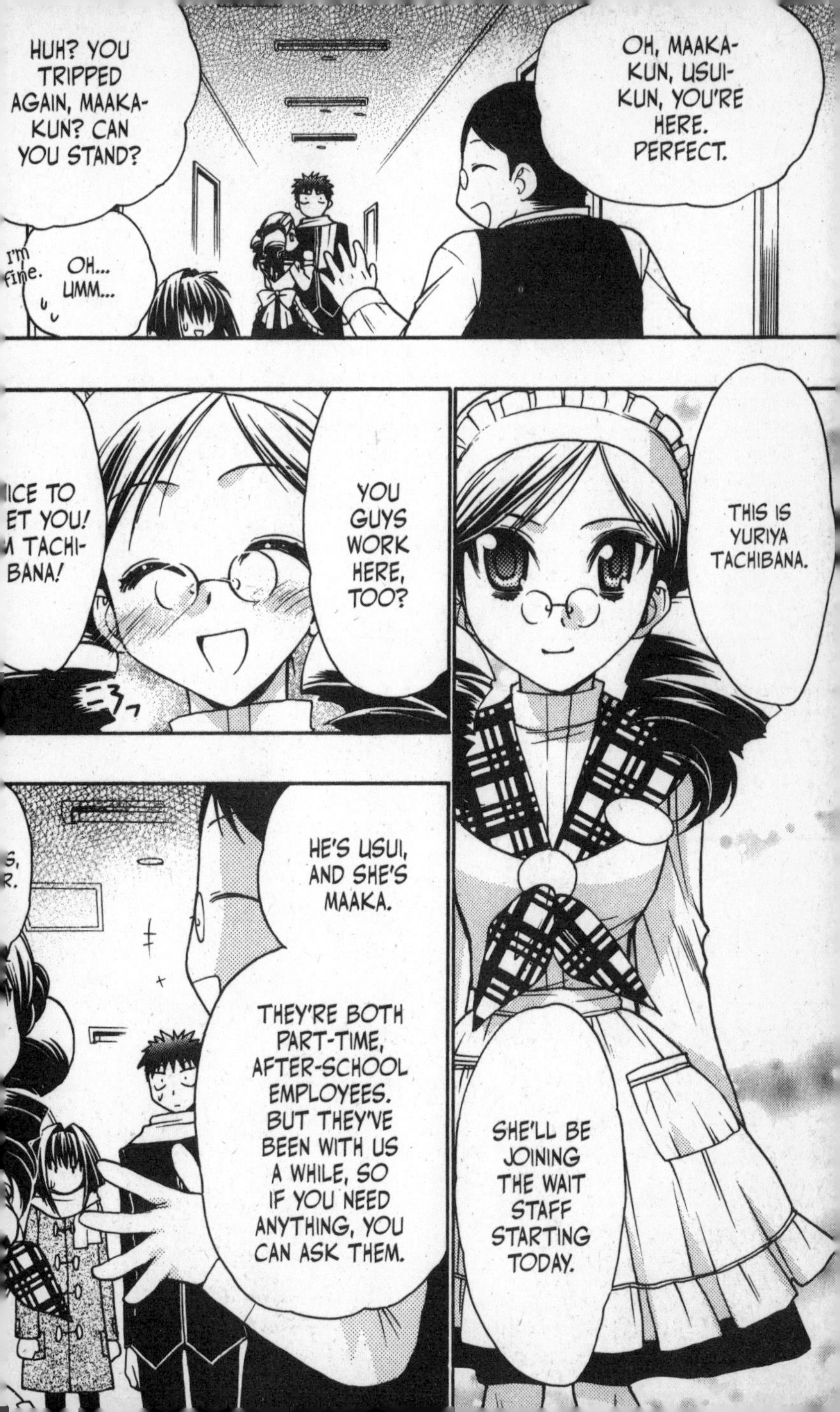
OH, MAAKA-KUN, USUI-KUN, YOU'RE HERE. PERFECT.
HUH? YOU TRIPPED AGAIN, MAAKA-KUN? CAN YOU STAND?
OH... UMM...
I'm fine.
THIS IS YURIYA TACHIBANA.
SHE'LL BE JOINING THE WAIT STAFF STARTING TODAY.
YOU GUYS WORK HERE, TOO?
ICE TO ET YOU! M TACHI-BANA!
HE'S USUI, AND SHE'S MAAKA.
THEY'RE BOTH PART-TIME, AFTER-SCHOOL EMPLOYEES. BUT THEY'VE BEEN WITH US A WHILE, SO IF YOU NEED ANYTHING, YOU CAN ASK THEM.

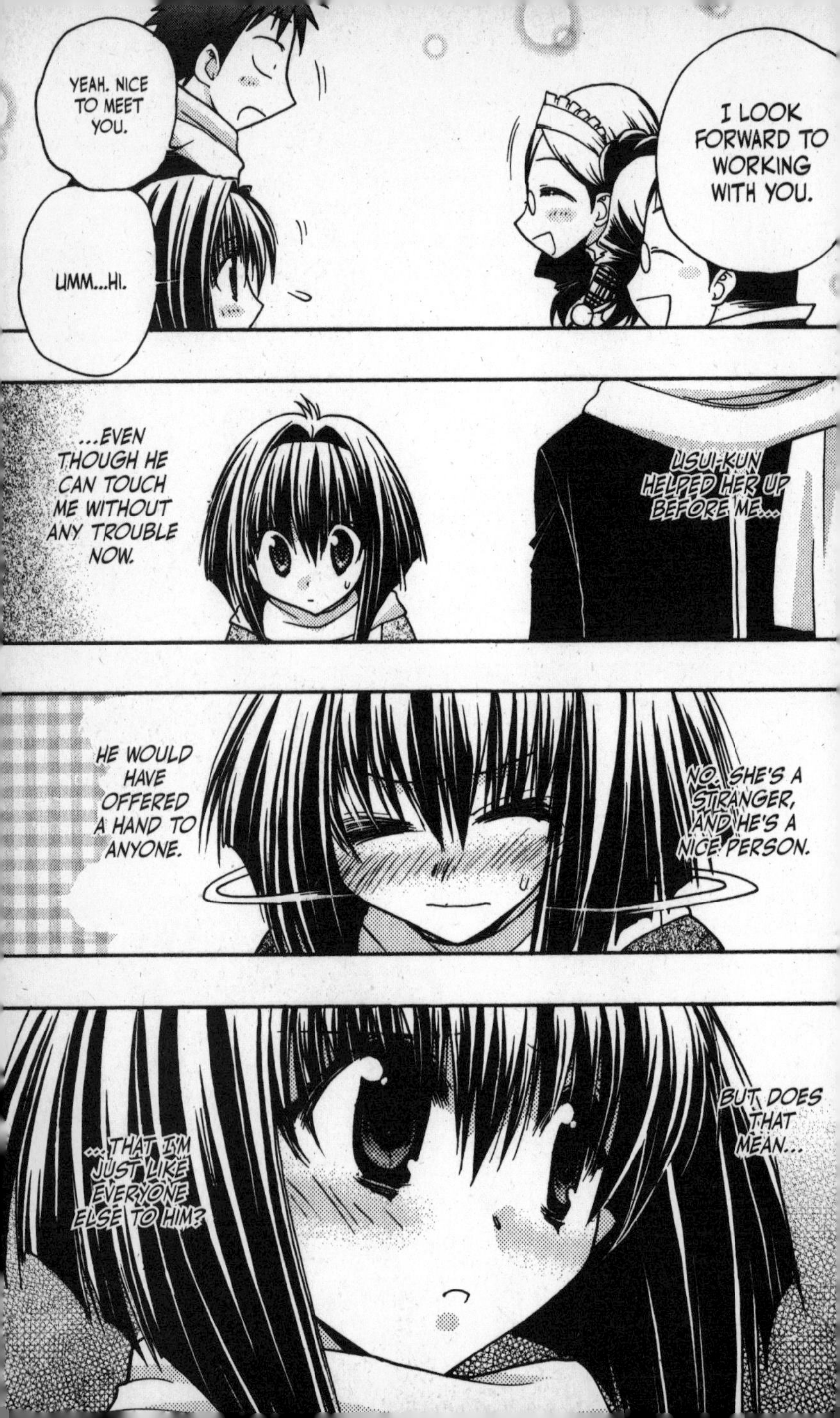
I LOOK FORWARD TO WORKING WITH YOU.
YEAH. NICE TO MEET YOU.
UMM...HI.
USUI-KUN HELPED HER UP BEFORE ME...
...EVEN THOUGH HE CAN TOUCH ME WITHOUT ANY TROUBLE NOW.
NO. SHE'S A STRANGER, AND HE'S A NICE PERSON.
HE WOULD HAVE OFFERED A HAND TO ANYONE.
BUT DOES THAT MEAN...
...THAT I'M JUST LIKE EVERYONE ELSE TO HIM?

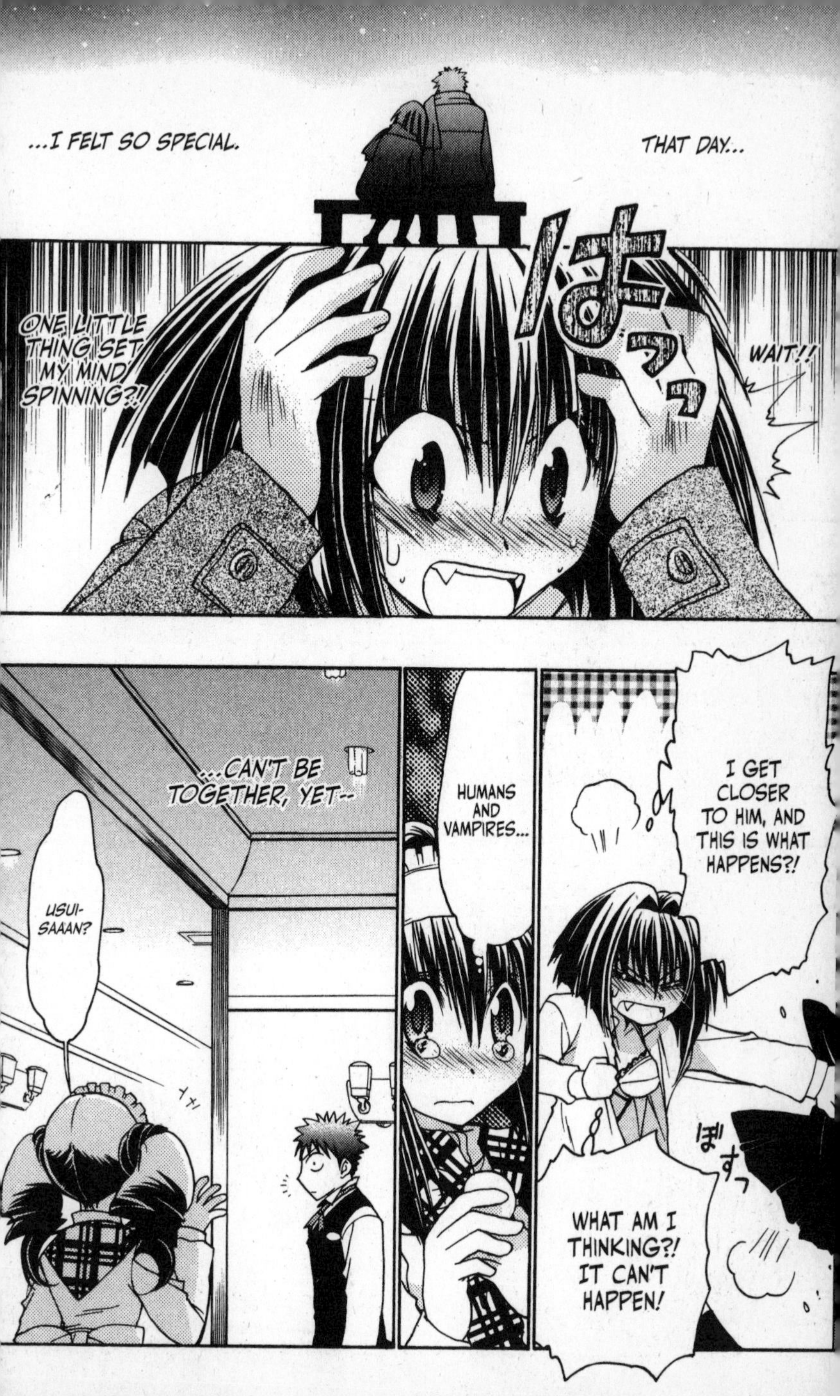
THAT DAY...
...I FELT SO SPECIAL.
はっっ
WAIT!!
ONE LITTLE THING SET MY MIND SPINNING?!
I GET CLOSER TO HIM, AND THIS IS WHAT HAPPENS?!
ぼすっ
WHAT AM I THINKING?! IT CAN'T HAPPEN!
HUMANS AND VAMPIRES...
...CAN'T BE TOGETHER, YET--
USUI-SAAAN?

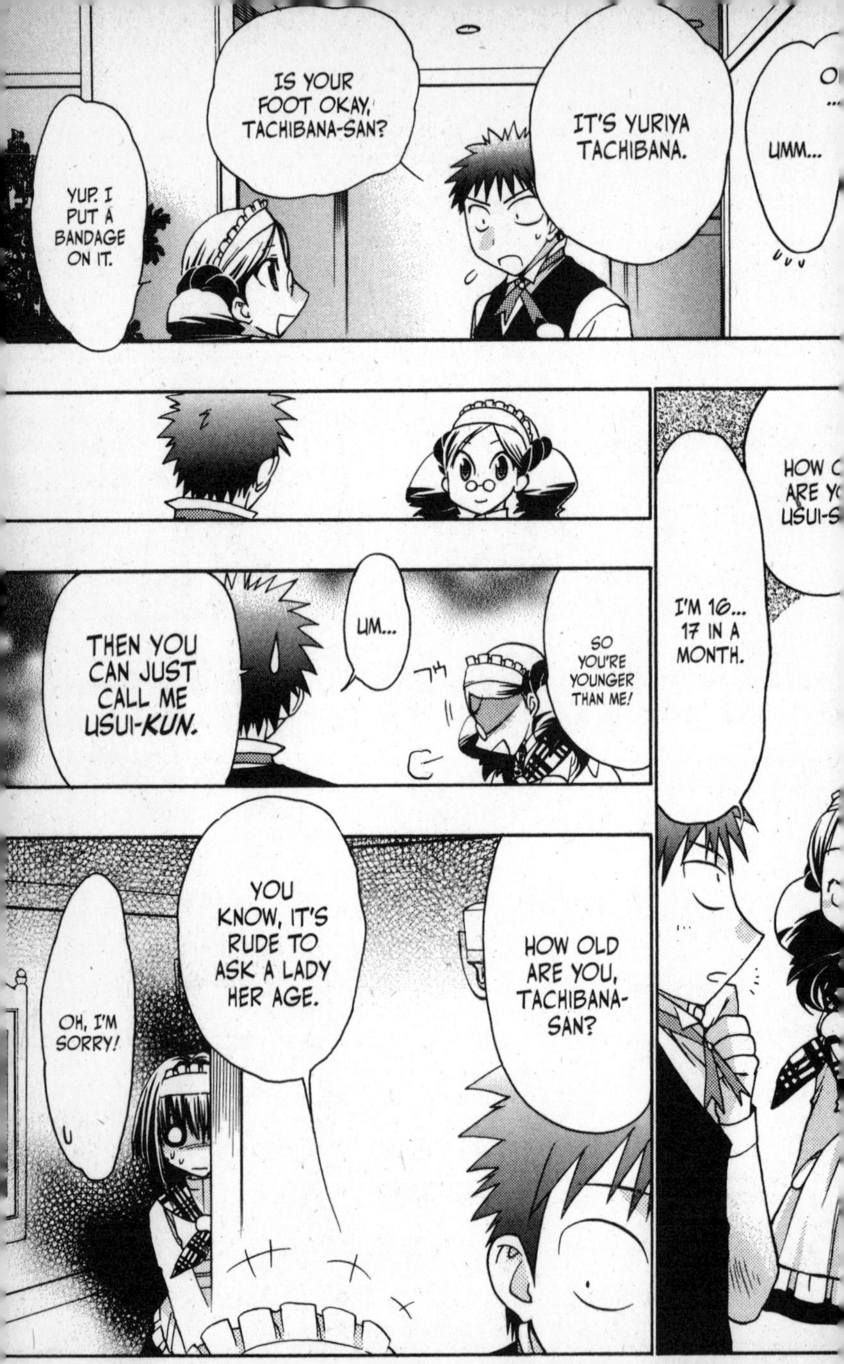
UMM...
IT'S YURIYA TACHIBANA.
IS YOUR FOOT OKAY, TACHIBANA-SAN?
YUP. I PUT A BANDAGE ON IT.
HOW O ARE YO USUI-S
I'M 16... 17 IN A MONTH.
SO YOU'RE YOUNGER THAN ME!
UM...
THEN YOU CAN JUST CALL ME USUI-*KUN*.
HOW OLD ARE YOU, TACHIBANA-SAN?
YOU KNOW, IT'S RUDE TO ASK A LADY HER AGE.
OH, I'M SORRY!

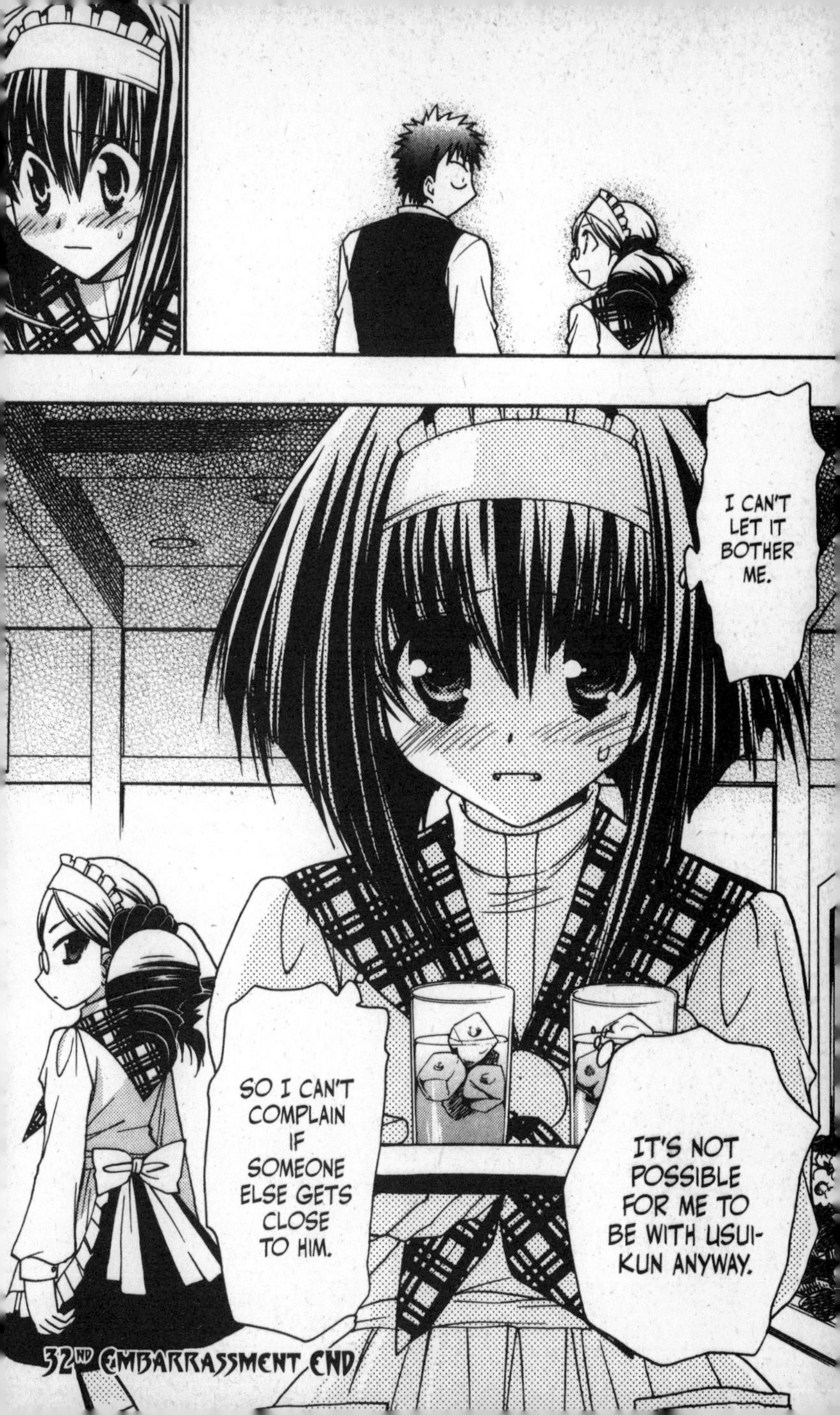
I CAN'T LET IT BOTHER ME.
IT'S NOT POSSIBLE FOR ME TO BE WITH USUI-KUN ANYWAY.
SO I CAN'T COMPLAIN IF SOMEONE ELSE GETS CLOSE TO HIM.
32ND EMBARRASSMENT END

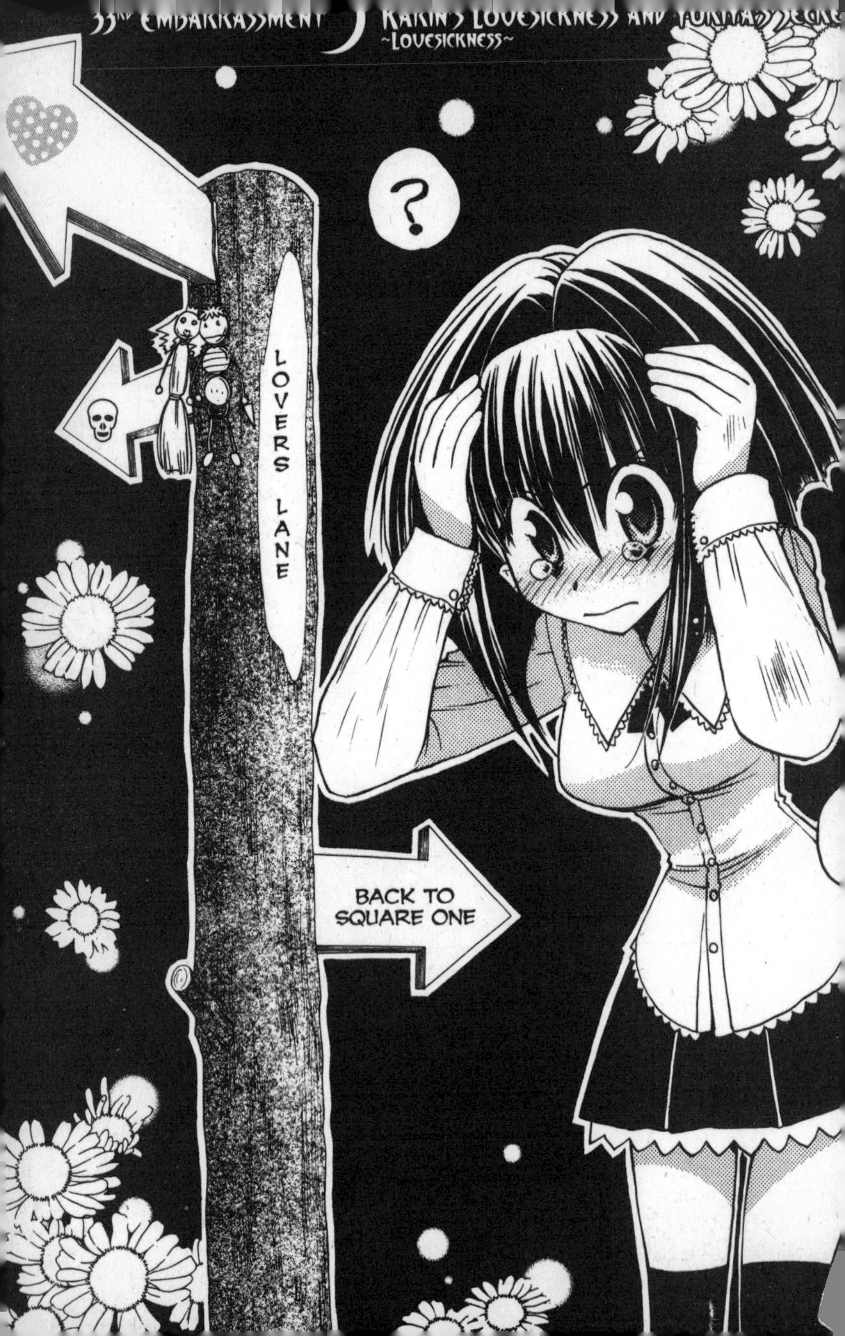
33RD EMBARRASSMENT
KARIN'S LOVESICKNESS AND
~LOVESICKNESS~
?
LOVERS LANE
BACK TO SQUARE ONE

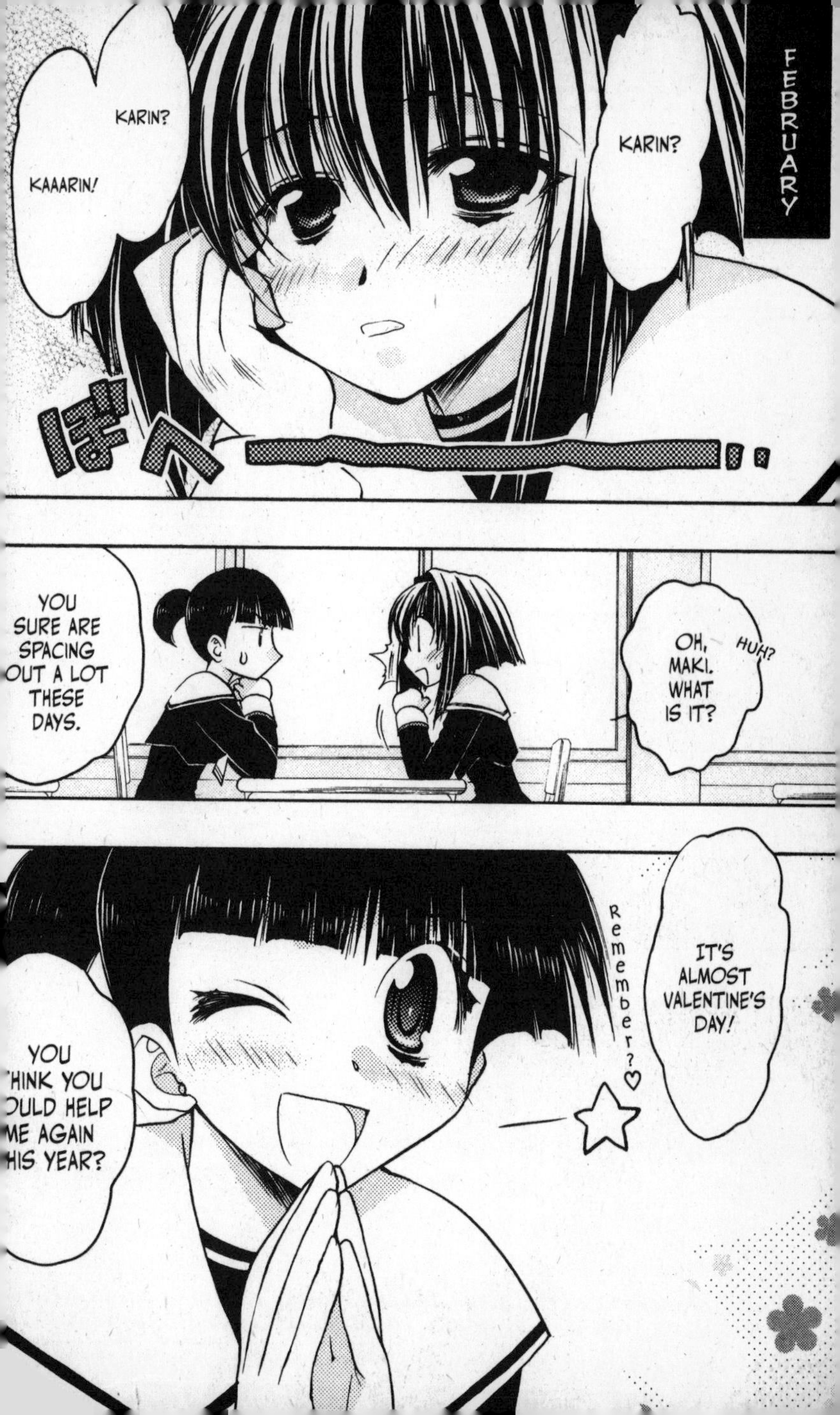
FEBRUARY
KARIN?
KARIN?
KAAARIN!
ぼへーーー!!
HUH?
OH, MAKI. WHAT IS IT?
YOU SURE ARE SPACING OUT A LOT THESE DAYS.
IT'S ALMOST VALENTINE'S DAY!
Remember?♡
YOU HINK YOU OULD HELP ME AGAIN HIS YEAR?

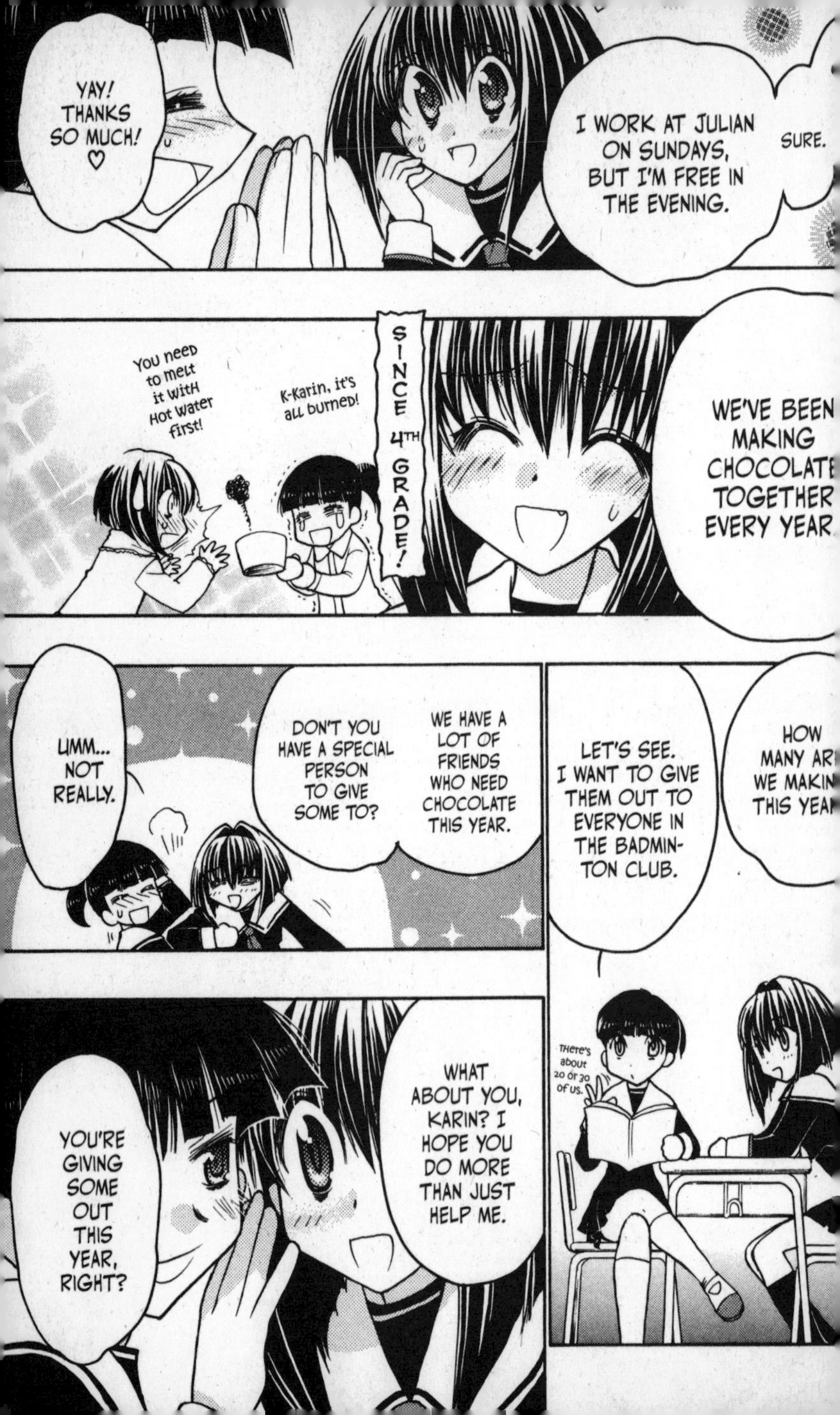
SURE.
I WORK AT JULIAN ON SUNDAYS, BUT I'M FREE IN THE EVENING.
YAY! THANKS SO MUCH! ♡
WE'VE BEEN MAKING CHOCOLATE TOGETHER EVERY YEAR.
SINCE 4TH GRADE!
K-Karin, it's all burned!
You need to melt it with hot water first!
HOW MANY AR WE MAKIN THIS YEA
LET'S SEE. I WANT TO GIVE THEM OUT TO EVERYONE IN THE BADMIN-TON CLUB.
There's about 20 or 30 of us.
WE HAVE A LOT OF FRIENDS WHO NEED CHOCOLATE THIS YEAR.
DON'T YOU HAVE A SPECIAL PERSON TO GIVE SOME TO?
UMM... NOT REALLY.
WHAT ABOUT YOU, KARIN? I HOPE YOU DO MORE THAN JUST HELP ME.
YOU'RE GIVING SOME OUT THIS YEAR, RIGHT?

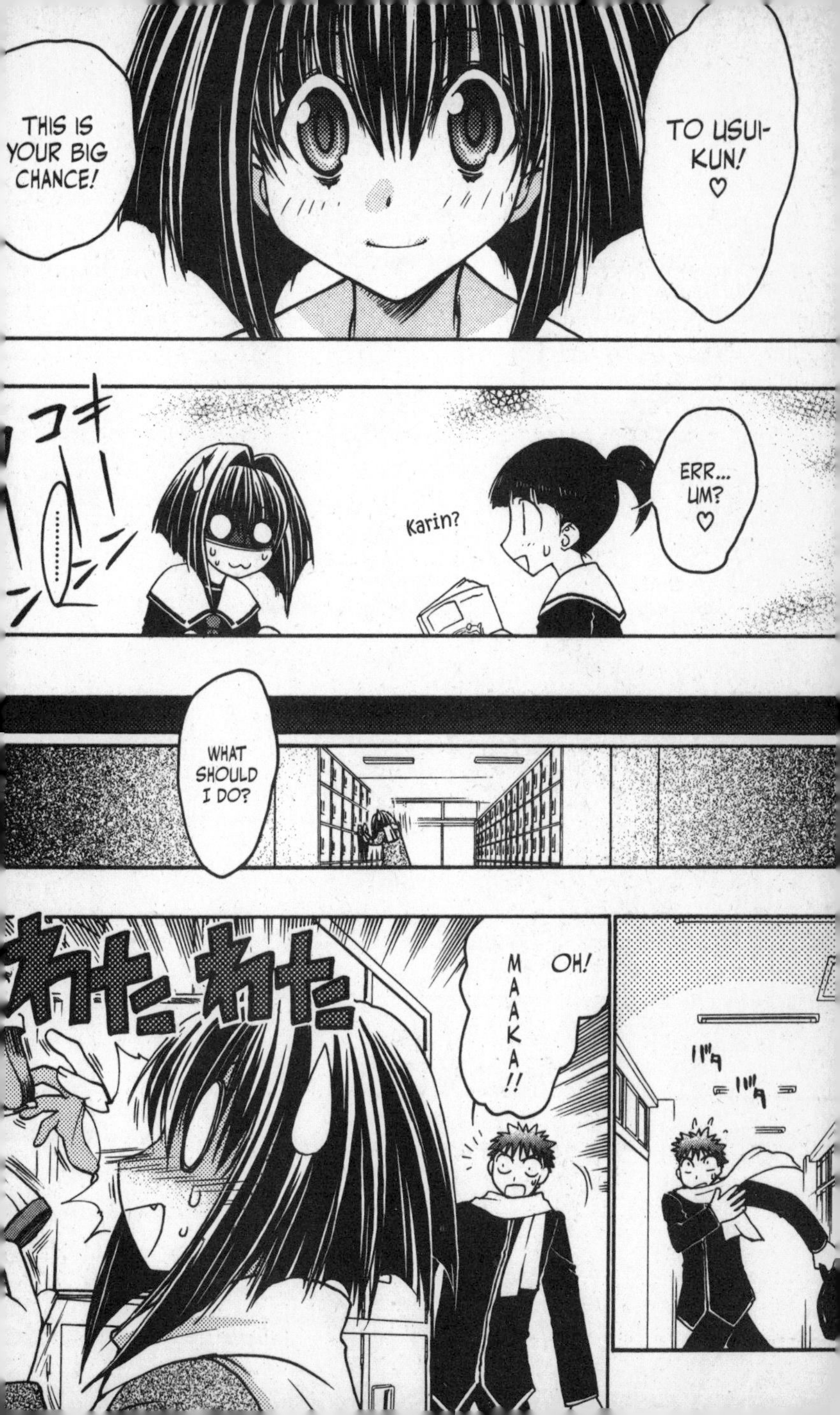
TO USUI-KUN! ♡
THIS IS YOUR BIG CHANCE!
ERR... UM? ♡
Karin?
......
コキ
WHAT SHOULD I DO?
バタ バタ
OH!
MAAKA!!
わたわた

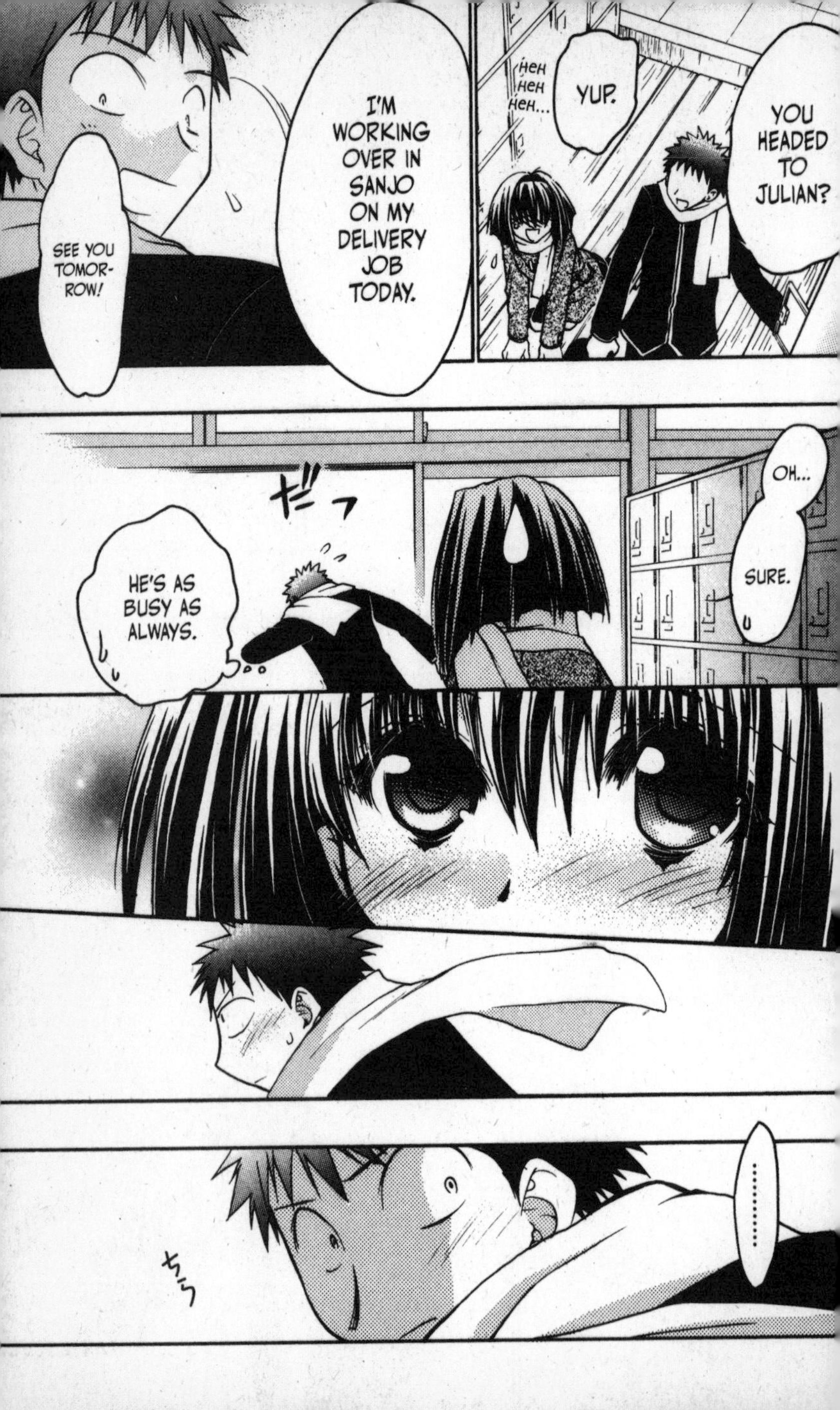
YOU HEADED TO JULIAN?
YUP.
HEH HEH HEH...
I'M WORKING OVER IN SANJO ON MY DELIVERY JOB TODAY.
SEE YOU TOMOR-ROW!
OH... SURE.
ダッ
HE'S AS BUSY AS ALWAYS.
......

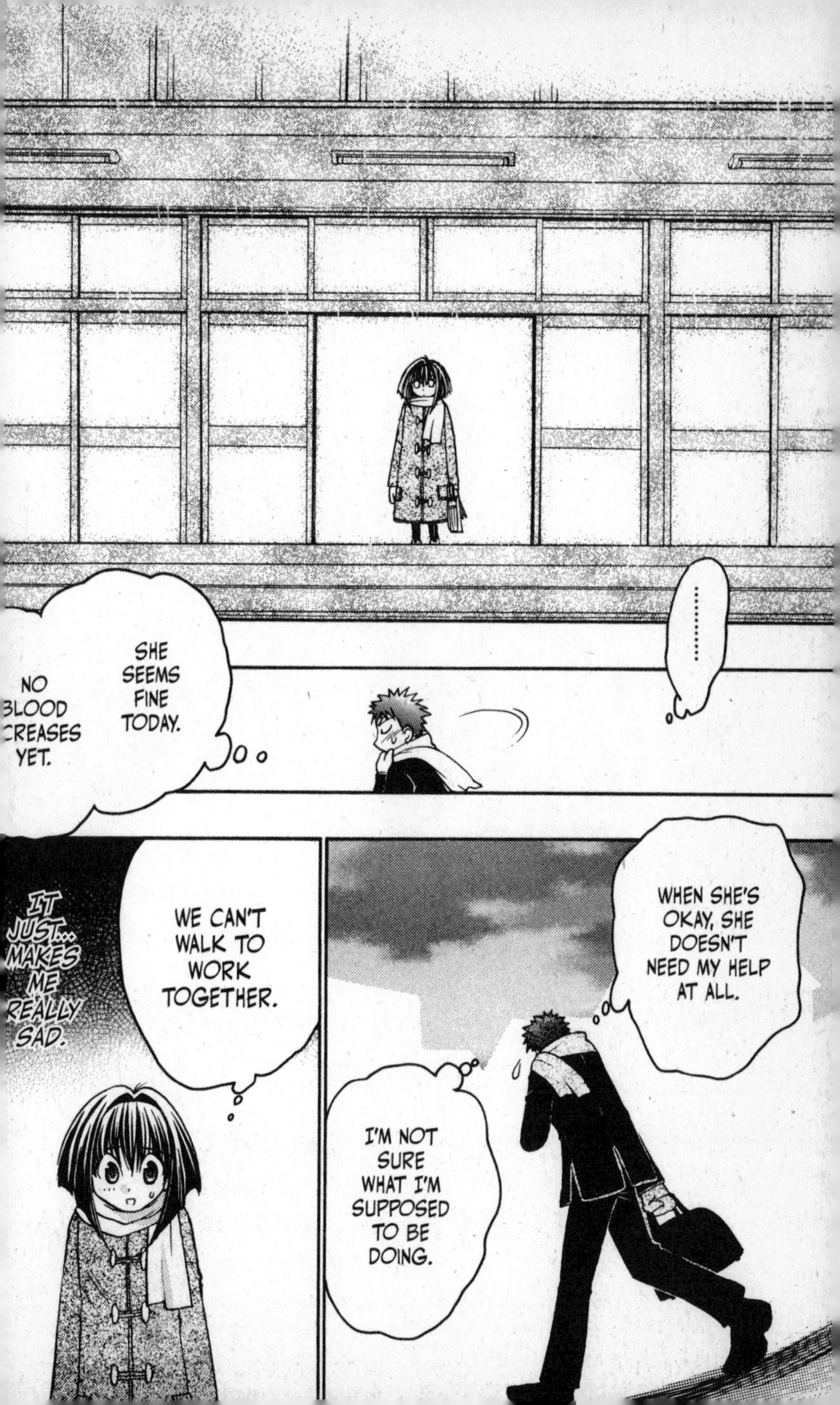
......
SHE SEEMS FINE TODAY.
NO BLOOD CREASES YET.
WHEN SHE'S OKAY, SHE DOESN'T NEED MY HELP AT ALL.
I'M NOT SURE WHAT I'M SUPPOSED TO BE DOING.
WE CAN'T WALK TO WORK TOGETHER.
IT JUST... MAKES ME REALLY SAD.

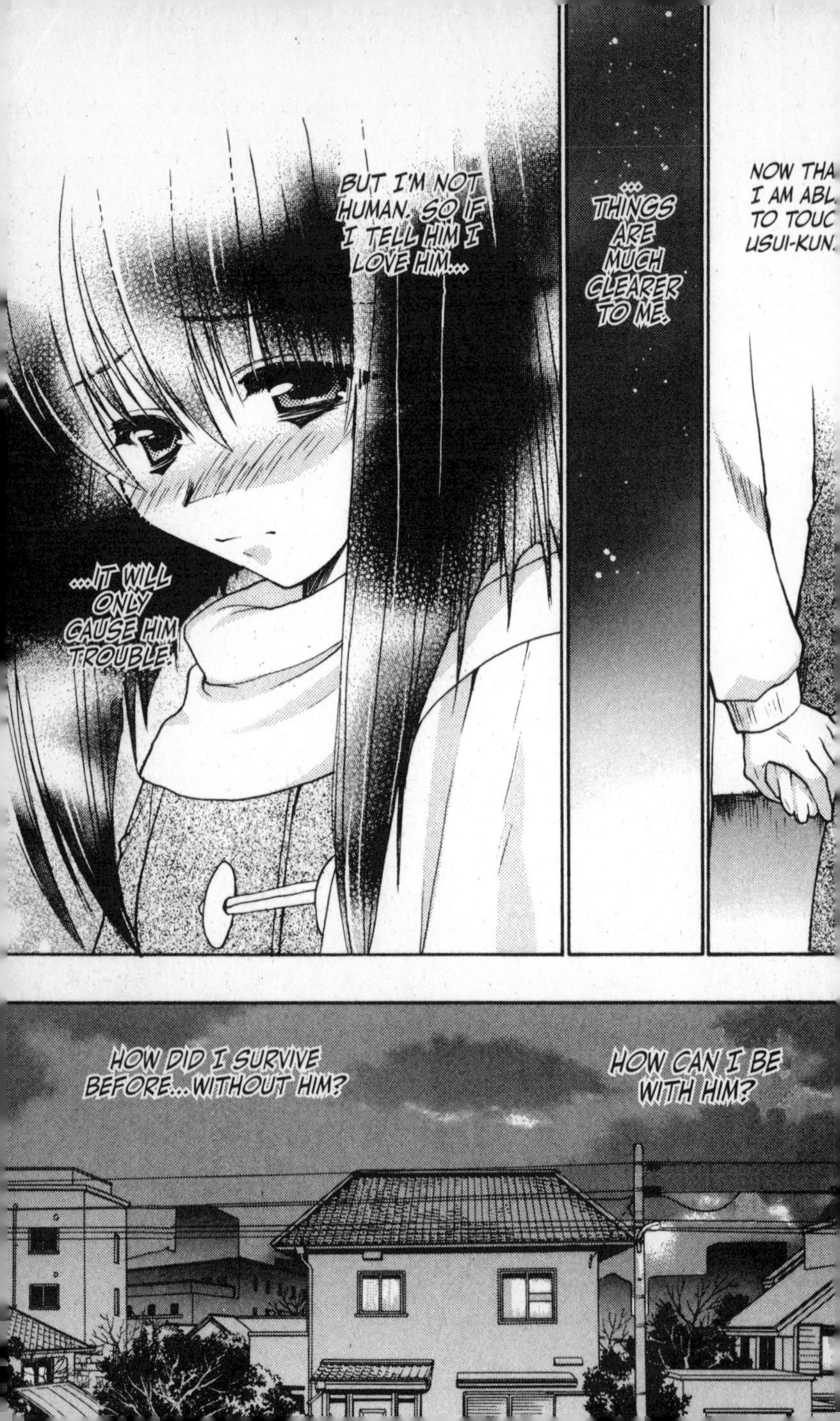
NOW THA I AM ABL TO TOUC USUI-KUN.
...THINGS ARE MUCH CLEARER TO ME.
BUT I'M NOT HUMAN. SO IF I TELL HIM I LOVE HIM...
...IT WILL ONLY CAUSE HIM TROUBLE.
HOW CAN I BE WITH HIM?
HOW DID I SURVIVE BEFORE...WITHOUT HIM?

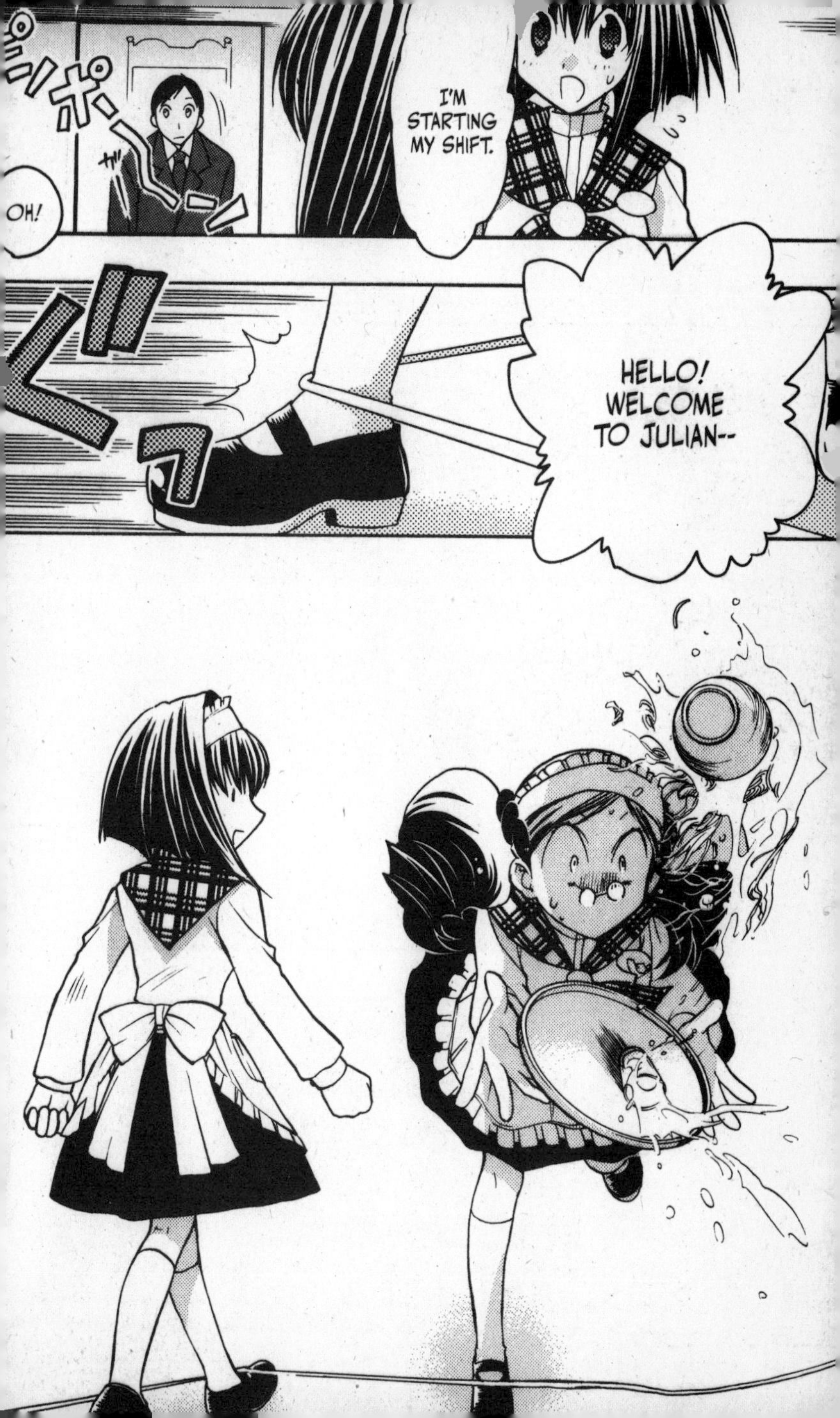
I'M STARTING MY SHIFT.
OH!
HELLO! WELCOME TO JULIAN--

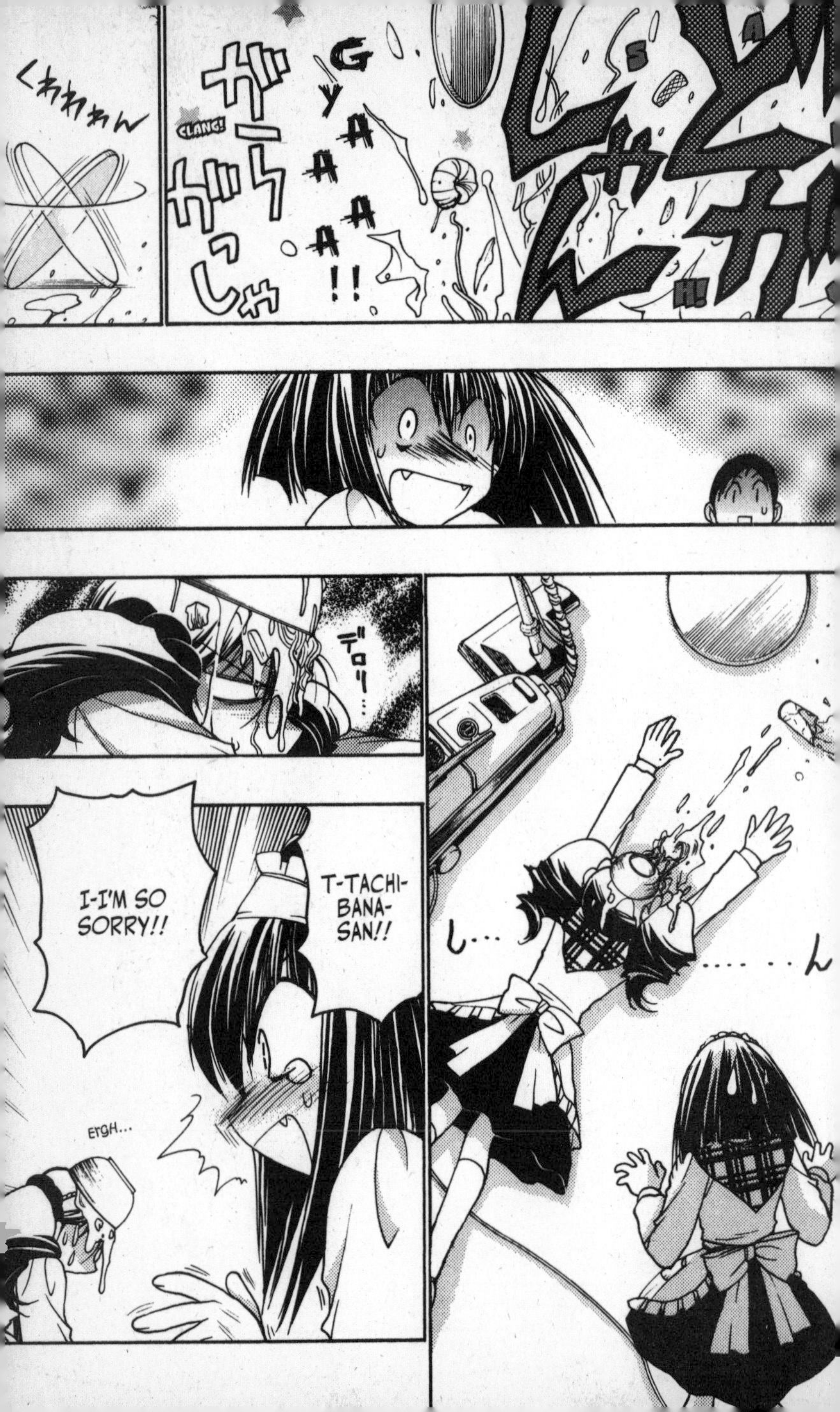
CLANG!
GYAAAAA!!
くわわぁん
し…
……ん
デロリ…
T-TACHI-BANA-SAN!!
I-I'M SO SORRY!!
ERGH...

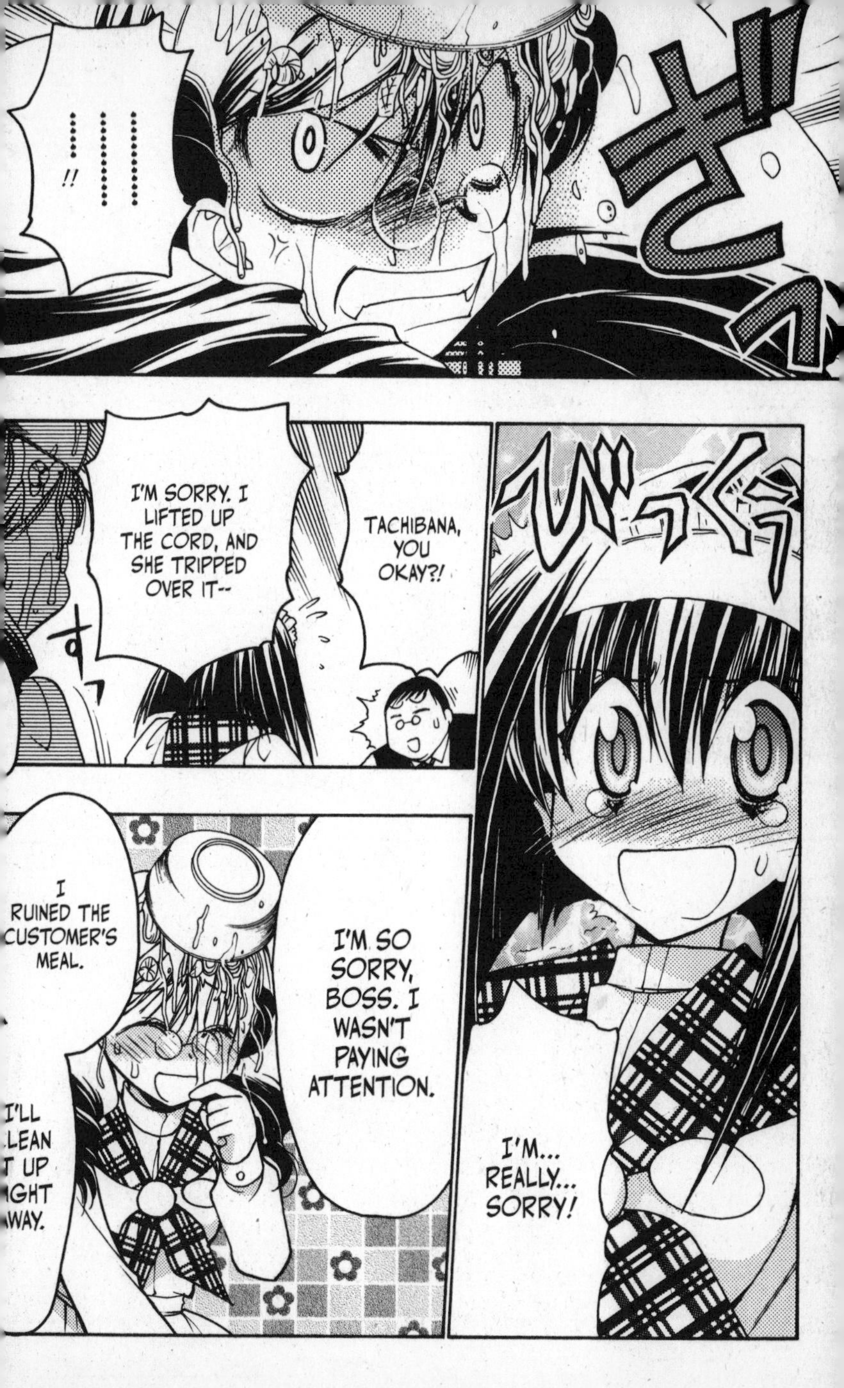
......!!
I'M... REALLY... SORRY!
TACHIBANA, YOU OKAY?!
I'M SORRY. I LIFTED UP THE CORD, AND SHE TRIPPED OVER IT--
I'M SO SORRY, BOSS. I WASN'T PAYING ATTENTION.
I RUINED THE CUSTOMER'S MEAL.
I'LL LEAN T UP IGHT WAY.

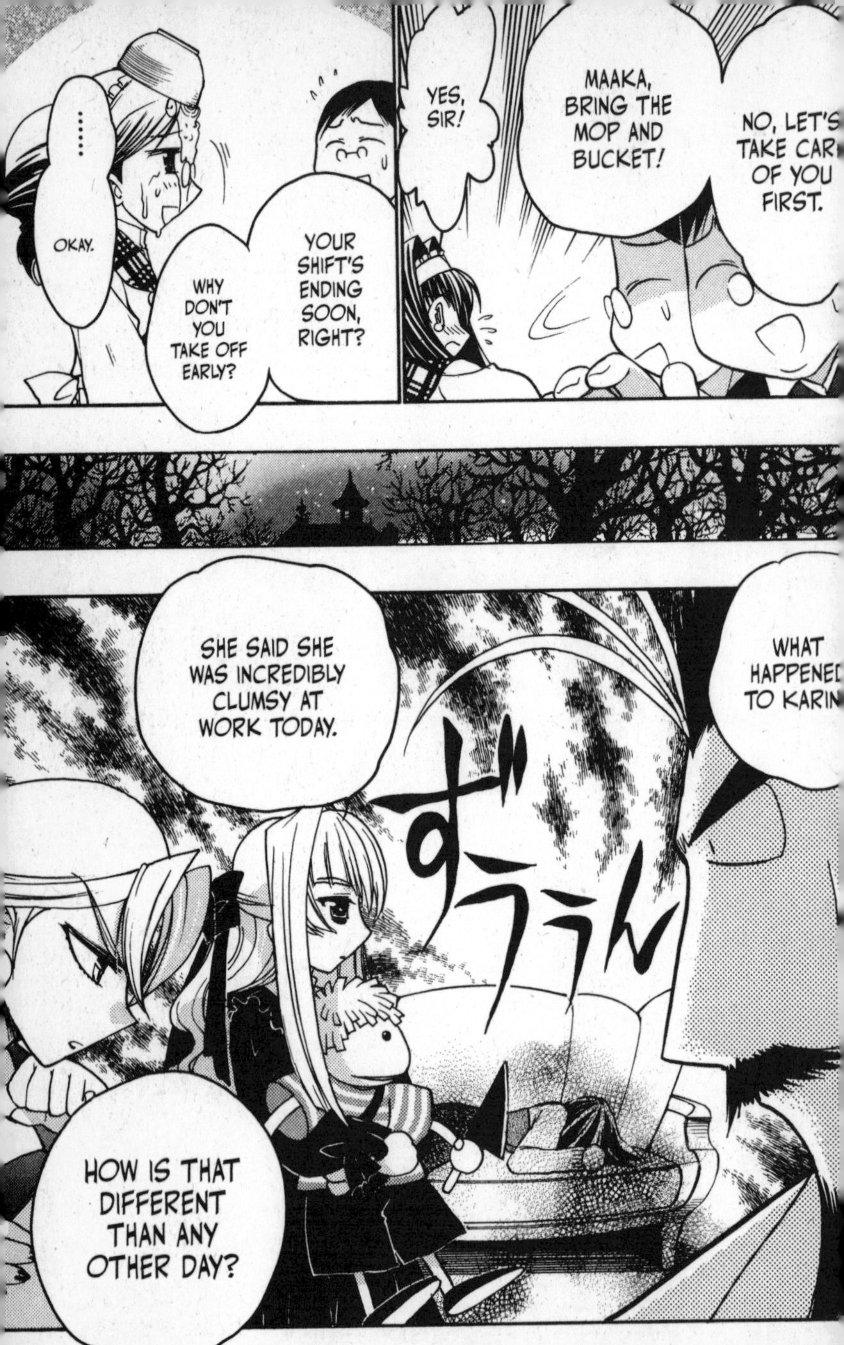
NO, LET'S TAKE CAR OF YOU FIRST.
MAAKA, BRING THE MOP AND BUCKET!
YES, SIR!
YOUR SHIFT'S ENDING SOON, RIGHT?
WHY DON'T YOU TAKE OFF EARLY?
......
OKAY.
WHAT HAPPENED TO KARIN
SHE SAID SHE WAS INCREDIBLY CLUMSY AT WORK TODAY.
ずううん
HOW IS THAT DIFFERENT THAN ANY OTHER DAY?

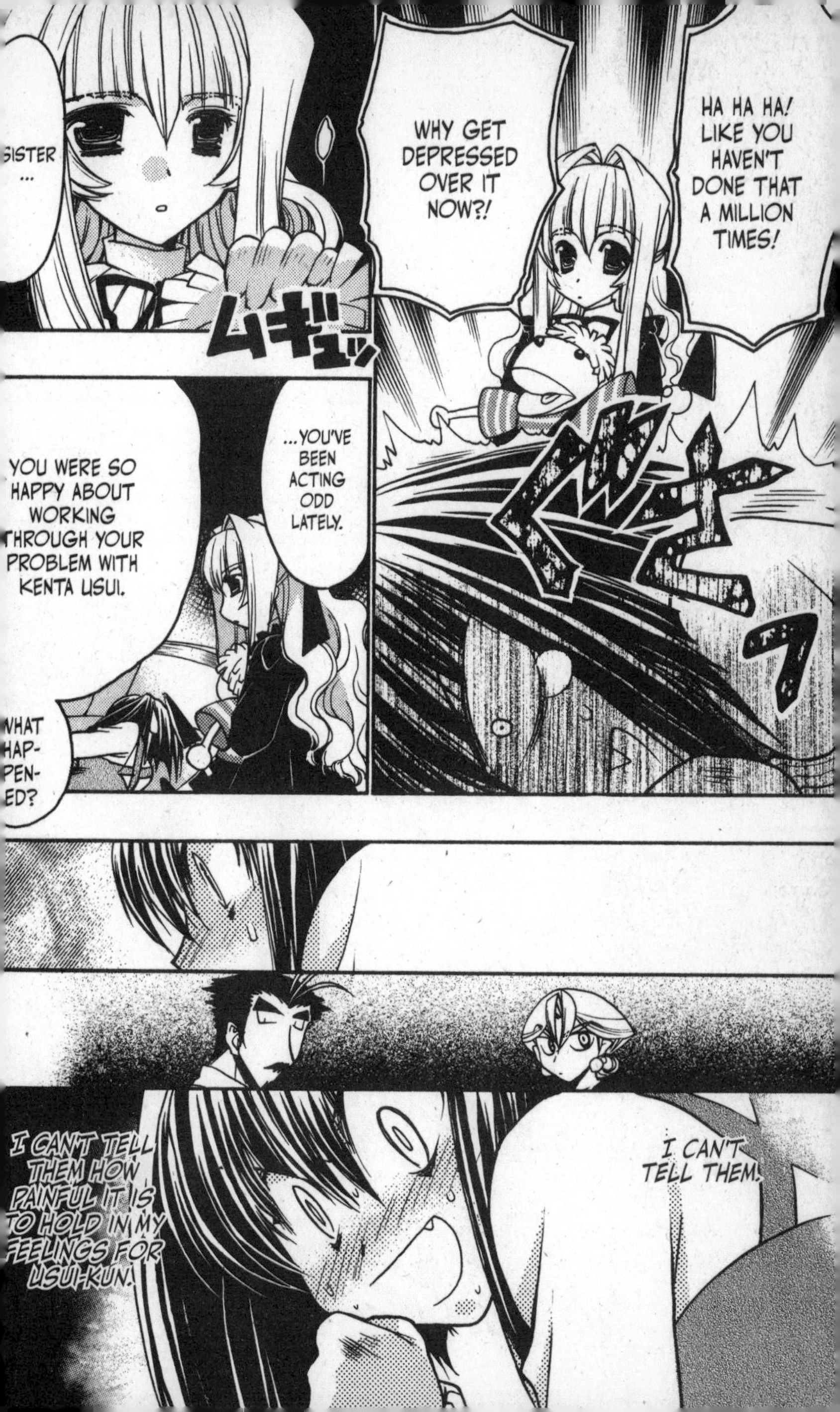
HA HA HA! LIKE YOU HAVEN'T DONE THAT A MILLION TIMES!
WHY GET DEPRESSED OVER IT NOW?!
SISTER ...
ムギュッ
...YOU'VE BEEN ACTING ODD LATELY.
YOU WERE SO HAPPY ABOUT WORKING THROUGH YOUR PROBLEM WITH KENTA USUI.
WHAT HAPPENED?
I CAN'T TELL THEM!
I CAN'T TELL THEM HOW PAINFUL IT IS TO HOLD IN MY FEELINGS FOR USUI-KUN!

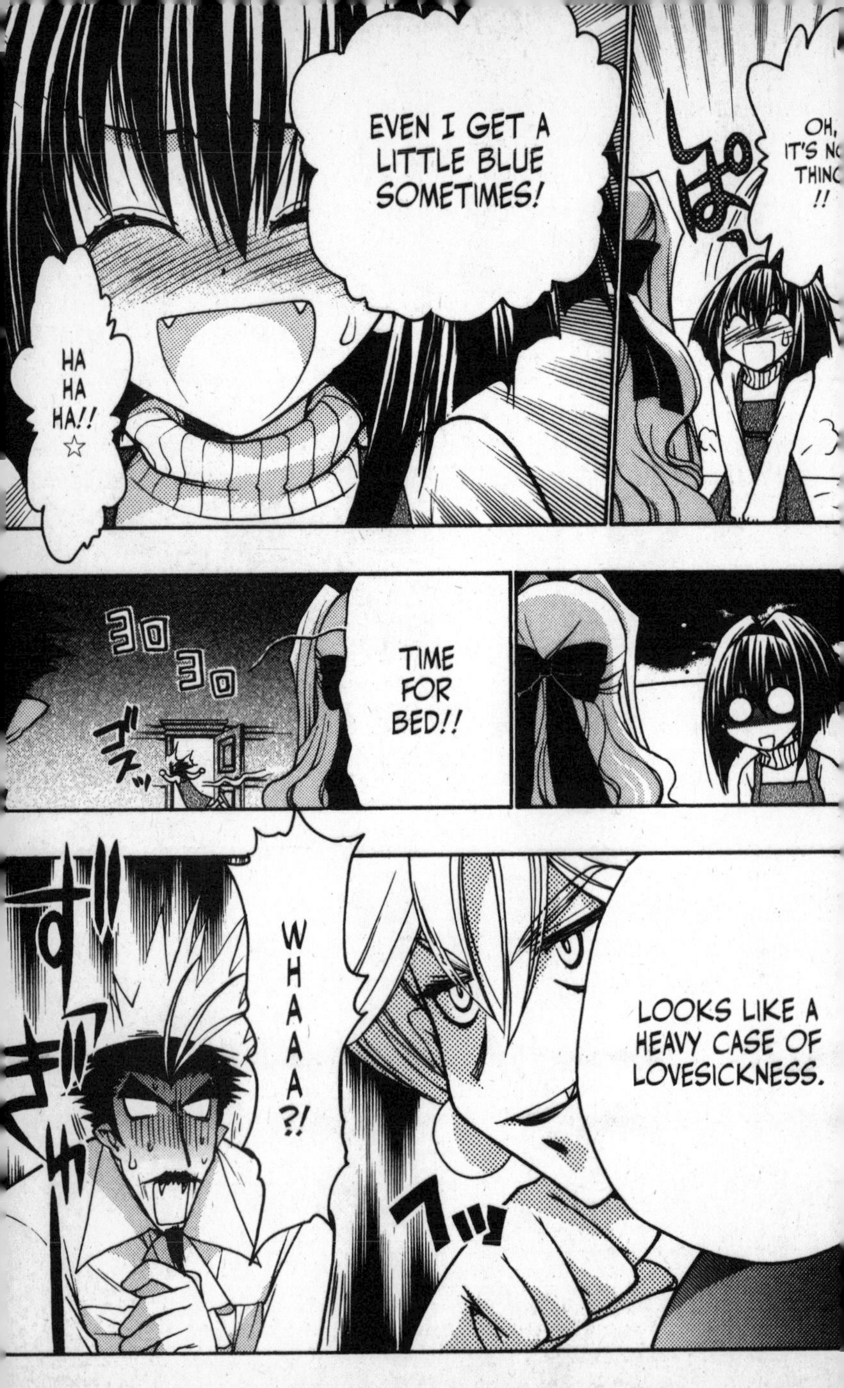
ぱっ
OH, IT'S NO THING !!
EVEN I GET A LITTLE BLUE SOMETIMES!
HA HA HA!! ☆
TIME FOR BED!!
ヨロ ヨロ
ゴズッ
LOOKS LIKE A HEAVY CASE OF LOVESICKNESS.
WHAAAA?!
ずーーん!!

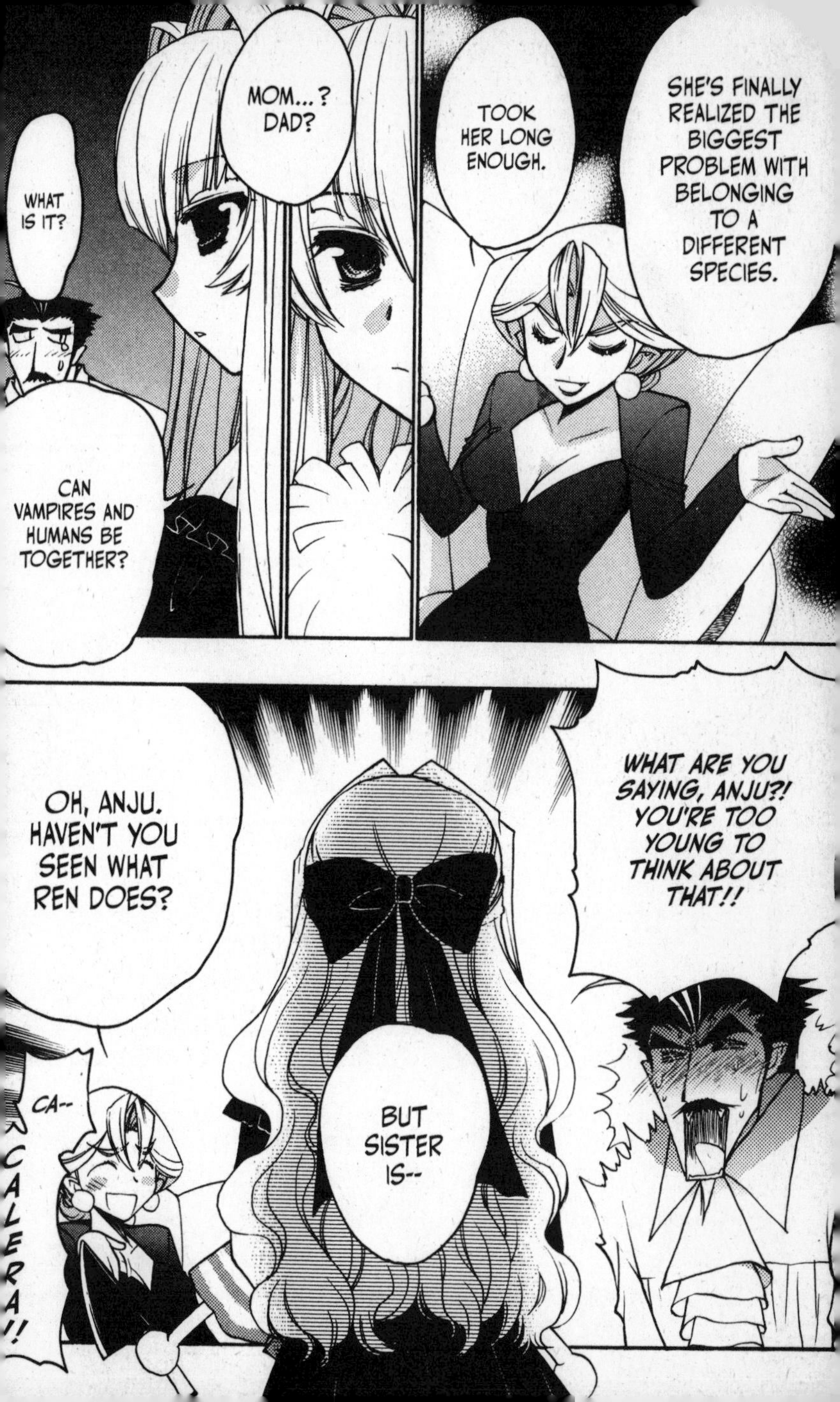
SHE'S FINALLY REALIZED THE BIGGEST PROBLEM WITH BELONGING TO A DIFFERENT SPECIES.
TOOK HER LONG ENOUGH.
MOM...? DAD?
WHAT IS IT?
CAN VAMPIRES AND HUMANS BE TOGETHER?
WHAT ARE YOU SAYING, ANJU?! YOU'RE TOO YOUNG TO THINK ABOUT THAT!!
OH, ANJU. HAVEN'T YOU SEEN WHAT REN DOES?
BUT SISTER IS--
CA--
CALERA!!

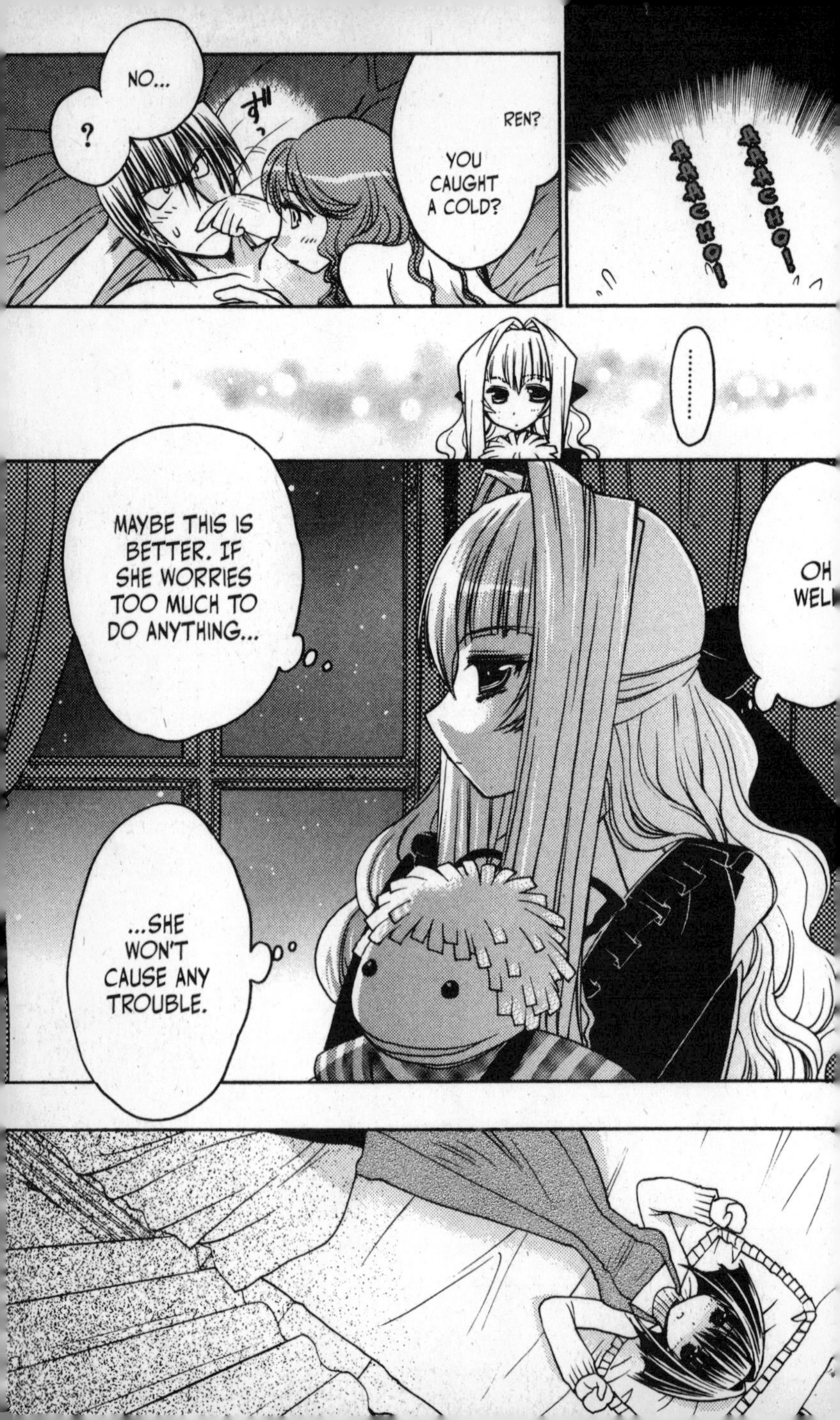

AAACHOO!
AAACHOO!
REN? YOU CAUGHT A COLD?
NO...
?
......
OH WELL
MAYBE THIS IS BETTER. IF SHE WORRIES TOO MUCH TO DO ANYTHING...
...SHE WON'T CAUSE ANY TROUBLE.

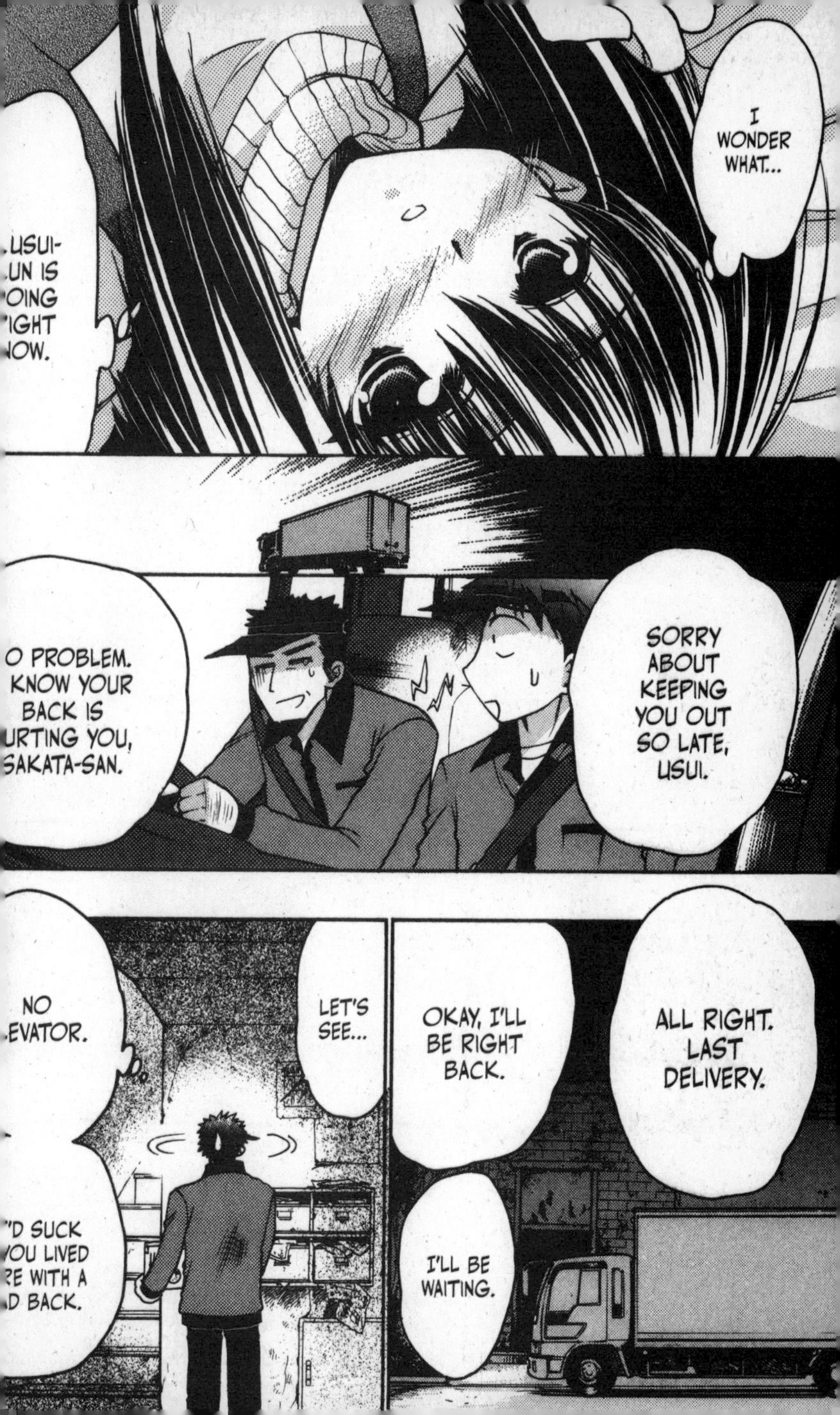
I WONDER WHAT...
USUI- UN IS OING IGHT NOW.
SORRY ABOUT KEEPING YOU OUT SO LATE, USUI.
O PROBLEM. KNOW YOUR BACK IS URTING YOU, SAKATA-SAN.
ALL RIGHT. LAST DELIVERY.
OKAY, I'LL BE RIGHT BACK.
I'LL BE WAITING.
LET'S SEE...
NO EVATOR.
'D SUCK OU LIVED E WITH A D BACK.

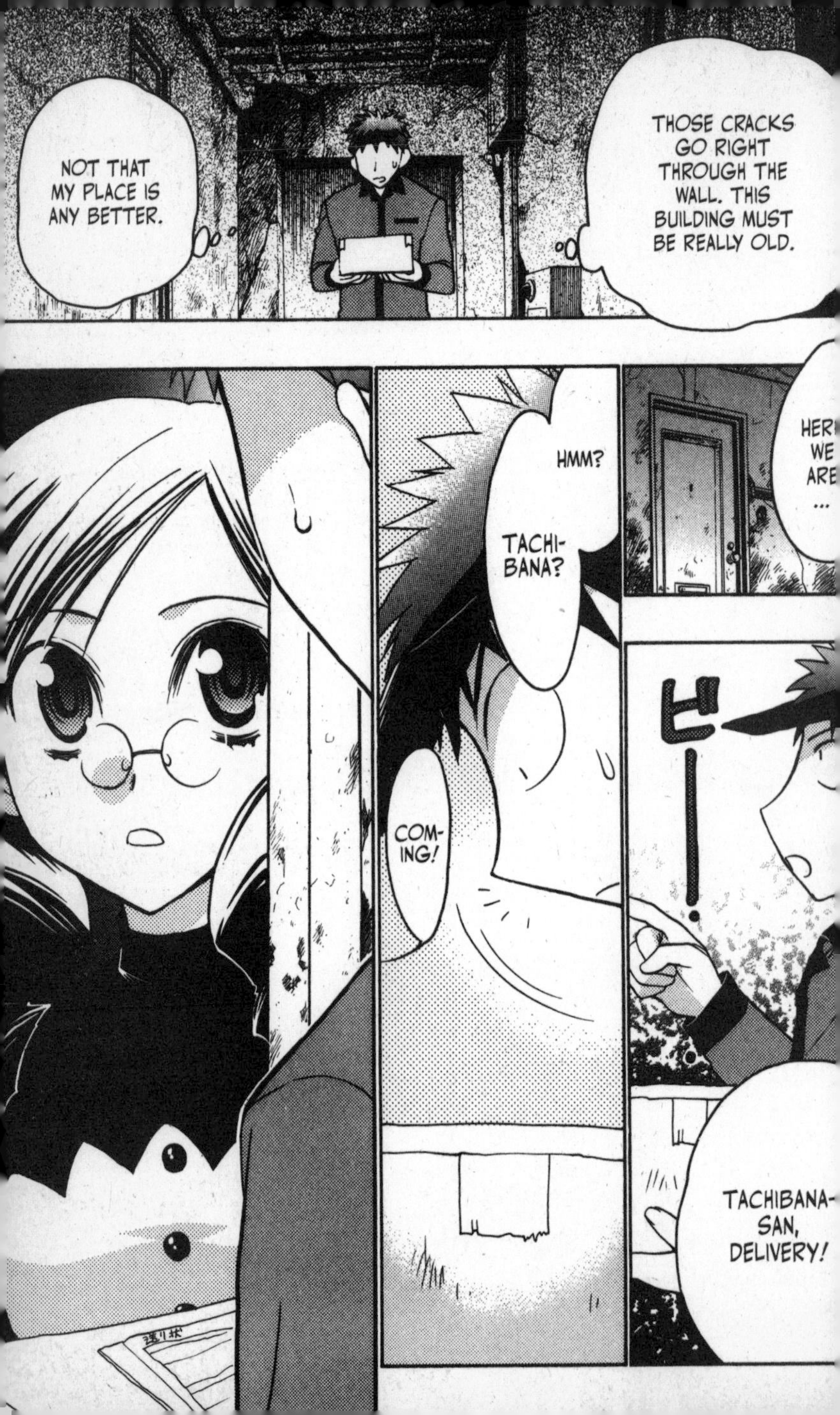
THOSE CRACKS GO RIGHT THROUGH THE WALL. THIS BUILDING MUST BE REALLY OLD.
NOT THAT MY PLACE IS ANY BETTER.
HER WE ARE ...
ビー!
TACHIBANA-SAN, DELIVERY!
HMM?
TACHIBANA?
COMING!

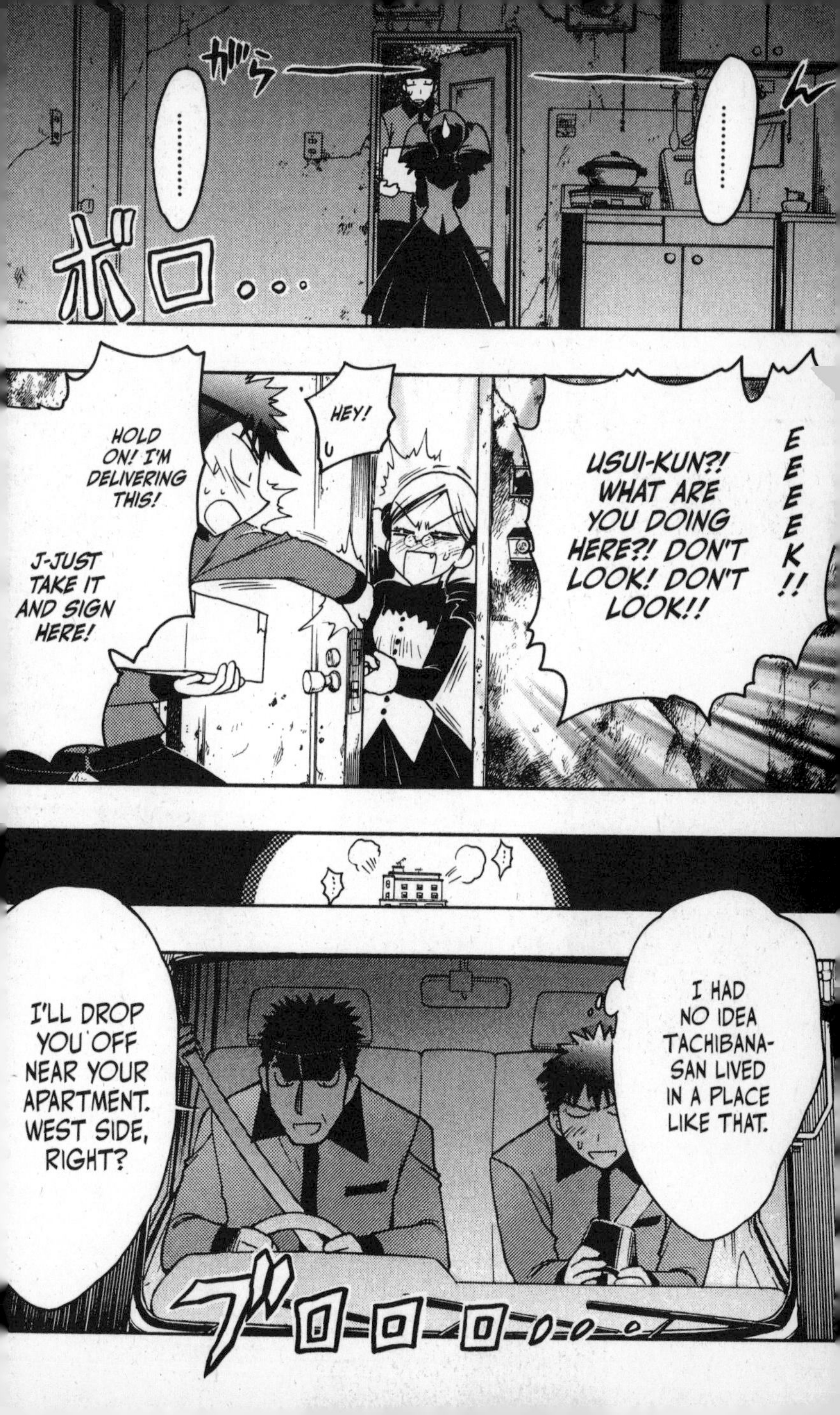
……
ガらーーーーーーん
……
ボロ…
EEEEEK!!
USUI-KUN?! WHAT ARE YOU DOING HERE?! DON'T LOOK! DON'T LOOK!!
HEY!
HOLD ON! I'M DELIVERING THIS!
J-JUST TAKE IT AND SIGN HERE!
I HAD NO IDEA TACHIBANA-SAN LIVED IN A PLACE LIKE THAT.
I'LL DROP YOU OFF NEAR YOUR APARTMENT. WEST SIDE, RIGHT?
ブロロロロ…

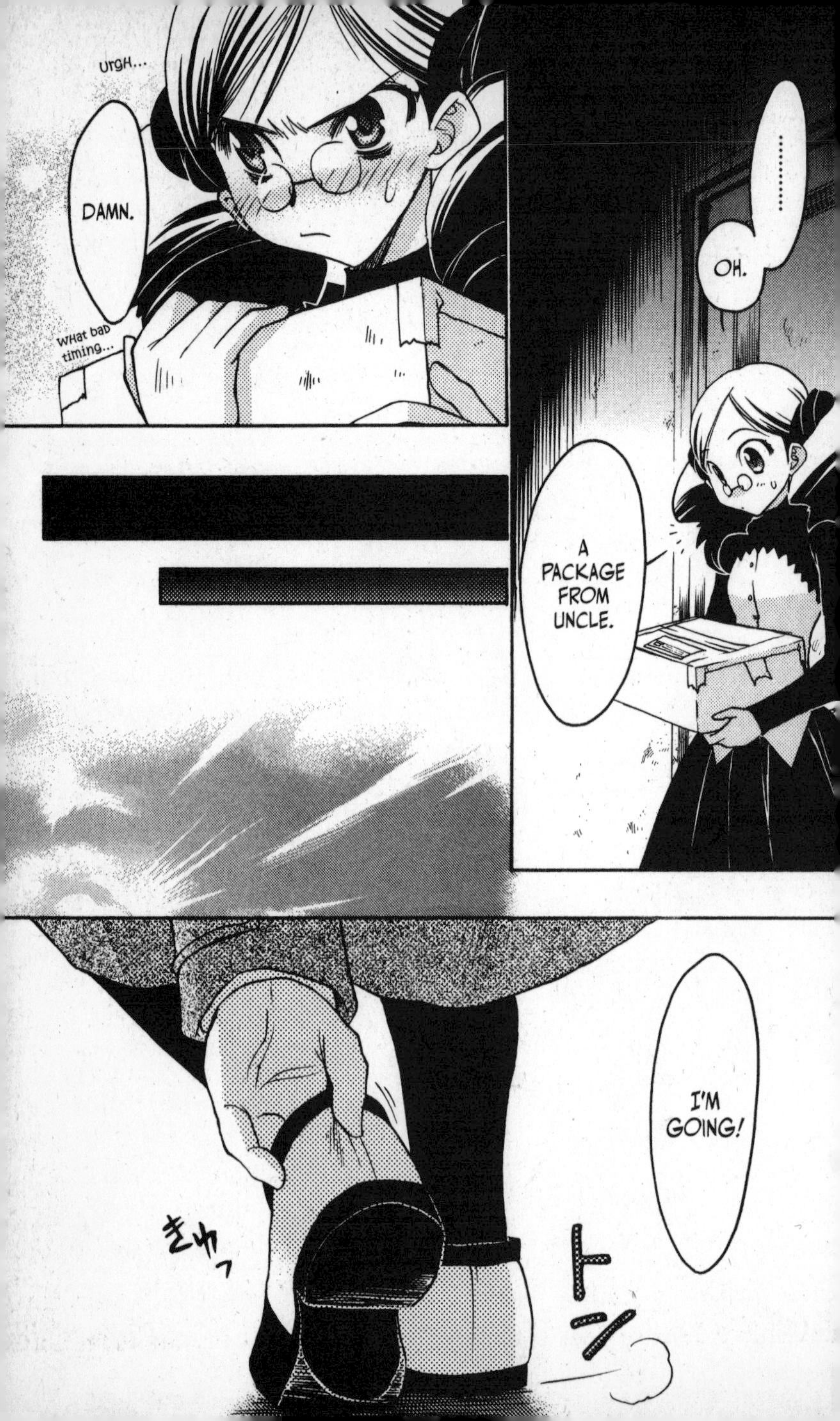
......
OH.
A PACKAGE FROM UNCLE.
Urgh...
DAMN.
What bad timing...
I'M GOING!
トンッ
きゅっ

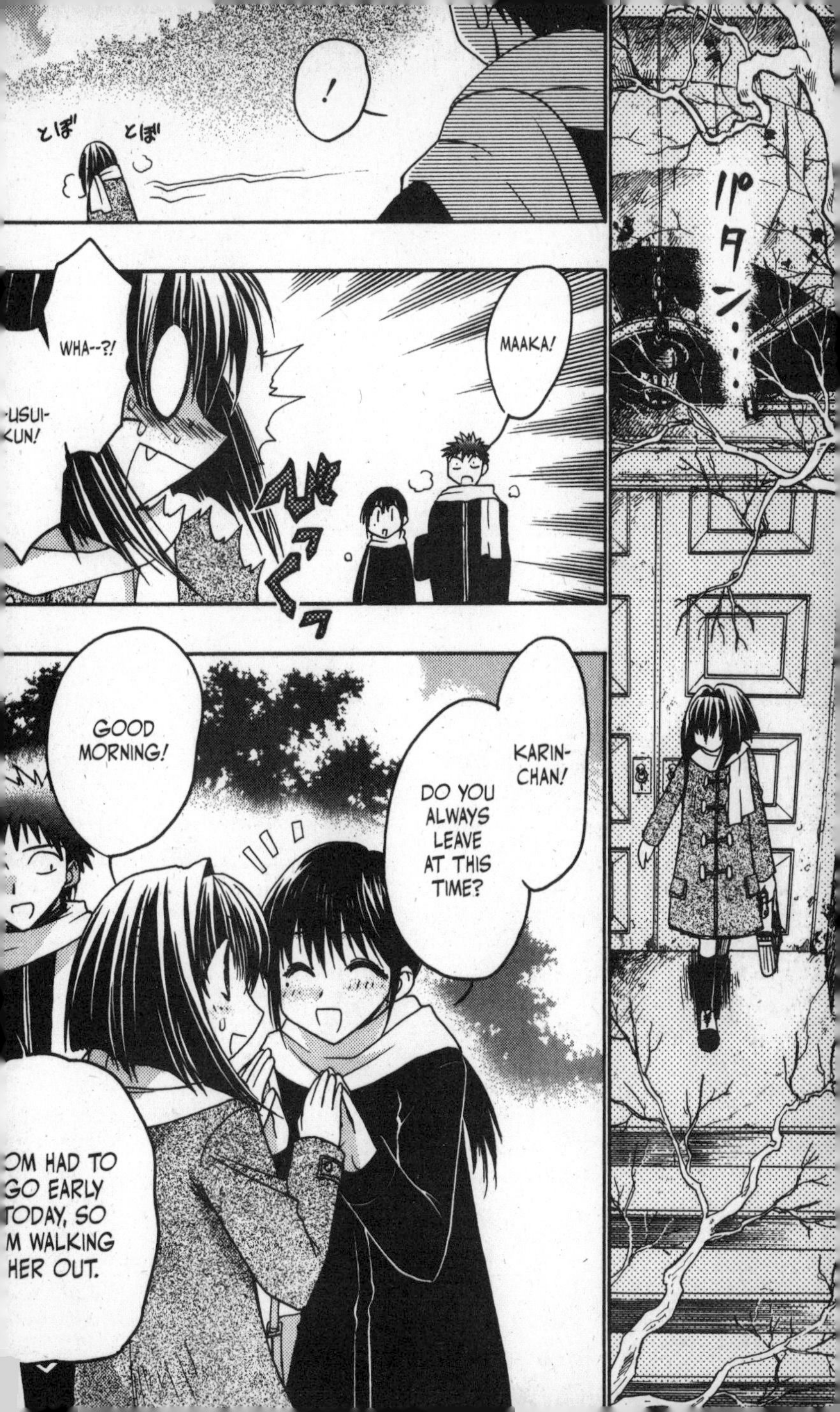

パタン・・・
!
とぼ とぼ
MAAKA!
WHA--?!
USUI-KUN!
KARIN-CHAN!
DO YOU ALWAYS LEAVE AT THIS TIME?
GOOD MORNING!
OM HAD TO GO EARLY TODAY, SO M WALKING HER OUT.

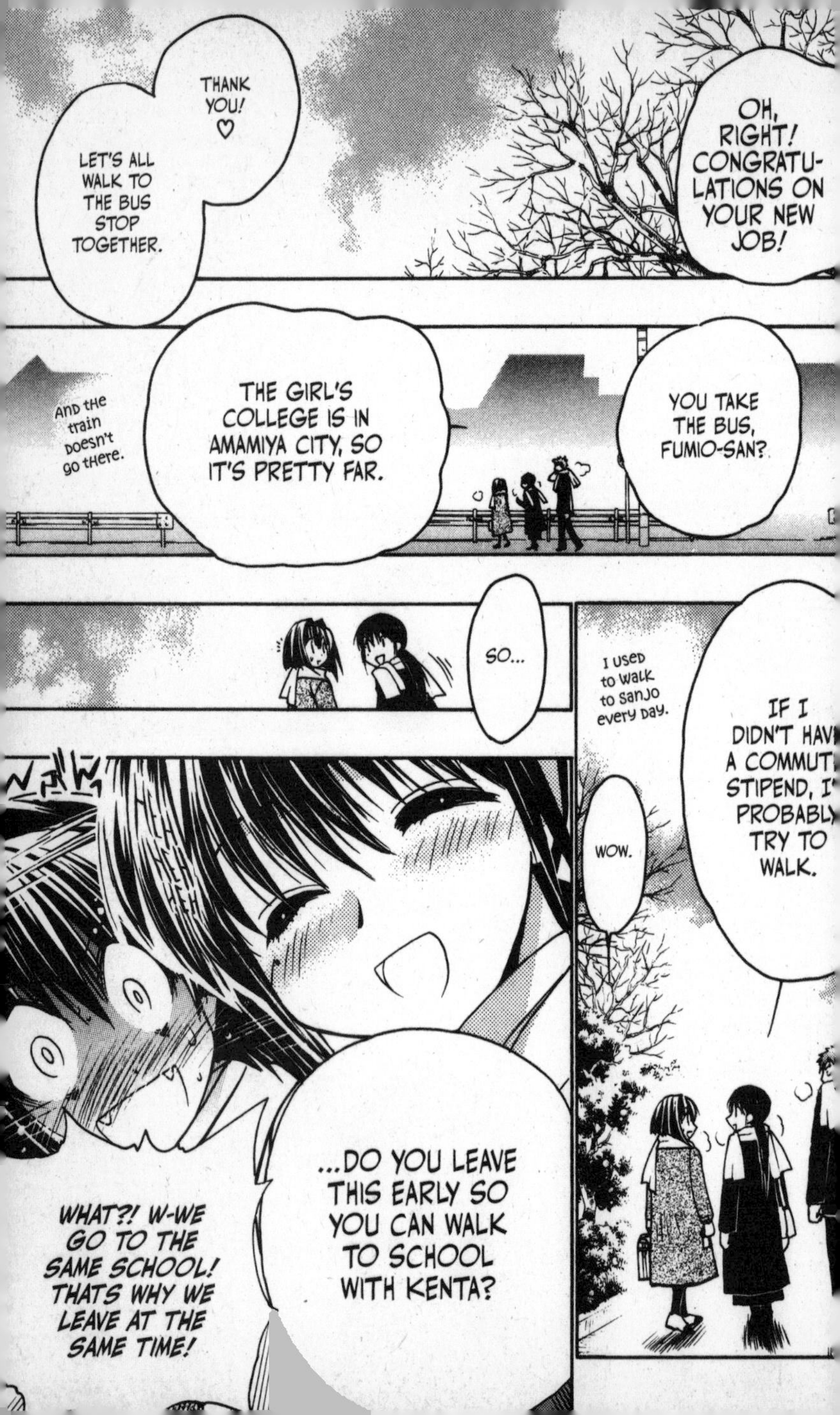
OH, RIGHT! CONGRATULATIONS ON YOUR NEW JOB!
THANK YOU! ♡
LET'S ALL WALK TO THE BUS STOP TOGETHER.
YOU TAKE THE BUS, FUMIO-SAN?
THE GIRL'S COLLEGE IS IN AMAMIYA CITY, SO IT'S PRETTY FAR.
And the train doesn't go there.
IF I DIDN'T HAV A COMMUT STIPEND, I' PROBABL TRY TO WALK.
I used to walk to Sanjo every day.
WOW.
SO...
...DO YOU LEAVE THIS EARLY SO YOU CAN WALK TO SCHOOL WITH KENTA?
WHAT?! W-WE GO TO THE SAME SCHOOL! THATS WHY WE LEAVE AT THE SAME TIME!

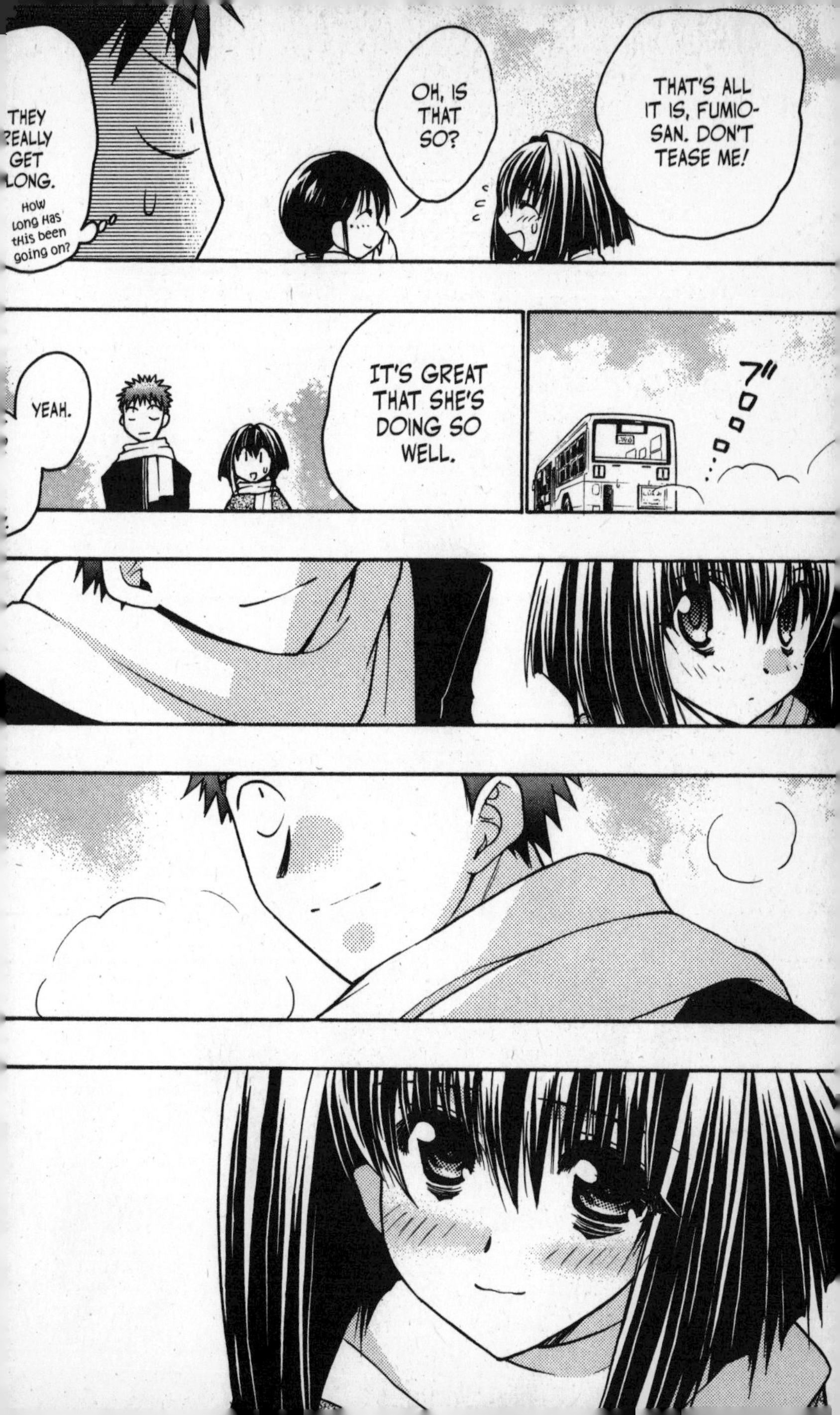
THAT'S ALL IT IS, FUMIO-SAN. DON'T TEASE ME!
OH, IS THAT SO?
THEY REALLY GET LONG.
HOW LONG HAS THIS BEEN GOING ON?
ブロロロ…
IT'S GREAT THAT SHE'S DOING SO WELL.
YEAH.

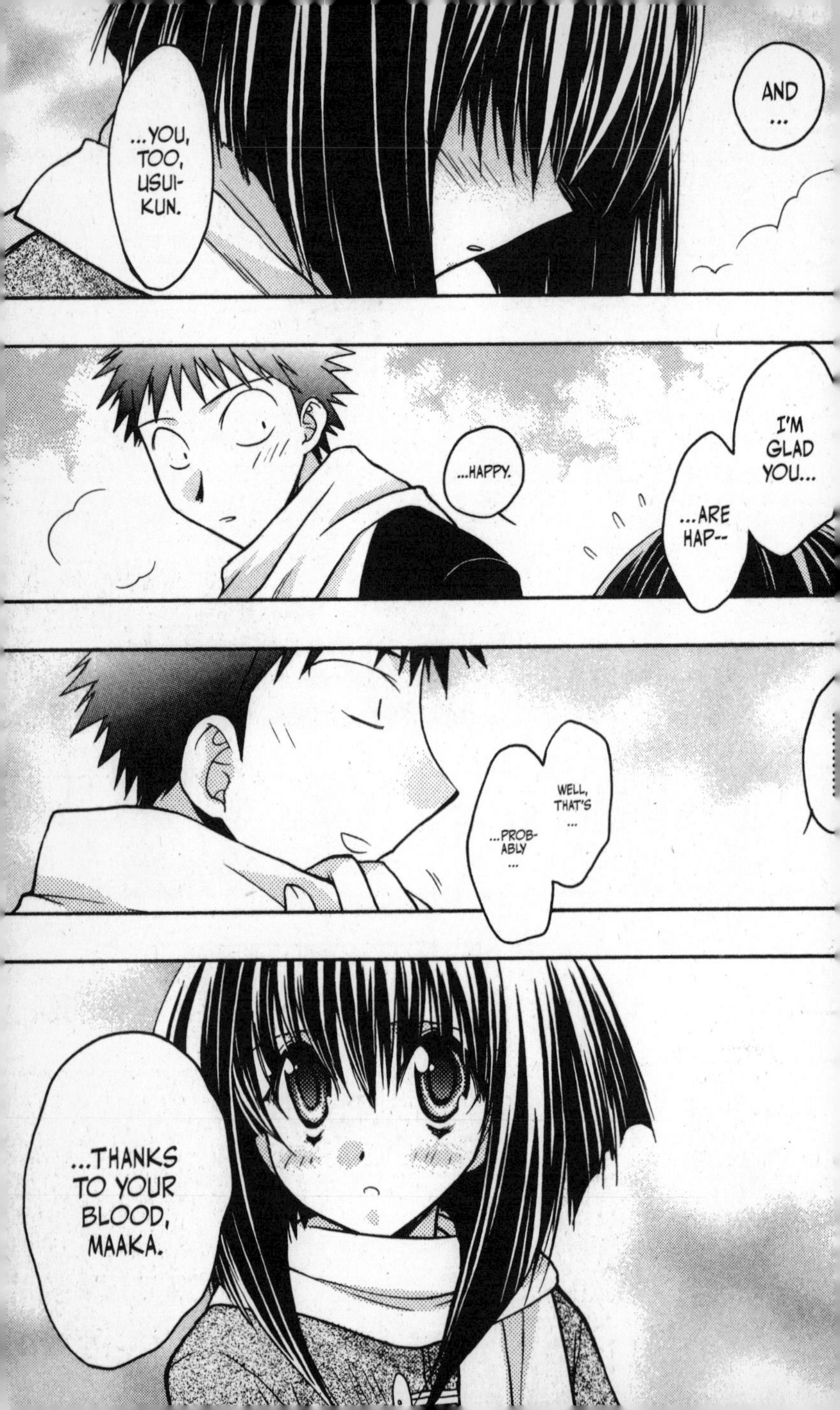
AND ...
...YOU, TOO, USUI-KUN.
I'M GLAD YOU...
...ARE HAP--
...HAPPY.
WELL, THAT'S ...
...PROB-ABLY ...
...THANKS TO YOUR BLOOD, MAAKA.

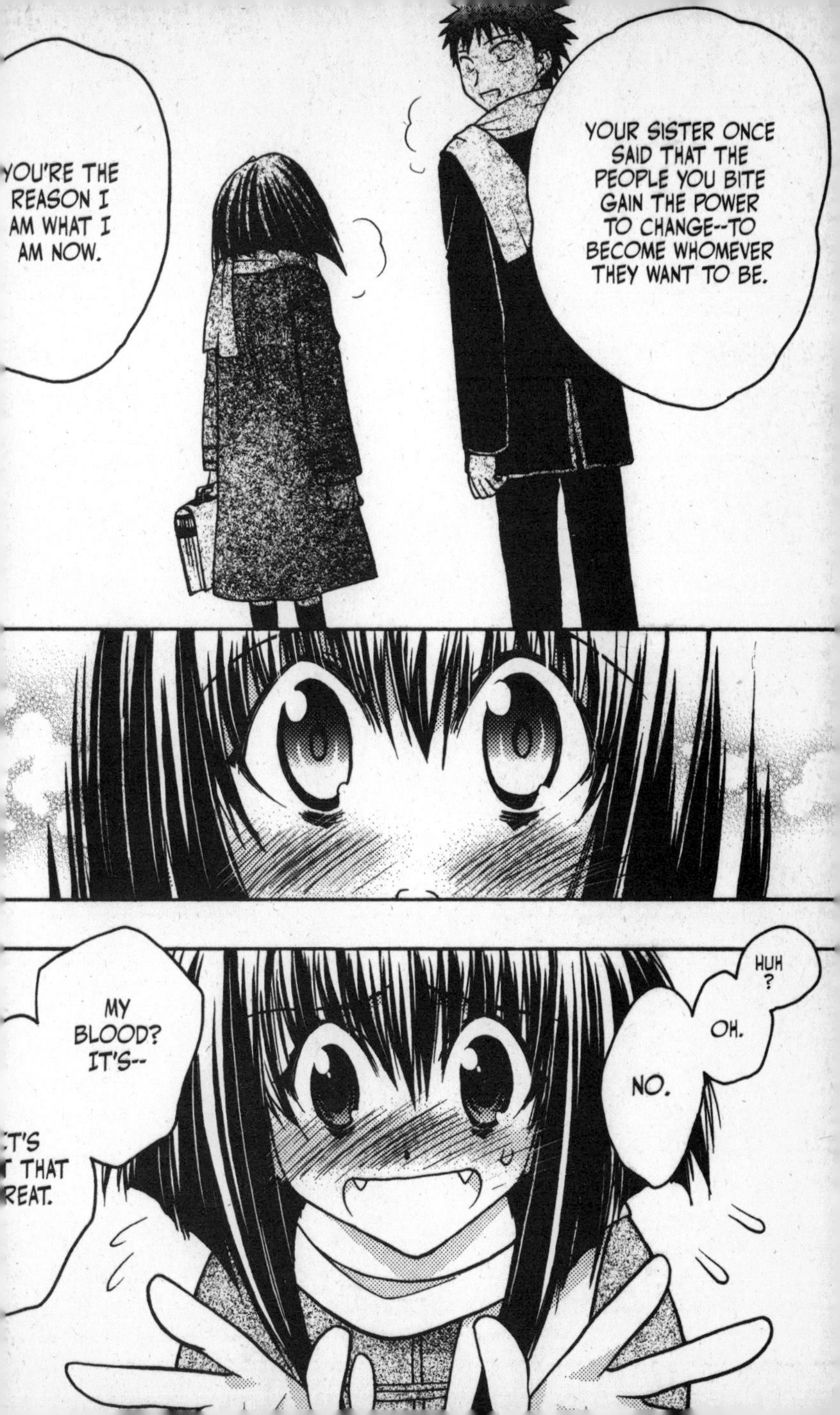
YOUR SISTER ONCE SAID THAT THE PEOPLE YOU BITE GAIN THE POWER TO CHANGE--TO BECOME WHOMEVER THEY WANT TO BE.
YOU'RE THE REASON I AM WHAT I AM NOW.
HUH?
OH.
NO.
MY BLOOD? IT'S--
T'S T THAT REAT.

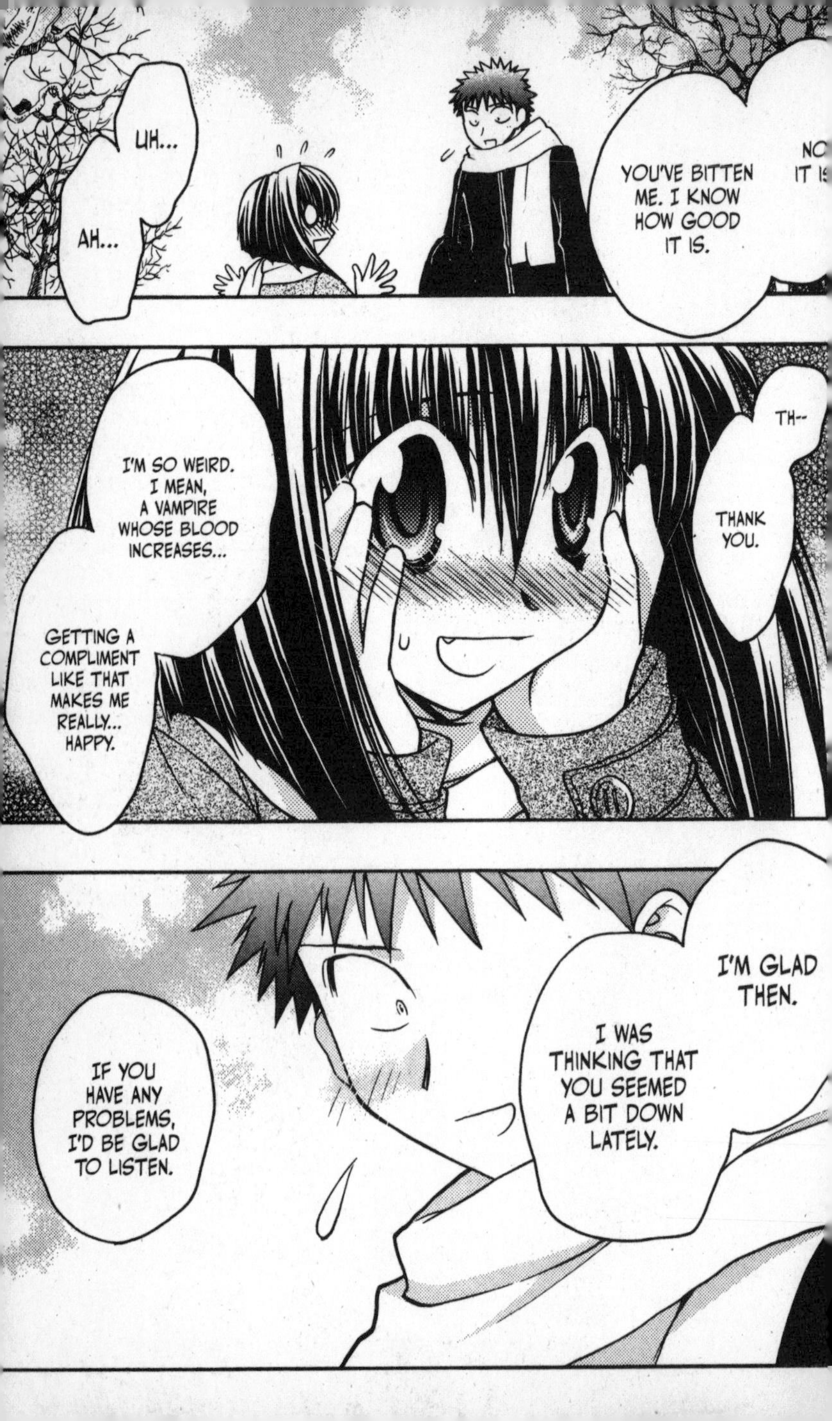
YOU'VE BITTEN ME. I KNOW HOW GOOD IT IS.
UH...
AH...
TH--
THANK YOU.
I'M SO WEIRD. I MEAN, A VAMPIRE WHOSE BLOOD INCREASES...
GETTING A COMPLIMENT LIKE THAT MAKES ME REALLY... HAPPY.
I'M GLAD THEN.
I WAS THINKING THAT YOU SEEMED A BIT DOWN LATELY.
IF YOU HAVE ANY PROBLEMS, I'D BE GLAD TO LISTEN.

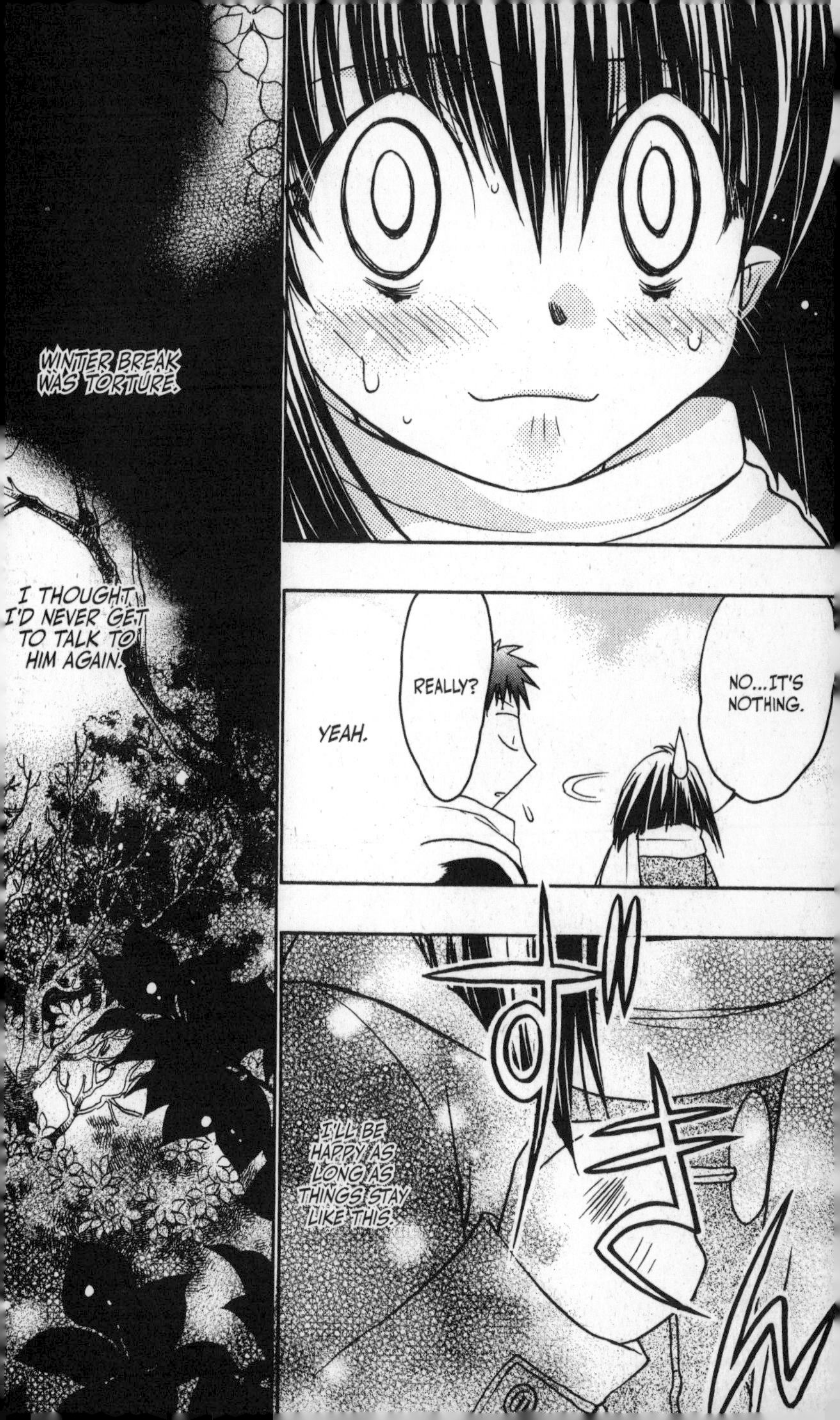
NO...IT'S NOTHING.
REALLY?
YEAH.
I'LL BE HAPPY AS LONG AS THINGS STAY LIKE THIS.
WINTER BREAK WAS TORTURE.
I THOUGHT I'D NEVER GET TO TALK TO HIM AGAIN.

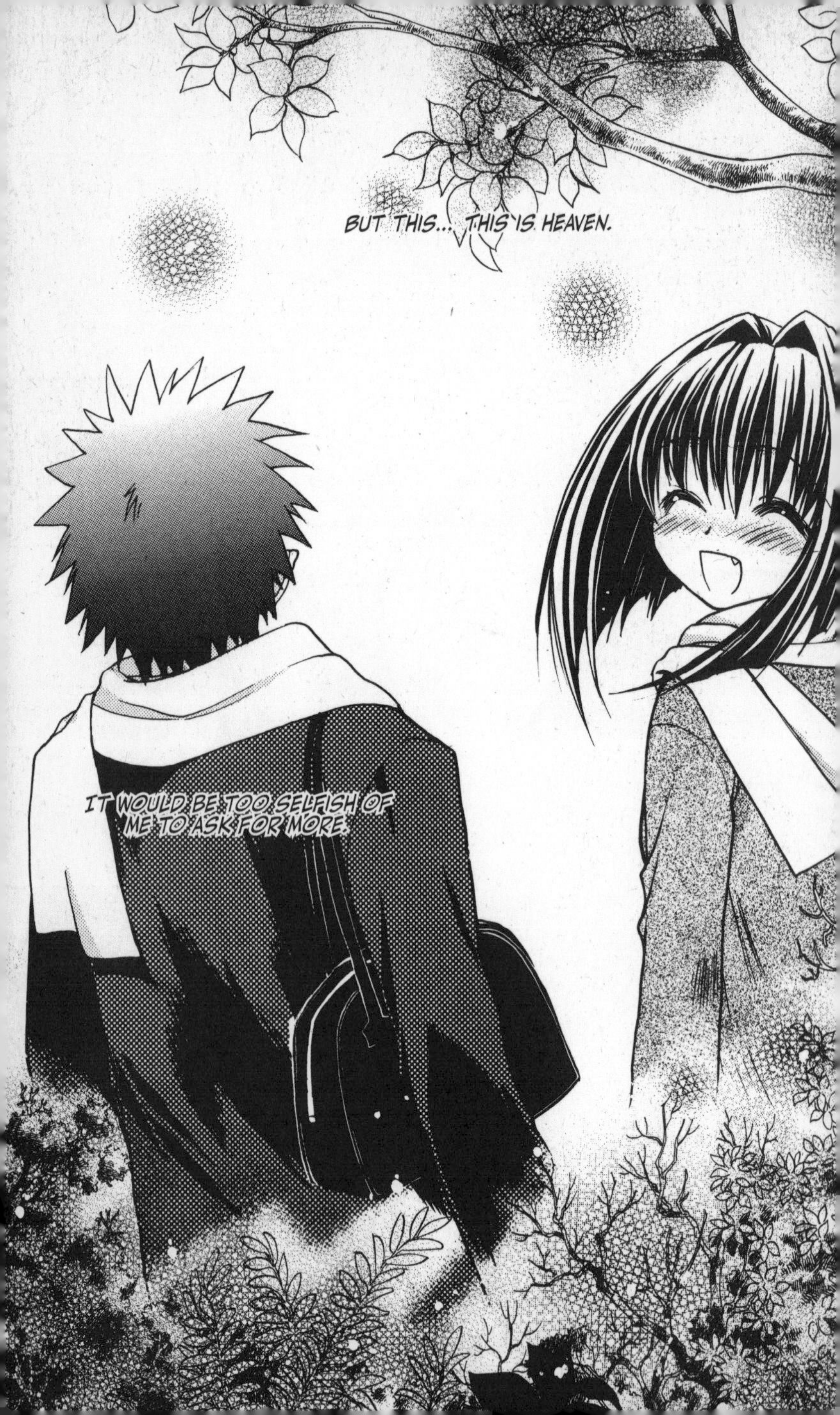
BUT THIS... THIS IS HEAVEN.
IT WOULD BE TOO SELFISH OF ME TO ASK FOR MORE.

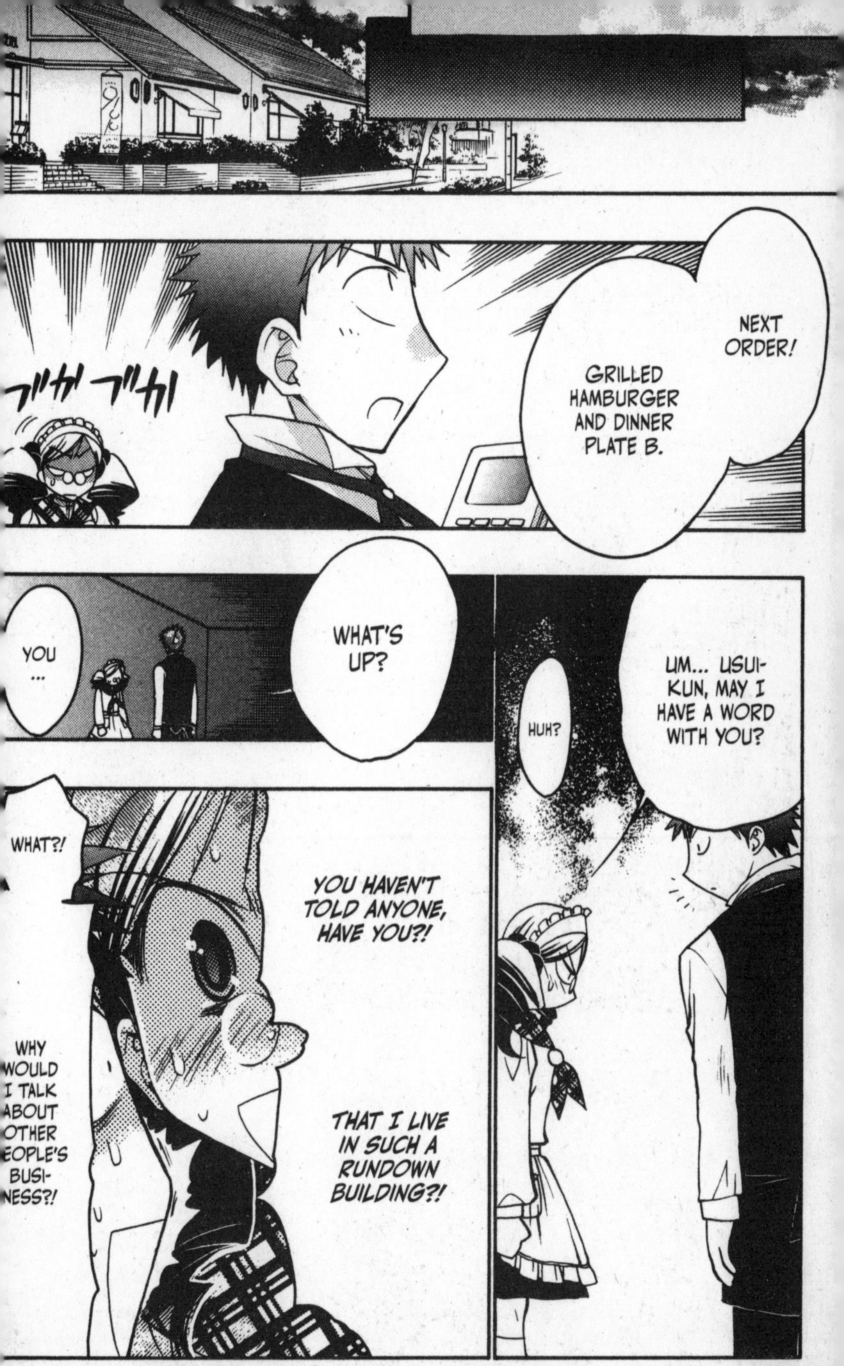
NEXT ORDER!
GRILLED HAMBURGER AND DINNER PLATE B.
ブガ ブガ
UM... USUI-KUN, MAY I HAVE A WORD WITH YOU?
HUH?
WHAT'S UP?
YOU ...
YOU HAVEN'T TOLD ANYONE, HAVE YOU?!
THAT I LIVE IN SUCH A RUNDOWN BUILDING?!
WHAT?!
WHY WOULD I TALK ABOUT OTHER EOPLE'S BUSI- NESS?!

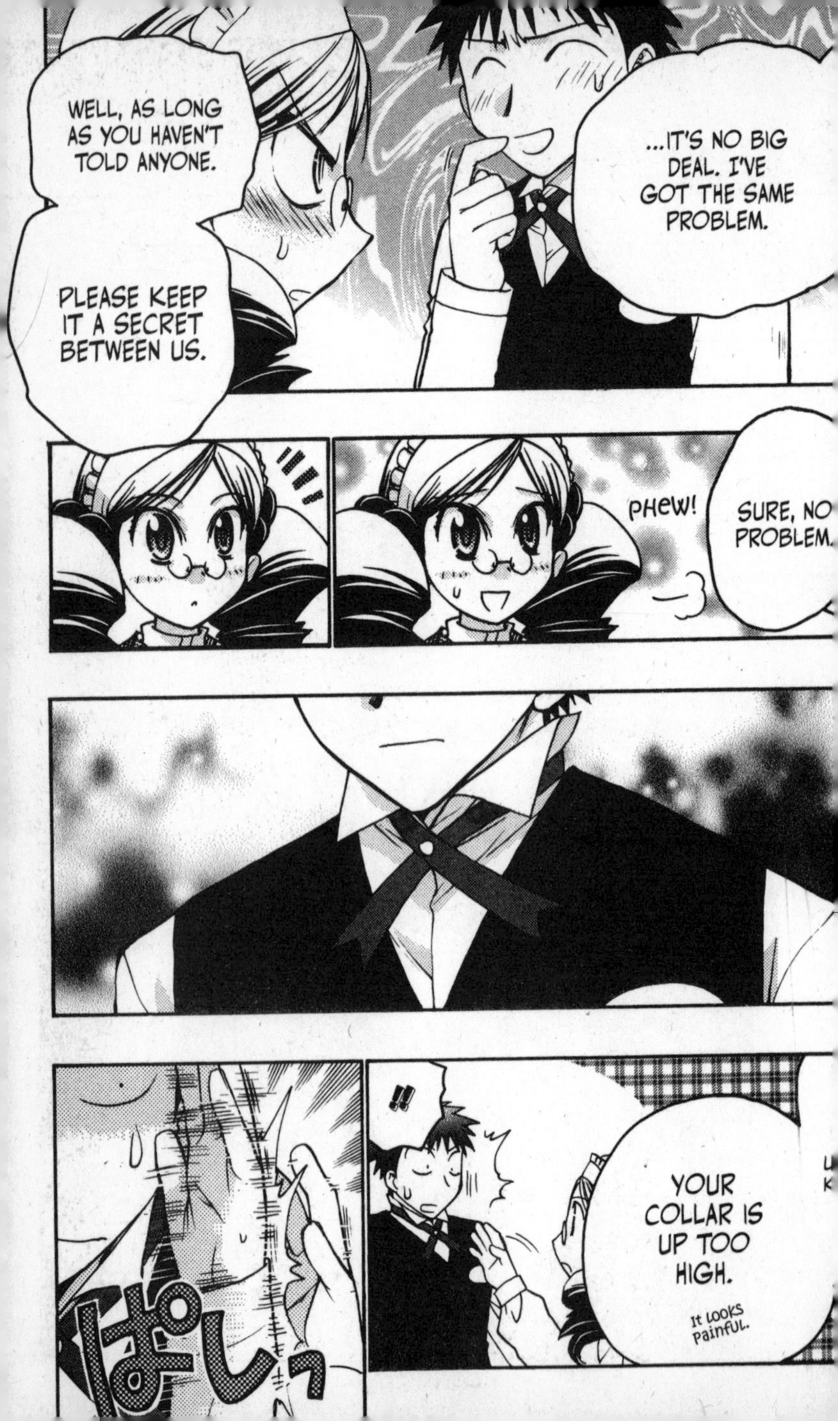
...IT'S NO BIG DEAL. I'VE GOT THE SAME PROBLEM.
WELL, AS LONG AS YOU HAVEN'T TOLD ANYONE.
PLEASE KEEP IT A SECRET BETWEEN US.
SURE, NO PROBLEM.
PHEW!
YOUR COLLAR IS UP TOO HIGH.
It looks painful.
ぱしっ

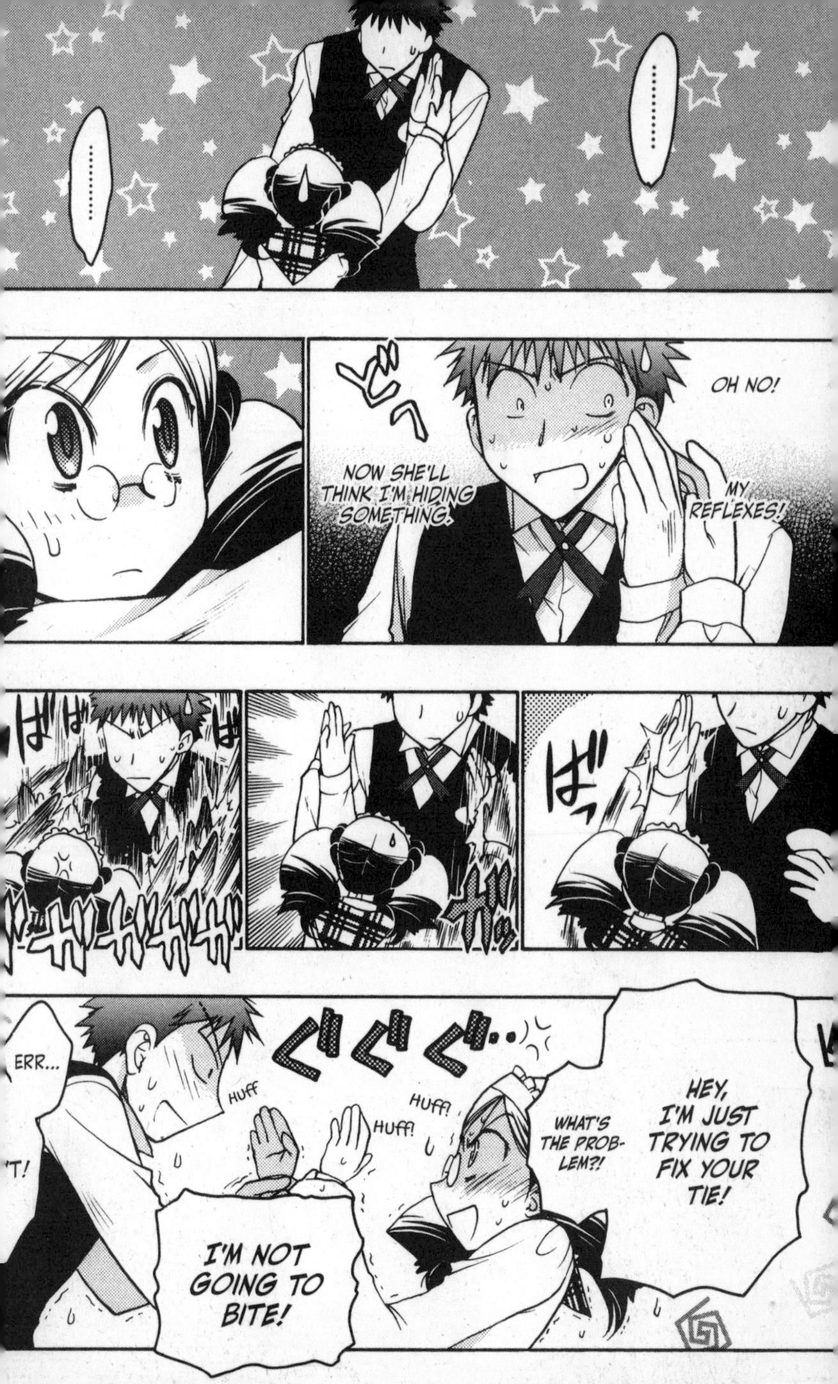
......
......
OH NO!
MY REFLEXES!
NOW SHE'LL THINK I'M HIDING SOMETHING.
HEY, I'M JUST TRYING TO FIX YOUR TIE!
WHAT'S THE PROB-LEM?!
HUFF!
HUFF!
HUFF
ERR...
I'M NOT GOING TO BITE!

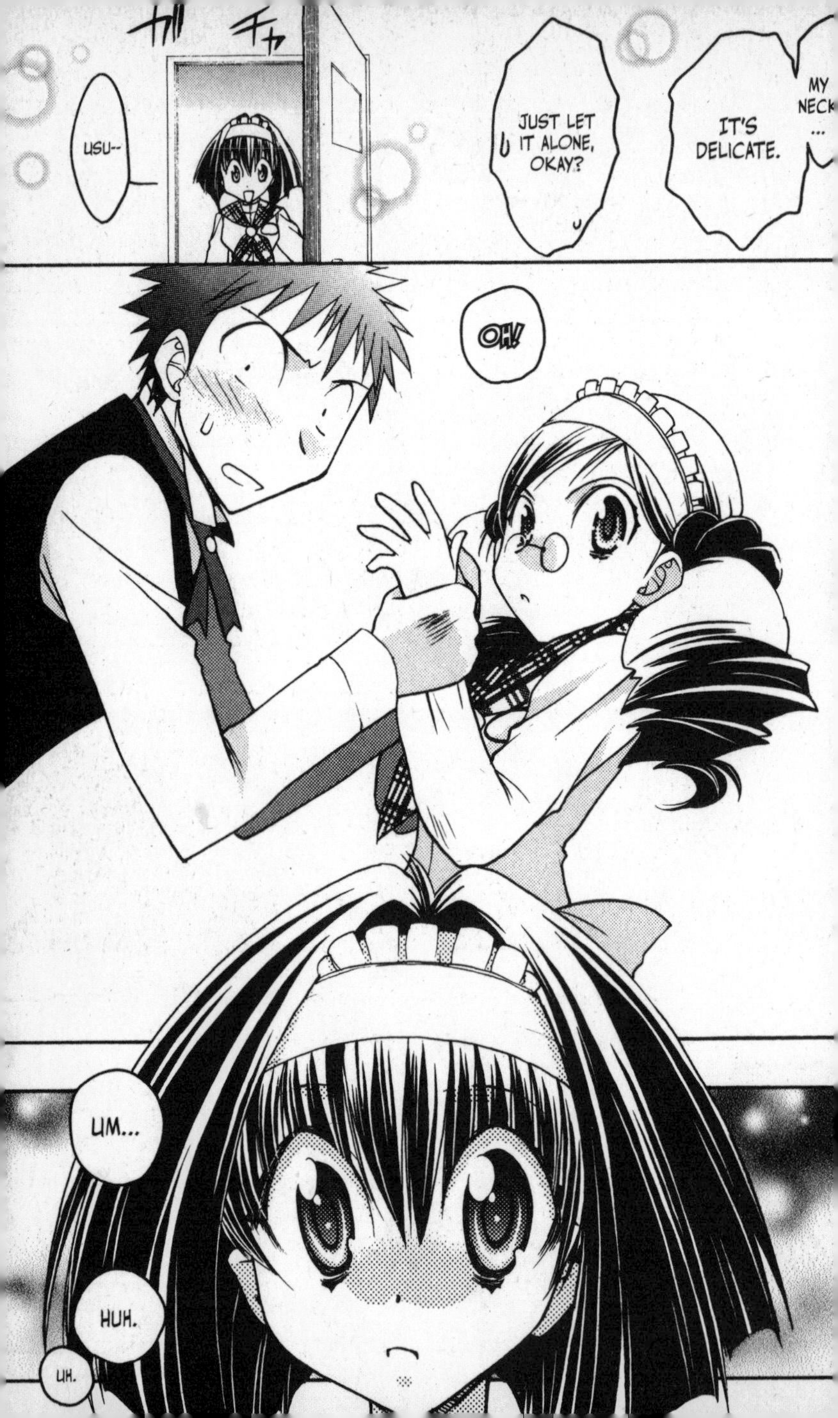
MY NECK...
IT'S DELICATE.
JUST LET IT ALONE, OKAY?
ガチャ
USU--
OH!
UM...
HUH.
UH.

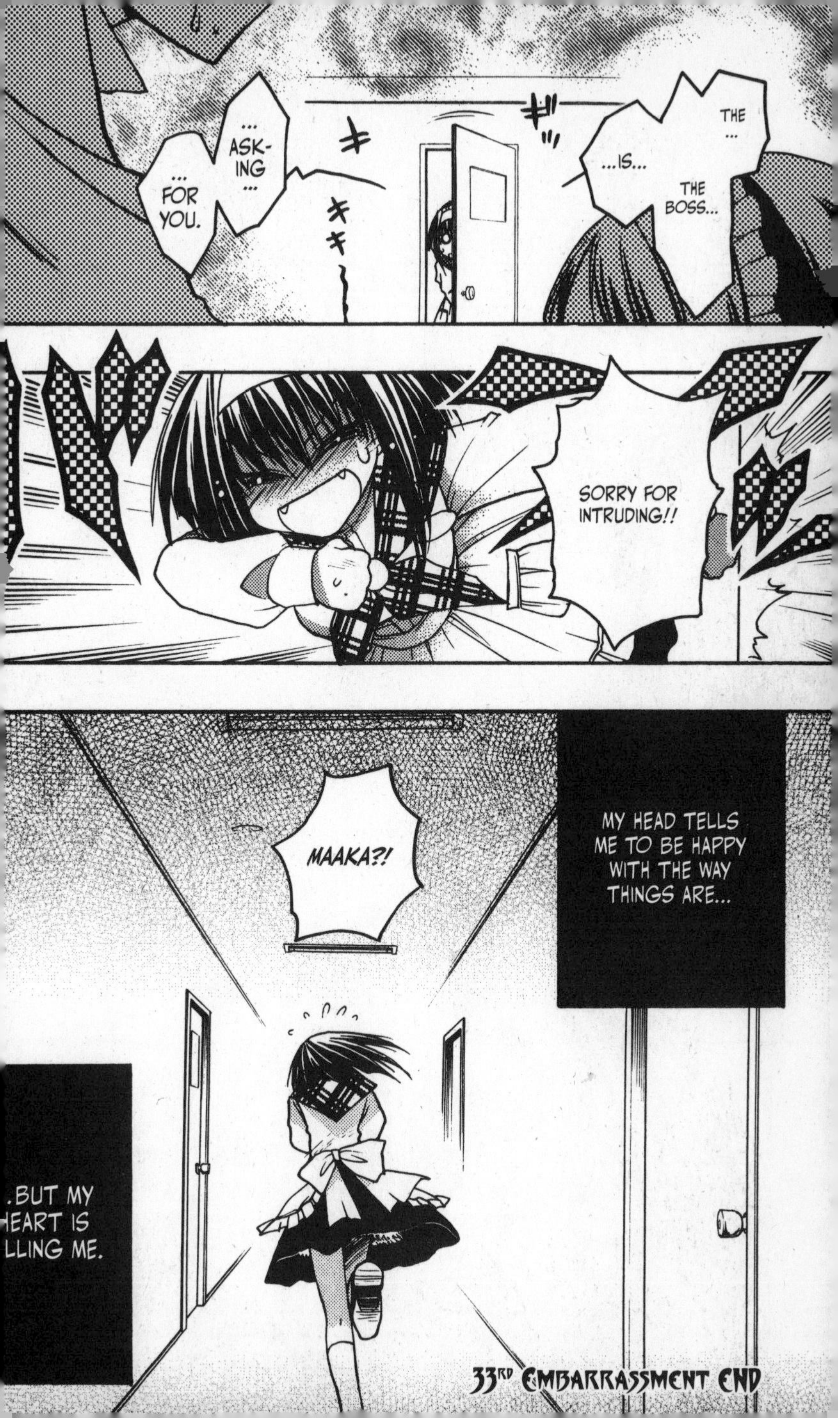
THE ... ...IS... THE BOSS...
ギッ
... ASK-ING ... ... FOR YOU.
SORRY FOR INTRUDING!!
MY HEAD TELLS ME TO BE HAPPY WITH THE WAY THINGS ARE...
MAAKA?!
.BUT MY HEART IS LLING ME.
33RD EMBARRASSMENT END

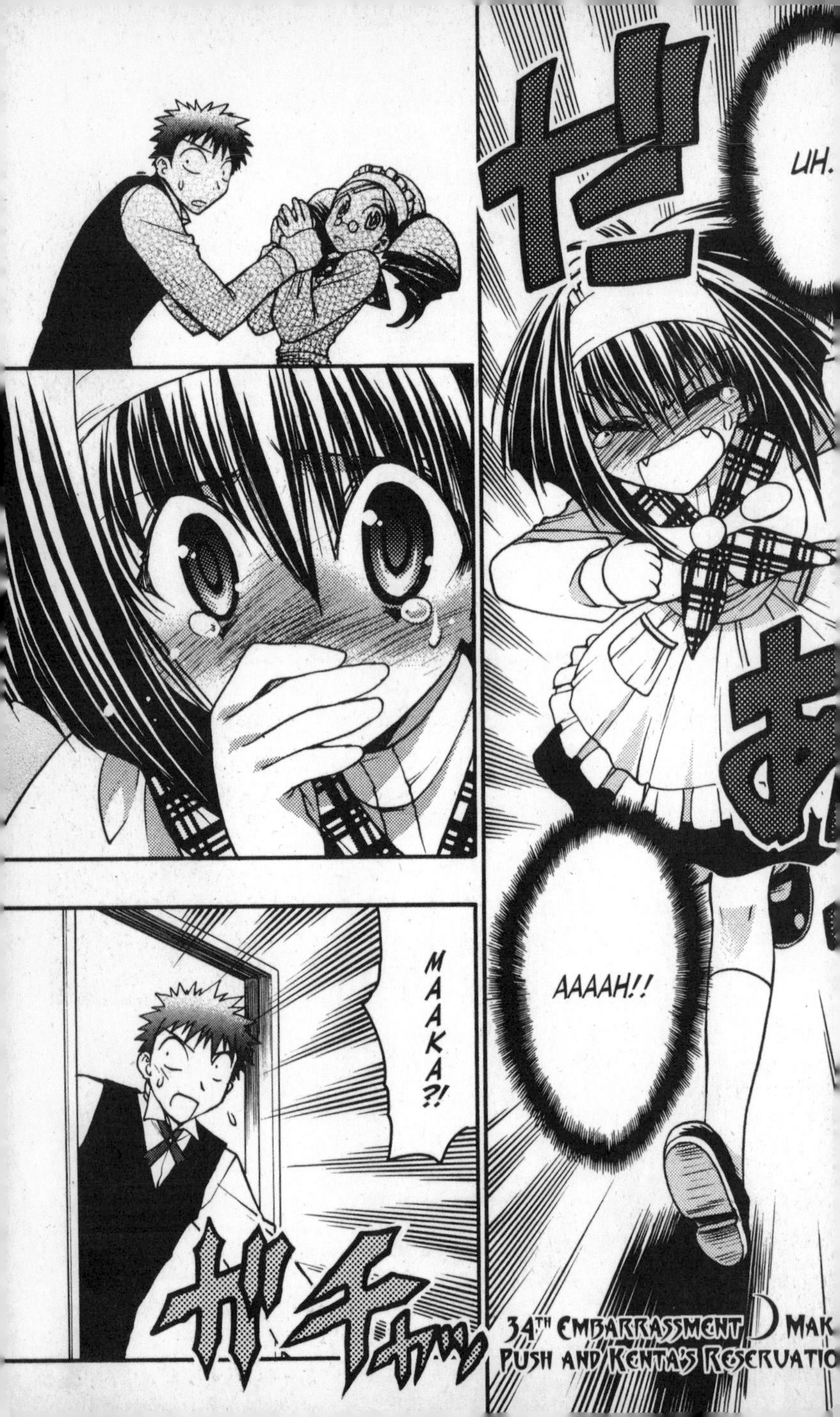
UH.
AAAAH!!
34TH EMBARRASSMENT MAK
PUSH AND KENTA'S RESERVATIO
MAAKA?!
ガチャ

34TH EMBARRASSMENT) MAKI'S PUSH AND KENTA'S RESERVATIONS
~RESERVE~

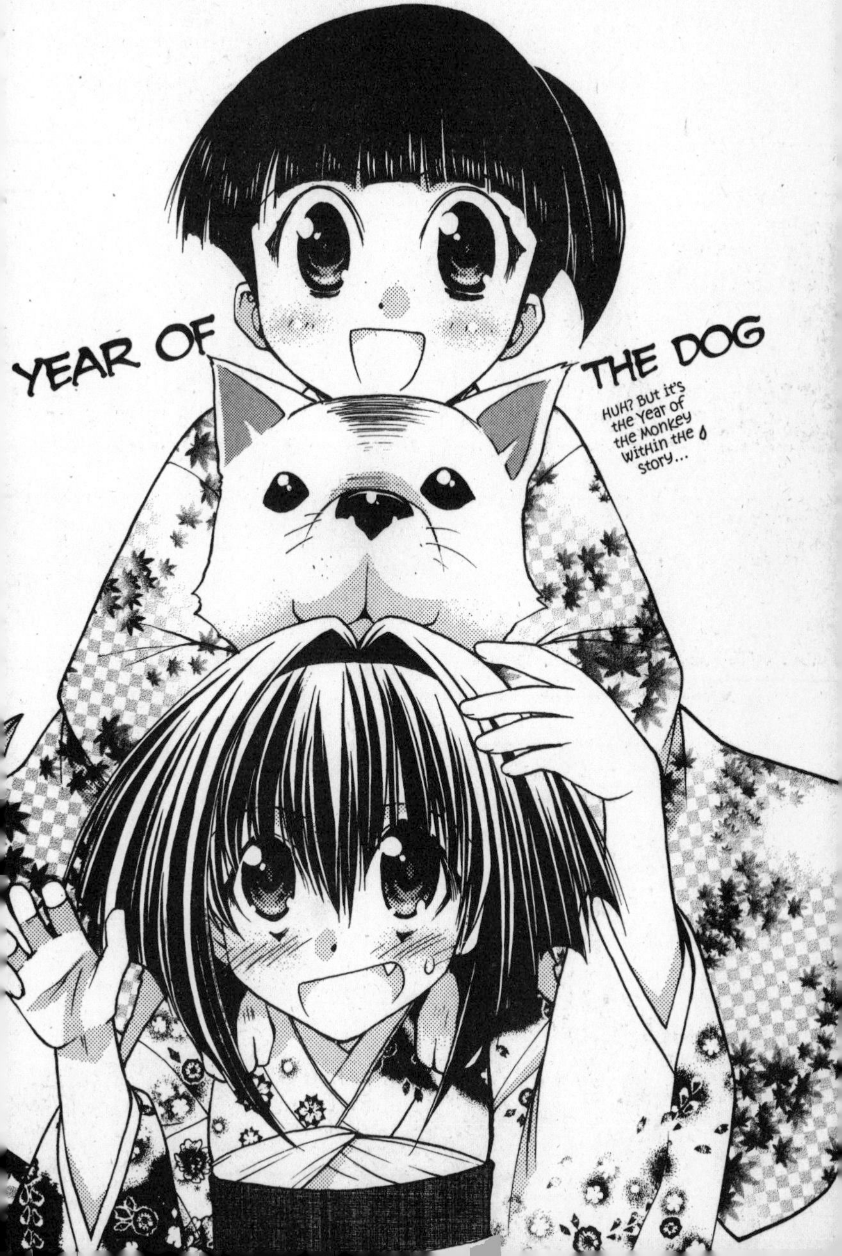

YEAR OF THE DOG
HUH? But it's the Year of the Monkey within the story...

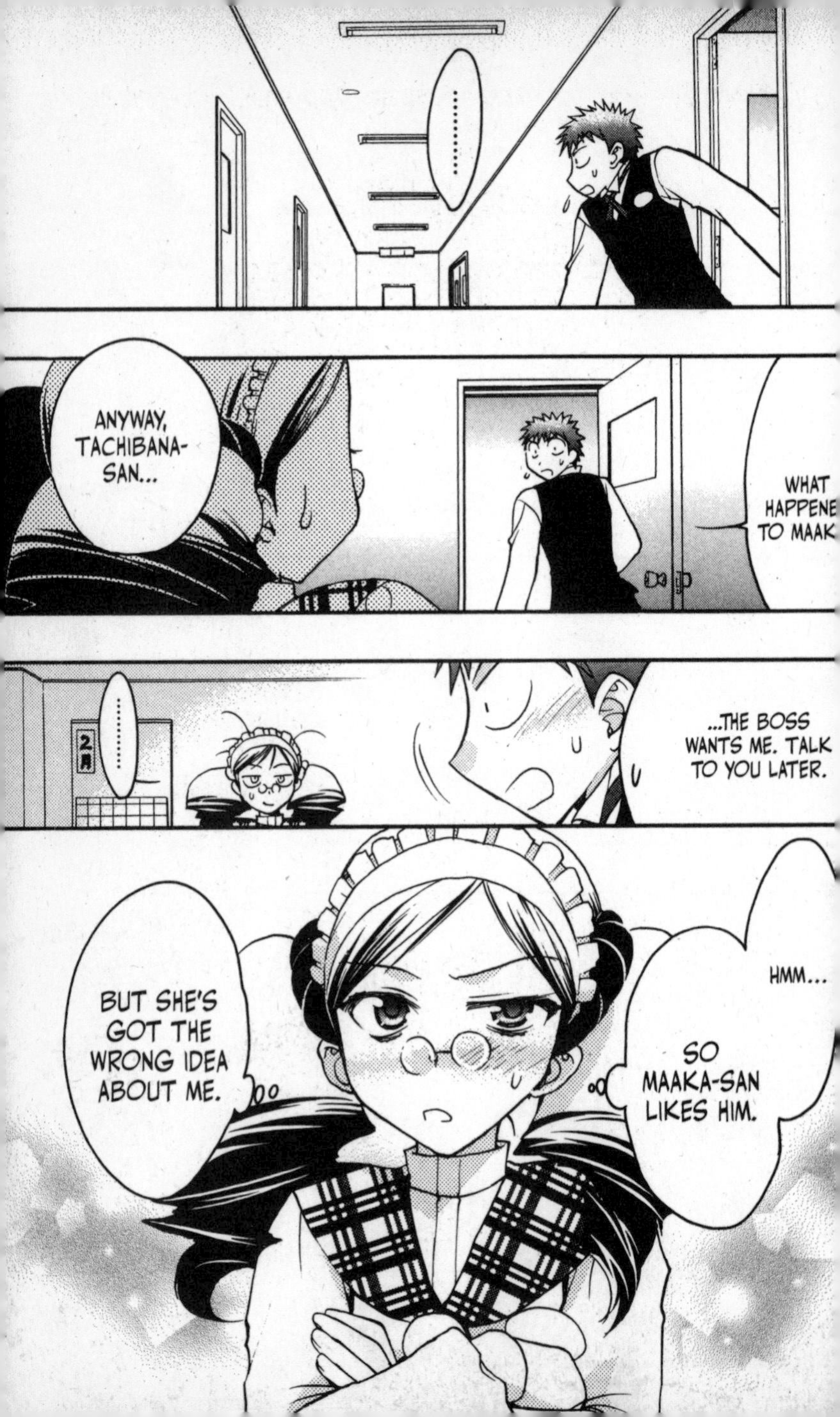
......
WHAT HAPPENE TO MAAK
ANYWAY, TACHIBANA-SAN...
...THE BOSS WANTS ME. TALK TO YOU LATER.
......
HMM...
SO MAAKA-SAN LIKES HIM.
BUT SHE'S GOT THE WRONG IDEA ABOUT ME.

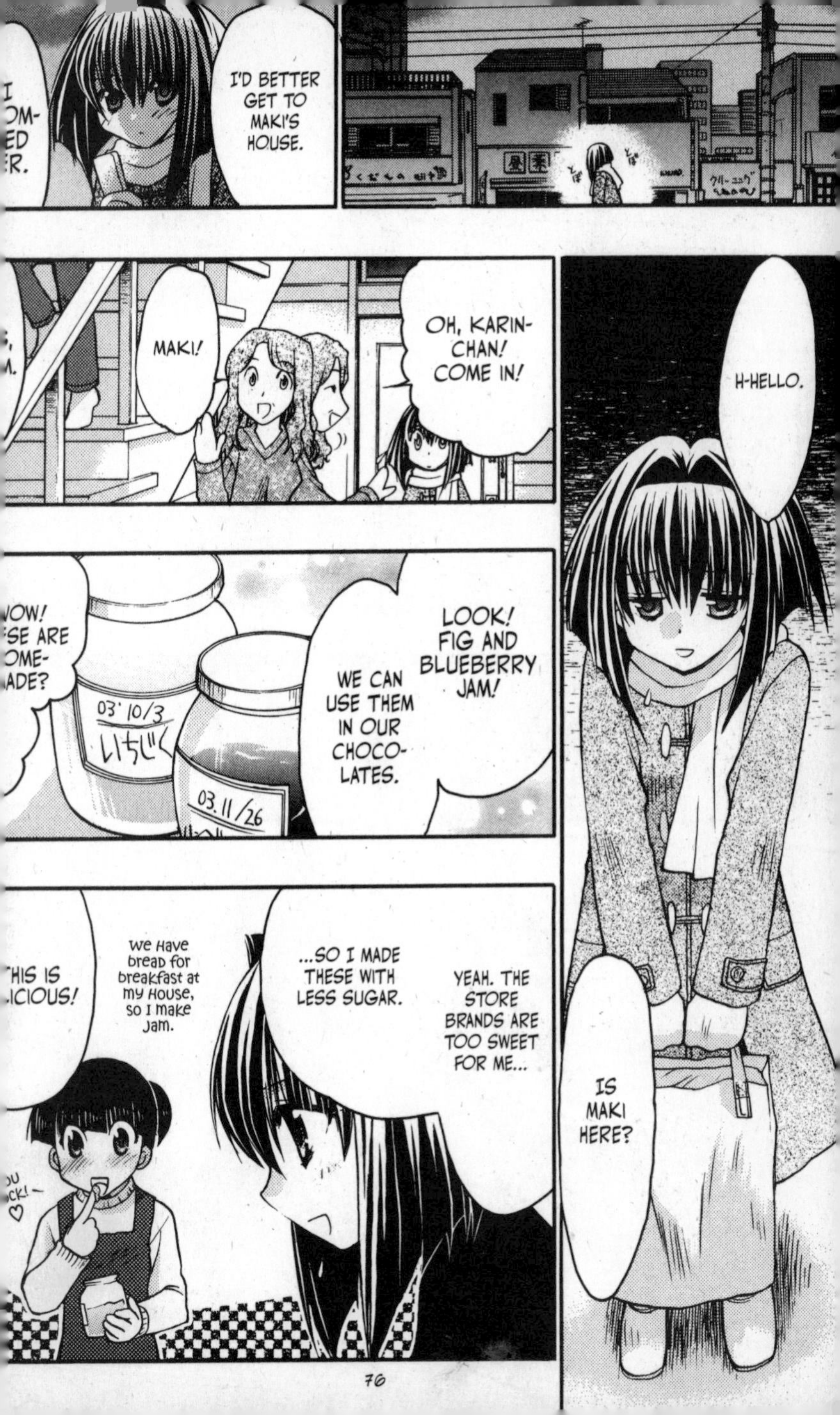

I'D BETTER GET TO MAKI'S HOUSE.
H-HELLO.
IS MAKI HERE?
OH, KARIN-CHAN! COME IN!
MAKI!
LOOK! FIG AND BLUEBERRY JAM!
WE CAN USE THEM IN OUR CHOCOLATES.
03' 10/3
いちじく
03.11/26
YEAH. THE STORE BRANDS ARE TOO SWEET FOR ME...
...SO I MADE THESE WITH LESS SUGAR.
We Have bread for breakfast at my House, so I make jam.

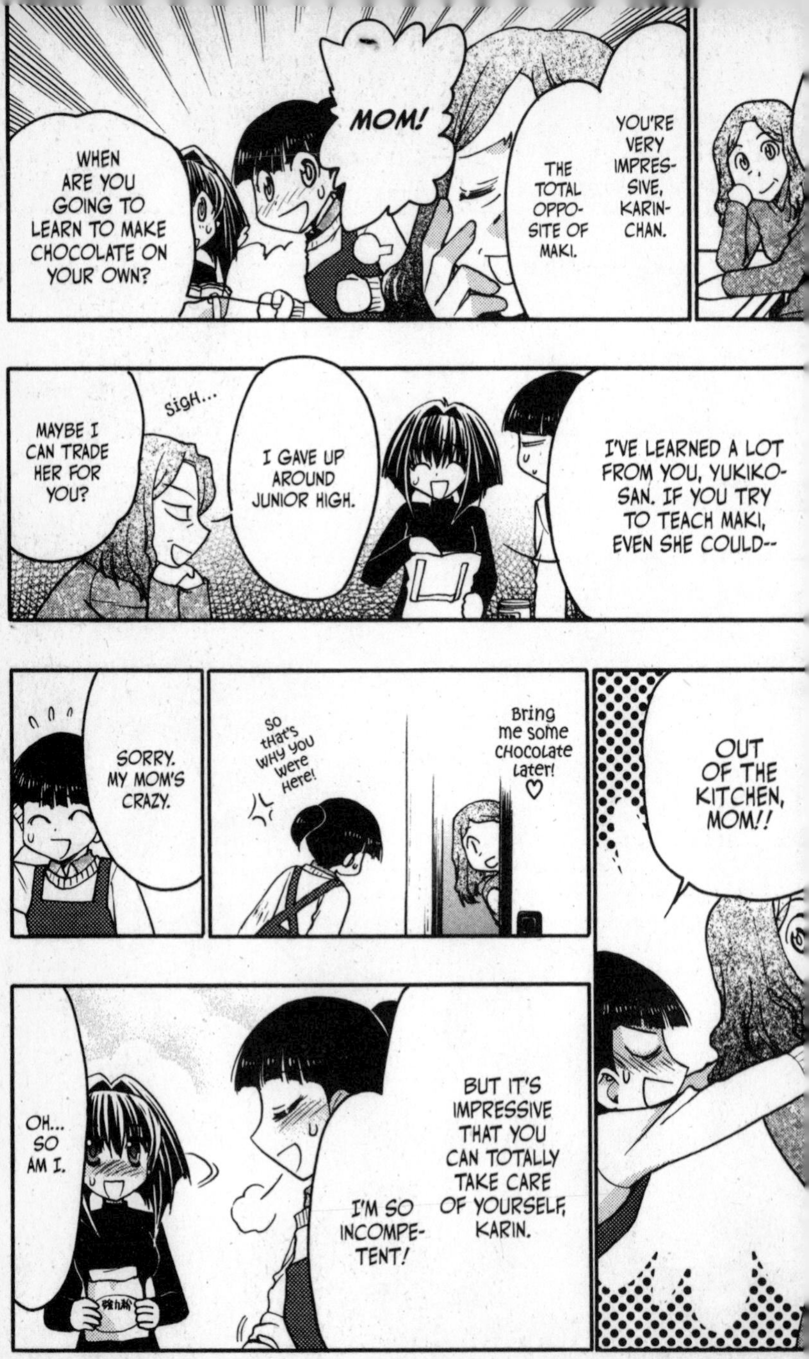
YOU'RE VERY IMPRESSIVE, KARIN-CHAN.
THE TOTAL OPPOSITE OF MAKI.
MOM!
WHEN ARE YOU GOING TO LEARN TO MAKE CHOCOLATE ON YOUR OWN?
I'VE LEARNED A LOT FROM YOU, YUKIKO-SAN. IF YOU TRY TO TEACH MAKI, EVEN SHE COULD--
I GAVE UP AROUND JUNIOR HIGH.
SIGH...
MAYBE I CAN TRADE HER FOR YOU?
OUT OF THE KITCHEN, MOM!!
Bring me some chocolate later! ♡
So that's why you were here!
SORRY. MY MOM'S CRAZY.
BUT IT'S IMPRESSIVE THAT YOU CAN TOTALLY TAKE CARE OF YOURSELF, KARIN.
I'M SO INCOMPETENT!
OH... SO AM I.

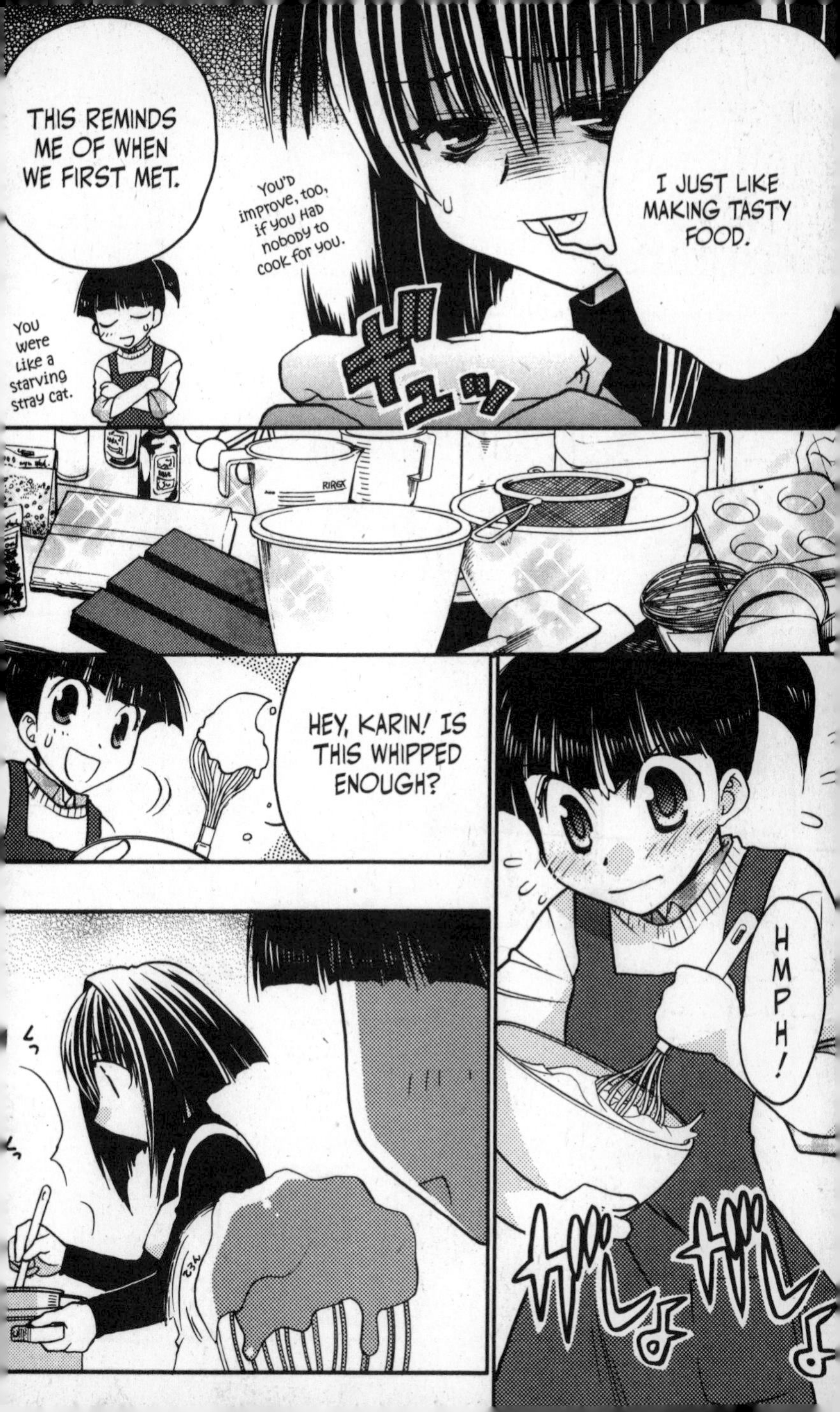
I JUST LIKE MAKING TASTY FOOD.
YOU'D improve, too, if you had nobody to cook for you.
ギュッ
THIS REMINDS ME OF WHEN WE FIRST MET.
You were like a starving stray cat.
HMPH!
HEY, KARIN! IS THIS WHIPPED ENOUGH?

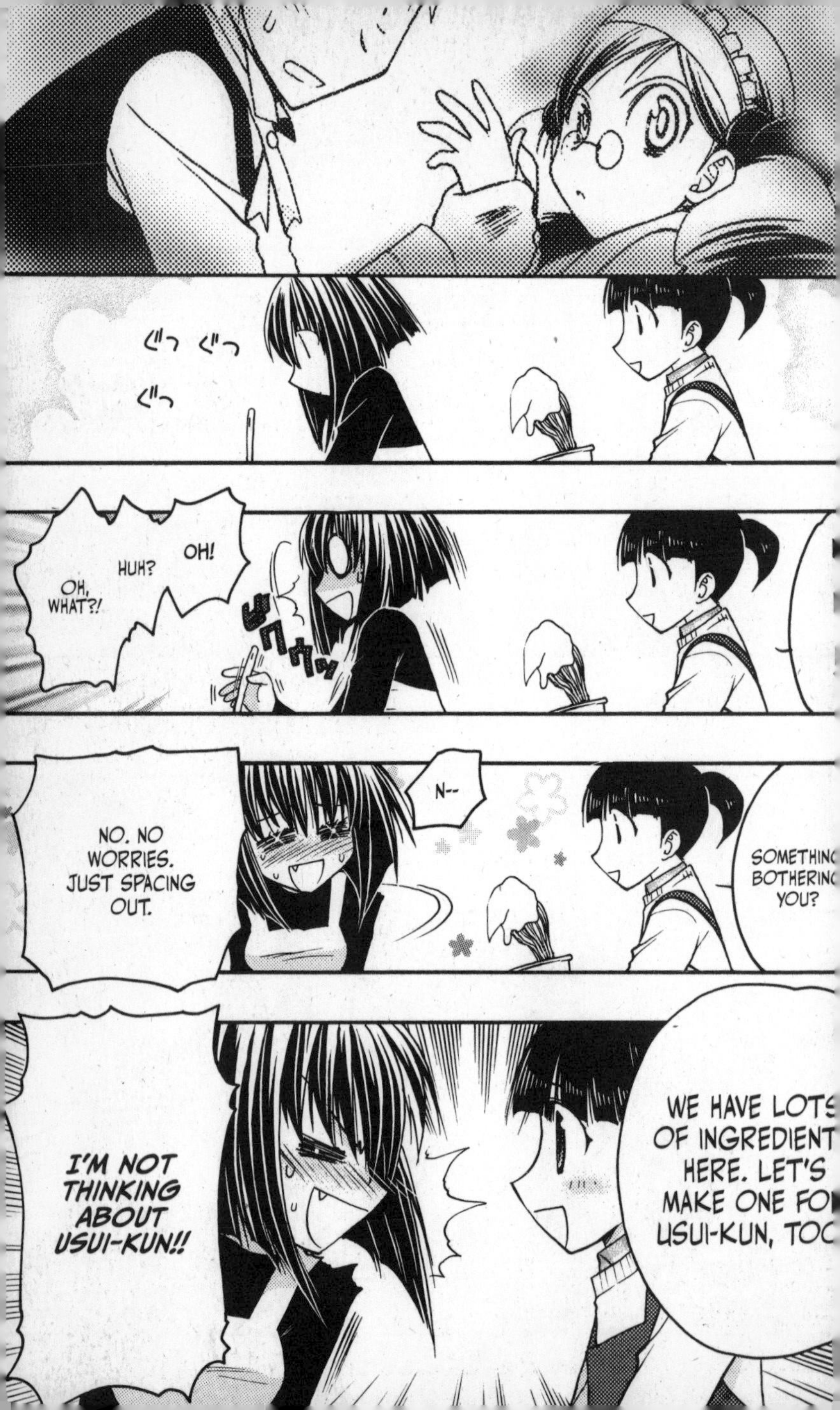
ぐっ ぐっ
ぐっ
OH!
HUH?
OH, WHAT?!
SOMETHIN BOTHERIN YOU?
N--
NO. NO WORRIES. JUST SPACING OUT.
WE HAVE LOTS OF INGREDIENT HERE. LET'S MAKE ONE FO USUI-KUN, TOO
I'M NOT THINKING ABOUT USUI-KUN!!

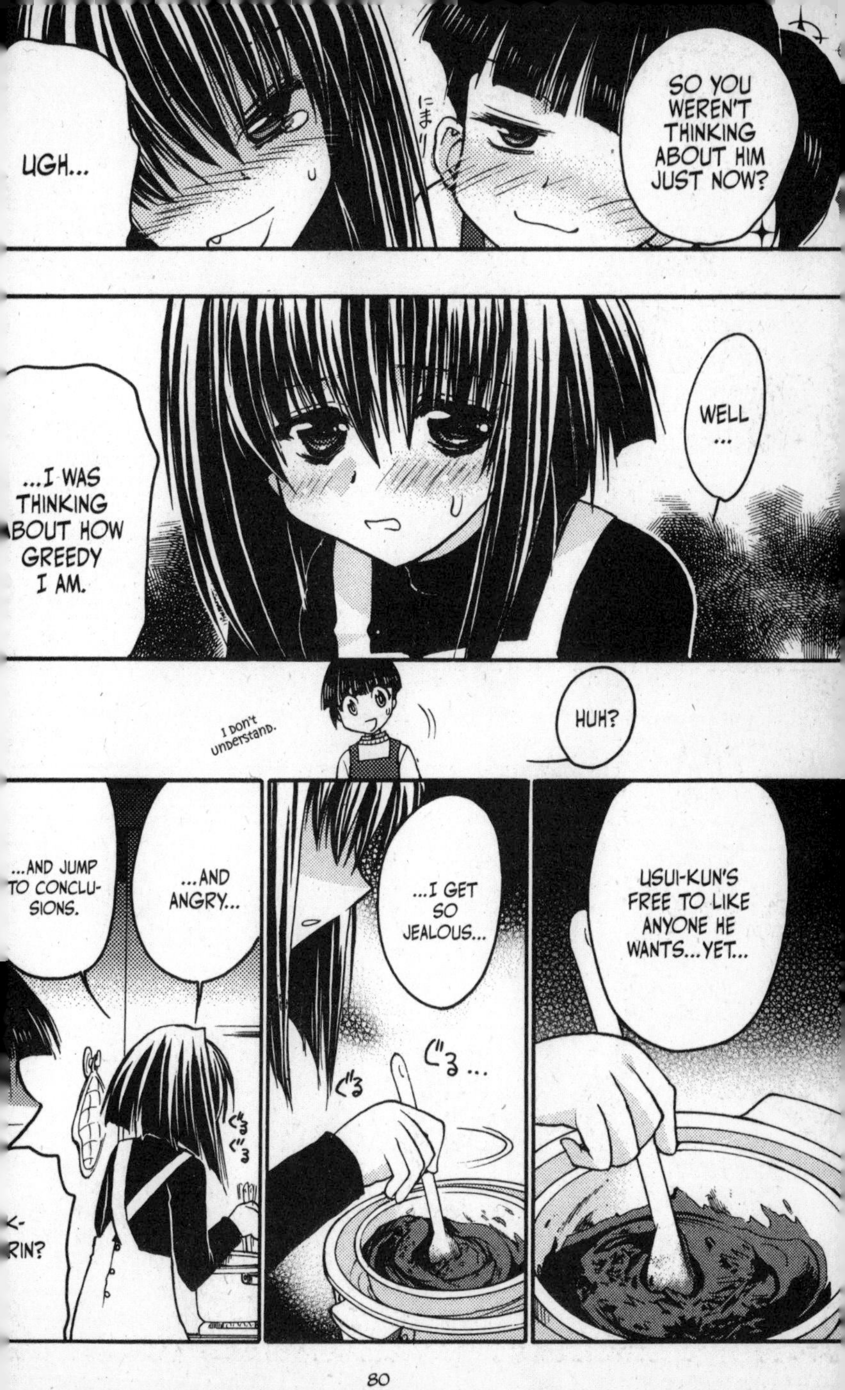

SO YOU WEREN'T THINKING ABOUT HIM JUST NOW?
UGH...
WELL ...
...I WAS THINKING BOUT HOW GREEDY I AM.
HUH?
I DON'T UNDERSTAND.
USUI-KUN'S FREE TO LIKE ANYONE HE WANTS...YET...
...I GET SO JEALOUS...
ぐる ...
ぐる
...AND ANGRY...
...AND JUMP TO CONCLUSIONS.
ぐる ぐる

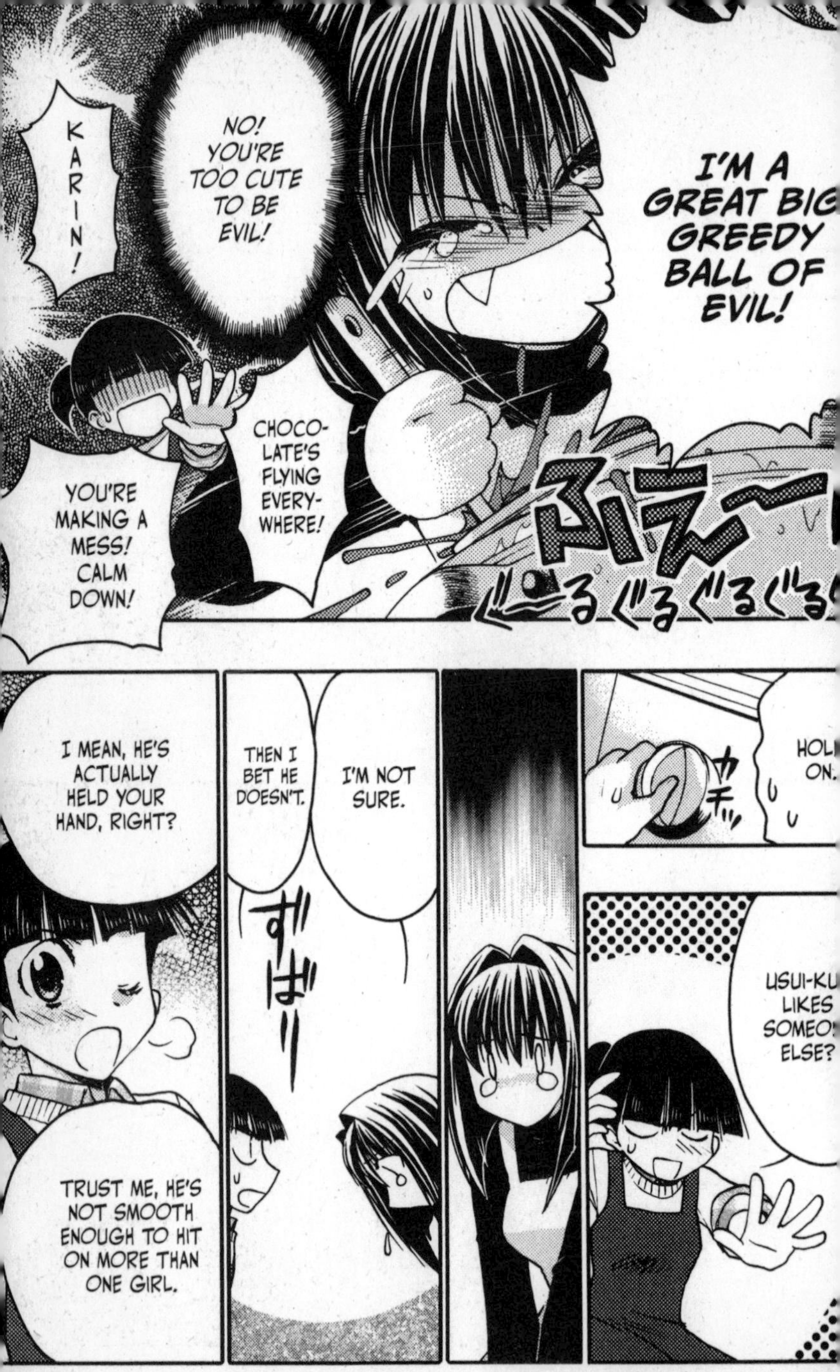
I'M A GREAT BIG GREEDY BALL OF EVIL!
ふえ～ん
ぐるぐるぐるぐる
KARIN!
NO! YOU'RE TOO CUTE TO BE EVIL!
CHOCOLATE'S FLYING EVERYWHERE!
YOU'RE MAKING A MESS! CALM DOWN!
HOL ON.
カチ
USUI-KU LIKES SOMEO ELSE?
I'M NOT SURE.
THEN I BET HE DOESN'T.
ずばー
I MEAN, HE'S ACTUALLY HELD YOUR HAND, RIGHT?
TRUST ME, HE'S NOT SMOOTH ENOUGH TO HIT ON MORE THAN ONE GIRL.

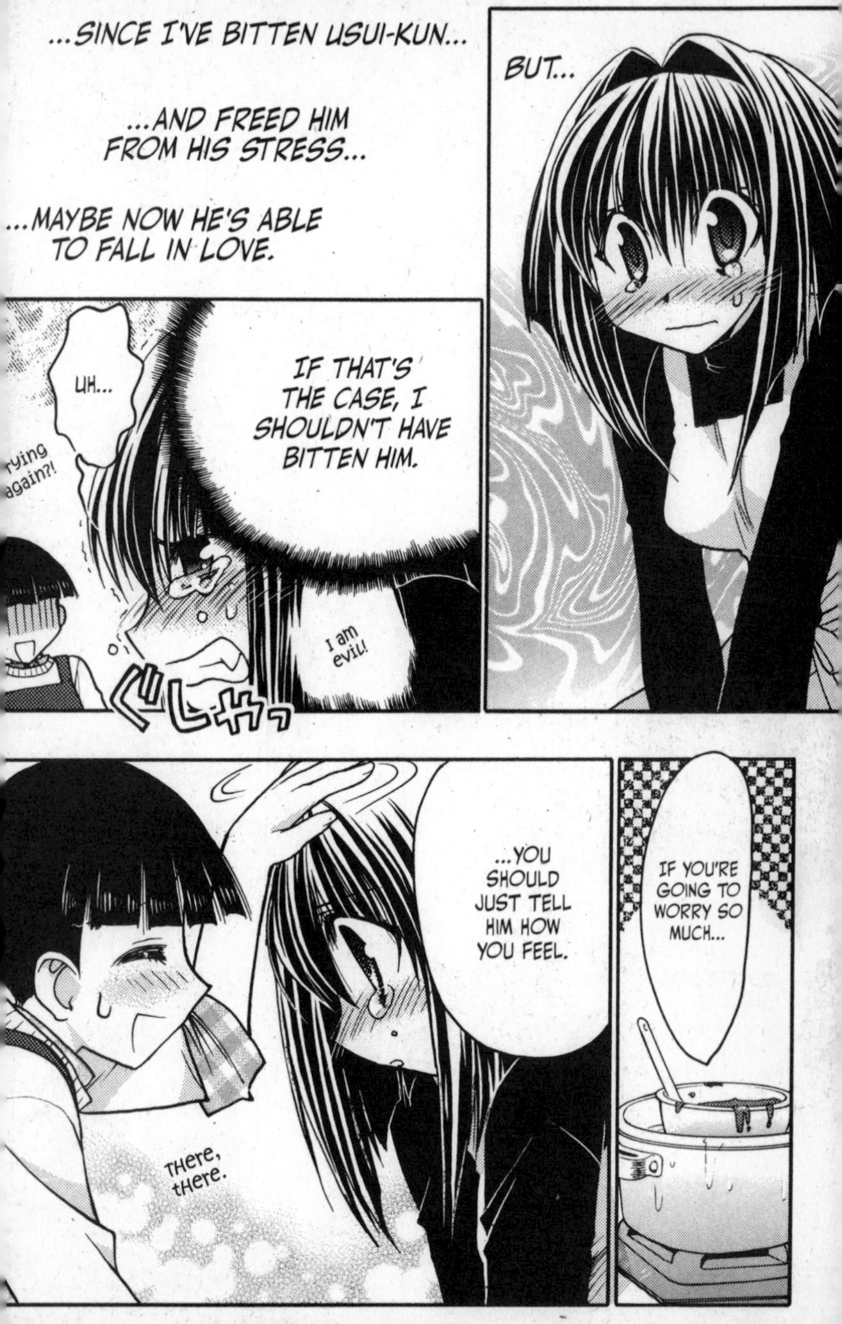
BUT...
...SINCE I'VE BITTEN USUI-KUN...
...AND FREED HIM FROM HIS STRESS...
...MAYBE NOW HE'S ABLE TO FALL IN LOVE.
IF THAT'S THE CASE, I SHOULDN'T HAVE BITTEN HIM.
UH...
rying again?!
I am evil!
IF YOU'RE GOING TO WORRY SO MUCH...
...YOU SHOULD JUST TELL HIM HOW YOU FEEL.
There, there.

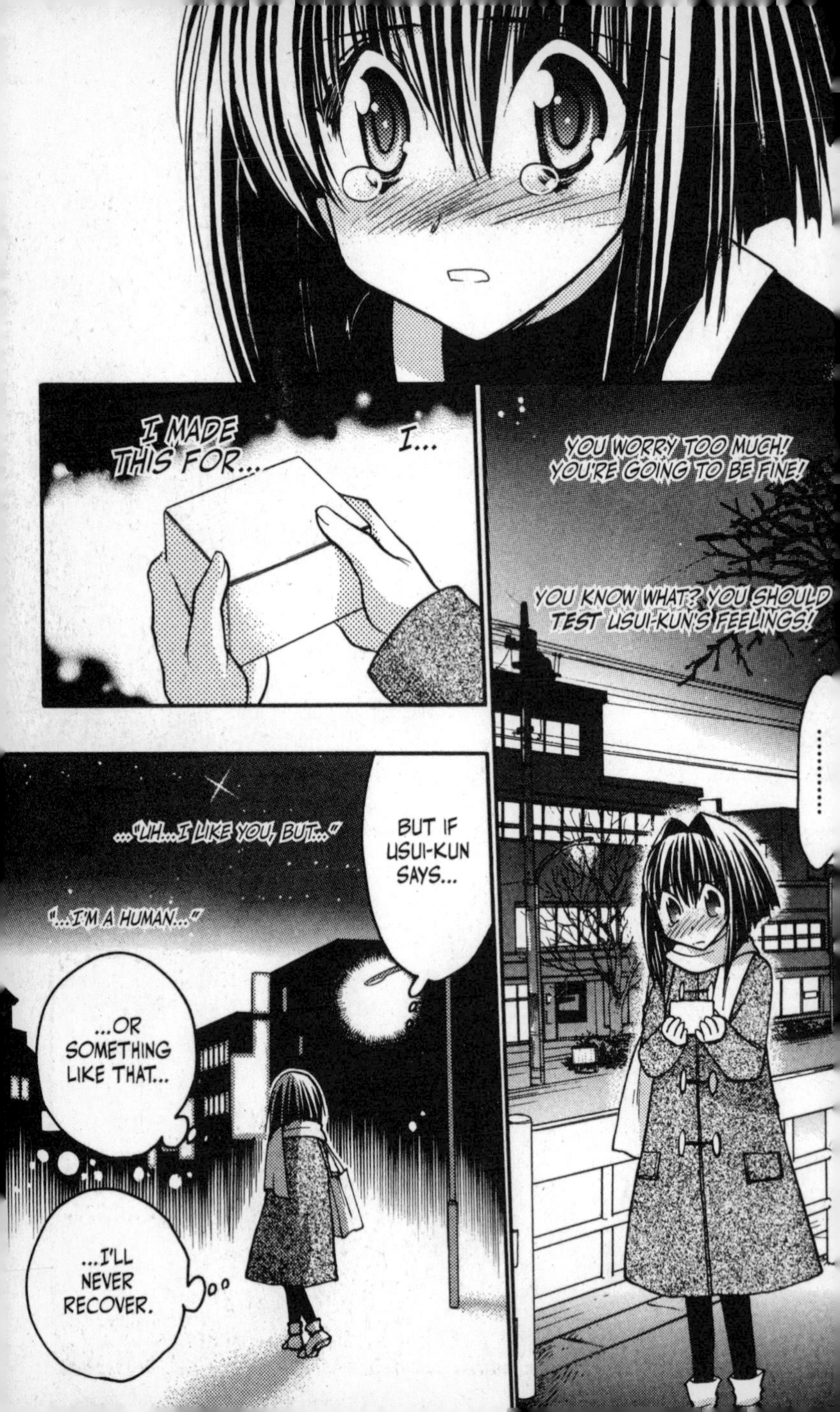
YOU WORRY TOO MUCH! YOU'RE GOING TO BE FINE!
YOU KNOW WHAT? YOU SHOULD TEST USUI-KUN'S FEELINGS!
......
I...
I MADE THIS FOR...
BUT IF USUI-KUN SAYS...
..."UH...I LIKE YOU, BUT..."
"...I'M A HUMAN..."
...OR SOMETHING LIKE THAT...
...I'LL NEVER RECOVER.

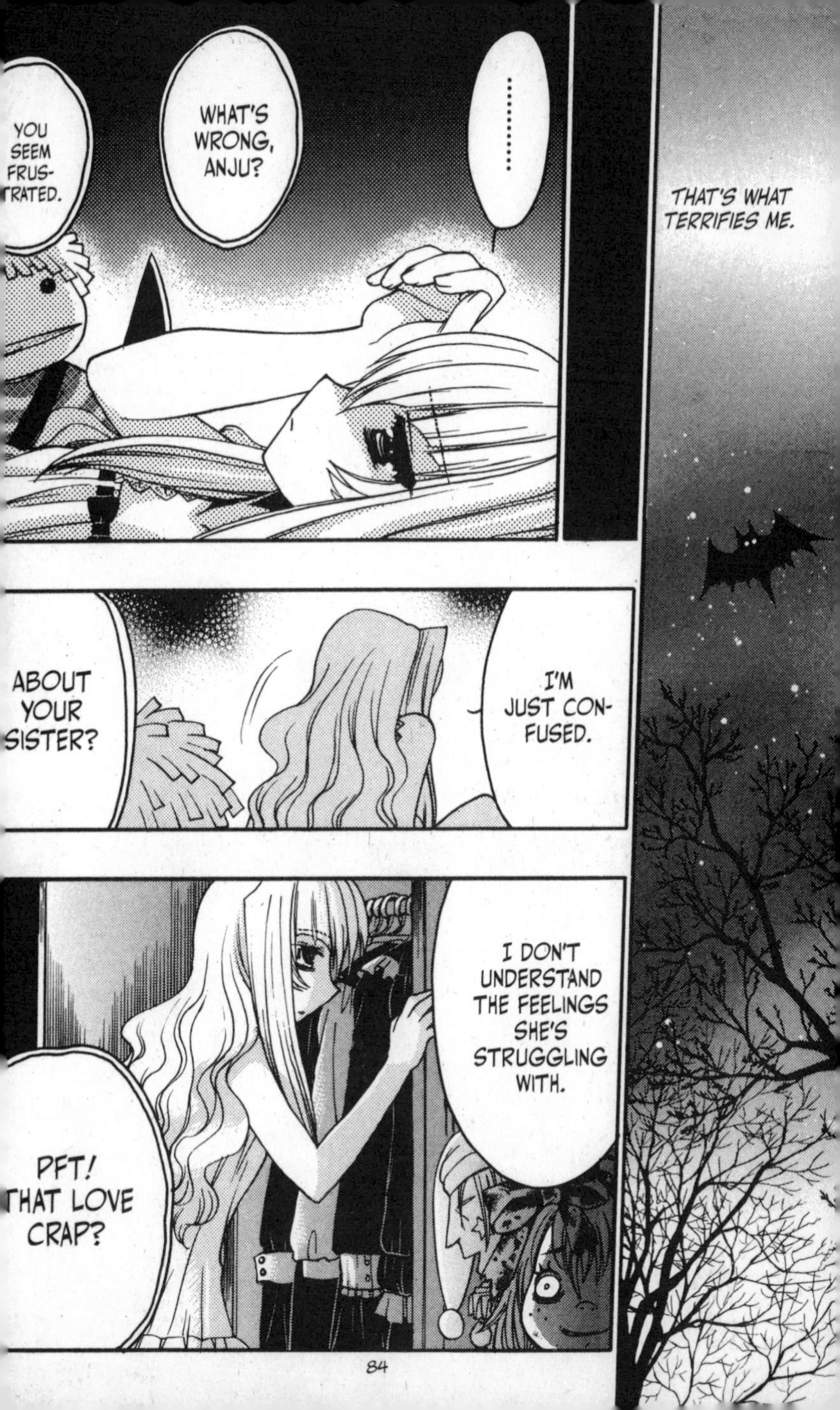
THAT'S WHAT TERRIFIES ME.
....
WHAT'S WRONG, ANJU?
YOU SEEM FRUS-TRATED.
I'M JUST CON-FUSED.
ABOUT YOUR SISTER?
I DON'T UNDERSTAND THE FEELINGS SHE'S STRUGGLING WITH.
PFT! THAT LOVE CRAP?

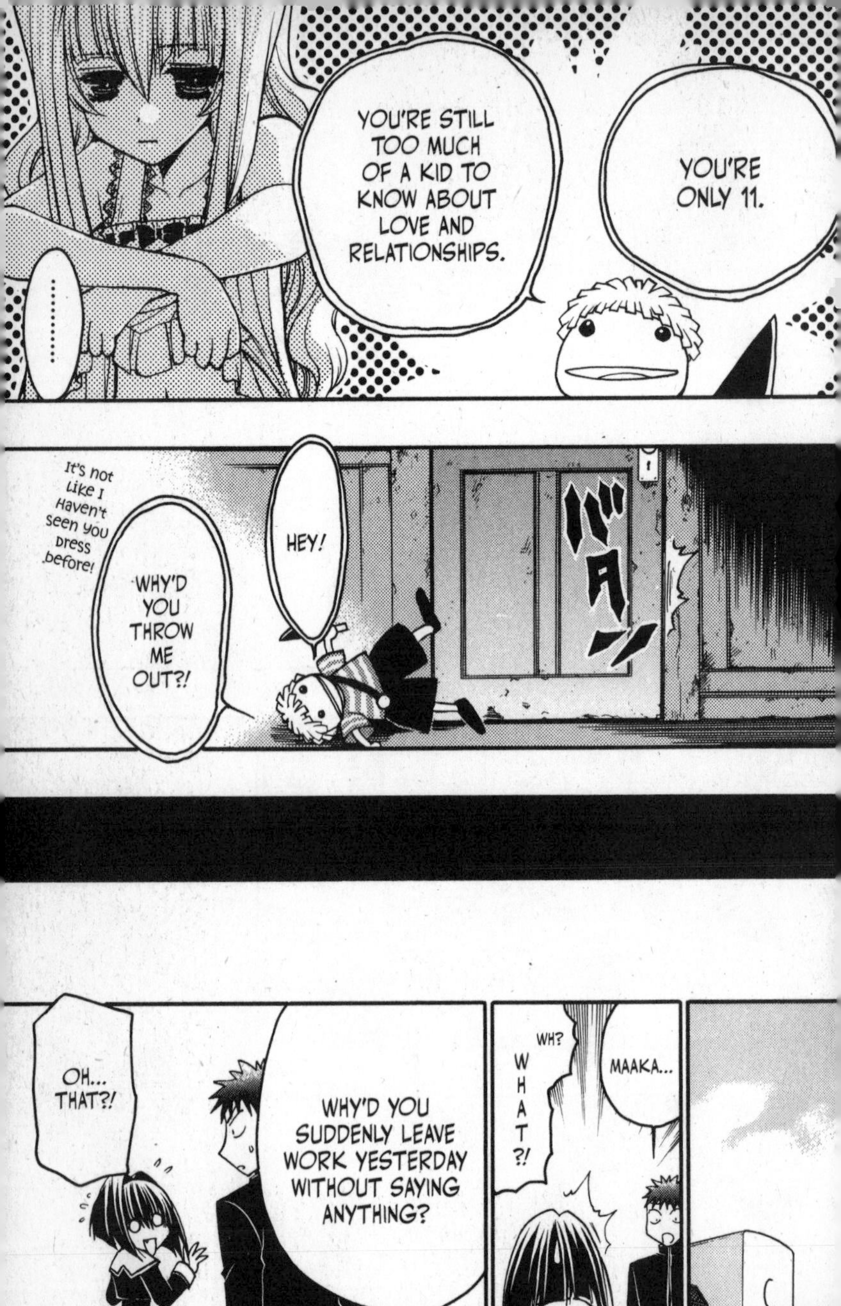
YOU'RE ONLY 11.
YOU'RE STILL TOO MUCH OF A KID TO KNOW ABOUT LOVE AND RELATIONSHIPS.
......
バターン
HEY!
WHY'D YOU THROW ME OUT?!
It's not like I haven't seen you dress before!
MAAKA...
WH?
WHAT?!
WHY'D YOU SUDDENLY LEAVE WORK YESTERDAY WITHOUT SAYING ANYTHING?
OH... THAT?!

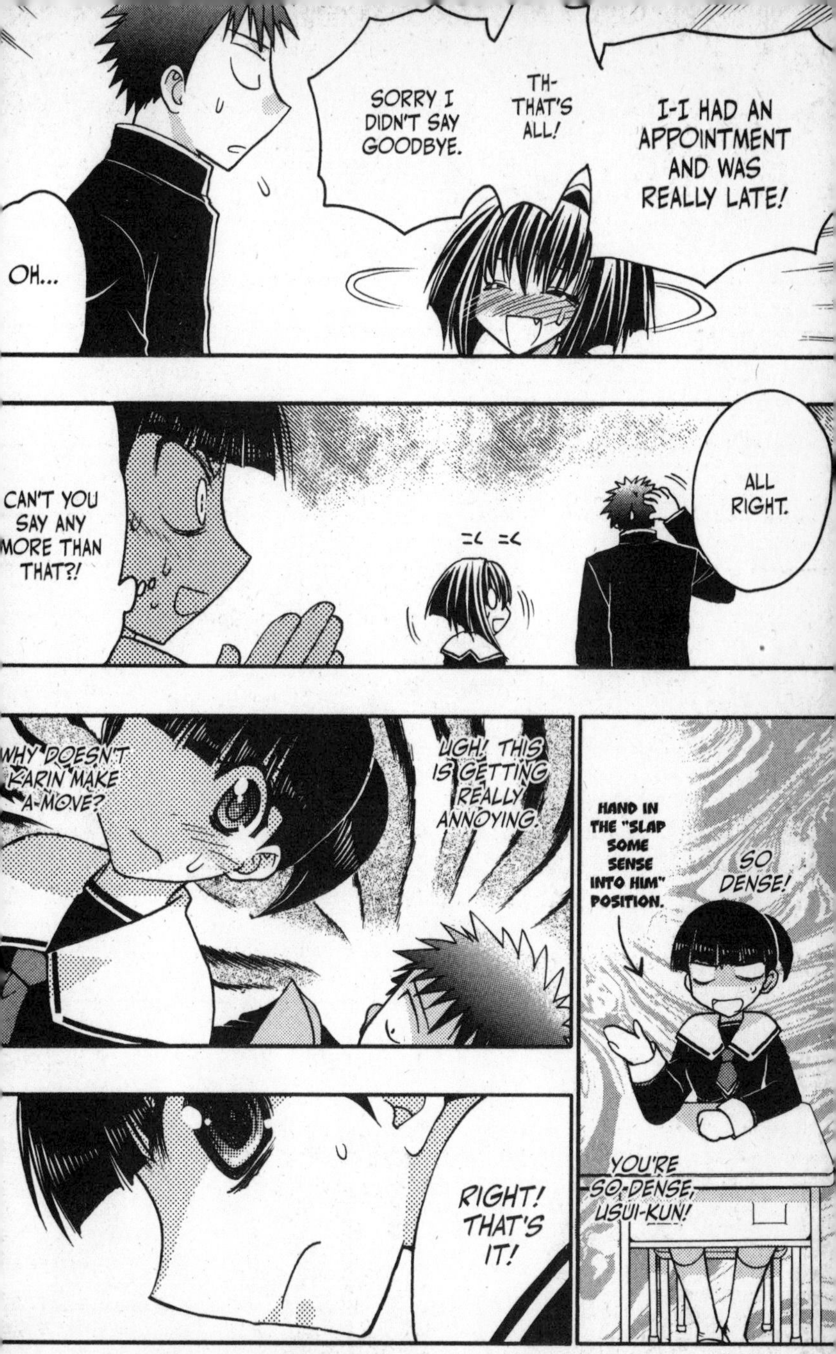
I-I HAD AN APPOINTMENT AND WAS REALLY LATE!
TH-THAT'S ALL!
SORRY I DIDN'T SAY GOODBYE.
OH...
ALL RIGHT.
CAN'T YOU SAY ANY MORE THAN THAT?!
SO DENSE!
HAND IN THE "SLAP SOME SENSE INTO HIM" POSITION.
YOU'RE SO-DENSE, USUI-KUN!
UGH! THIS IS GETTING REALLY ANNOYING.
WHY DOESN'T KARIN MAKE A MOVE?
RIGHT! THAT'S IT!

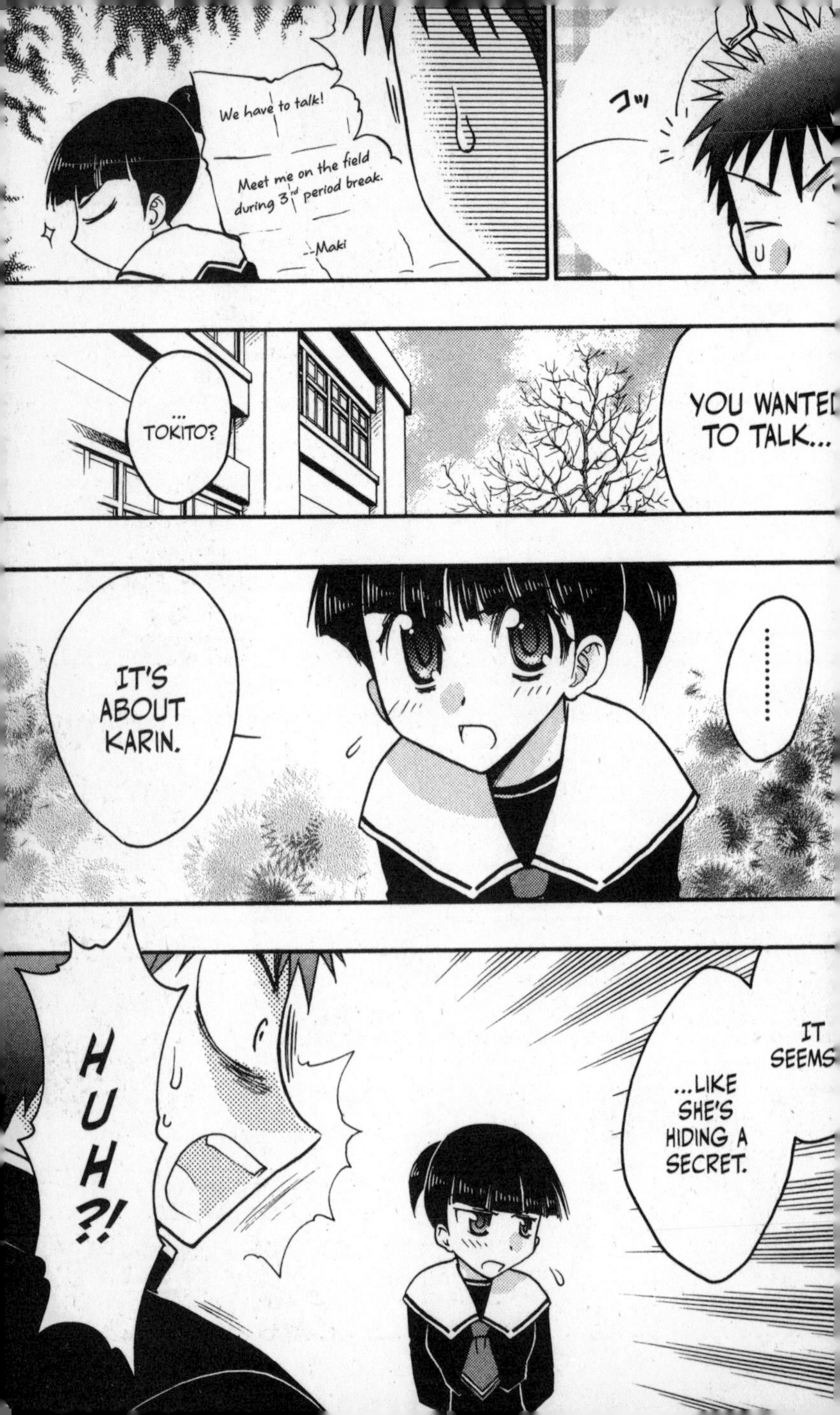

コッ
We have to talk!
Meet me on the field during 3rd period break.
--Maki
YOU WANTED TO TALK...
...TOKITO?
....
IT'S ABOUT KARIN.
IT SEEMS
...LIKE SHE'S HIDING A SECRET.
HUH?!

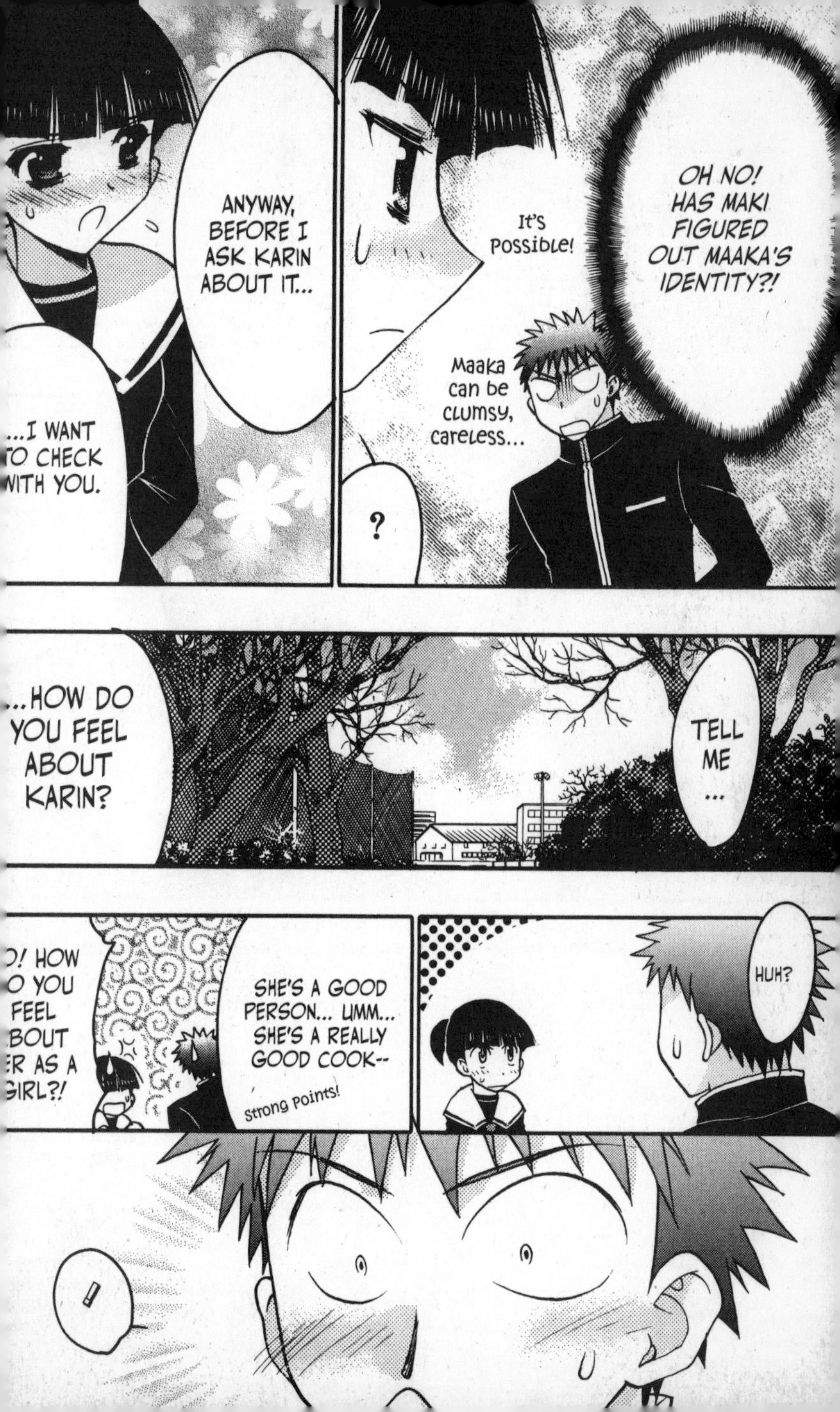
OH NO! HAS MAKI FIGURED OUT MAAKA'S IDENTITY?!
It's possible!
Maaka can be clumsy, careless...
?
ANYWAY, BEFORE I ASK KARIN ABOUT IT...
...I WANT TO CHECK WITH YOU.
TELL ME ...
...HOW DO YOU FEEL ABOUT KARIN?
HUH?
SHE'S A GOOD PERSON... UMM... SHE'S A REALLY GOOD COOK--
Strong Points!
O! HOW O YOU FEEL BOUT ER AS A GIRL?!
!

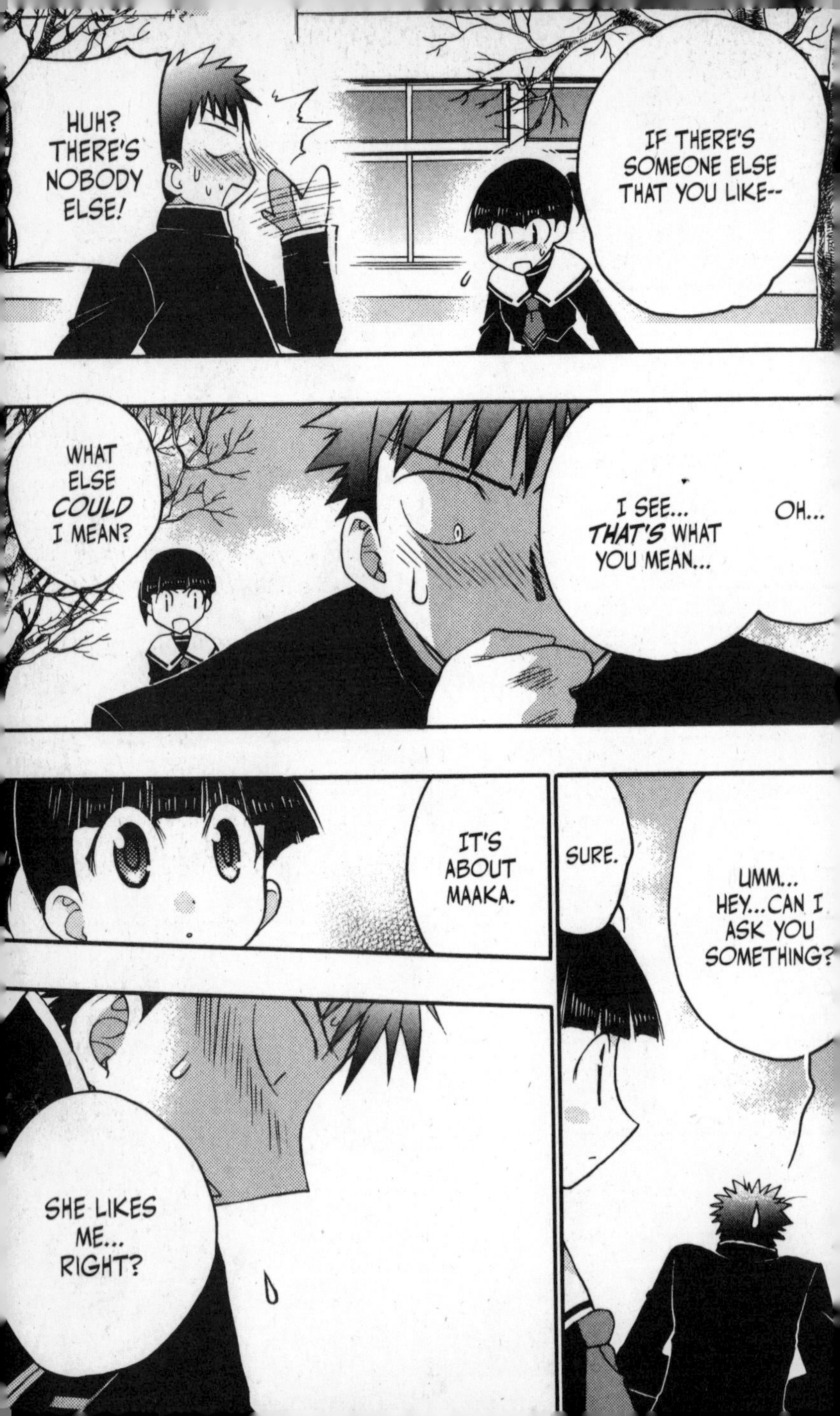
IF THERE'S SOMEONE ELSE THAT YOU LIKE--
HUH? THERE'S NOBODY ELSE!
OH...
I SEE... *THAT'S* WHAT YOU MEAN...
WHAT ELSE *COULD* I MEAN?
UMM... HEY...CAN I ASK YOU SOMETHING?
SURE.
IT'S ABOUT MAAKA.
SHE LIKES ME... RIGHT?

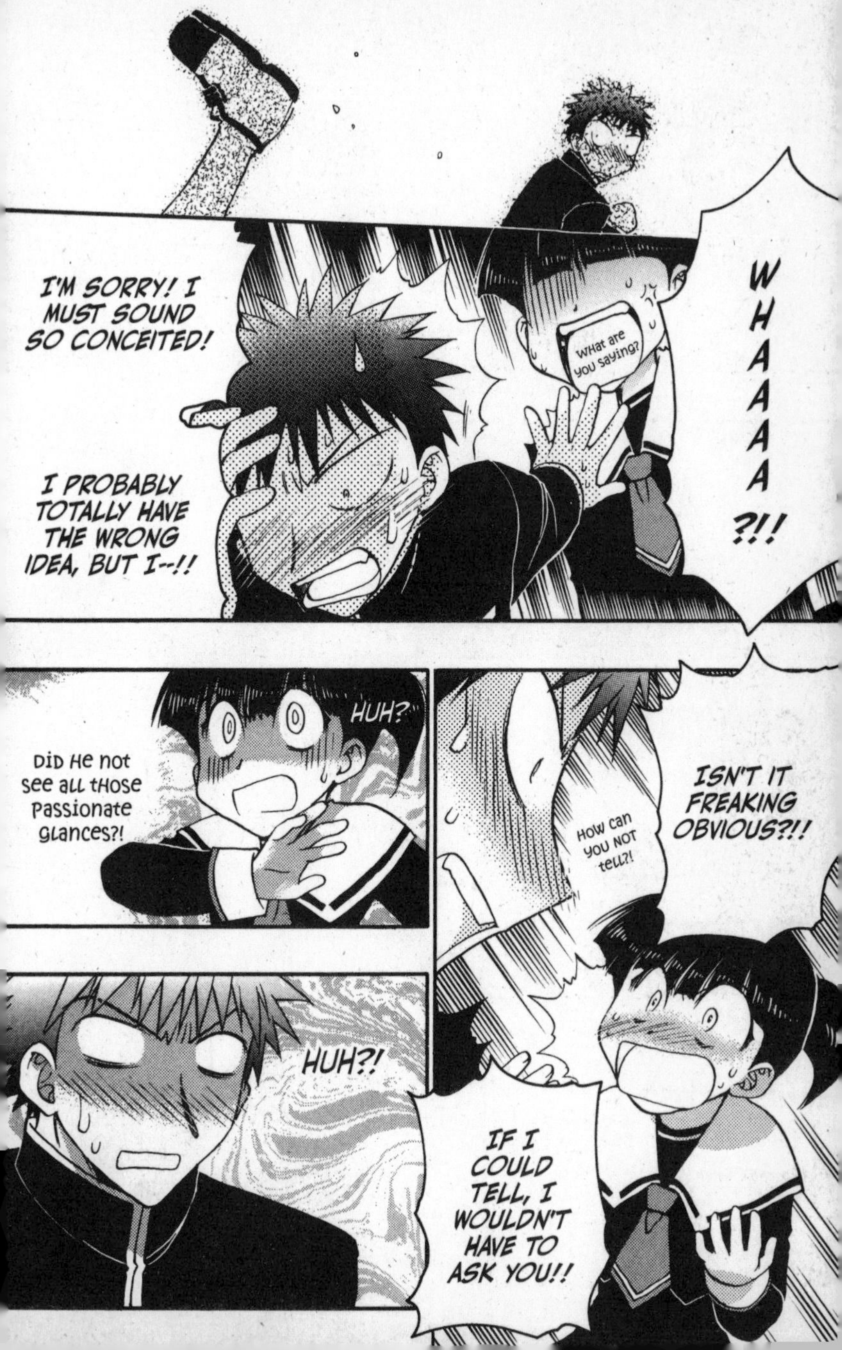
WHAAAAA?!!
What are you saying?
I'M SORRY! I MUST SOUND SO CONCEITED!
I PROBABLY TOTALLY HAVE THE WRONG IDEA, BUT I--!!
ISN'T IT FREAKING OBVIOUS?!!
How can you NOT tell?!
HUH?
Did he not see all those passionate glances?!
HUH?!
IF I COULD TELL, I WOULDN'T HAVE TO ASK YOU!!

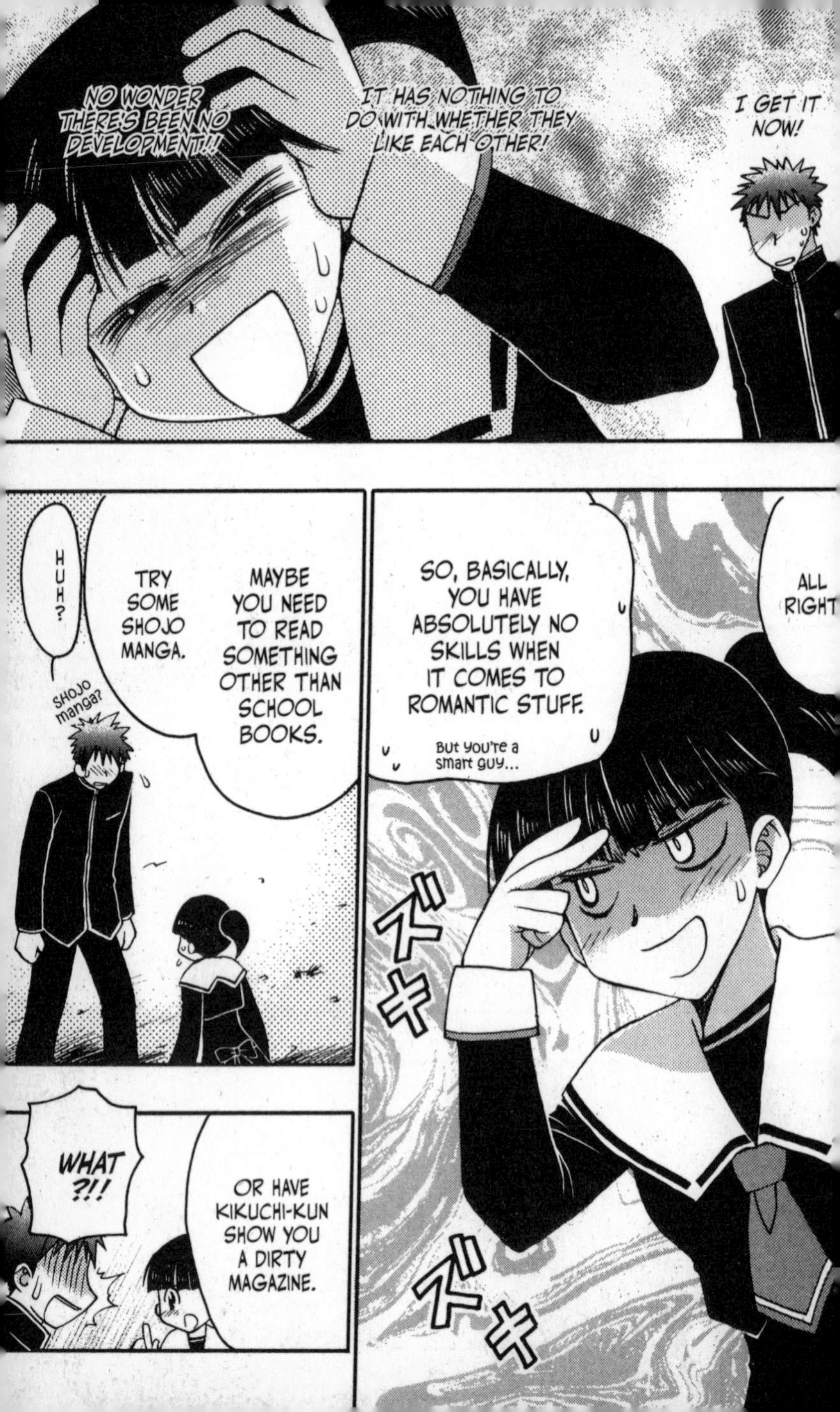
I GET IT NOW!
IT HAS NOTHING TO DO WITH WHETHER THEY LIKE EACH OTHER!
NO WONDER THERE'S BEEN NO DEVELOPMENT!!
ALL RIGHT
SO, BASICALLY, YOU HAVE ABSOLUTELY NO SKILLS WHEN IT COMES TO ROMANTIC STUFF.
But you're a smart guy...
ズキ
ズキ
MAYBE YOU NEED TO READ SOMETHING OTHER THAN SCHOOL BOOKS.
TRY SOME SHOJO MANGA.
HUH?
SHOJO manga?
OR HAVE KIKUCHI-KUN SHOW YOU A DIRTY MAGAZINE.
WHAT ?!!

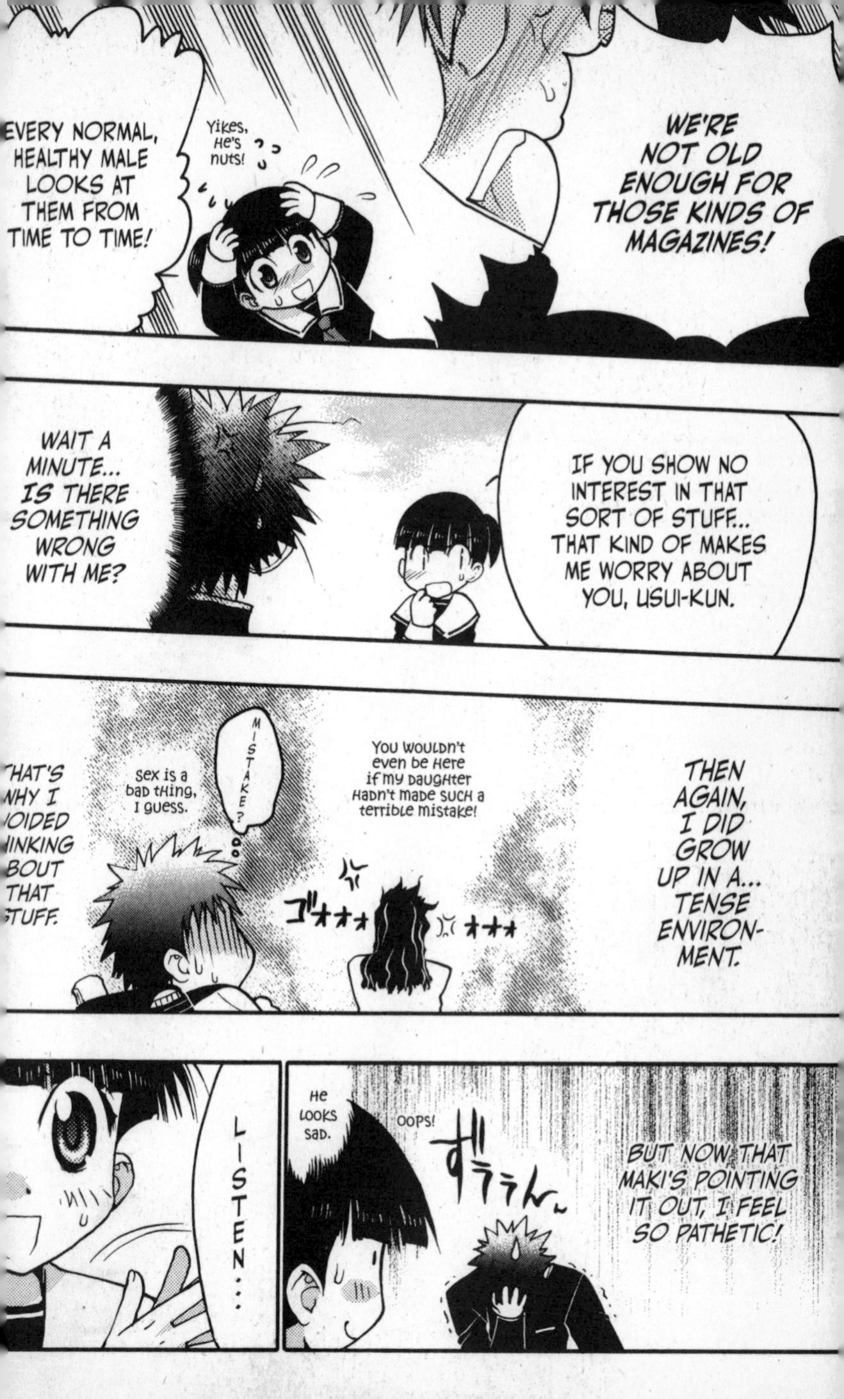
WE'RE NOT OLD ENOUGH FOR THOSE KINDS OF MAGAZINES!
Yikes, He's nuts!
EVERY NORMAL, HEALTHY MALE LOOKS AT THEM FROM TIME TO TIME!
IF YOU SHOW NO INTEREST IN THAT SORT OF STUFF... THAT KIND OF MAKES ME WORRY ABOUT YOU, USUI-KUN.
WAIT A MINUTE... IS THERE SOMETHING WRONG WITH ME?
THEN AGAIN, I DID GROW UP IN A... TENSE ENVIRONMENT.
You wouldn't even be Here if my daughter Hadn't made such a terrible mistake!
ゴオオオ
オオオ
MISTAKE?
sex is a bad thing, I guess.
HAT'S WHY I OIDED HINKING BOUT THAT TUFF.
BUT NOW THAT MAKI'S POINTING IT OUT, I FEEL SO PATHETIC!
OOPS!
He looks sad.
LISTEN...

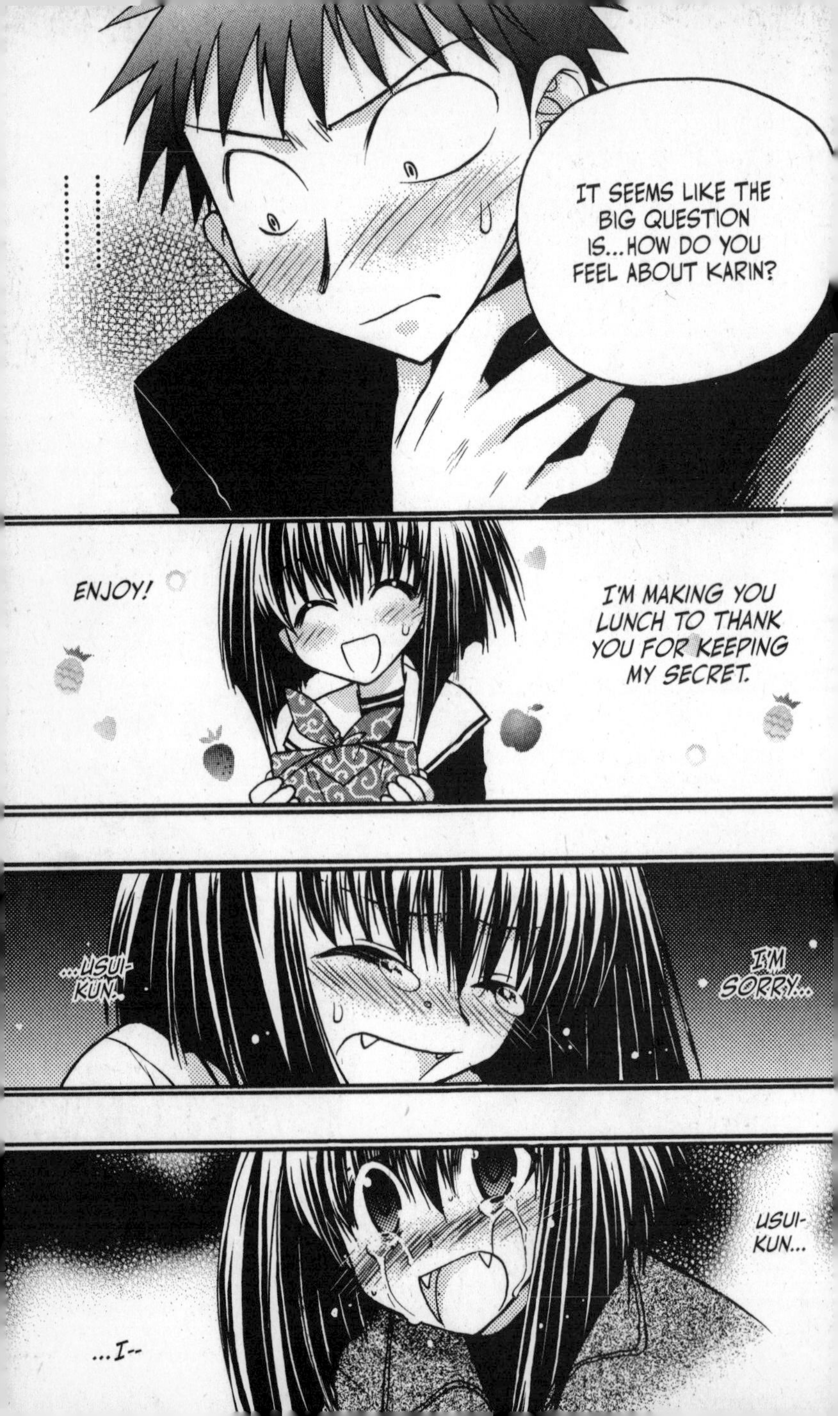
IT SEEMS LIKE THE BIG QUESTION IS...HOW DO YOU FEEL ABOUT KARIN?
......
I'M MAKING YOU LUNCH TO THANK YOU FOR KEEPING MY SECRET.
ENJOY!
I'M SORRY...
...USUI-KUN...
USUI-KUN...
...I--

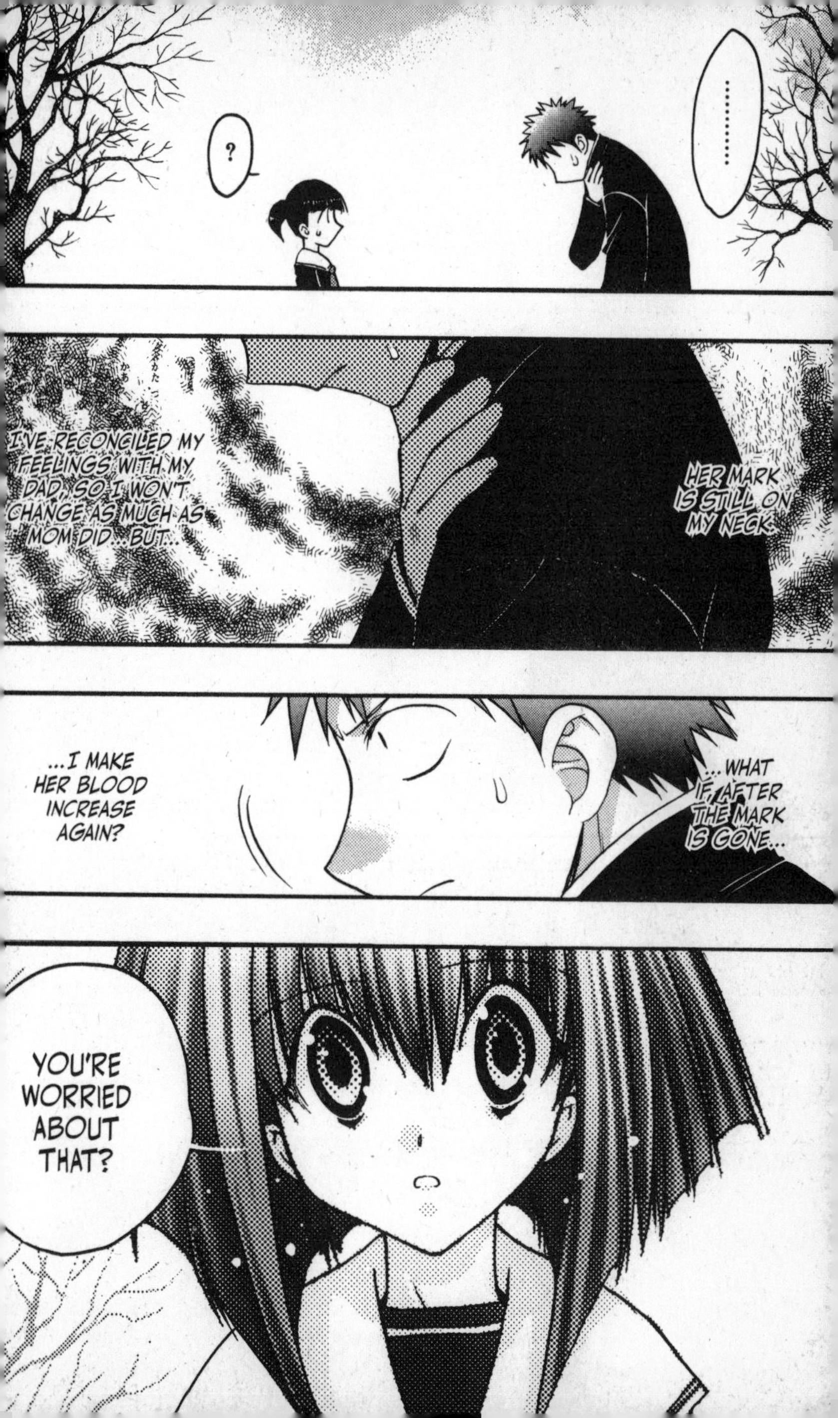
......
?
HER MARK IS STILL ON MY NECK.
I'VE RECONCILED MY FEELINGS WITH MY DAD, SO I WON'T CHANGE AS MUCH AS MOM DID... BUT...
...WHAT IF, AFTER THE MARK IS GONE...
...I MAKE HER BLOOD INCREASE AGAIN?
YOU'RE WORRIED ABOUT THAT?

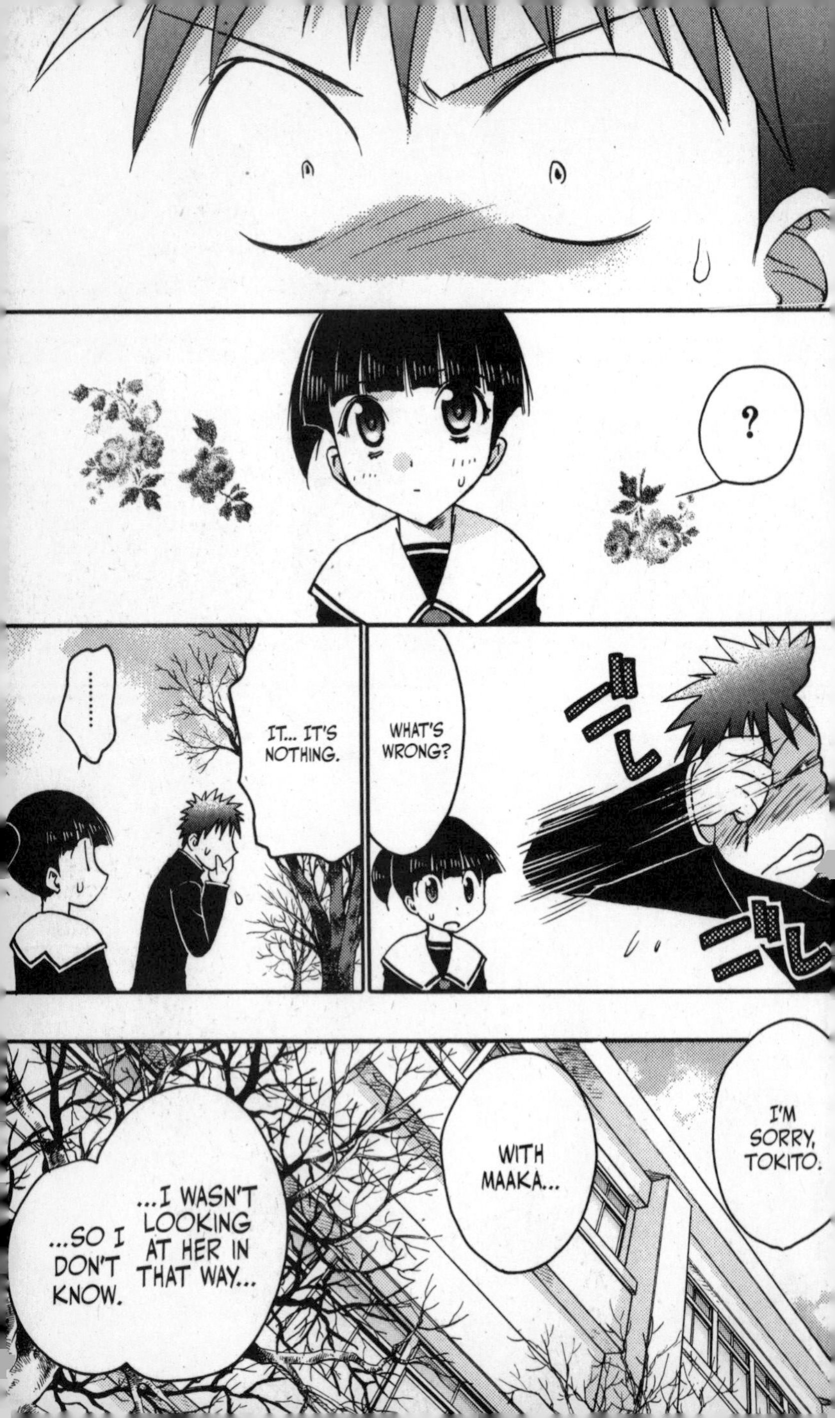
?
WHAT'S WRONG?
IT... IT'S NOTHING.
......
I'M SORRY, TOKITO.
WITH MAAKA...
...I WASN'T LOOKING AT HER IN THAT WAY...
...SO I DON'T KNOW.

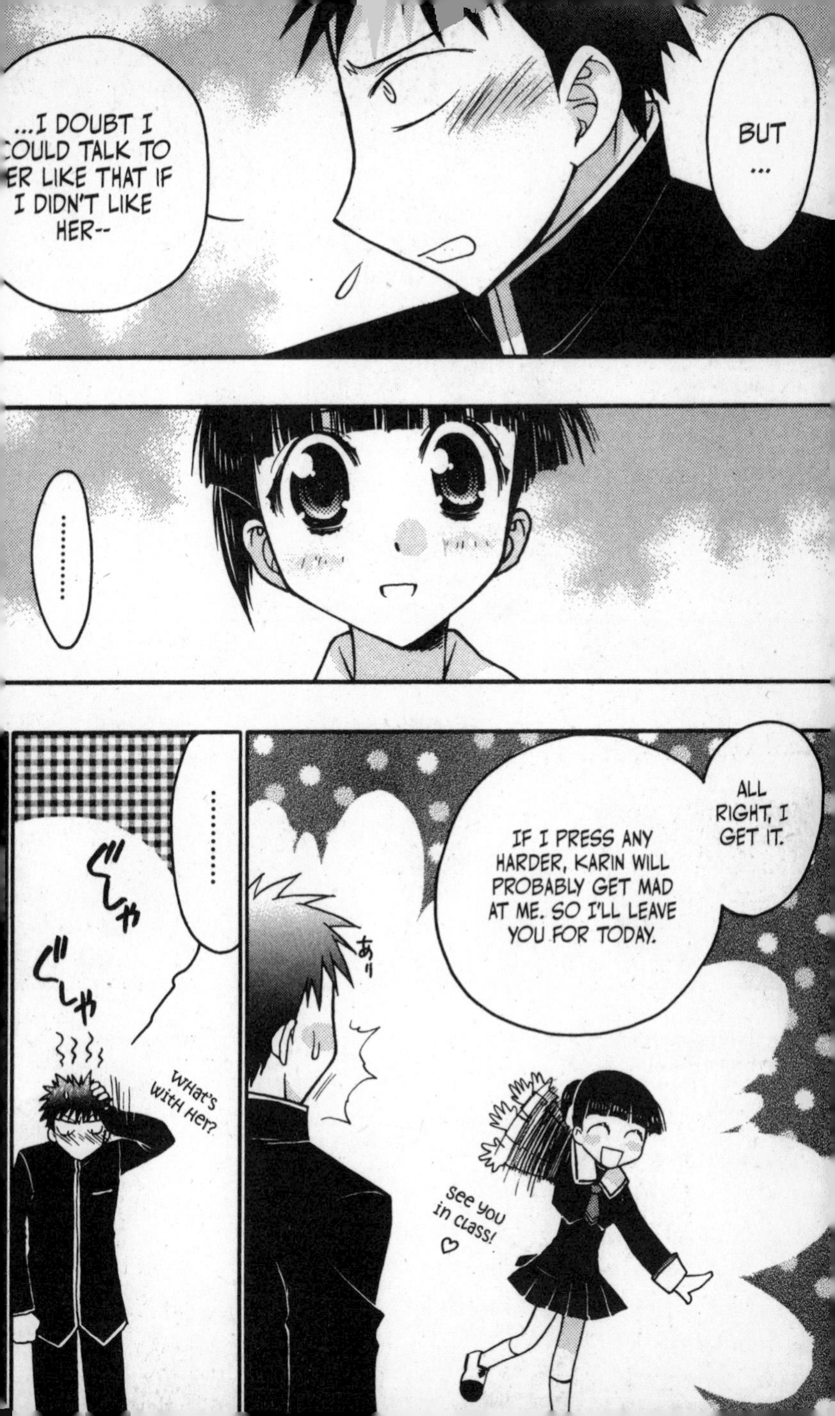
BUT ...
...I DOUBT I COULD TALK TO HER LIKE THAT IF I DIDN'T LIKE HER--
....
ALL RIGHT, I GET IT.
IF I PRESS ANY HARDER, KARIN WILL PROBABLY GET MAD AT ME. SO I'LL LEAVE YOU FOR TODAY.
あり
See you in class! ♡
....
ぐしゃ
ぐしゃ
WHat's witH Her?

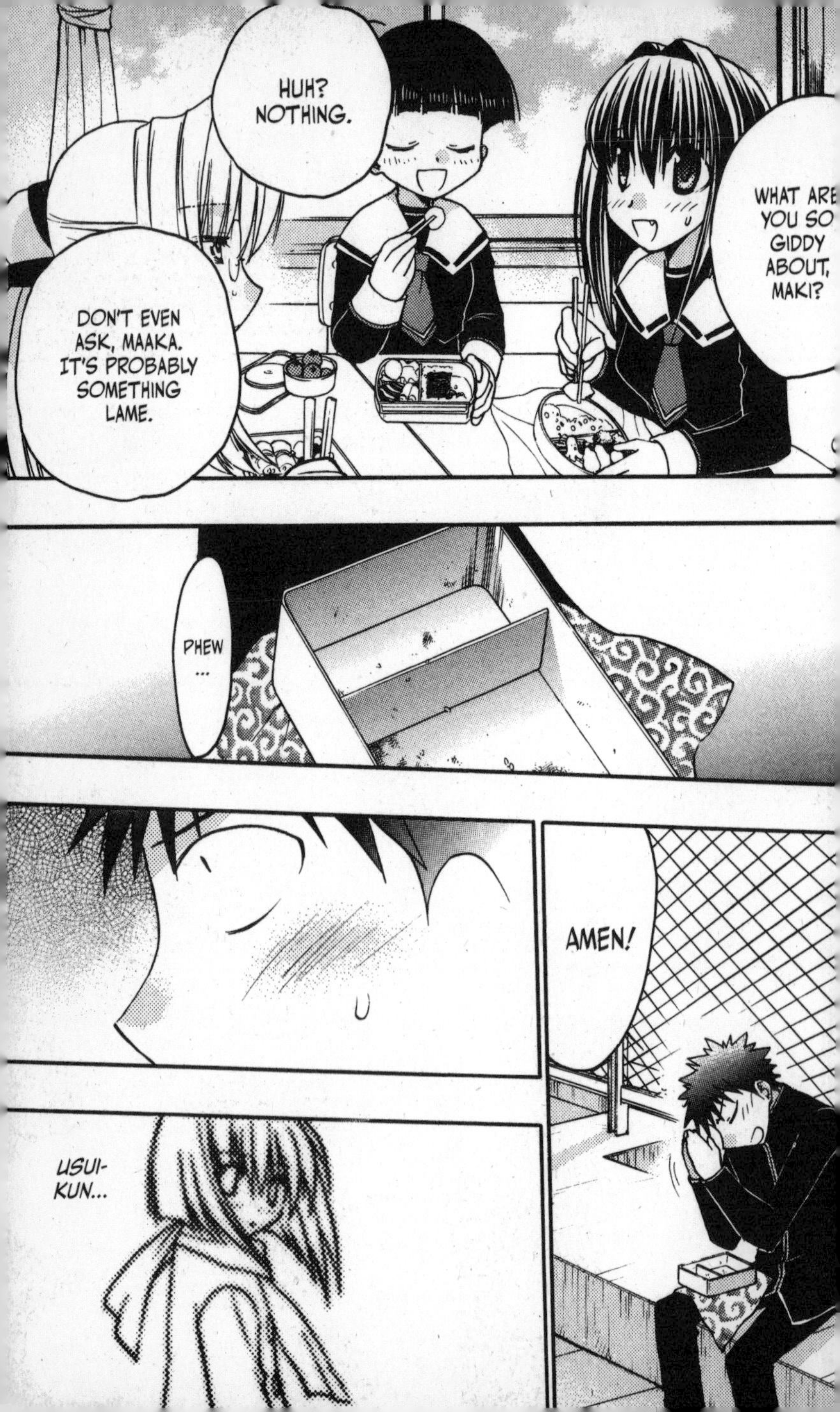
WHAT ARE YOU SO GIDDY ABOUT, MAKI?
HUH? NOTHING.
DON'T EVEN ASK, MAAKA. IT'S PROBABLY SOMETHING LAME.
PHEW ...
AMEN!
USUI-KUN...

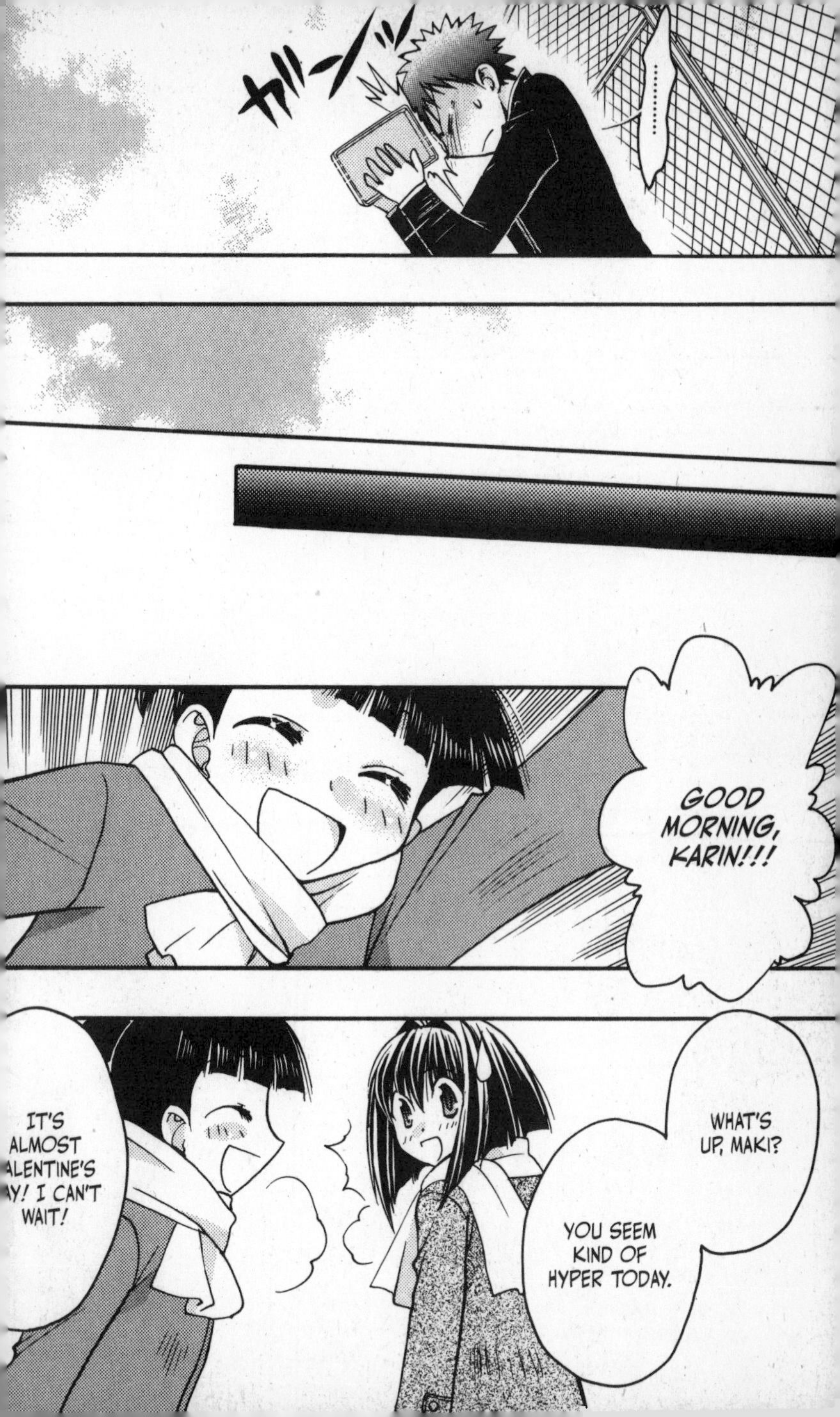
......
GOOD MORNING, KARIN!!!
WHAT'S UP, MAKI?
YOU SEEM KIND OF HYPER TODAY.
IT'S ALMOST ALENTINE'S Y! I CAN'T WAIT!

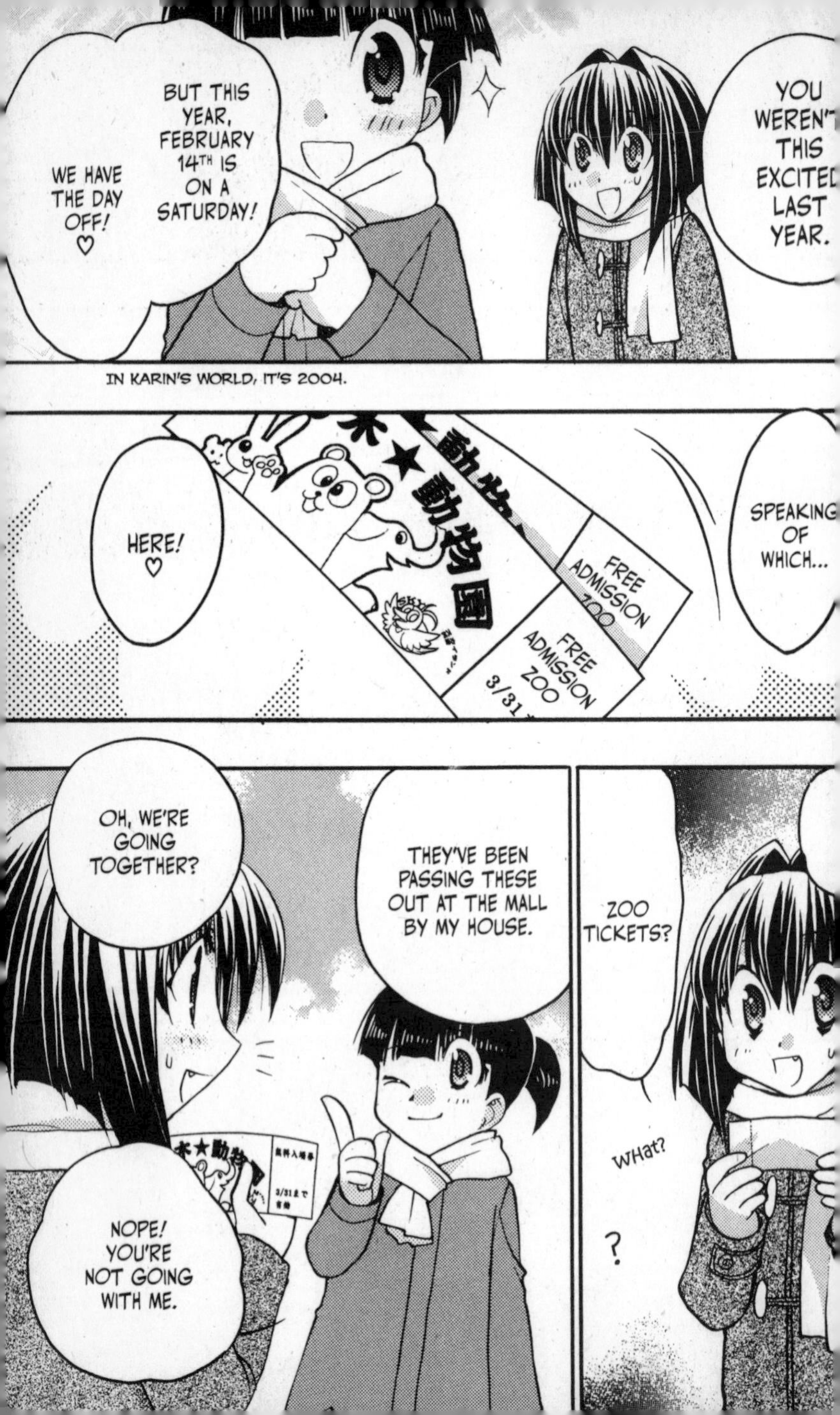
YOU WEREN'T THIS EXCITED LAST YEAR.
BUT THIS YEAR, FEBRUARY 14TH IS ON A SATURDAY!
WE HAVE THE DAY OFF! ♡
IN KARIN'S WORLD, IT'S 2004.
SPEAKING OF WHICH...
FREE ADMISSION ZOO
FREE ADMISSION ZOO 3/31
HERE! ♡
ZOO TICKETS?
WHAT?
?
THEY'VE BEEN PASSING THESE OUT AT THE MALL BY MY HOUSE.
OH, WE'RE GOING TOGETHER?
NOPE! YOU'RE NOT GOING WITH ME.

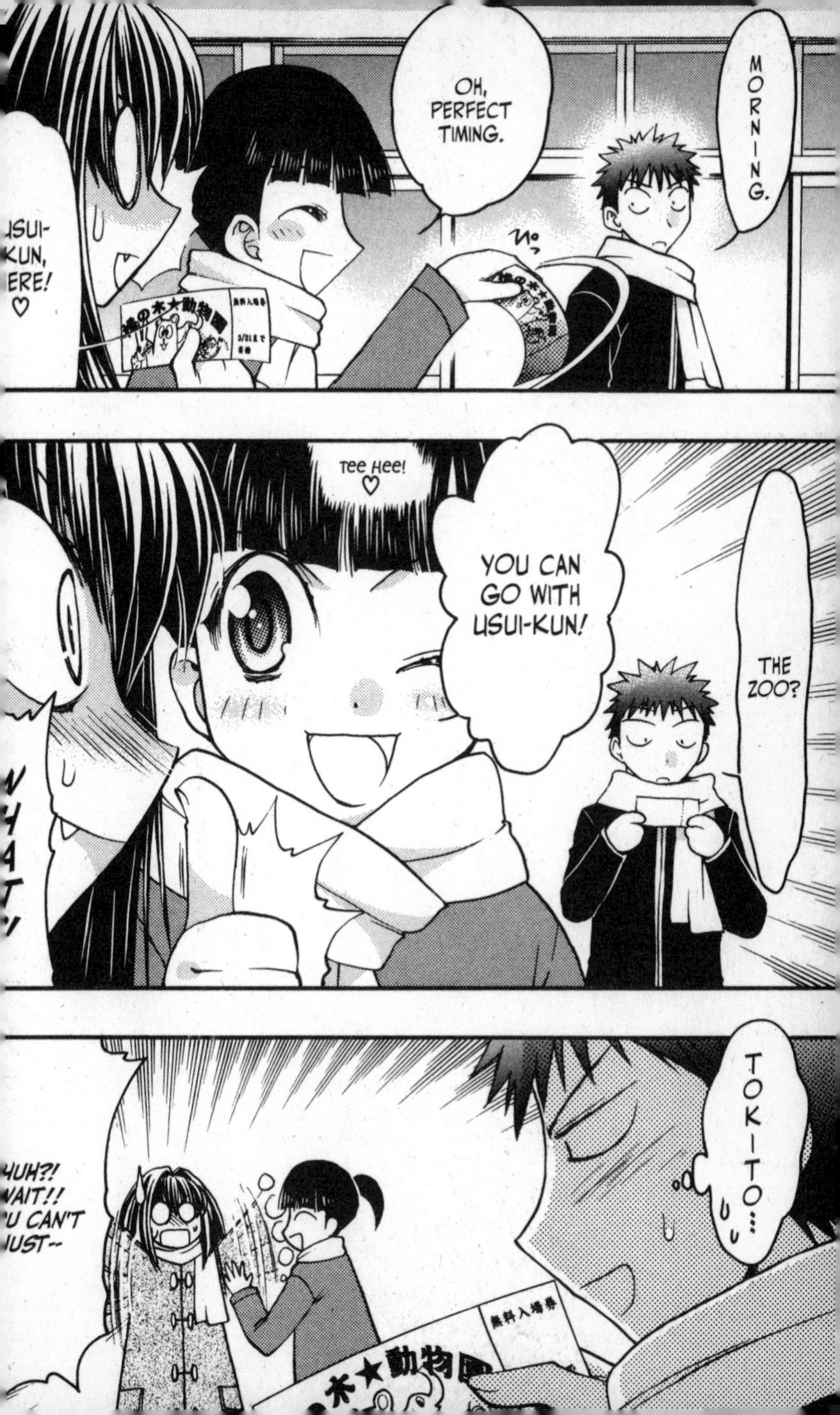
MORNING.
OH, PERFECT TIMING.
SUI-KUN, ERE! ♡
THE ZOO?
YOU CAN GO WITH USUI-KUN!
TEE HEE! ♡
TOKITO...
HUH?! WAIT!! U CAN'T JUST--

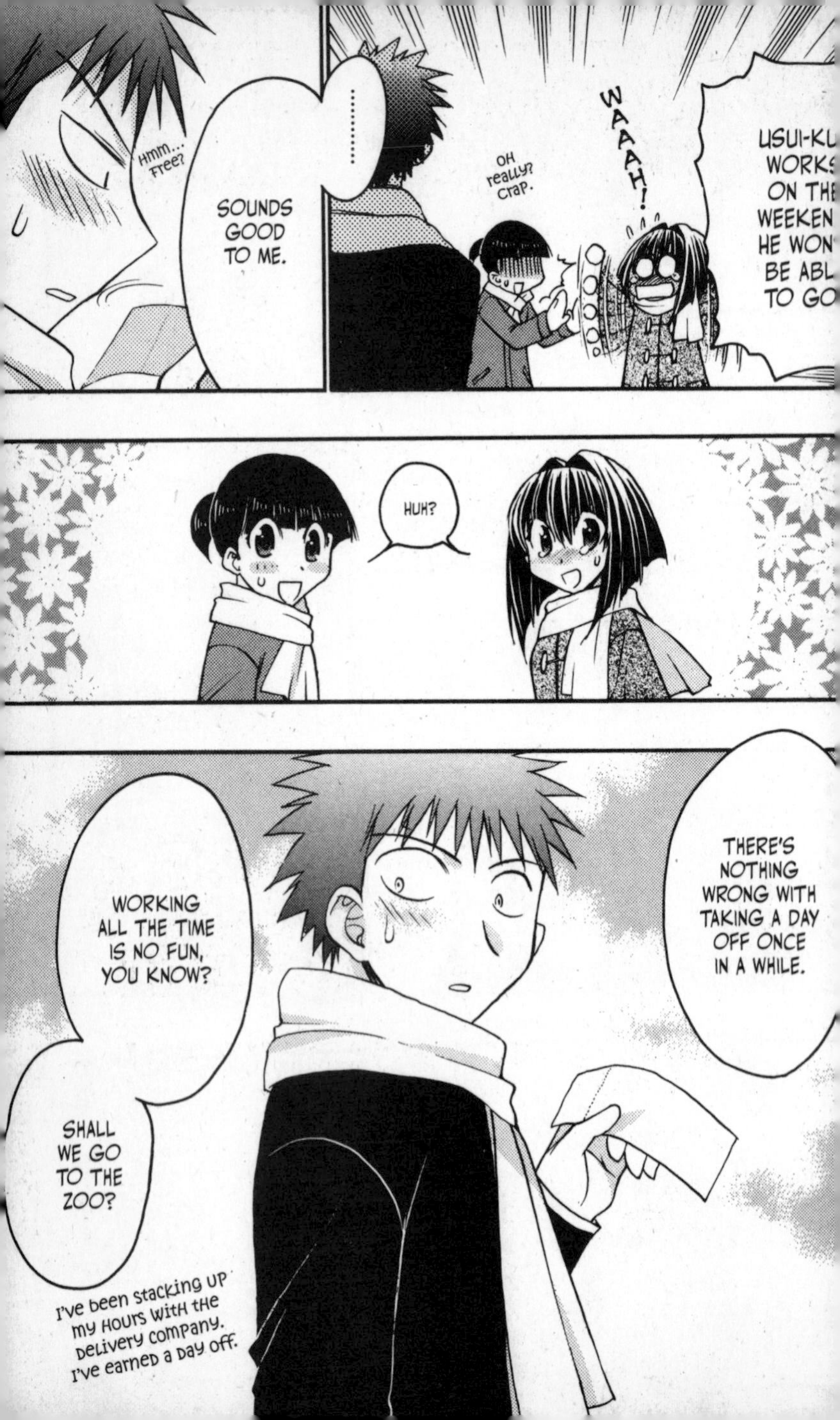
USUI-KU WORKS ON THE WEEKEN HE WON' BE ABL TO GO
WAAAH!
OH really? Crap.
......
SOUNDS GOOD TO ME.
Hmm... Free?
HUH?
THERE'S NOTHING WRONG WITH TAKING A DAY OFF ONCE IN A WHILE.
WORKING ALL THE TIME IS NO FUN, YOU KNOW?
SHALL WE GO TO THE ZOO?
I've been stacking up my hours with the delivery company. I've earned a day off.

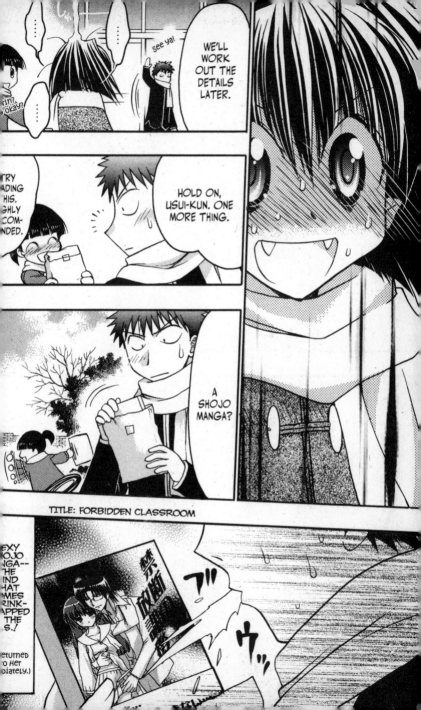

WE'LL WORK OUT THE DETAILS LATER.

See ya!

...rin? okay?

HOLD ON, USUI-KUN. ONE MORE THING.

TRY READING THIS. HIGHLY RECOM- MENDED.

A SHOJO MANGA?

TITLE: FORBIDDEN CLASSROOM

SEXY SHOJO MANGA-- THE KIND THAT COMES WRINK- WRAPPED THE S..!

(returned to her immediately.)

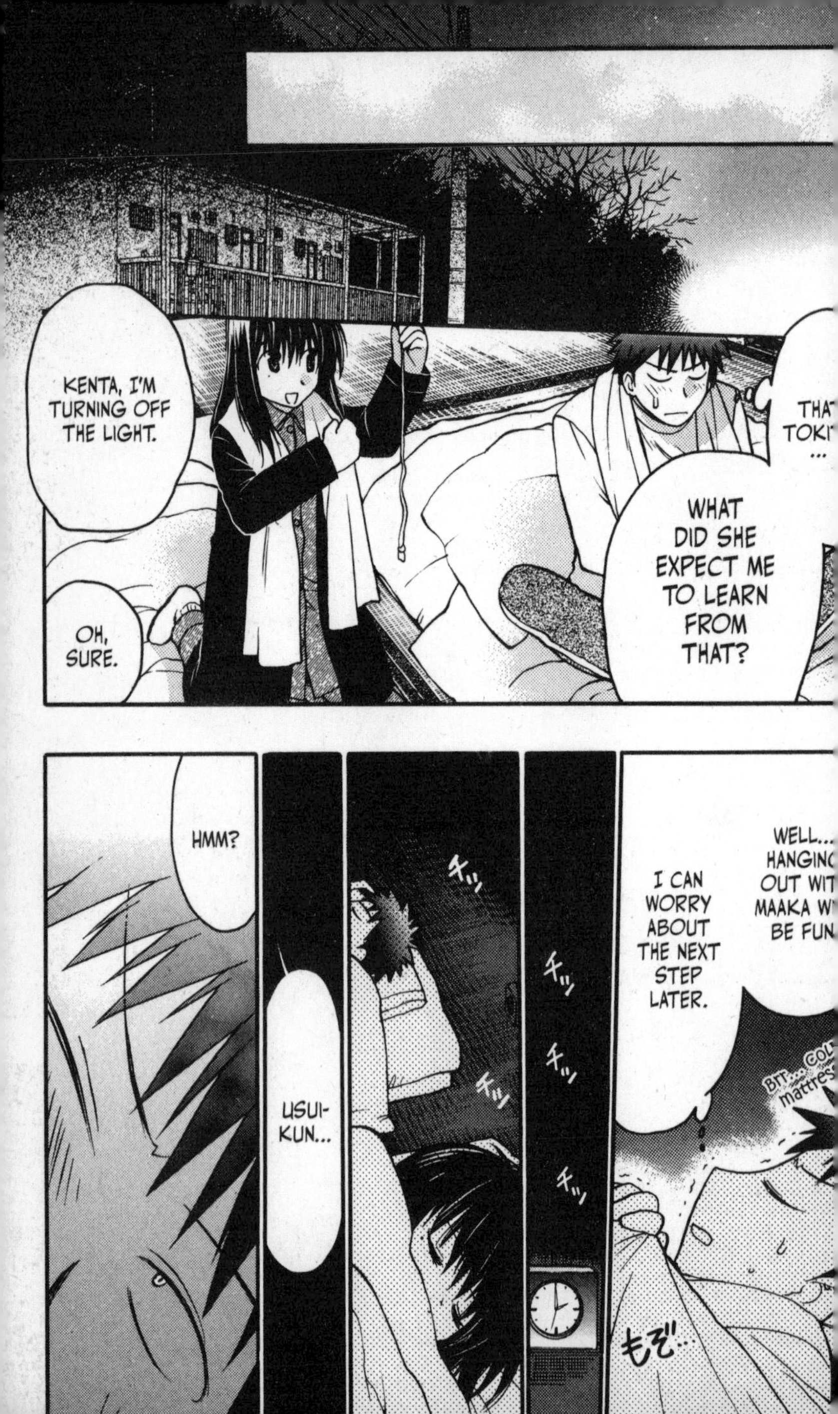

THAT TOKI...
WHAT DID SHE EXPECT ME TO LEARN FROM THAT?
KENTA, I'M TURNING OFF THE LIGHT.
OH, SURE.
WELL... HANGING OUT WIT MAAKA W BE FUN
I CAN WORRY ABOUT THE NEXT STEP LATER.
Brr... COL mattress
もぞ...
チッ
チッ
チッ
チッ
チッ
USUI-KUN...
HMM?

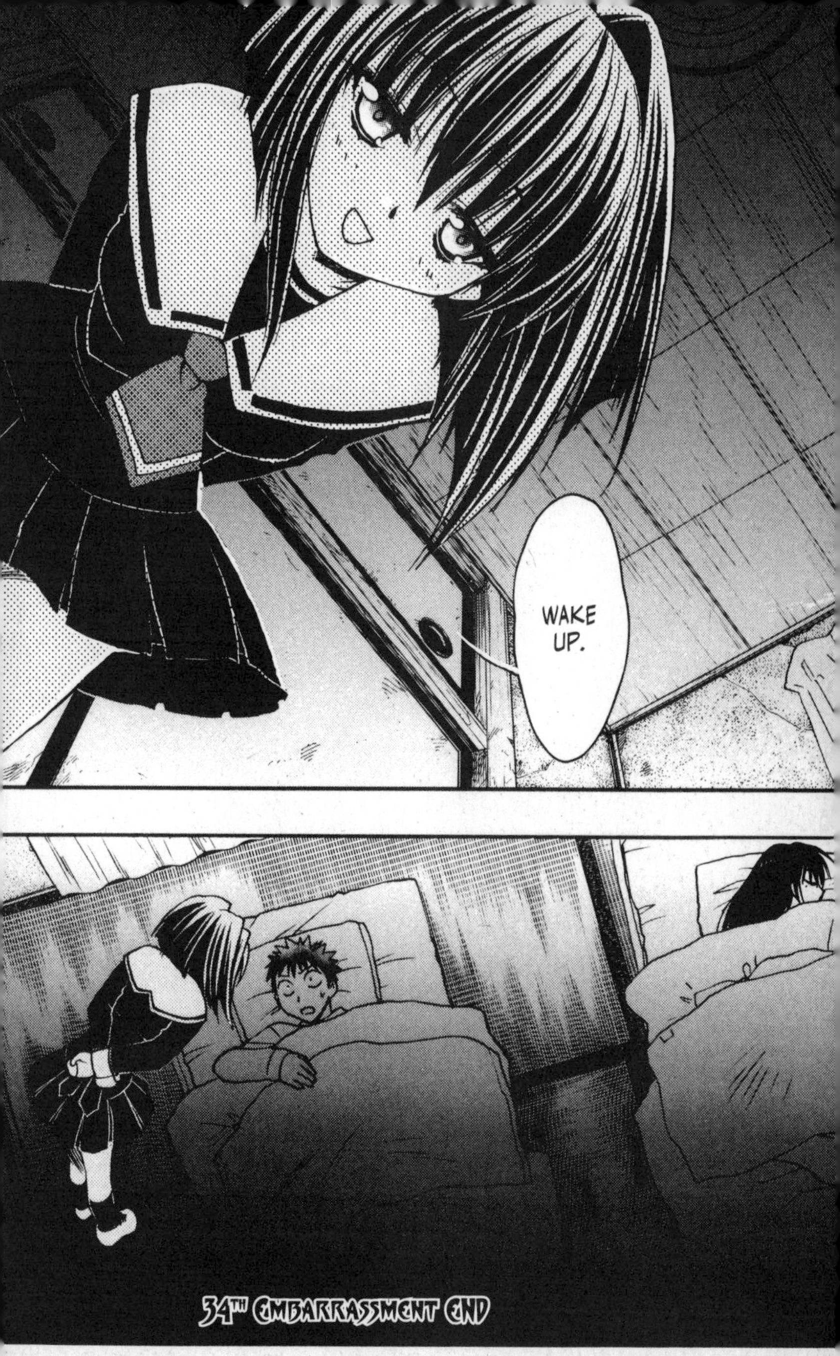
WAKE UP.
34TH EMBARRASSMENT END

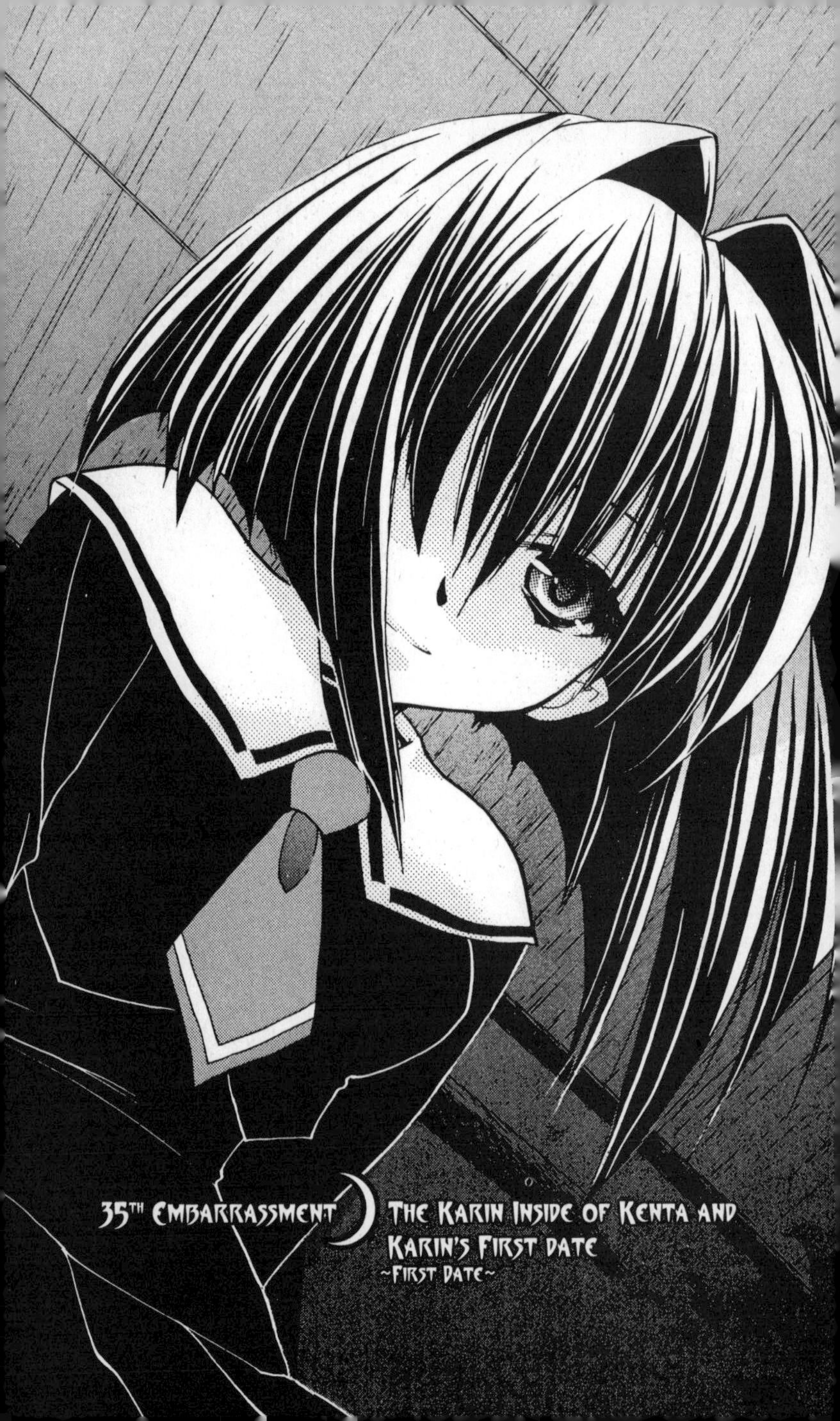
35TH EMBARRASSMENT
THE KARIN INSIDE OF KENTA AND KARIN'S FIRST DATE
~FIRST DATE~

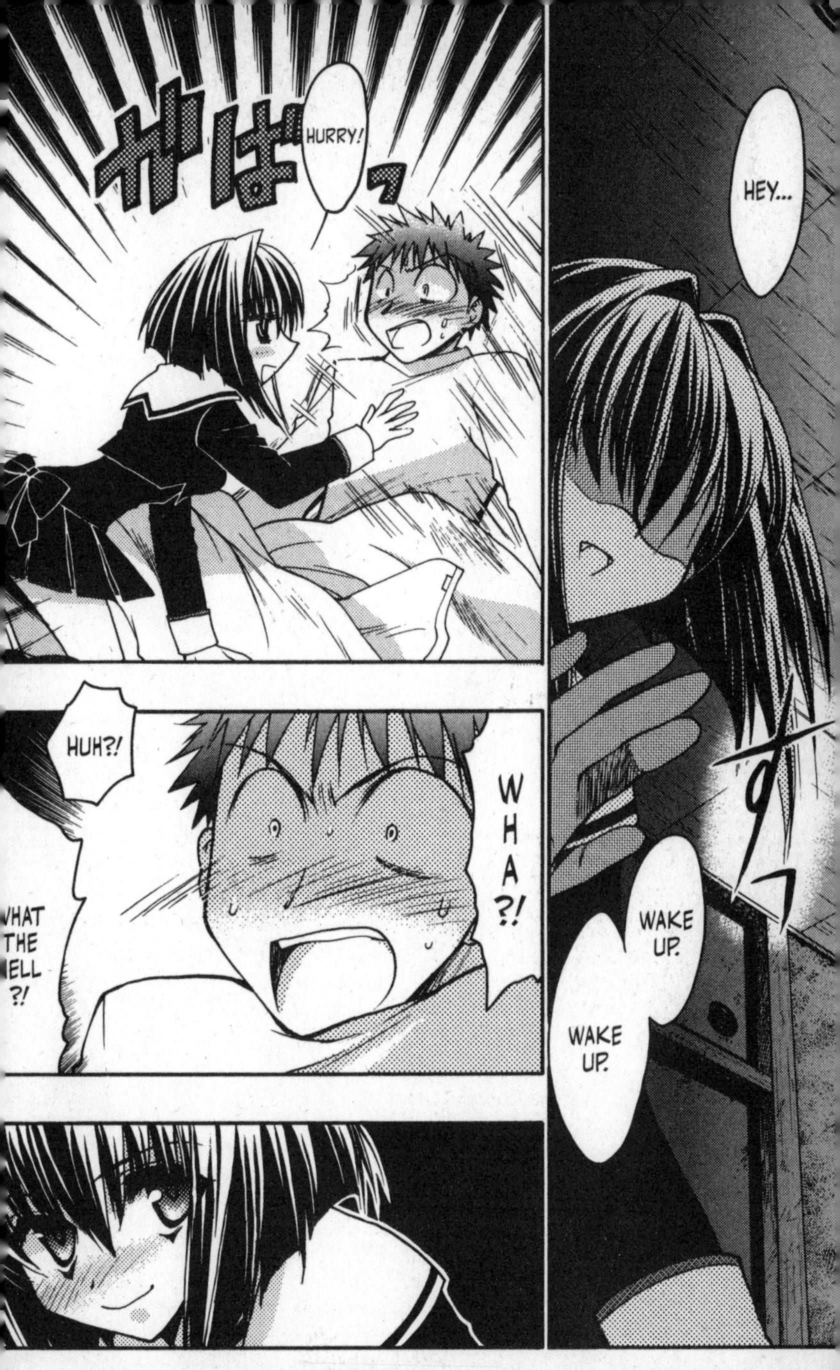

HEY...
WAKE UP.
WAKE UP.
がばっ
HURRY!
WHA?!
HUH?!
WHAT THE ELL ?!

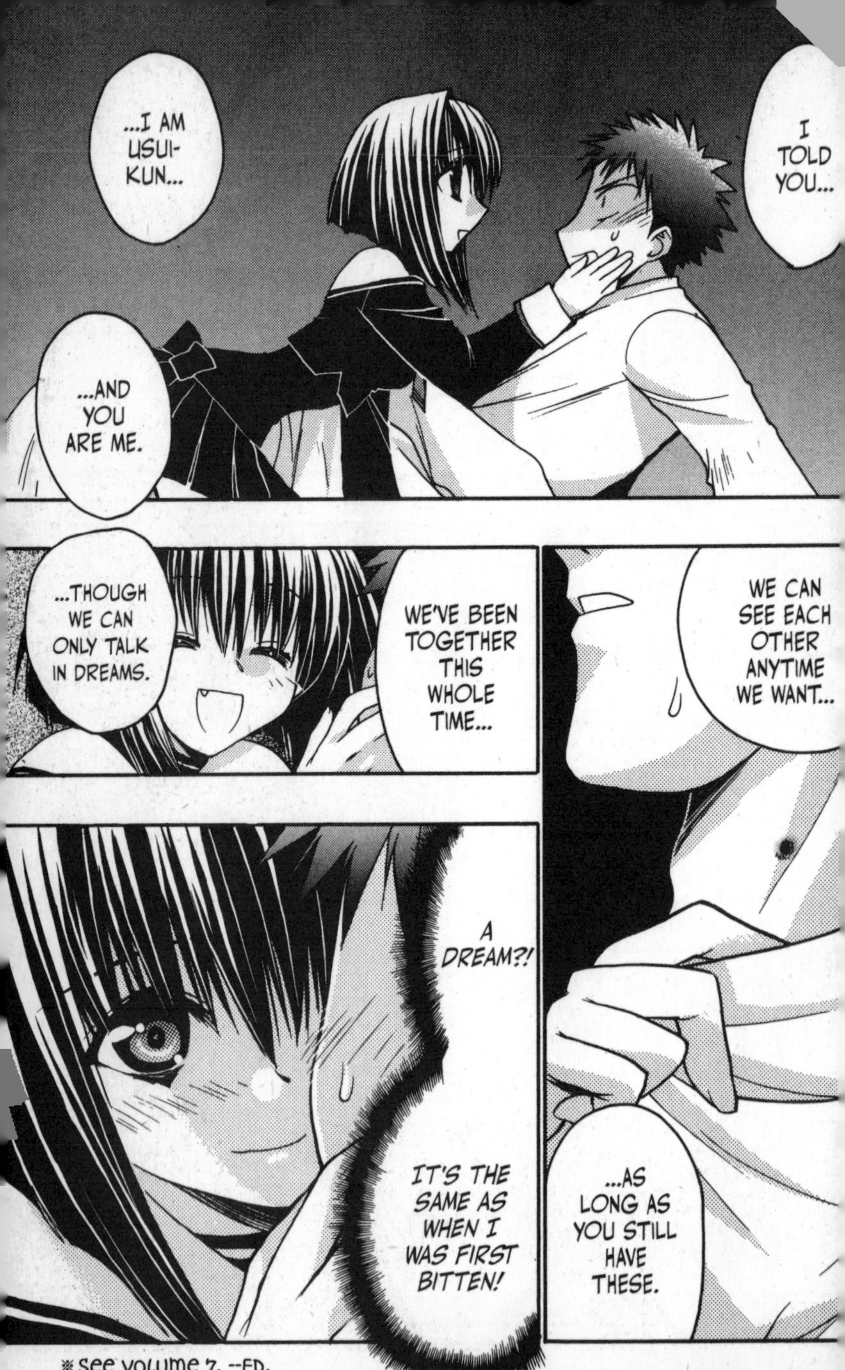
I TOLD YOU...
...I AM USUI-KUN...
...AND YOU ARE ME.
WE CAN SEE EACH OTHER ANYTIME WE WANT...
...AS LONG AS YOU STILL HAVE THESE.
WE'VE BEEN TOGETHER THIS WHOLE TIME...
...THOUGH WE CAN ONLY TALK IN DREAMS.
A DREAM?!
IT'S THE SAME AS WHEN I WAS FIRST BITTEN!

※see volume 7. --ED.

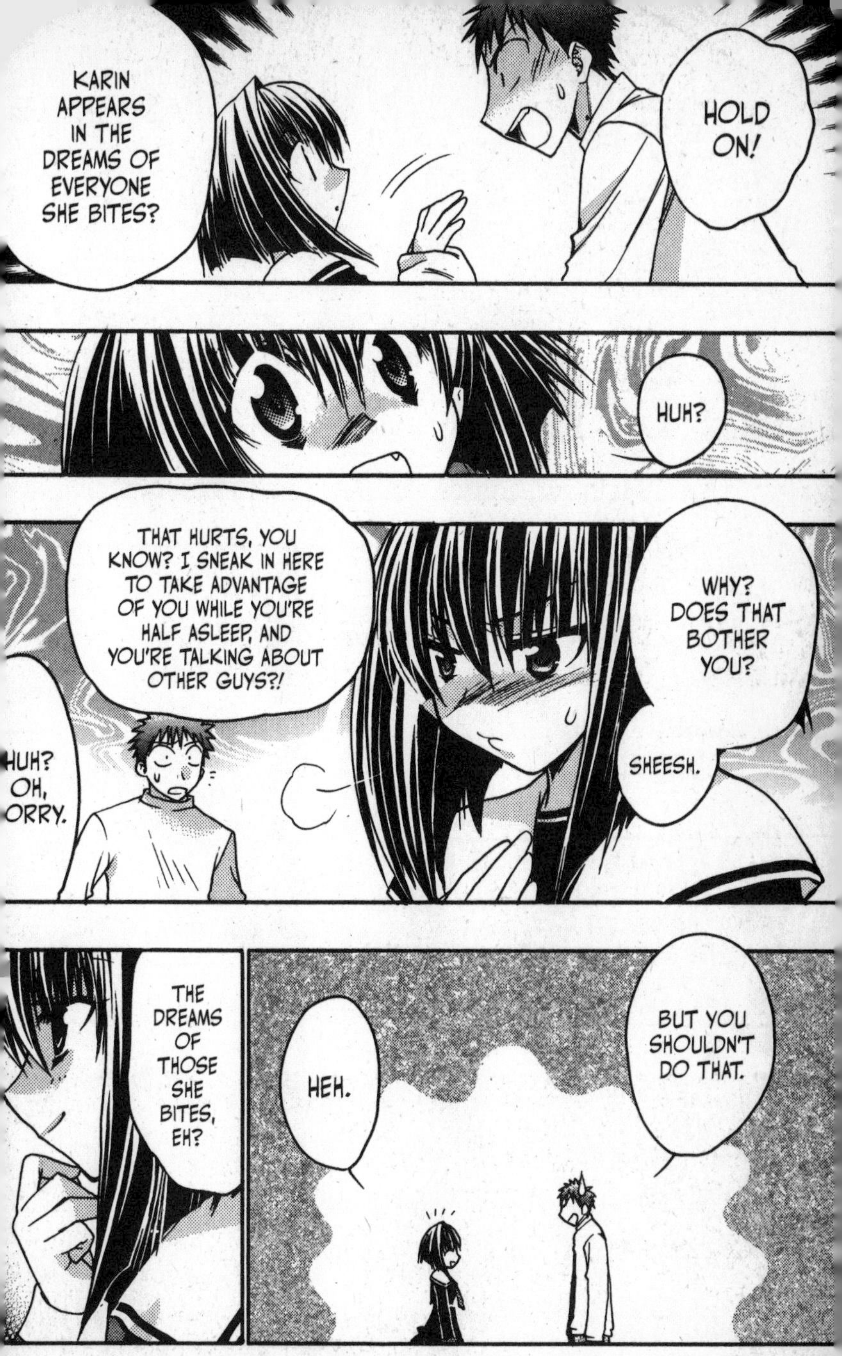
HOLD ON!
KARIN APPEARS IN THE DREAMS OF EVERYONE SHE BITES?
HUH?
WHY? DOES THAT BOTHER YOU?
SHEESH.
THAT HURTS, YOU KNOW? I SNEAK IN HERE TO TAKE ADVANTAGE OF YOU WHILE YOU'RE HALF ASLEEP, AND YOU'RE TALKING ABOUT OTHER GUYS?!
HUH? OH, ORRY.
BUT YOU SHOULDN'T DO THAT.
HEH.
THE DREAMS OF THOSE SHE BITES, EH?

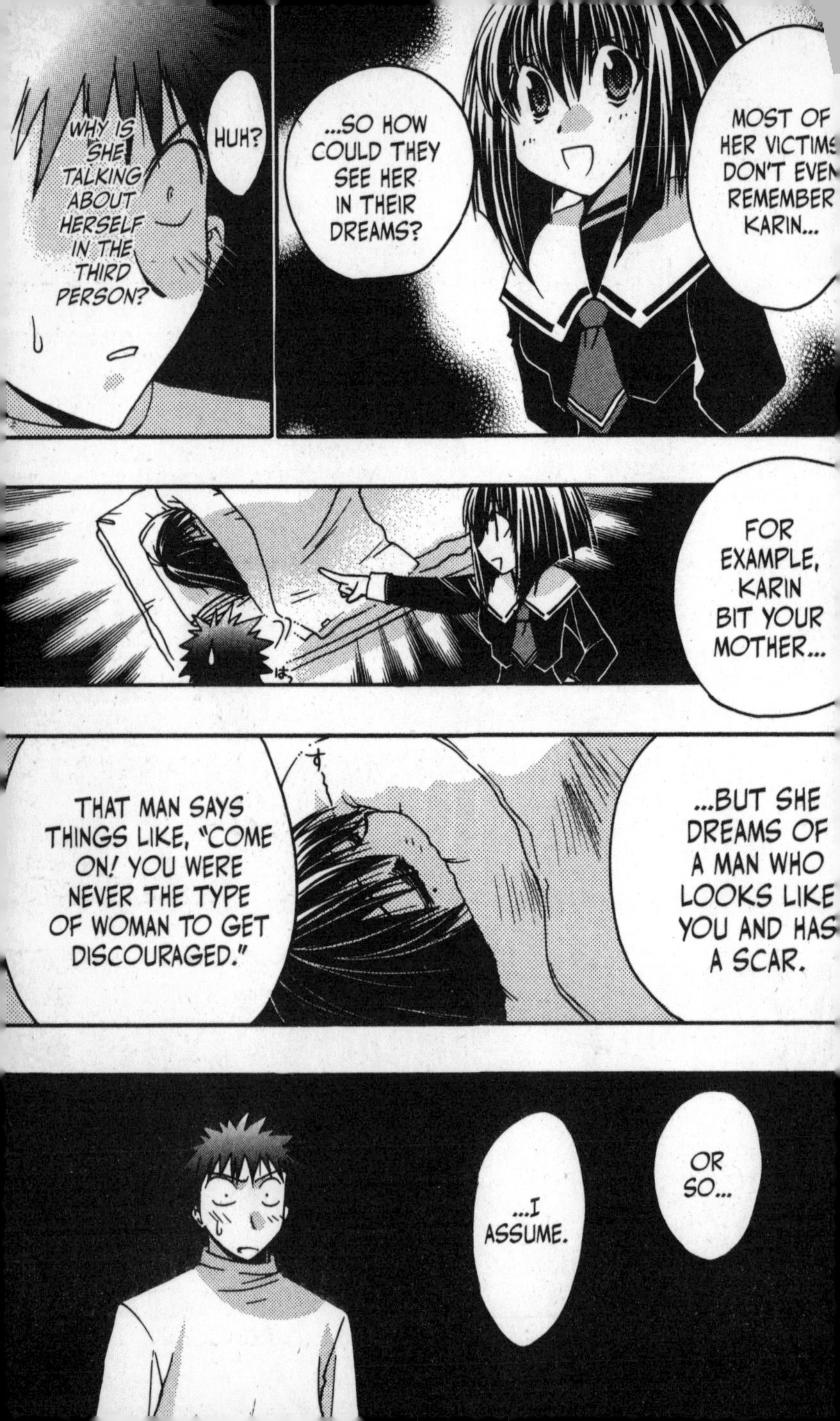
MOST OF HER VICTIMS DON'T EVEN REMEMBER KARIN...
...SO HOW COULD THEY SEE HER IN THEIR DREAMS?
HUH?
WHY IS SHE TALKING ABOUT HERSELF IN THE THIRD PERSON?
FOR EXAMPLE, KARIN BIT YOUR MOTHER...
...BUT SHE DREAMS OF A MAN WHO LOOKS LIKE YOU AND HAS A SCAR.
THAT MAN SAYS THINGS LIKE, "COME ON! YOU WERE NEVER THE TYPE OF WOMAN TO GET DISCOURAGED."
OR SO...
...I ASSUME.

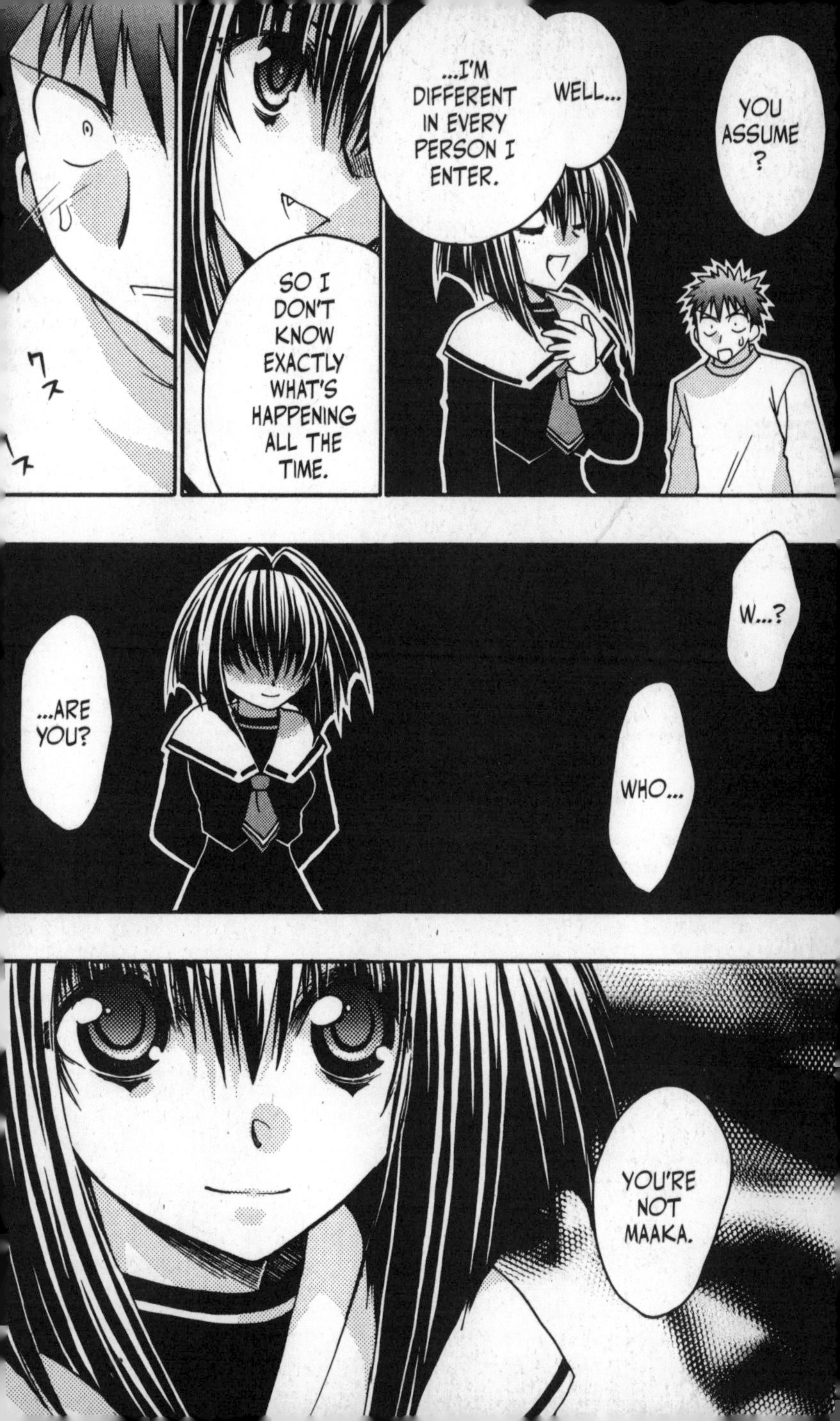
YOU ASSUME ?
WELL...
...I'M DIFFERENT IN EVERY PERSON I ENTER.
SO I DON'T KNOW EXACTLY WHAT'S HAPPENING ALL THE TIME.
クス
ス
W...?
WHO...
...ARE YOU?
YOU'RE NOT MAAKA.

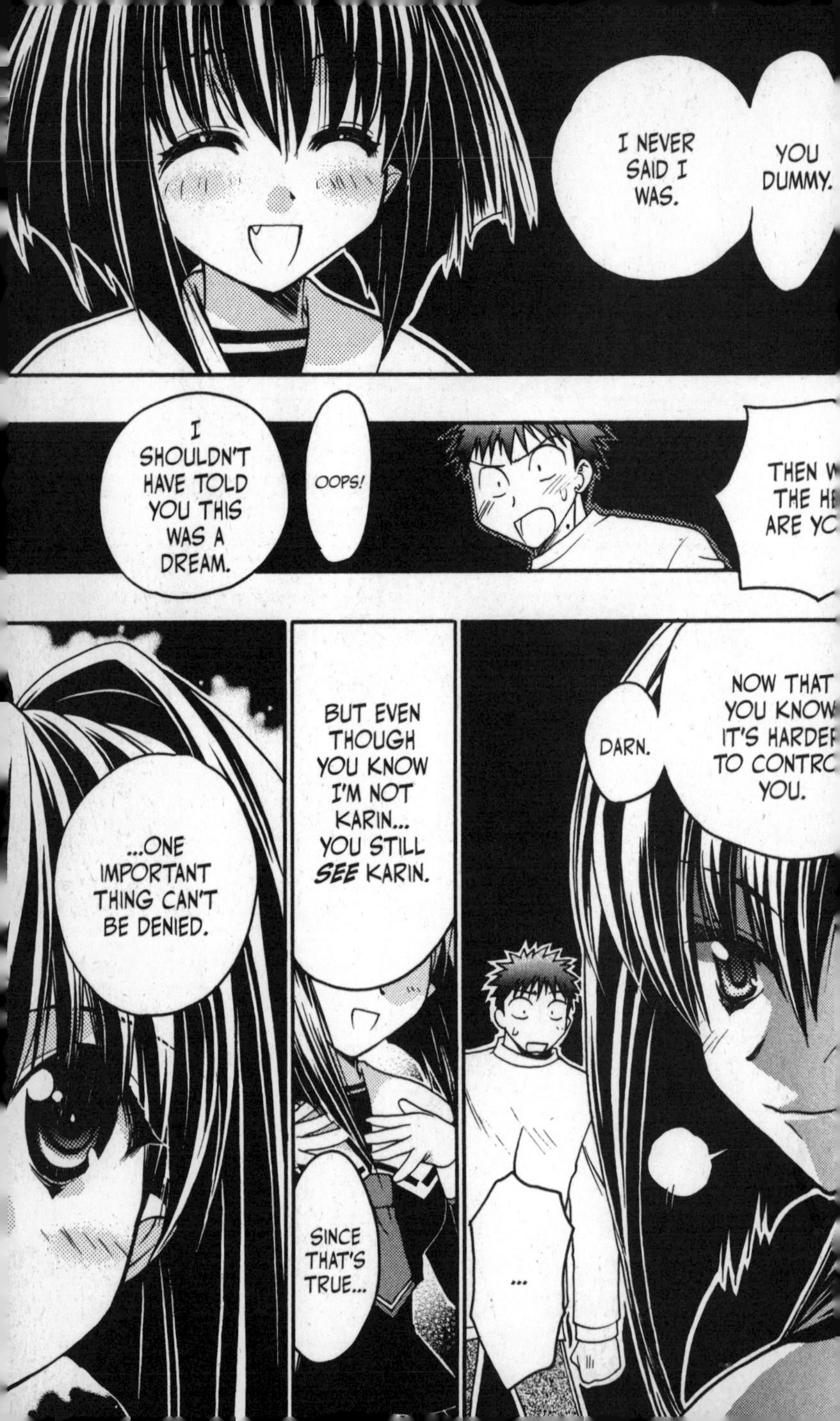
YOU DUMMY.
I NEVER SAID I WAS.
THEN W THE HE ARE YC
OOPS!
I SHOULDN'T HAVE TOLD YOU THIS WAS A DREAM.
NOW THAT YOU KNOW IT'S HARDEF TO CONTRC YOU.
DARN.
...
BUT EVEN THOUGH YOU KNOW I'M NOT KARIN... YOU STILL *SEE* KARIN.
SINCE THAT'S TRUE...
...ONE IMPORTANT THING CAN'T BE DENIED.

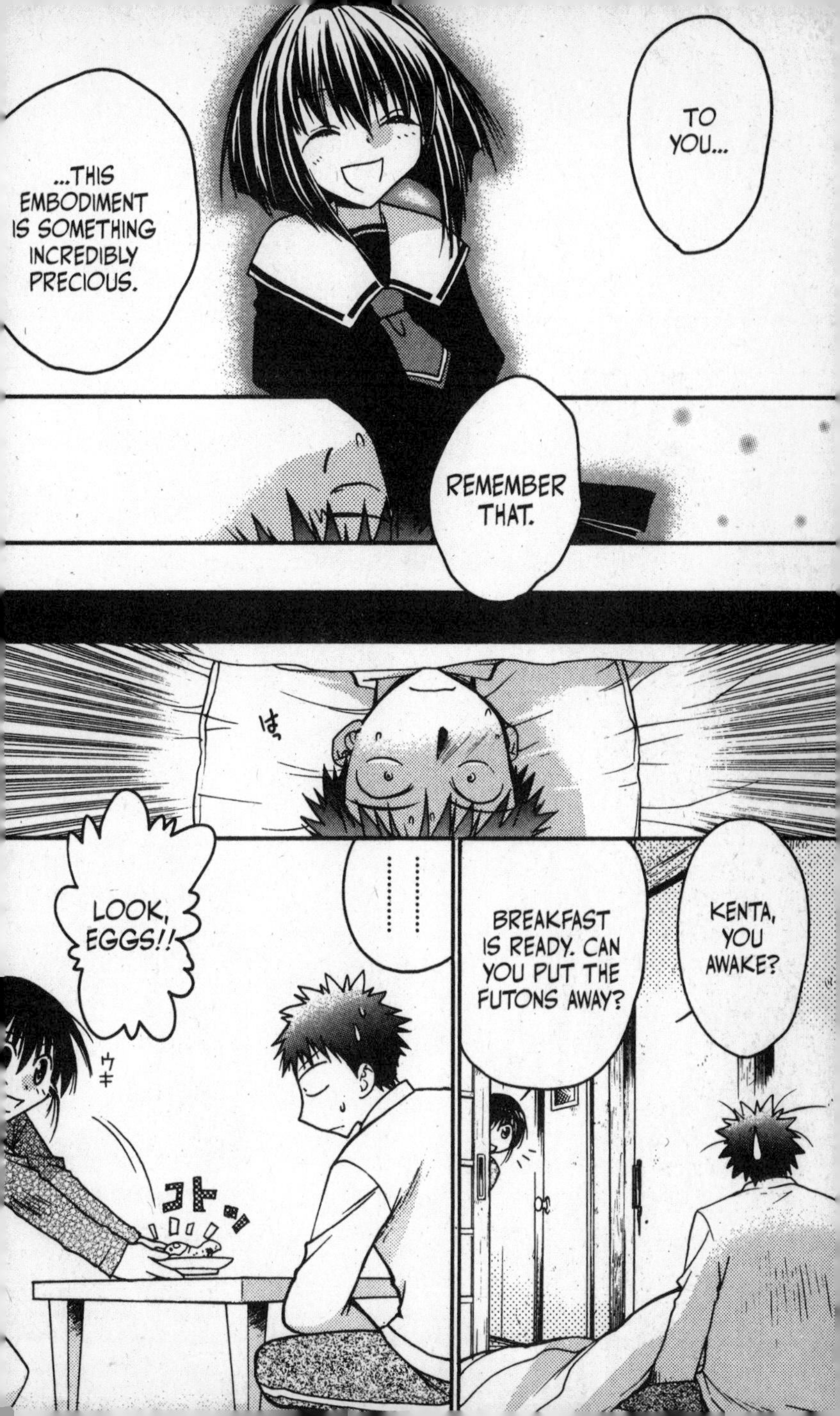
TO YOU...
...THIS EMBODIMENT IS SOMETHING INCREDIBLY PRECIOUS.
REMEMBER THAT.
はっ
KENTA, YOU AWAKE?
BREAKFAST IS READY. CAN YOU PUT THE FUTONS AWAY?
......
LOOK, EGGS!!
ウキ
コトッ

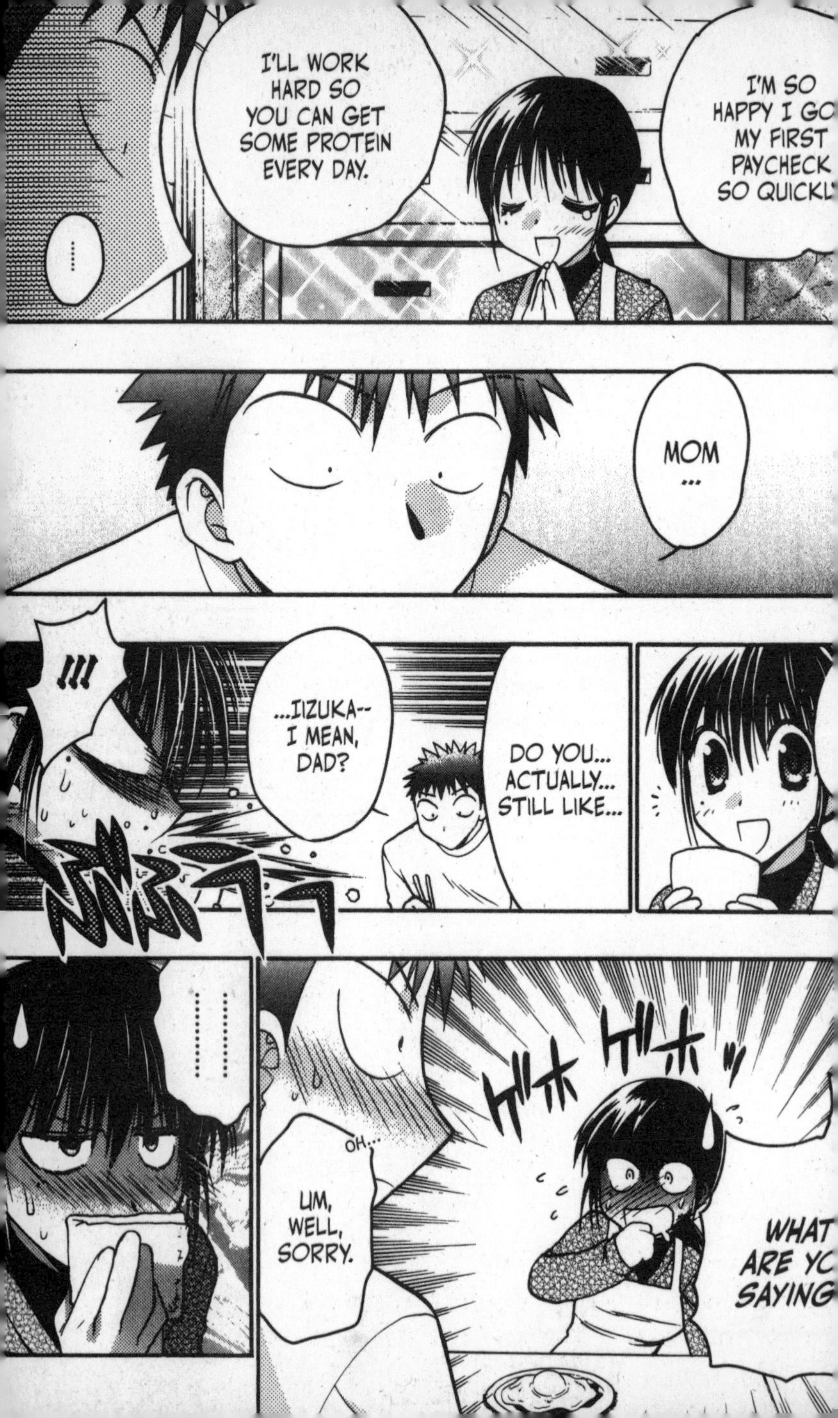

I'M SO HAPPY I GO MY FIRST PAYCHECK SO QUICKL
I'LL WORK HARD SO YOU CAN GET SOME PROTEIN EVERY DAY.
......
MOM ...
DO YOU... ACTUALLY... STILL LIKE...
...IIZUKA-- I MEAN, DAD?
!!!
WHAT ARE YO SAYING
OH...
UM, WELL, SORRY.
....

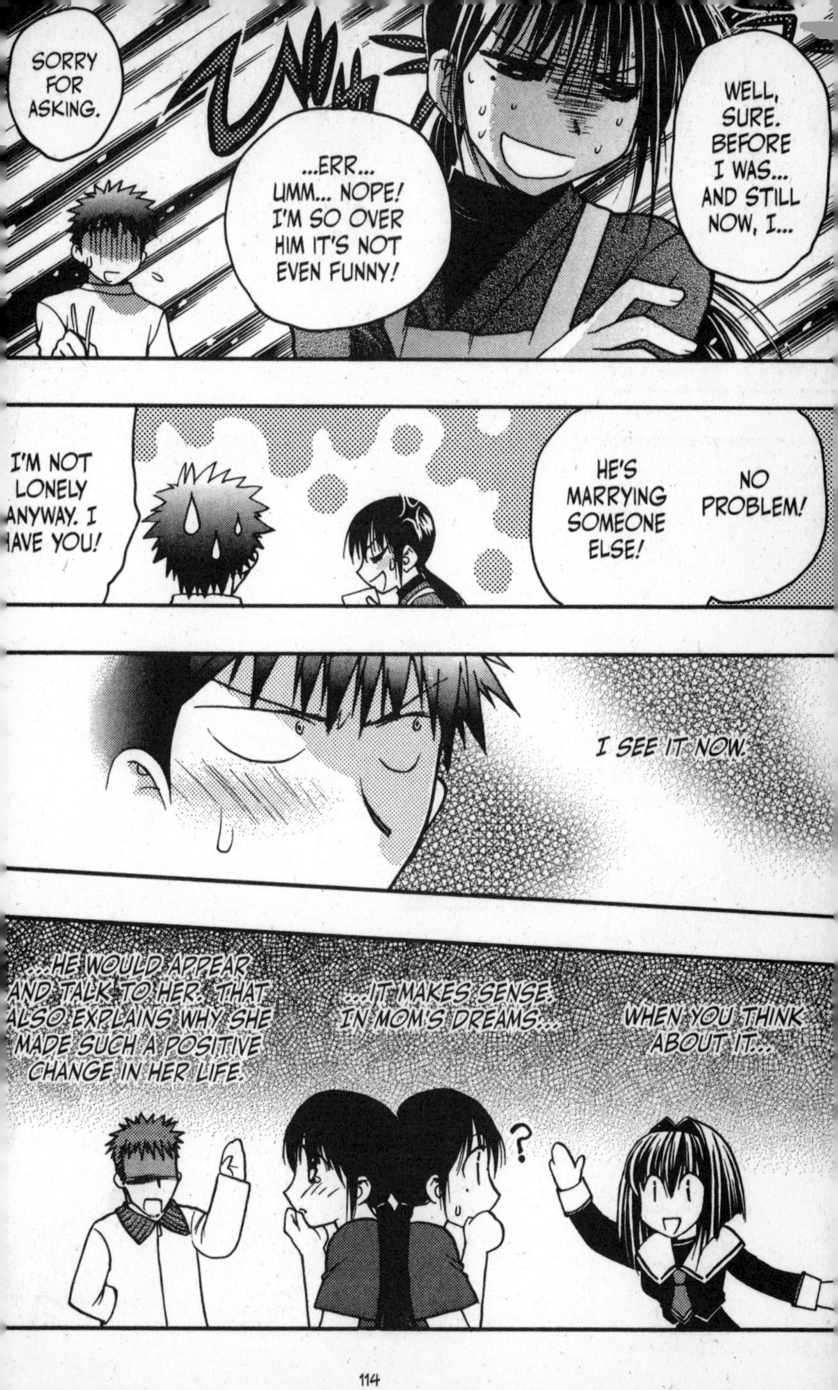
WELL, SURE. BEFORE I WAS... AND STILL NOW, I...
...ERR... UMM... NOPE! I'M SO OVER HIM IT'S NOT EVEN FUNNY!
SORRY FOR ASKING.
NO PROBLEM!
HE'S MARRYING SOMEONE ELSE!
I'M NOT LONELY ANYWAY. I HAVE YOU!
I SEE IT NOW.
WHEN YOU THINK ABOUT IT...
...IT MAKES SENSE. IN MOM'S DREAMS...
...HE WOULD APPEAR AND TALK TO HER. THAT ALSO EXPLAINS WHY SHE MADE SUCH A POSITIVE CHANGE IN HER LIFE.
?

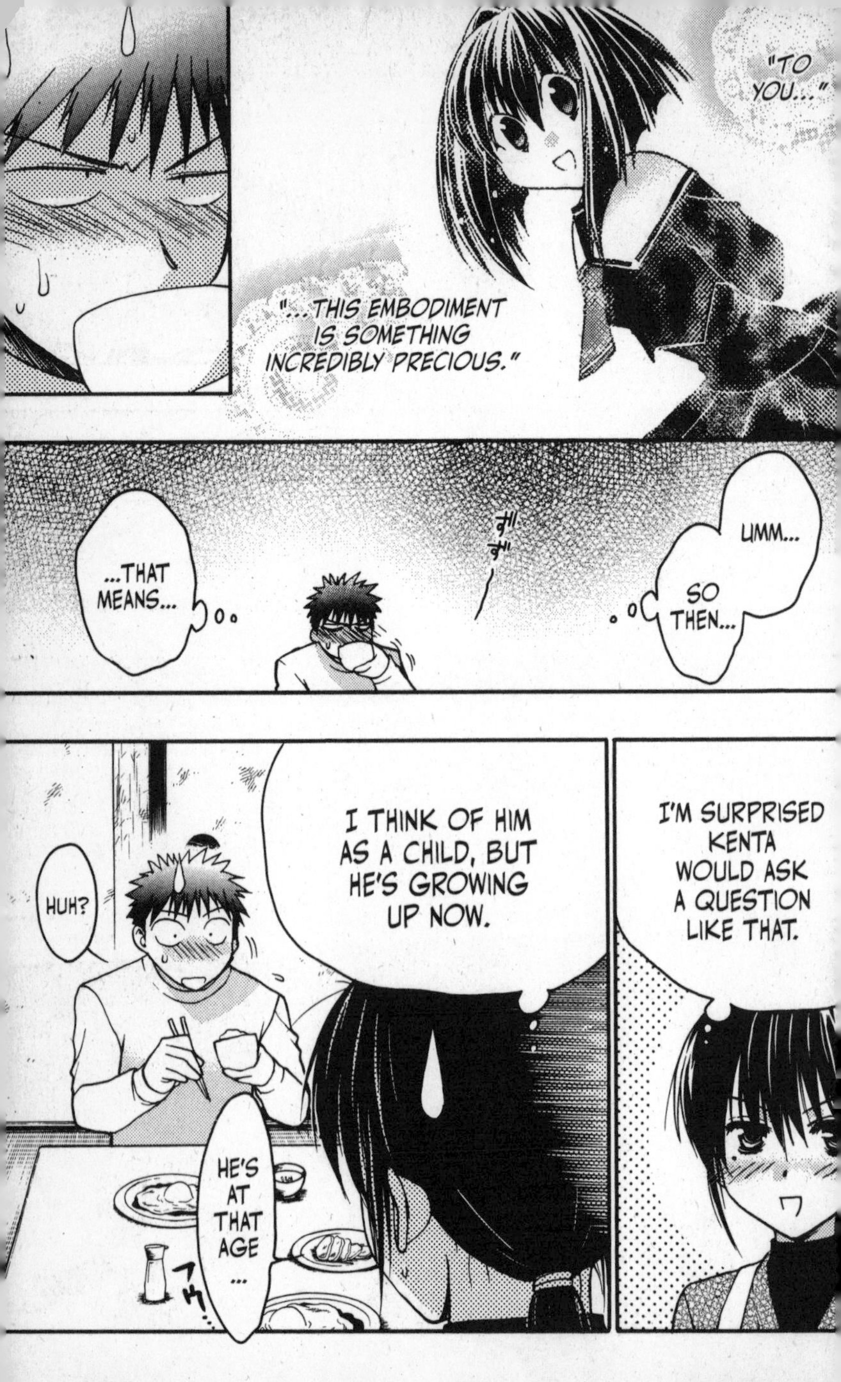
"TO YOU..."
"...THIS EMBODIMENT IS SOMETHING INCREDIBLY PRECIOUS."
UMM... SO THEN...
ずず
...THAT MEANS...
I'M SURPRISED KENTA WOULD ASK A QUESTION LIKE THAT.
I THINK OF HIM AS A CHILD, BUT HE'S GROWING UP NOW.
HUH?
HE'S AT THAT AGE ...

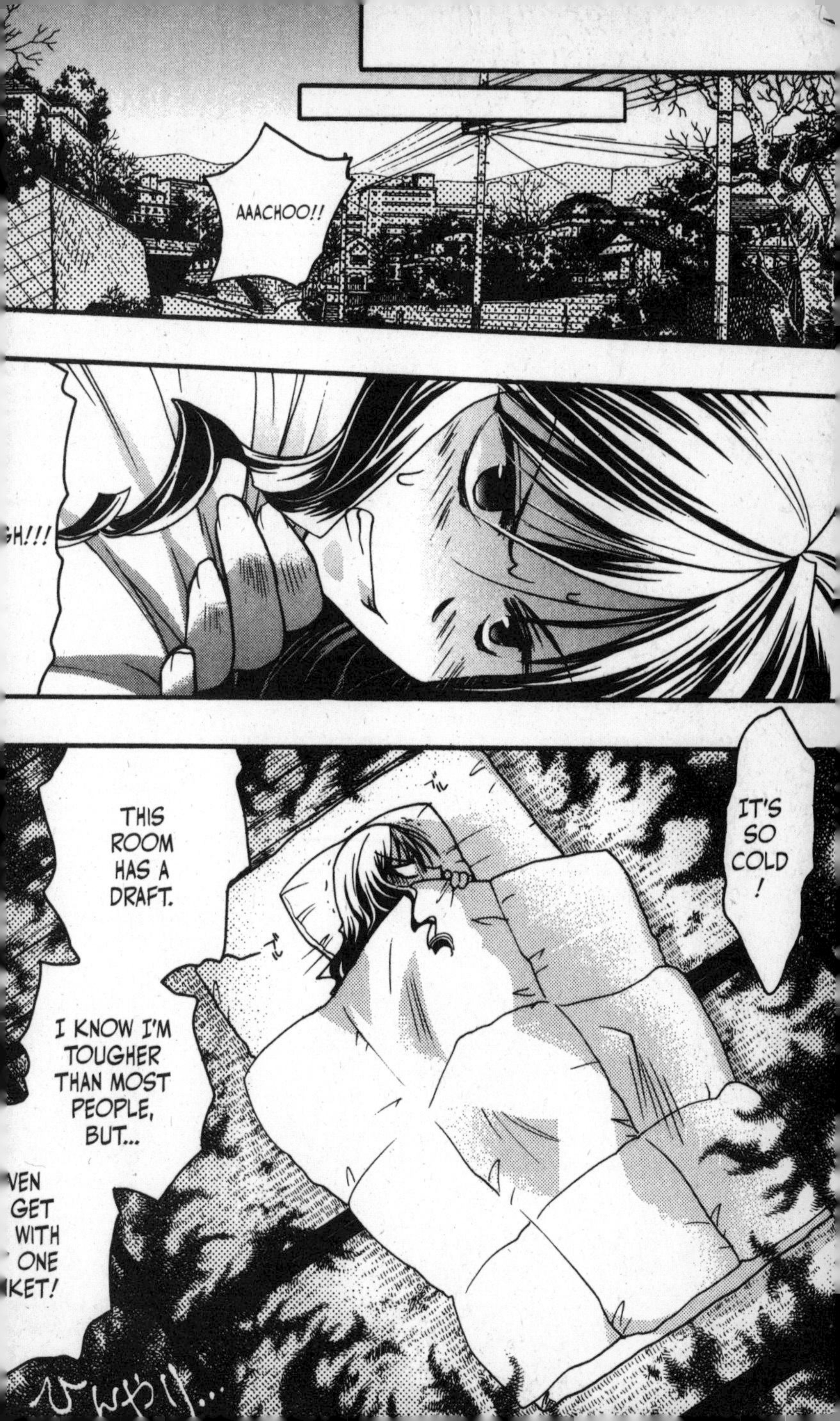
AAACHOO!!
GH!!!
IT'S SO COLD!
THIS ROOM HAS A DRAFT.
I KNOW I'M TOUGHER THAN MOST PEOPLE, BUT...
VEN GET WITH ONE KET!

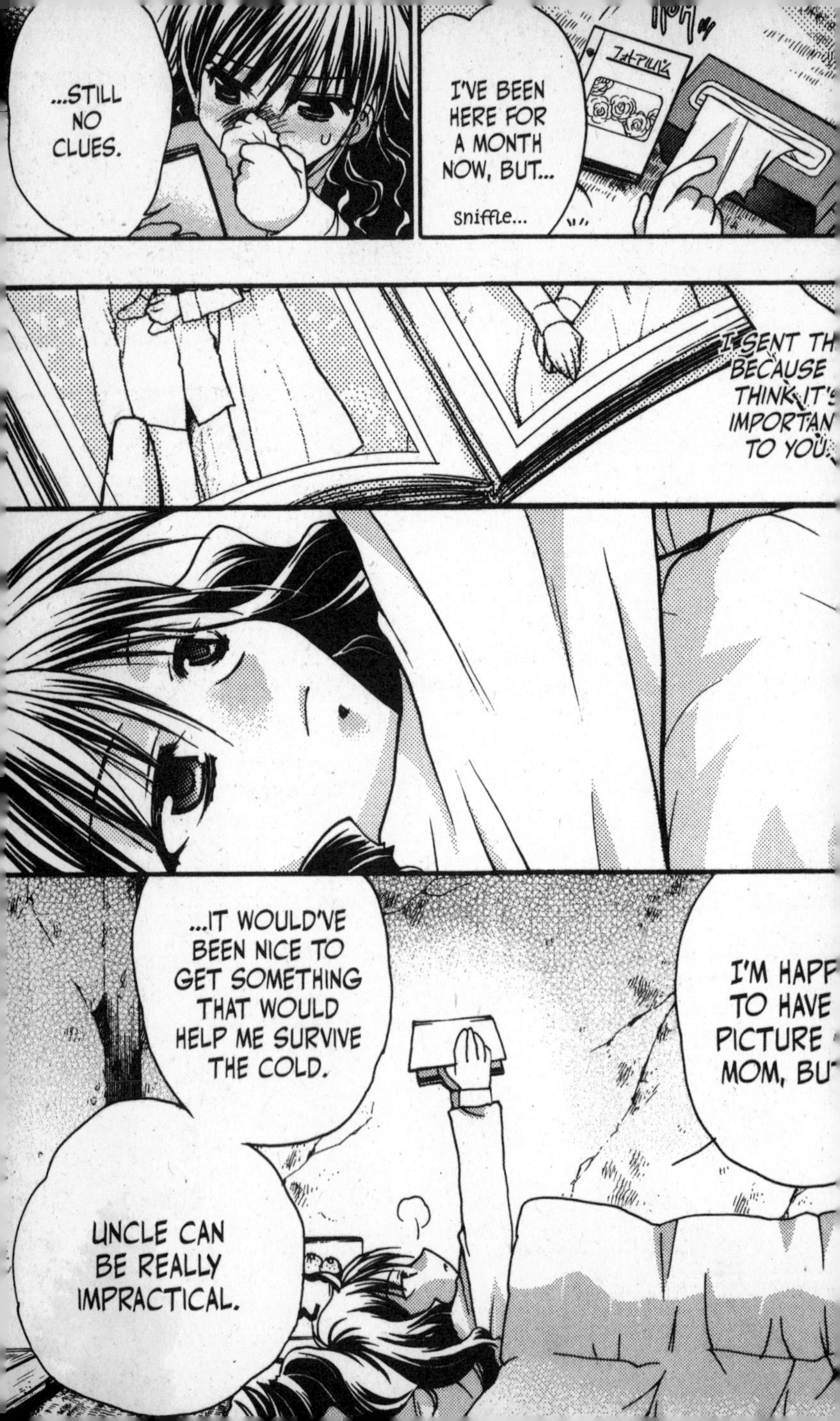
I'VE BEEN HERE FOR A MONTH NOW, BUT...
sniffle...
...STILL NO CLUES.
I SENT TH BECAUSE THINK IT'S IMPORTAN TO YOU.
I'M HAPP TO HAVE PICTURE MOM, BU
...IT WOULD'VE BEEN NICE TO GET SOMETHING THAT WOULD HELP ME SURVIVE THE COLD.
UNCLE CAN BE REALLY IMPRACTICAL.

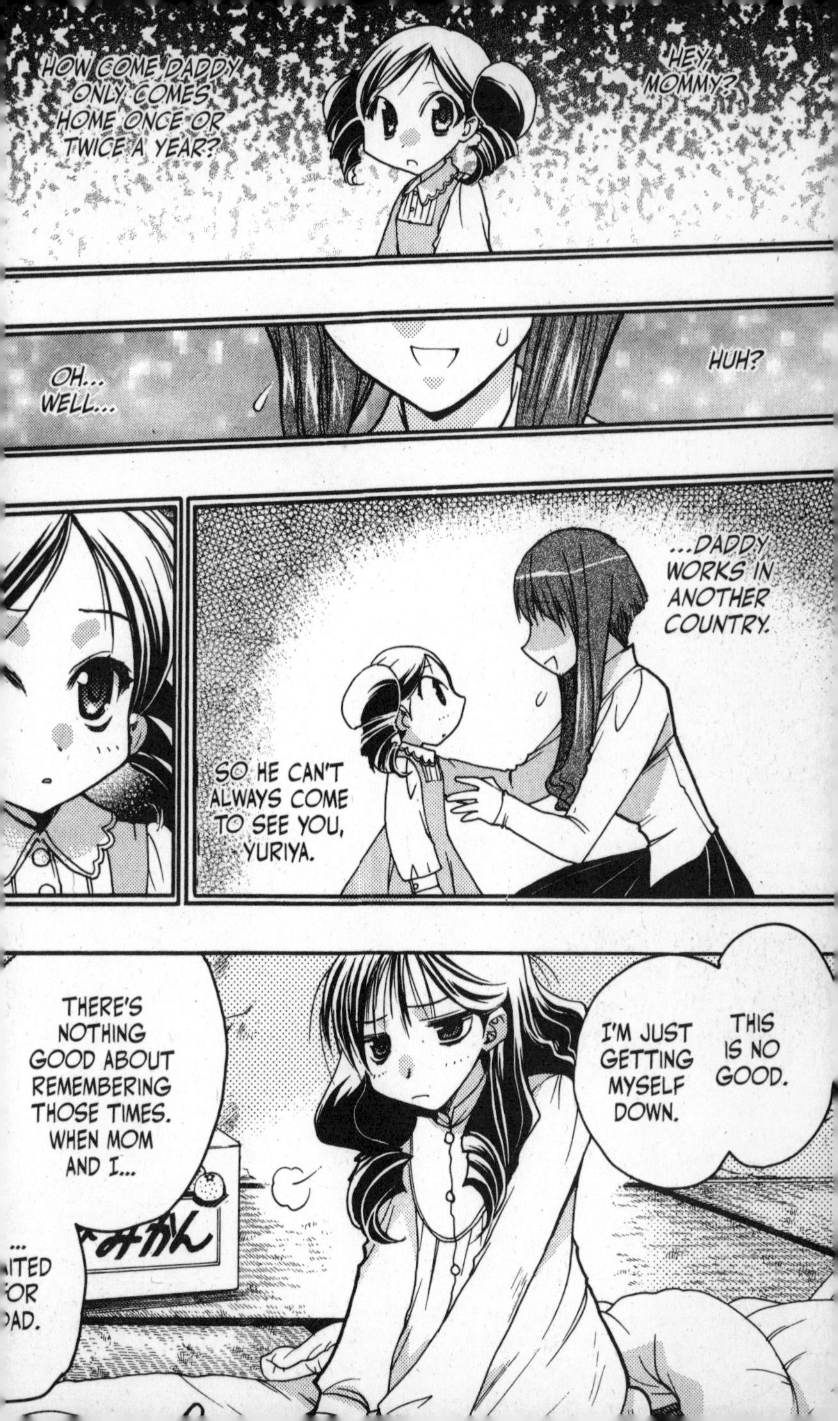
HEY, MOMMY?
HOW COME DADDY ONLY COMES HOME ONCE OR TWICE A YEAR?
HUH?
OH... WELL...
...DADDY WORKS IN ANOTHER COUNTRY.
SO HE CAN'T ALWAYS COME TO SEE YOU, YURIYA.
THIS IS NO GOOD.
I'M JUST GETTING MYSELF DOWN.
THERE'S NOTHING GOOD ABOUT REMEMBERING THOSE TIMES. WHEN MOM AND I...
...ITED FOR AD.

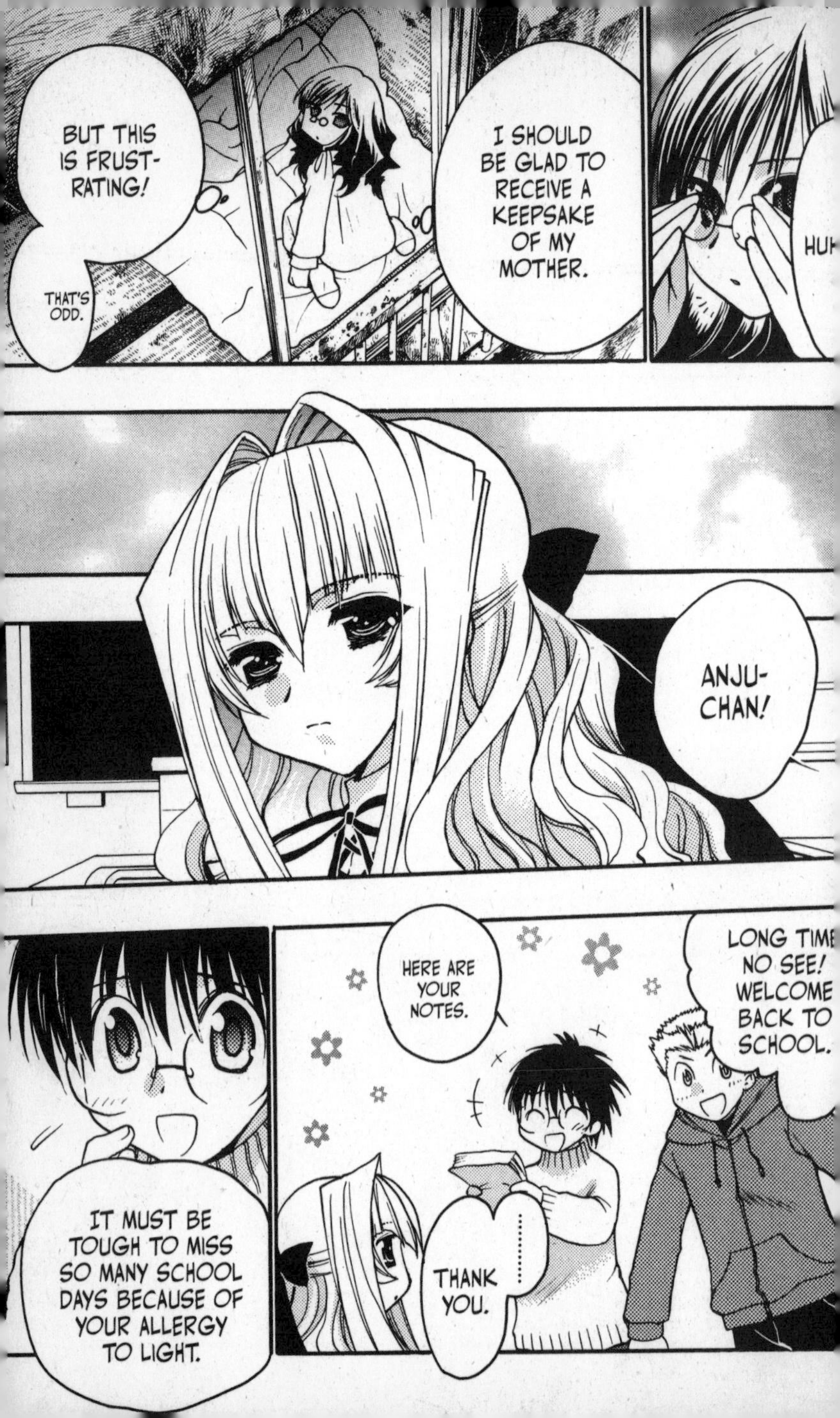
HU…
I SHOULD BE GLAD TO RECEIVE A KEEPSAKE OF MY MOTHER.
BUT THIS IS FRUST-RATING!
THAT'S ODD.
ANJU-CHAN!
LONG TIME NO SEE! WELCOME BACK TO SCHOOL.
HERE ARE YOUR NOTES.
......
THANK YOU.
IT MUST BE TOUGH TO MISS SO MANY SCHOOL DAYS BECAUSE OF YOUR ALLERGY TO LIGHT.

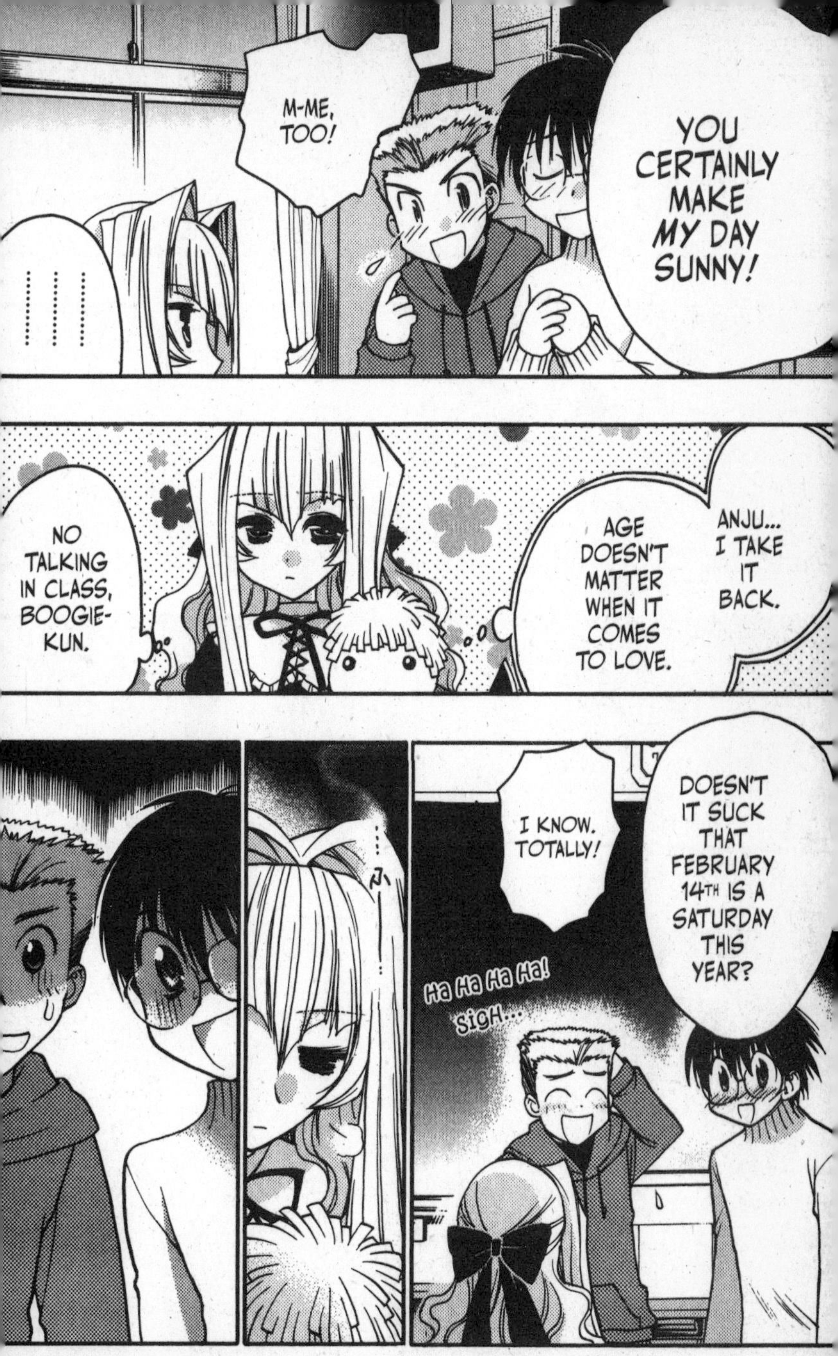
YOU CERTAINLY MAKE MY DAY SUNNY!
M-ME, TOO!
......
ANJU... I TAKE IT BACK.
AGE DOESN'T MATTER WHEN IT COMES TO LOVE.
NO TALKING IN CLASS, BOOGIE-KUN.
DOESN'T IT SUCK THAT FEBRUARY 14TH IS A SATURDAY THIS YEAR?
I KNOW. TOTALLY!
HA HA HA HA!
SIGH...

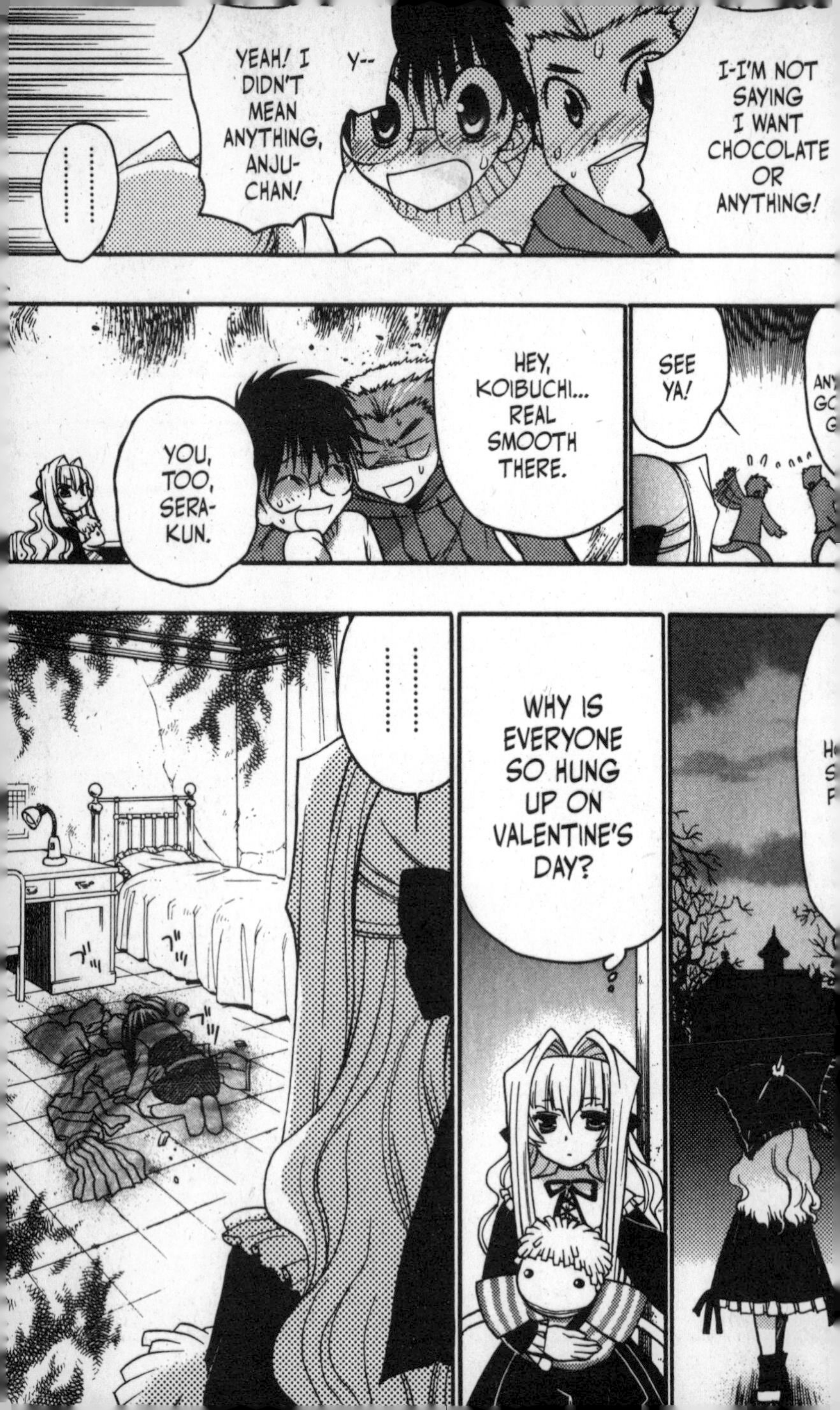

I-I'M NOT SAYING I WANT CHOCOLATE OR ANYTHING!
Y--
YEAH! I DIDN'T MEAN ANYTHING, ANJU-CHAN!
......
SEE YA!
HEY, KOIBUCHI... REAL SMOOTH THERE.
YOU, TOO, SERA-KUN.
WHY IS EVERYONE SO HUNG UP ON VALENTINE'S DAY?
......

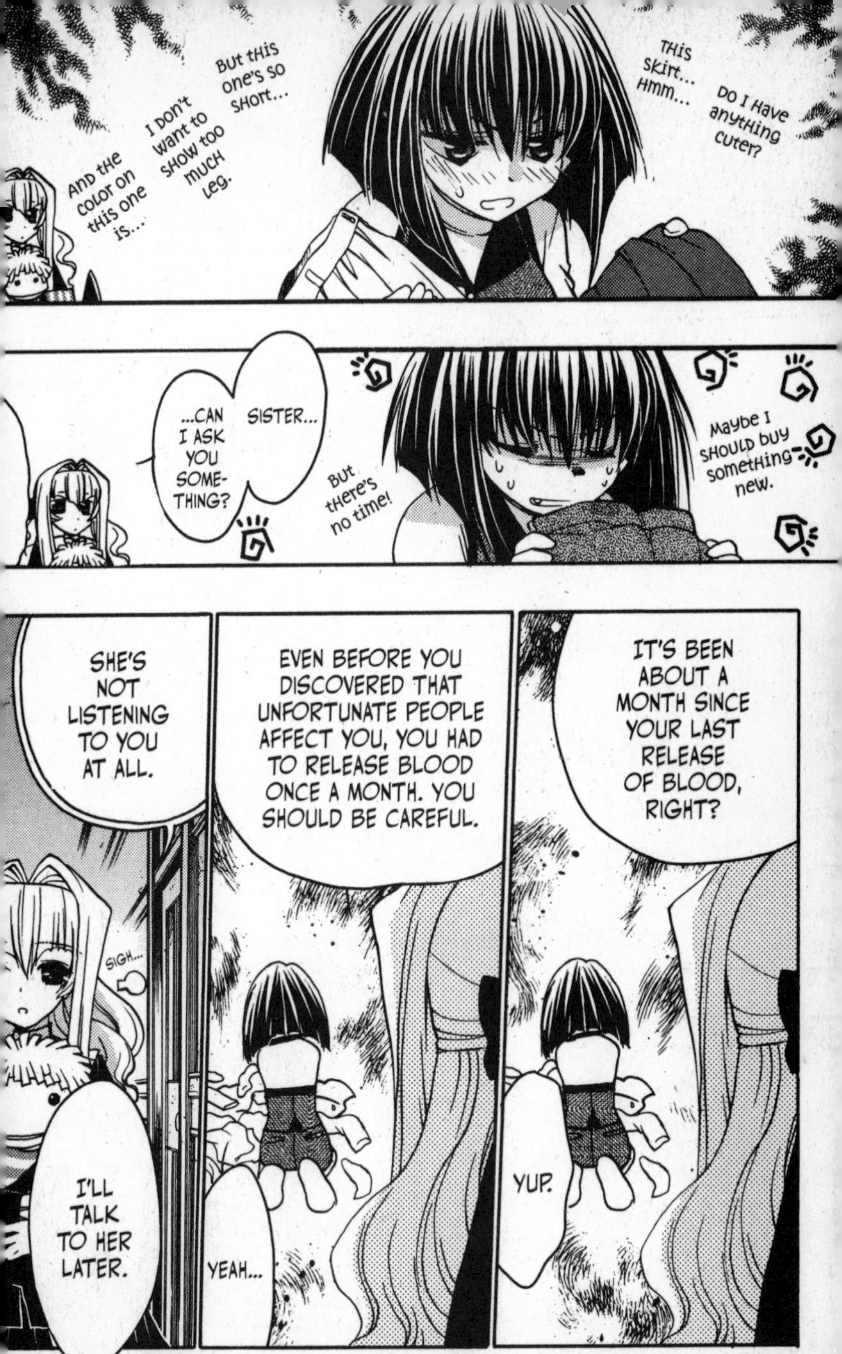
This skirt... Hmm...
Do I have anything cuter?
But this one's so short...
I don't want to show too much leg.
And the color on this one is...
Maybe I should buy something new.
But there's no time!
Sister...
...Can I ask you something?
It's been about a month since your last release of blood, right?
Yup.
Even before you discovered that unfortunate people affect you, you had to release blood once a month. You should be careful.
Yeah...
She's not listening to you at all.
Sigh...
I'll talk to her later.

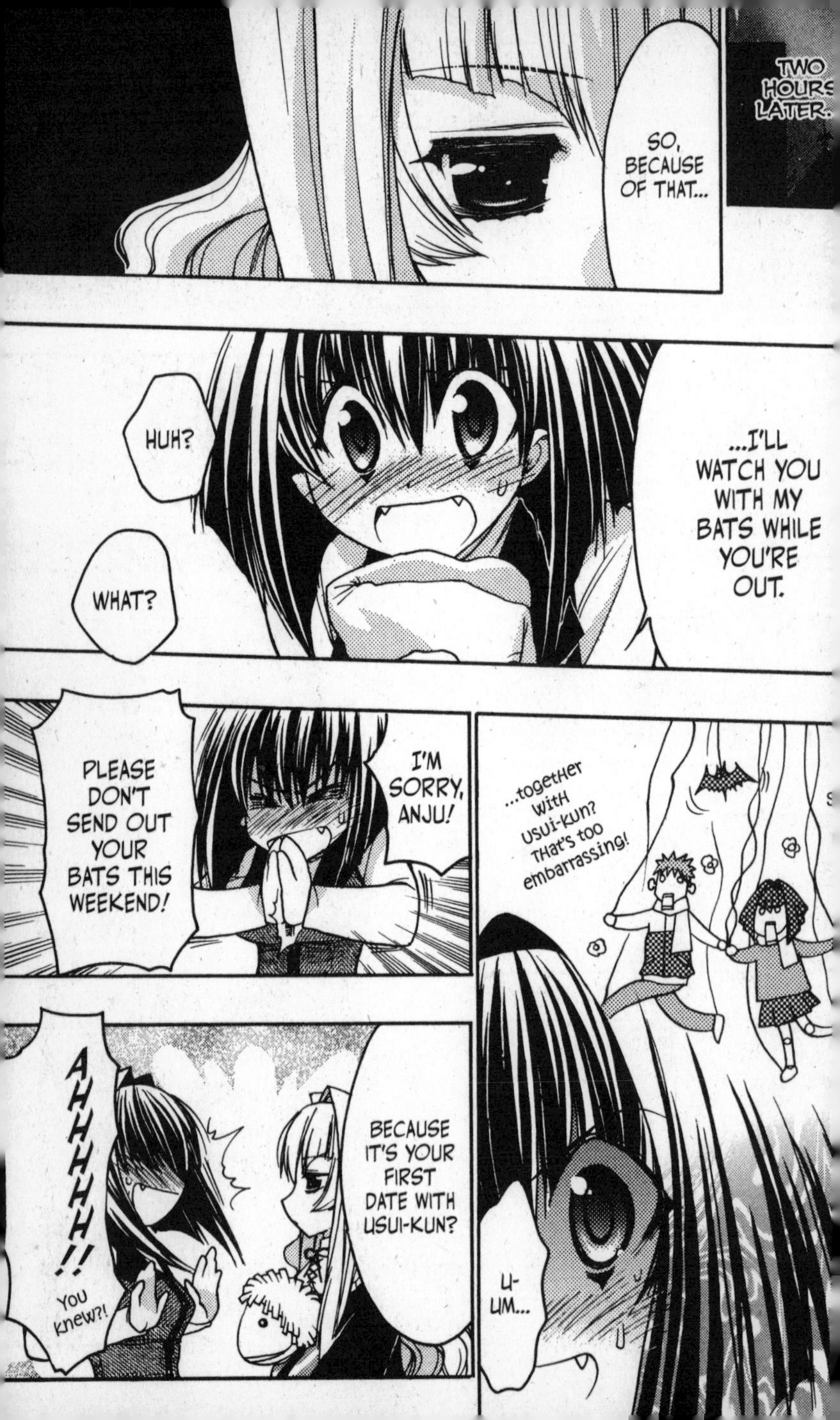
TWO HOURS LATER.
SO, BECAUSE OF THAT...
...I'LL WATCH YOU WITH MY BATS WHILE YOU'RE OUT.
HUH?
WHAT?
...together with Usui-kun? That's too embarrassing!
U-UM...
I'M SORRY, ANJU!
PLEASE DON'T SEND OUT YOUR BATS THIS WEEKEND!
BECAUSE IT'S YOUR FIRST DATE WITH USUI-KUN?
AHHHHH!!
You knew?!

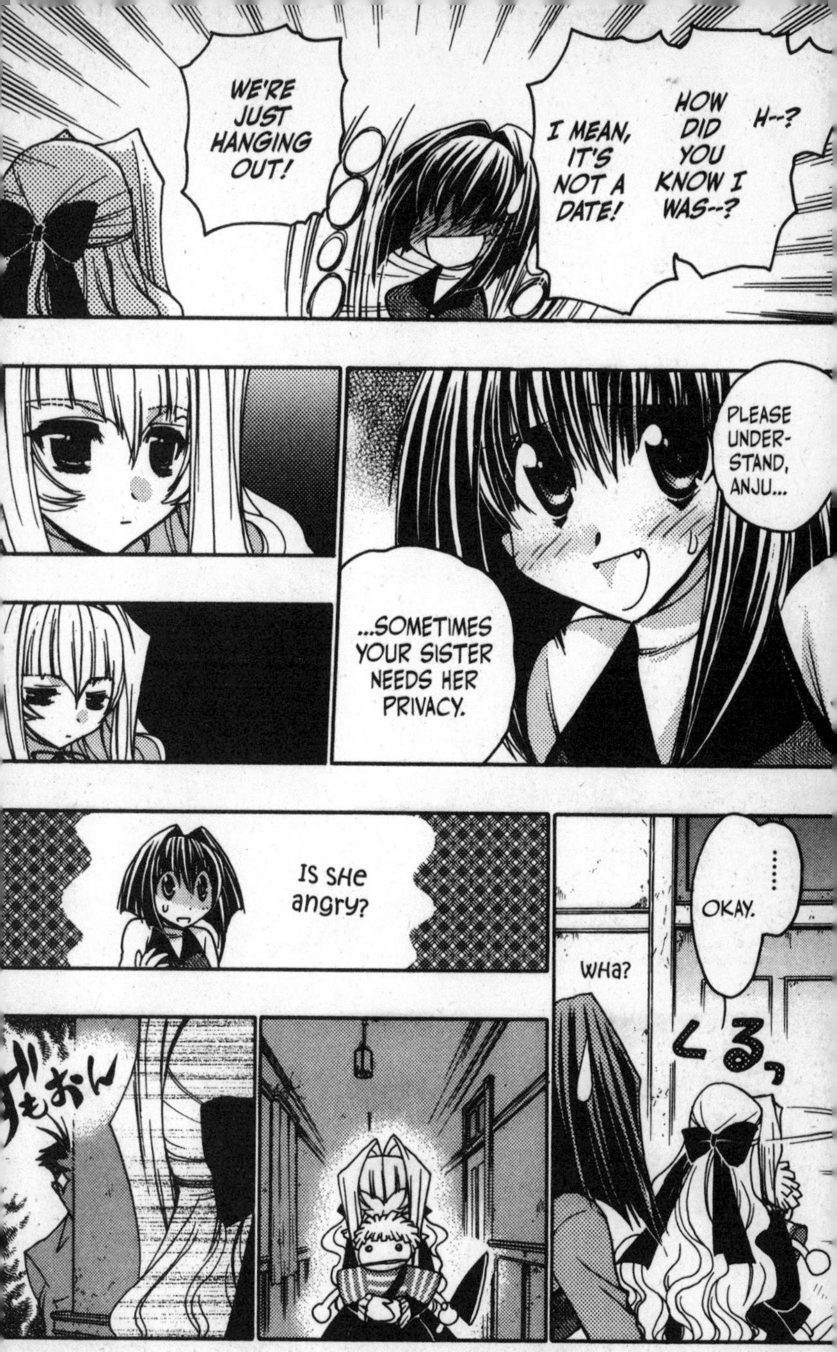

H--? HOW DID YOU KNOW I WAS--?
I MEAN, IT'S NOT A DATE!
WE'RE JUST HANGING OUT!
PLEASE UNDERSTAND, ANJU...
...SOMETIMES YOUR SISTER NEEDS HER PRIVACY.
......
OKAY.
WHA?
くるっ
IS SHE angry?
ずもおん

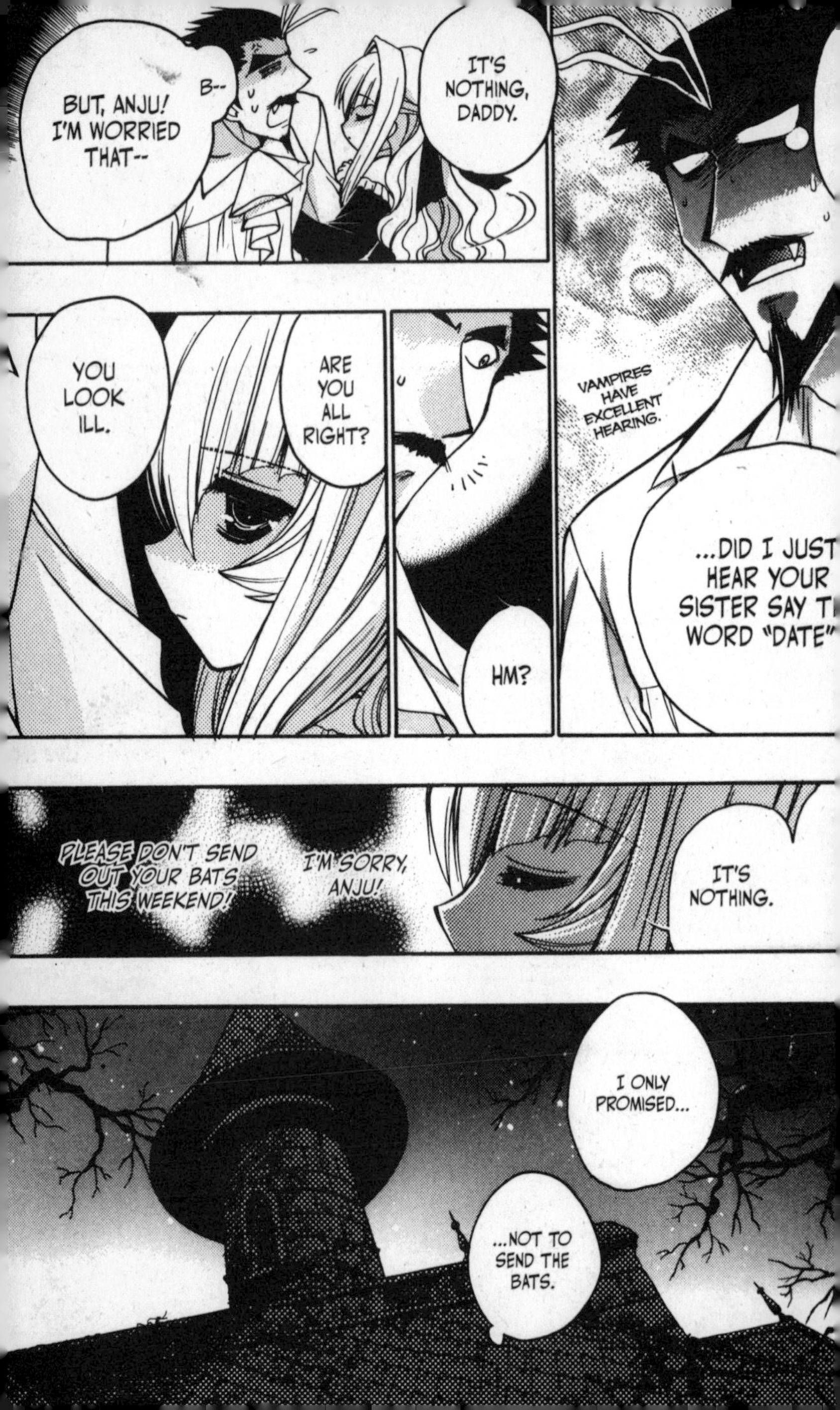
VAMPIRES HAVE EXCELLENT HEARING.
...DID I JUST HEAR YOUR SISTER SAY T WORD "DATE"
IT'S NOTHING, DADDY.
B--
BUT, ANJU! I'M WORRIED THAT--
HM?
ARE YOU ALL RIGHT?
YOU LOOK ILL.
IT'S NOTHING.
I'M SORRY, ANJU!
PLEASE DON'T SEND OUT YOUR BATS THIS WEEKEND!
I ONLY PROMISED...
...NOT TO SEND THE BATS.

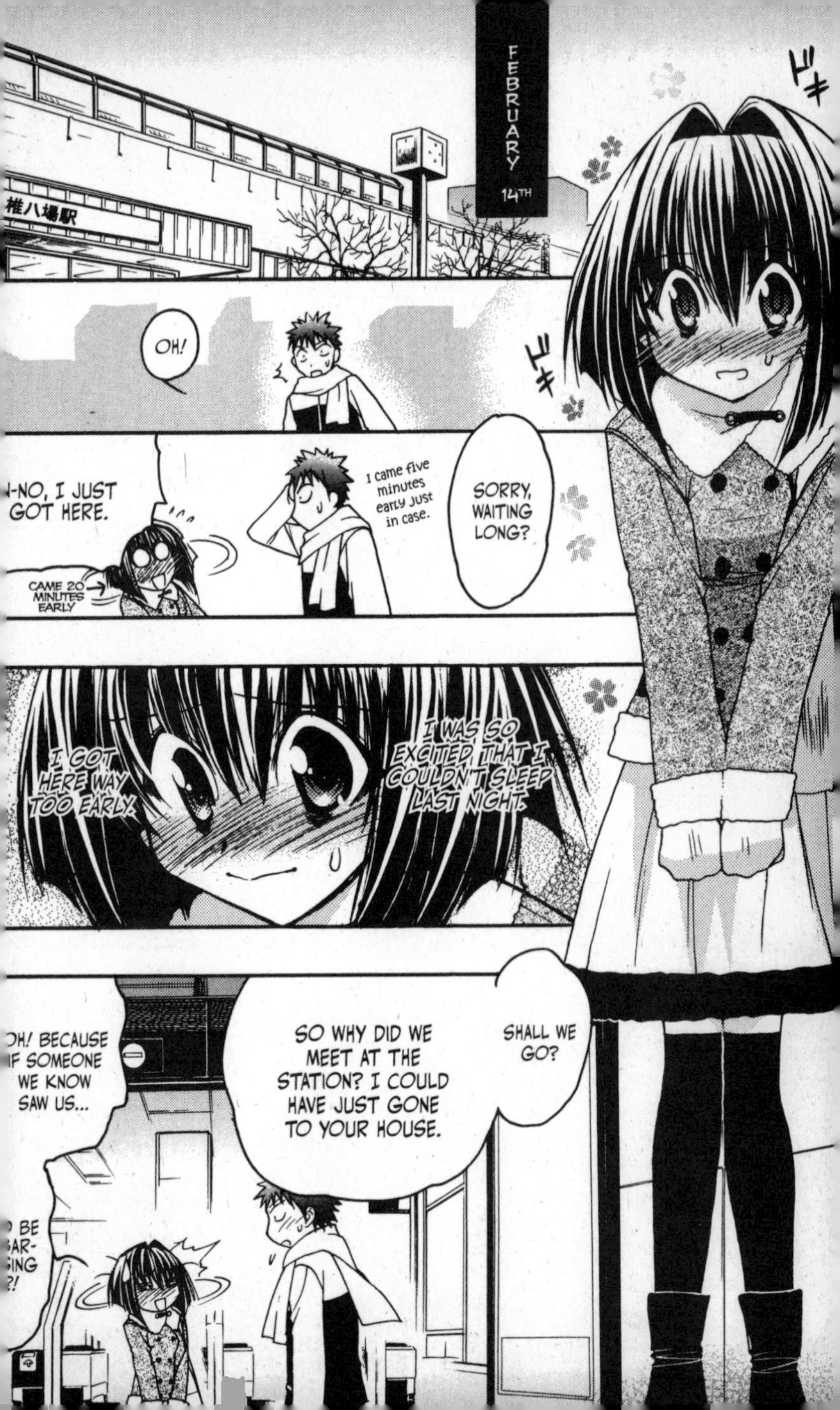

ドキ
ドキ
FEBRUARY 14TH
椎八場駅
OH!
SORRY, WAITING LONG?
I came five minutes early just in case.
-NO, I JUST GOT HERE.
CAME 20 MINUTES EARLY
I WAS SO EXCITED THAT I COULDN'T SLEEP LAST NIGHT.
I GOT HERE WAY TOO EARLY.
SHALL WE GO?
SO WHY DID WE MEET AT THE STATION? I COULD HAVE JUST GONE TO YOUR HOUSE.
OH! BECAUSE IF SOMEONE WE KNOW SAW US...

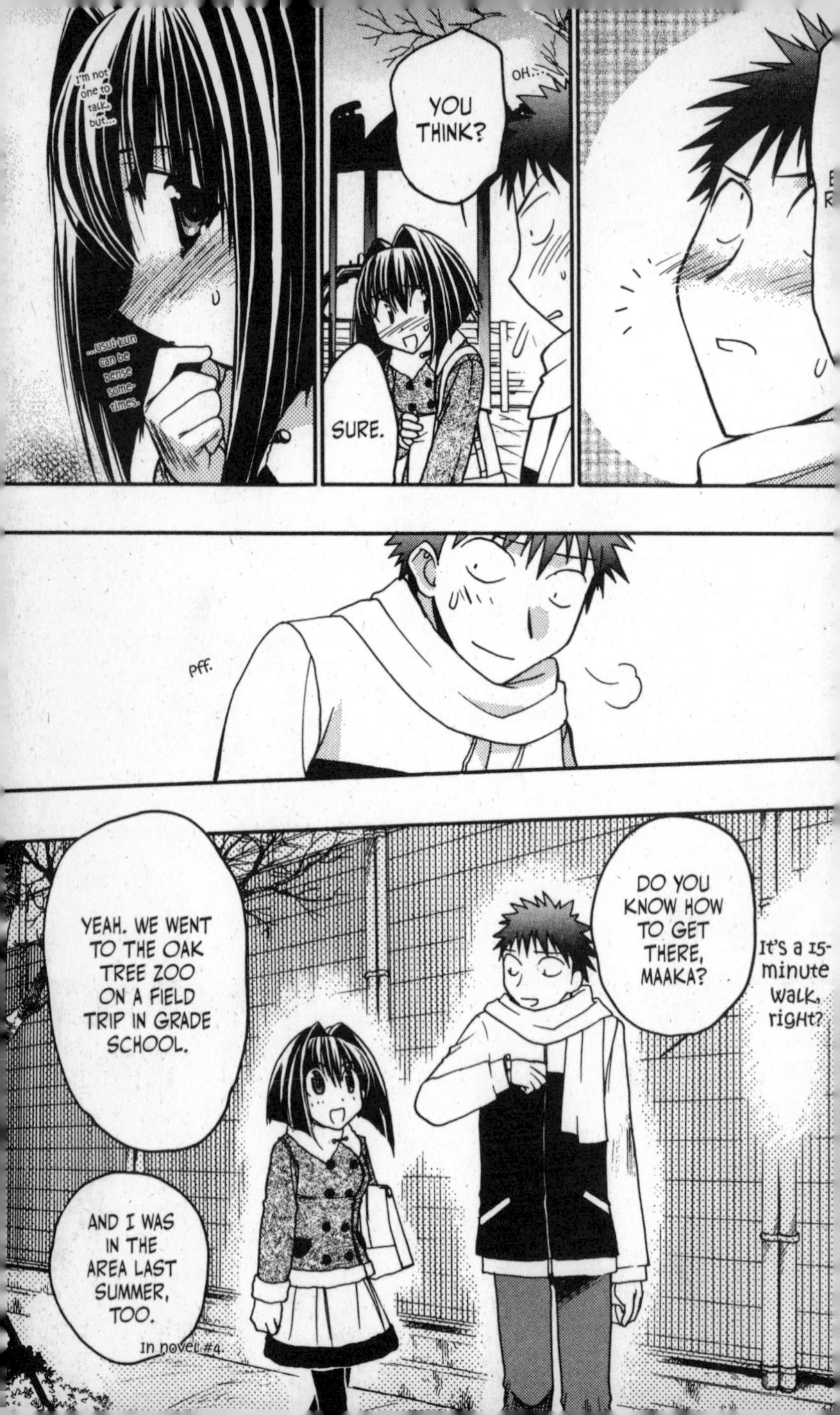
OH...
YOU THINK?
SURE.
I'm not one to talk, but...
...Usui-kun can be dense sometimes.
pff.
DO YOU KNOW HOW TO GET THERE, MAAKA?
It's a 15-minute walk, right?
YEAH. WE WENT TO THE OAK TREE ZOO ON A FIELD TRIP IN GRADE SCHOOL.
AND I WAS IN THE AREA LAST SUMMER, TOO.
In novel #4

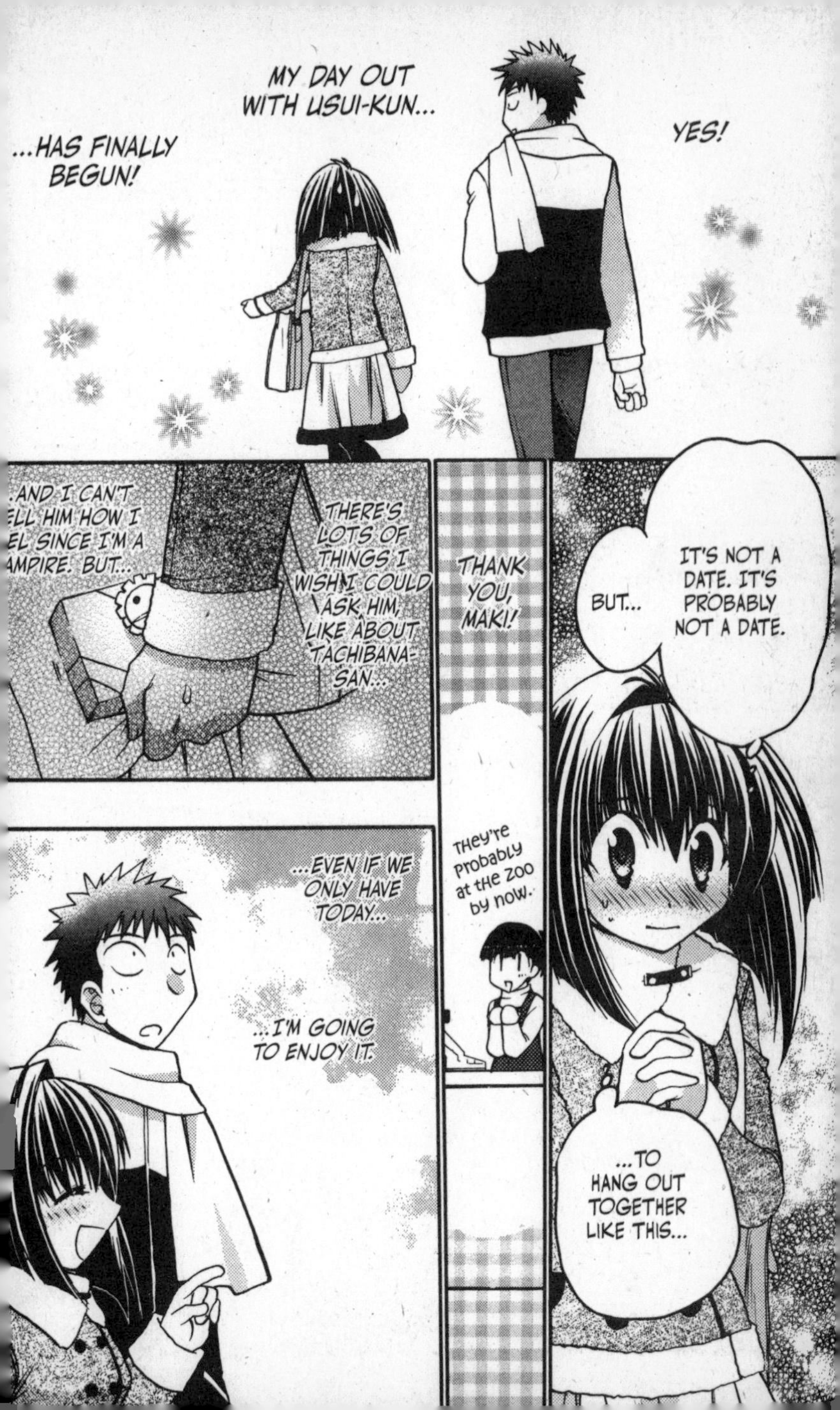

MY DAY OUT WITH USUI-KUN...
...HAS FINALLY BEGUN!
YES!
IT'S NOT A DATE. IT'S PROBABLY NOT A DATE.
BUT...
...TO HANG OUT TOGETHER LIKE THIS...
THANK YOU, MAKI!
They're probably at the zoo by now.
THERE'S LOTS OF THINGS I WISH I COULD ASK HIM, LIKE ABOUT TACHIBANA-SAN...
.AND I CAN'T ELL HIM HOW I EL SINCE I'M A AMPIRE. BUT...
...EVEN IF WE ONLY HAVE TODAY...
...I'M GOING TO ENJOY IT.

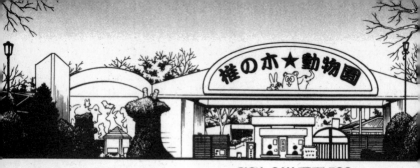

SIGN: OAK TREE ZOO

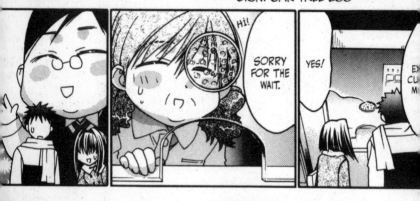

Hi!

SORRY FOR THE WAIT.

YES!

EX CU MI

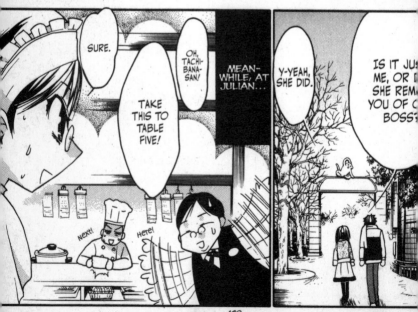

SURE.

OH, TACHI-BANA-SAN!

TAKE THIS TO TABLE FIVE!

MEAN-WHILE, AT JULIAN...

Y-YEAH, SHE DID.

IS IT JUS ME, OR D SHE REM YOU OF BOSS?

NEXT!

HERE!

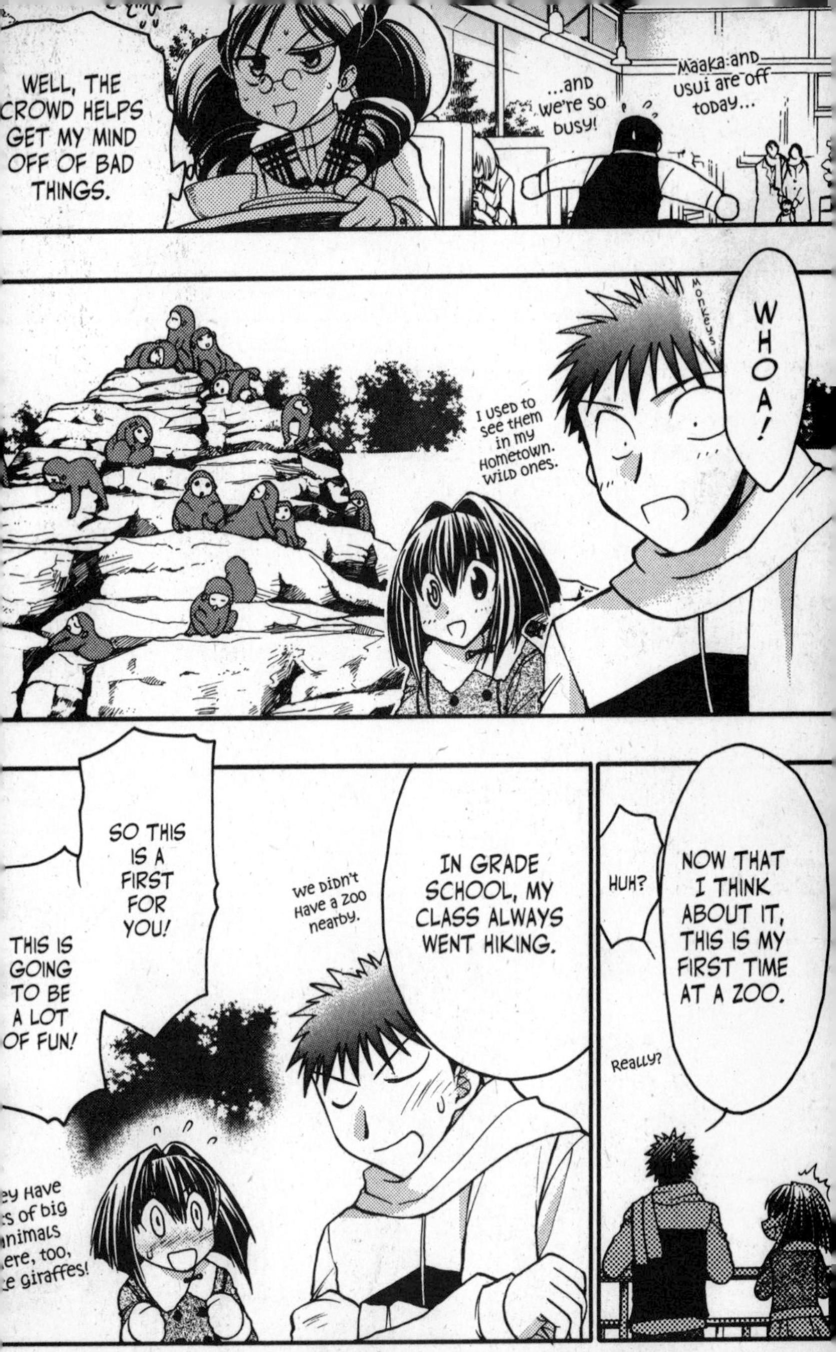
Maaka and Usui are off today...
...and we're so busy!
WELL, THE CROWD HELPS GET MY MIND OFF OF BAD THINGS.
WHOA!
Monkeys!
I used to see them in my hometown. Wild ones.
NOW THAT I THINK ABOUT IT, THIS IS MY FIRST TIME AT A ZOO.
HUH?
Really?
IN GRADE SCHOOL, MY CLASS ALWAYS WENT HIKING.
We didn't have a zoo nearby.
SO THIS IS A FIRST FOR YOU!
THIS IS GOING TO BE A LOT OF FUN!
ey have s of big nimals ere, too, e giraffes!

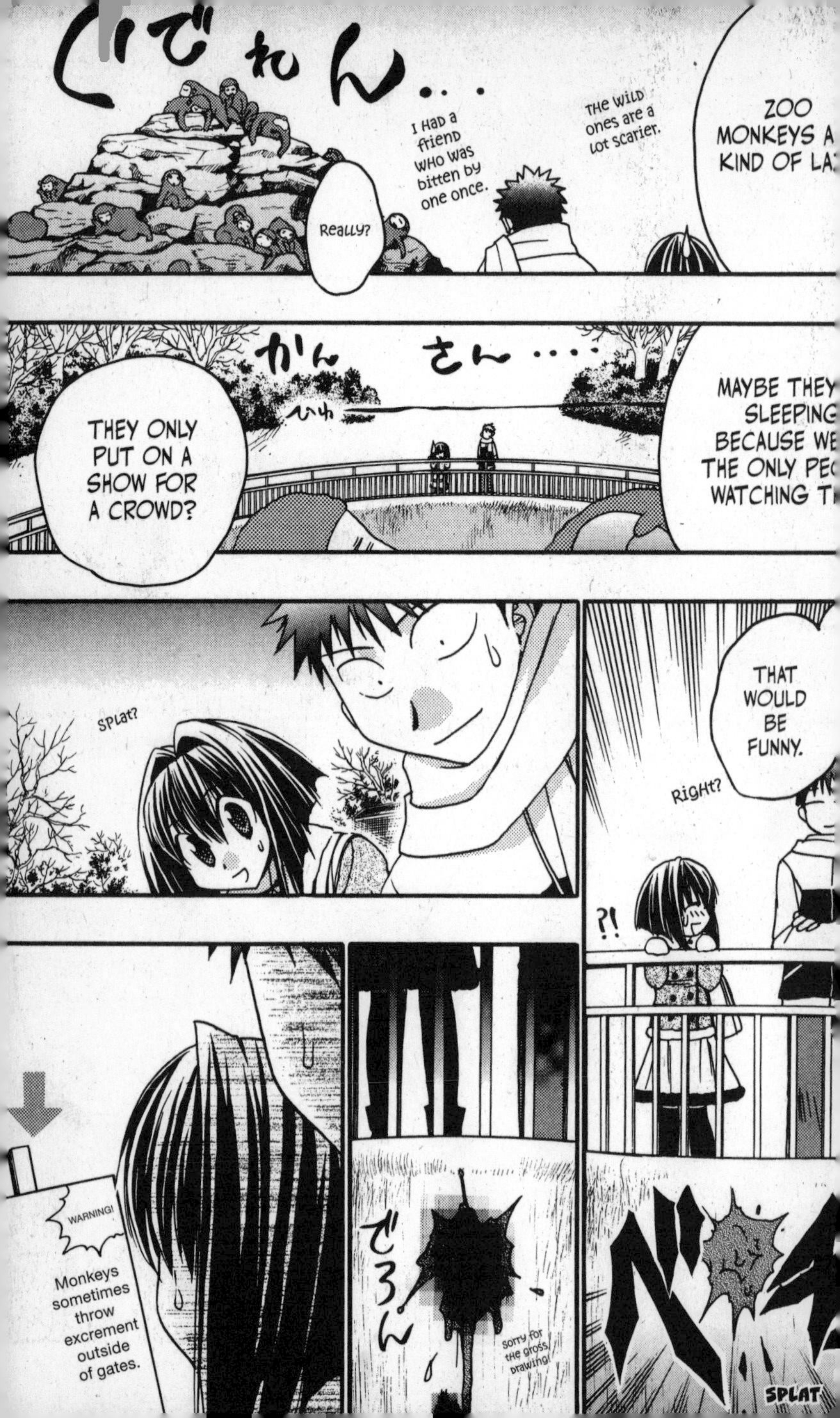
ZOO MONKEYS A KIND OF LA
THE WILD ones are a lot scarier.
I HAD a friend WHO WAS bitten by one once.
Really?
ぐでれん...
MAYBE THEY SLEEPING BECAUSE WE THE ONLY PE WATCHING T
かん さん....
ひゅ
THEY ONLY PUT ON A SHOW FOR A CROWD?
THAT WOULD BE FUNNY.
Right?
?!
Splat?
SPLAT
でろん
Sorry for the gross drawing!
WARNING!
Monkeys sometimes throw excrement outside of gates.

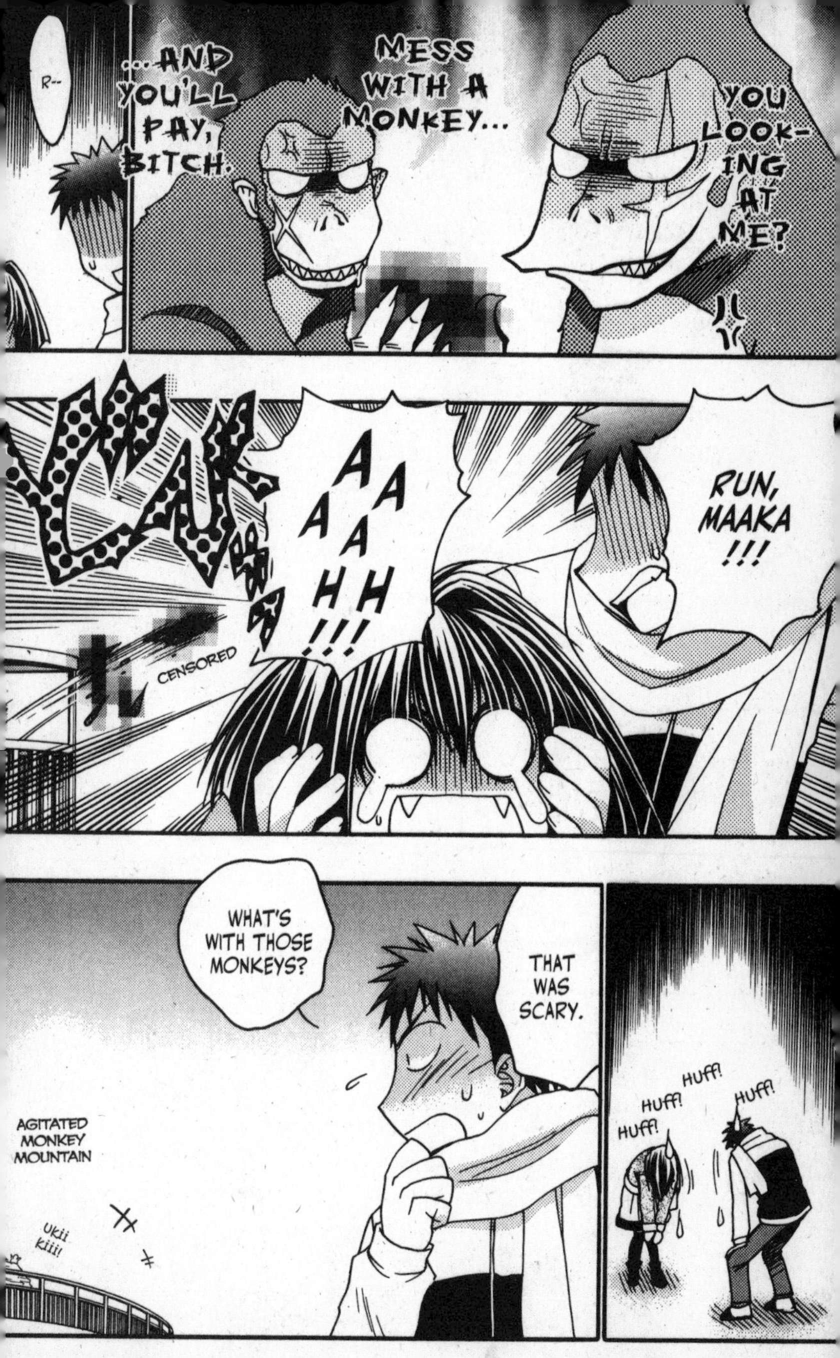
YOU LOOKING AT ME?
MESS WITH A MONKEY...
...AND YOU'LL PAY, BITCH.
R--
RUN, MAAKA!!!
AAAAHH!!!
CENSORED
HUFF! HUFF! HUFF! HUFF!
THAT WAS SCARY.
WHAT'S WITH THOSE MONKEYS?
AGITATED MONKEY MOUNTAIN
Ukii kiii!

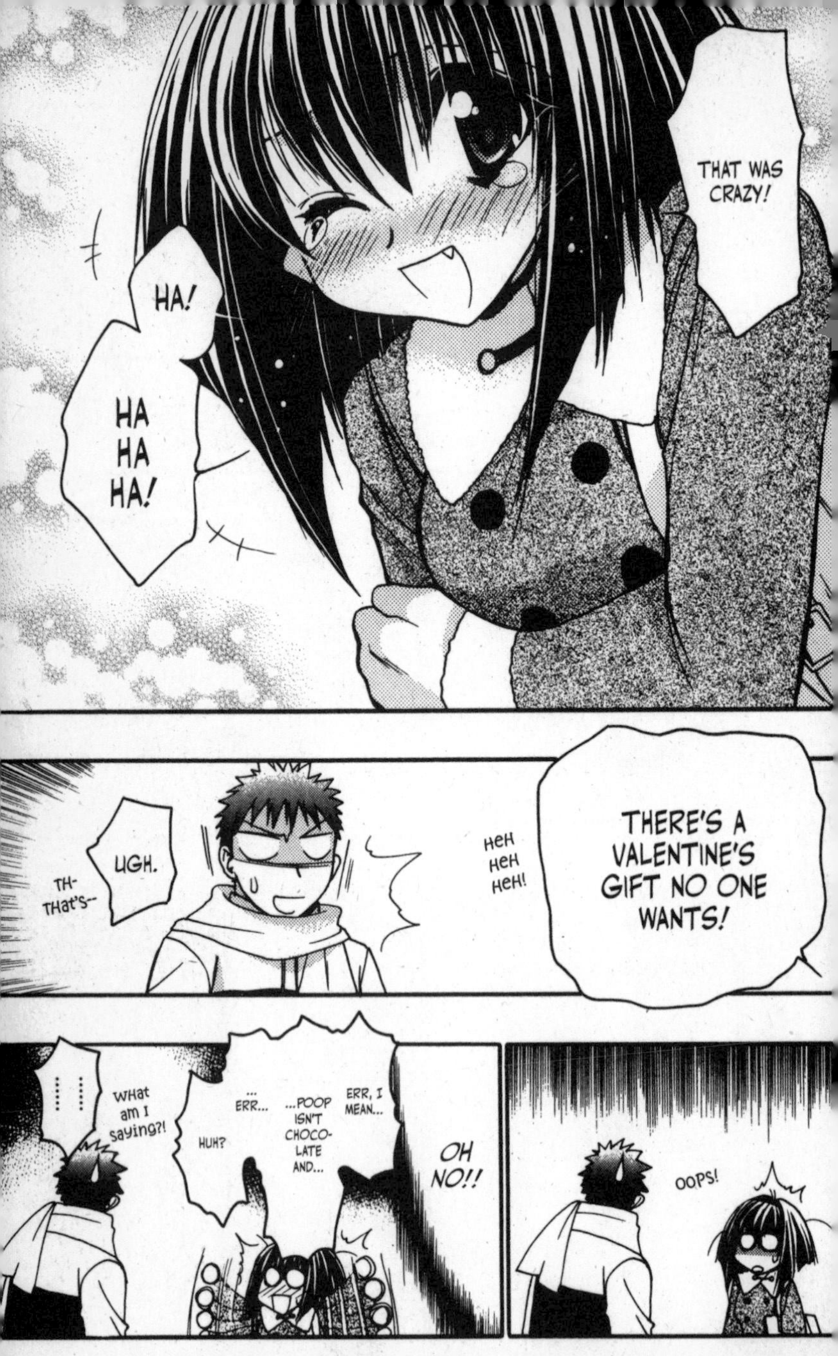
THAT WAS CRAZY!
HA!
HA HA HA!
THERE'S A VALENTINE'S GIFT NO ONE WANTS!
HEH HEH HEH!
UGH.
TH- THAT'S--
OOPS!
OH NO!!
ERR, I MEAN...
...POOP ISN'T CHOCO-LATE AND...
... ERR...
HUH?
WHAT AM I SAYING?!
......

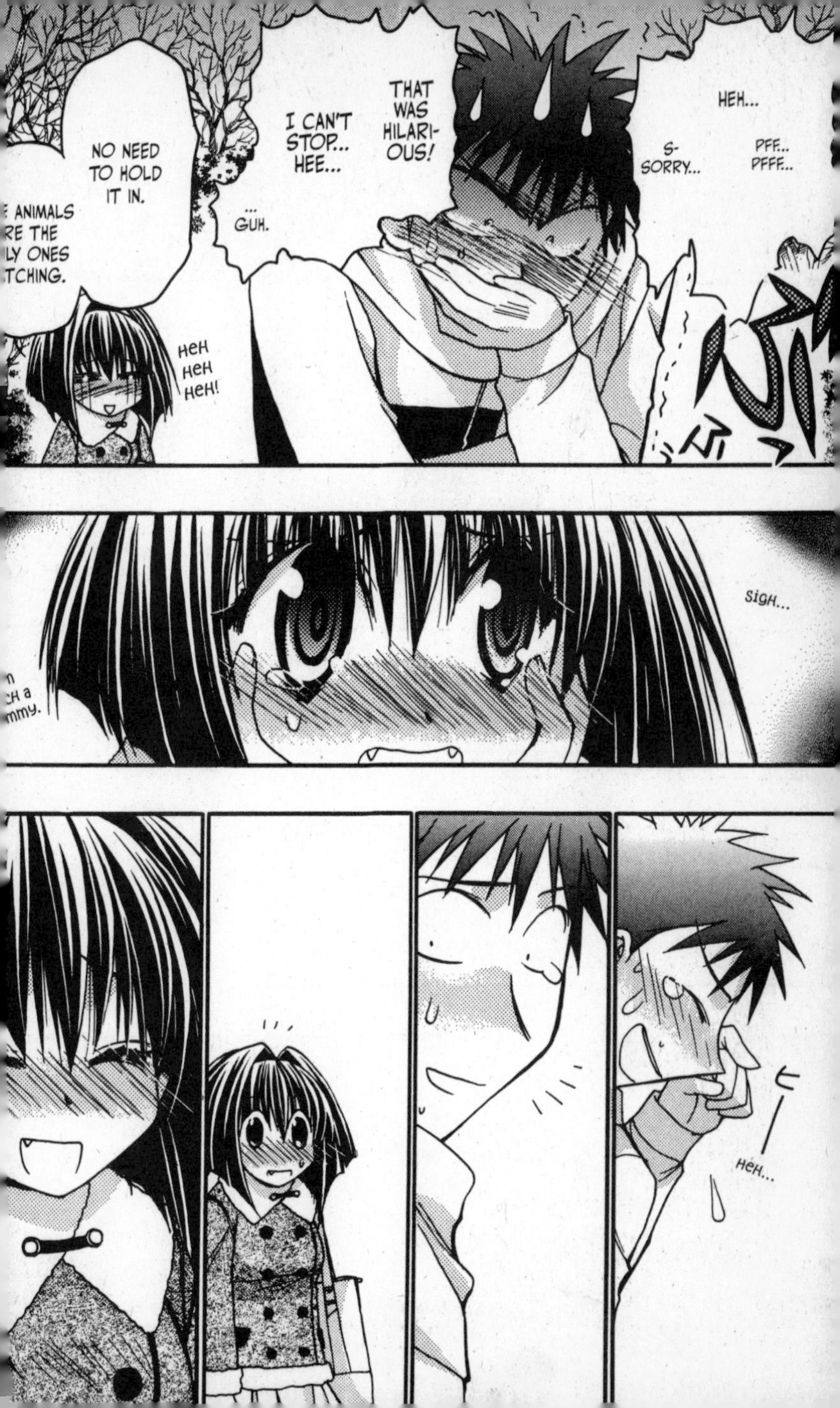

HEH...
PFF... PFFF...
S-SORRY...
THAT WAS HILARI-OUS!
I CAN'T STOP... HEE...
... GUH.
NO NEED TO HOLD IT IN.
E ANIMALS RE THE LY ONES TCHING.
HEH HEH HEH!
SIGH...
n ch a mmy.
HEH...

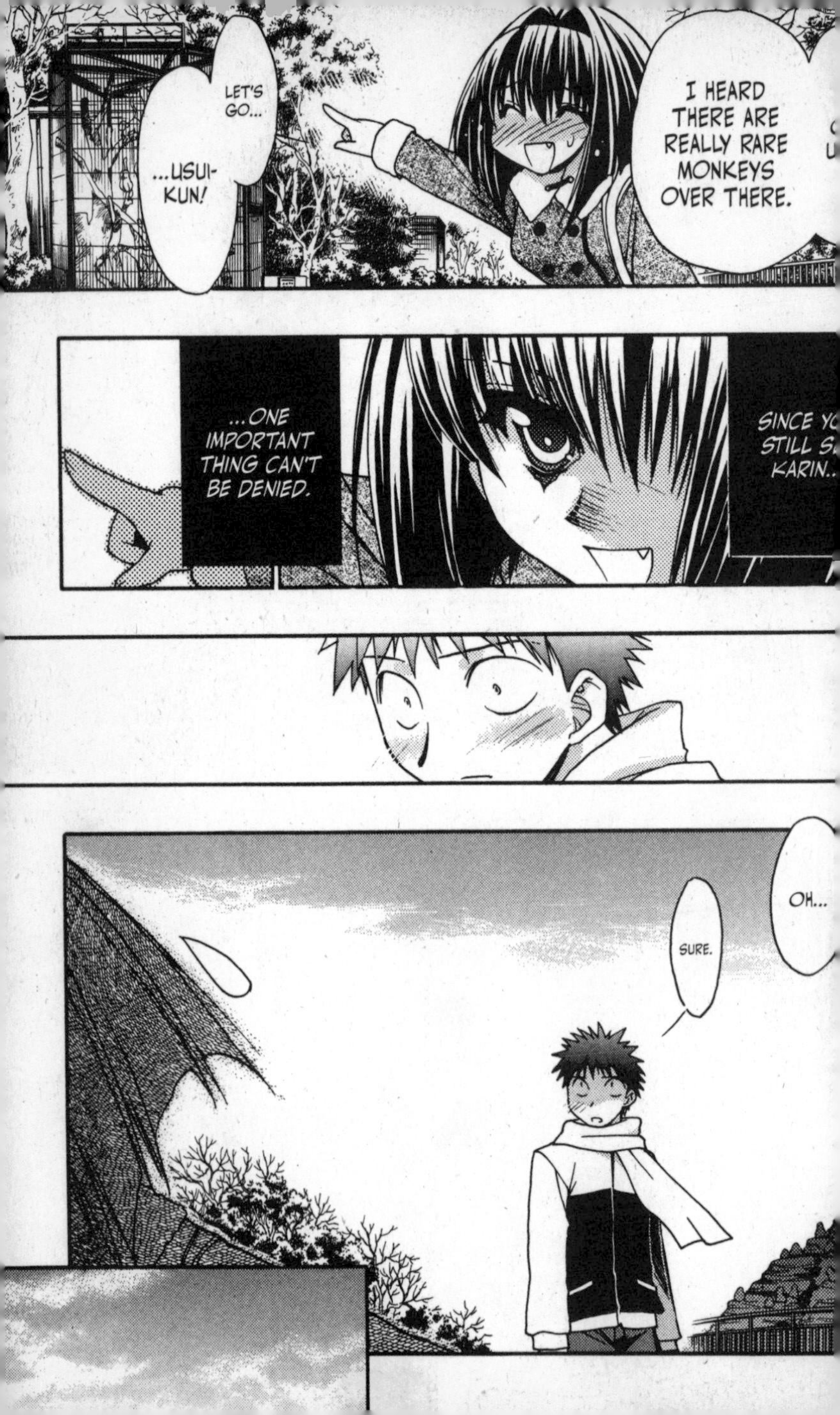
I HEARD THERE ARE REALLY RARE MONKEYS OVER THERE.
LET'S GO...
...USUI-KUN!
SINCE YO STILL S KARIN..
...ONE IMPORTANT THING CAN'T BE DENIED.
OH...
SURE.

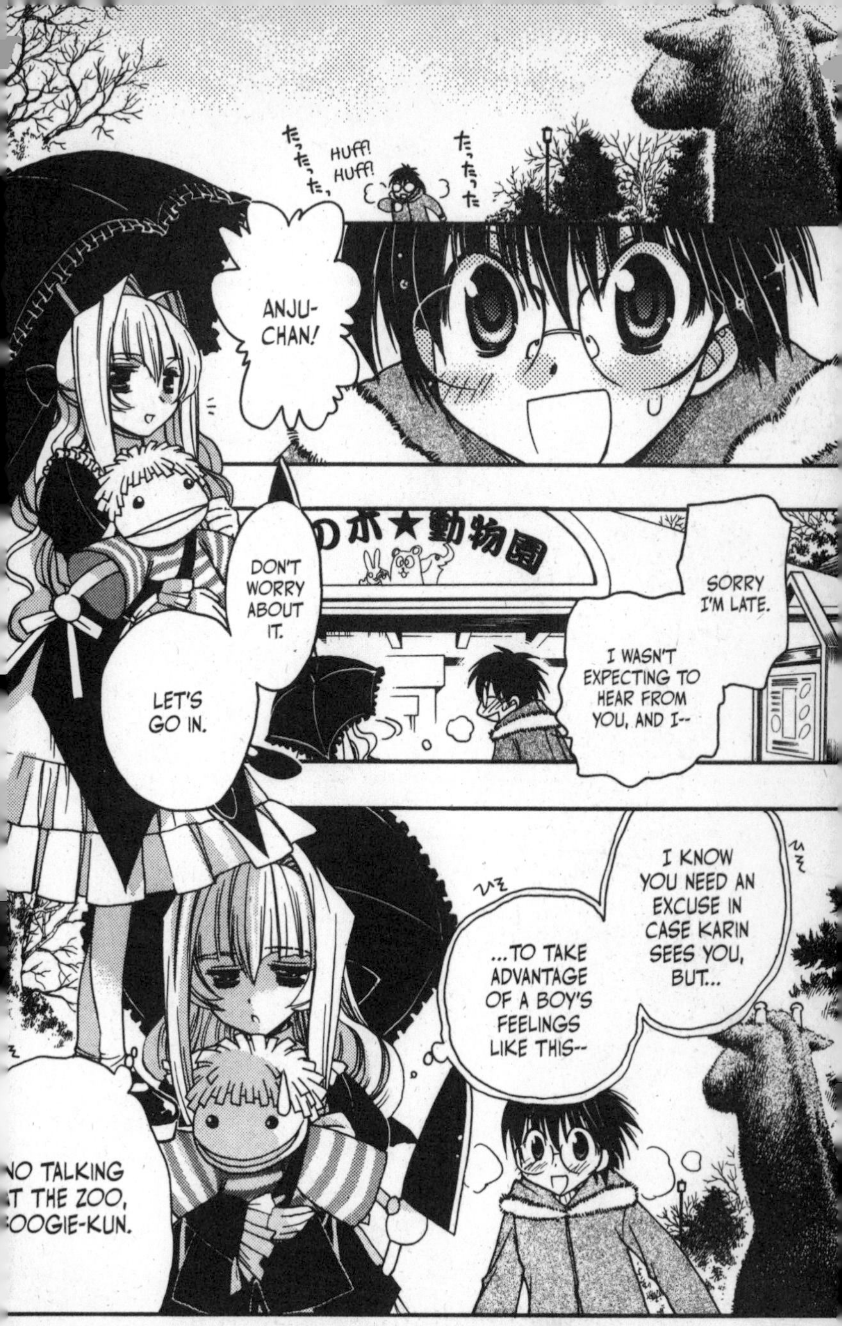
たったった
HUFF! HUFF!
たったった、
ANJU-CHAN!
SORRY I'M LATE.
I WASN'T EXPECTING TO HEAR FROM YOU, AND I--
DON'T WORRY ABOUT IT.
LET'S GO IN.
ひそ
I KNOW YOU NEED AN EXCUSE IN CASE KARIN SEES YOU, BUT...
ひそ
...TO TAKE ADVANTAGE OF A BOY'S FEELINGS LIKE THIS--
NO TALKING
T THE ZOO,
OOGIE-KUN.

35TH EMBARRASSMENT END

4TH BONUS STORY
MAKI WHO DOESN'T KNOW AND KARIN WHO CANNOT SAY ~MAKI SPECIAL~

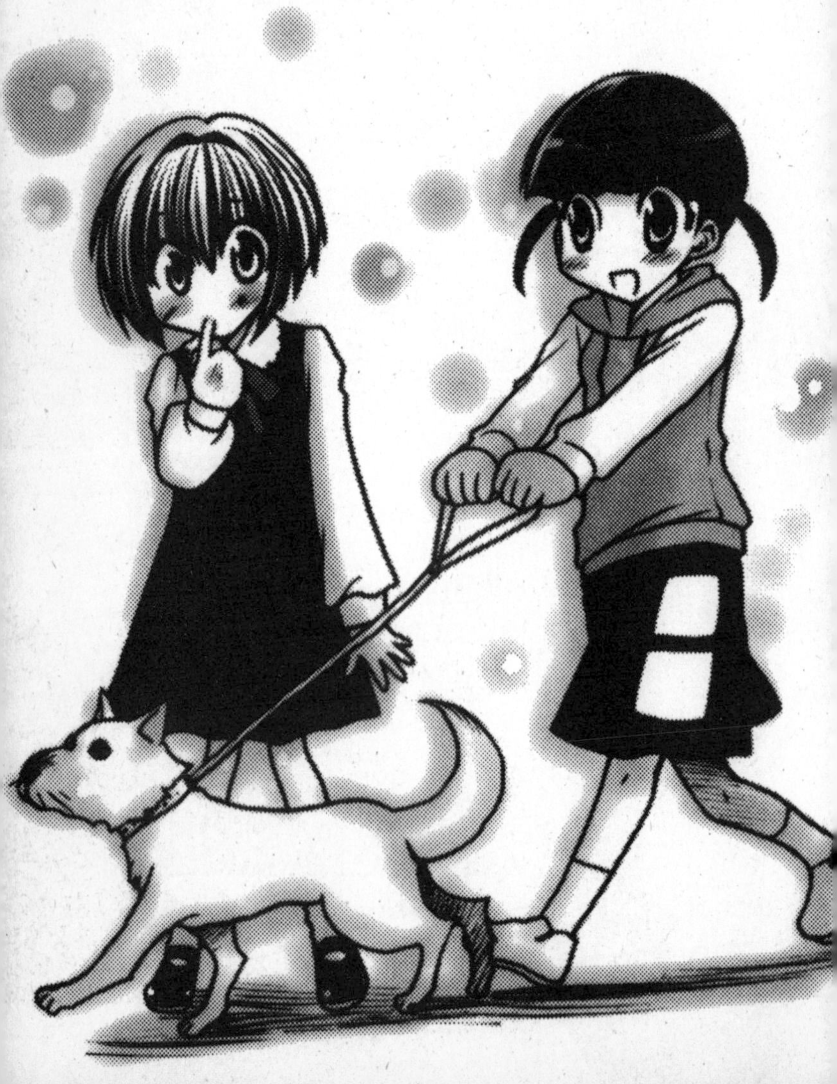

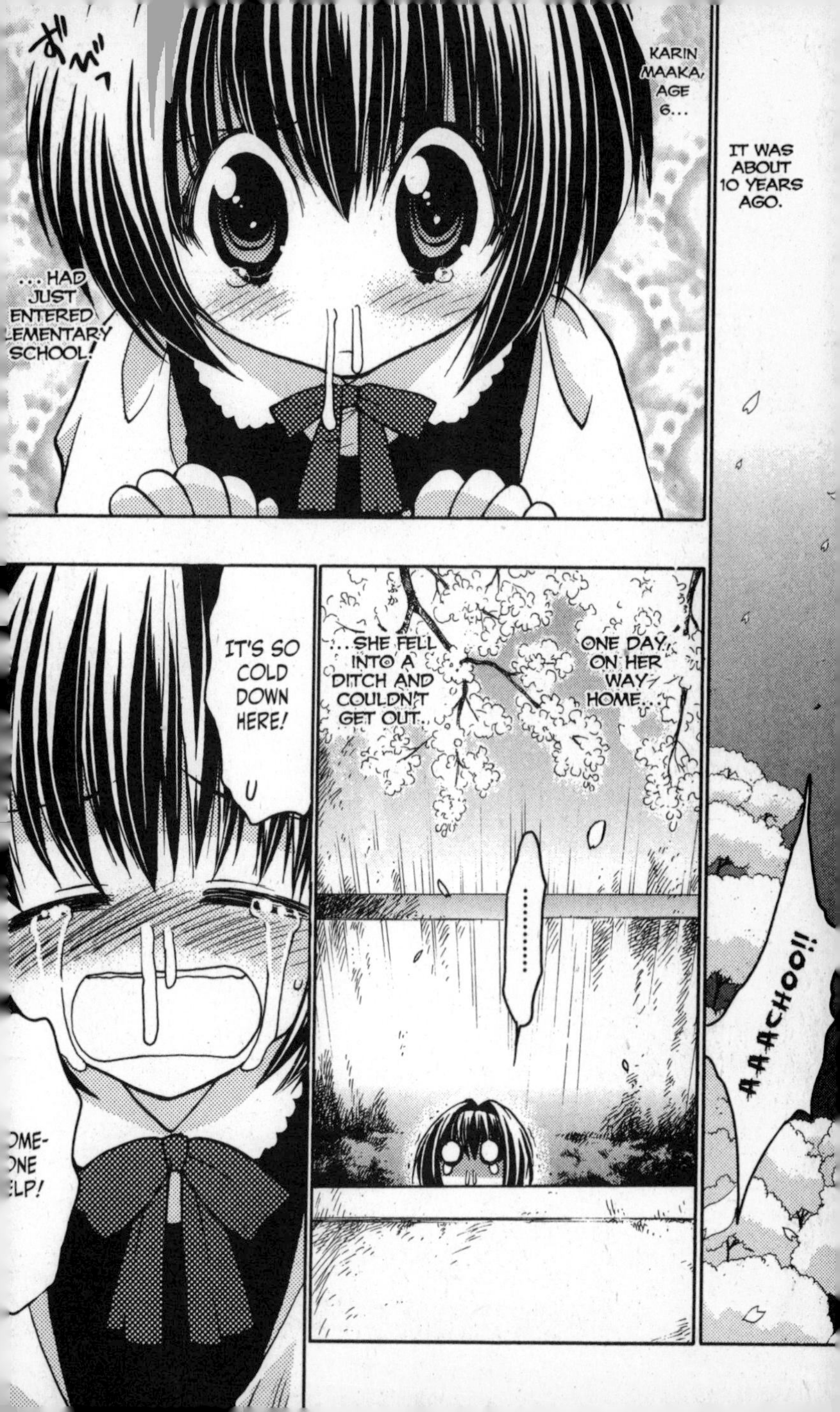
IT WAS ABOUT 10 YEARS AGO.
AAACHOO!!
ずびっ
KARIN MAAKA, AGE 6...
...HAD JUST ENTERED ELEMENTARY SCHOOL!
ONE DAY, ON HER WAY HOME...
...SHE FELL INTO A DITCH AND COULDN'T GET OUT...
......
IT'S SO COLD DOWN HERE!
OME-ONE ELP!

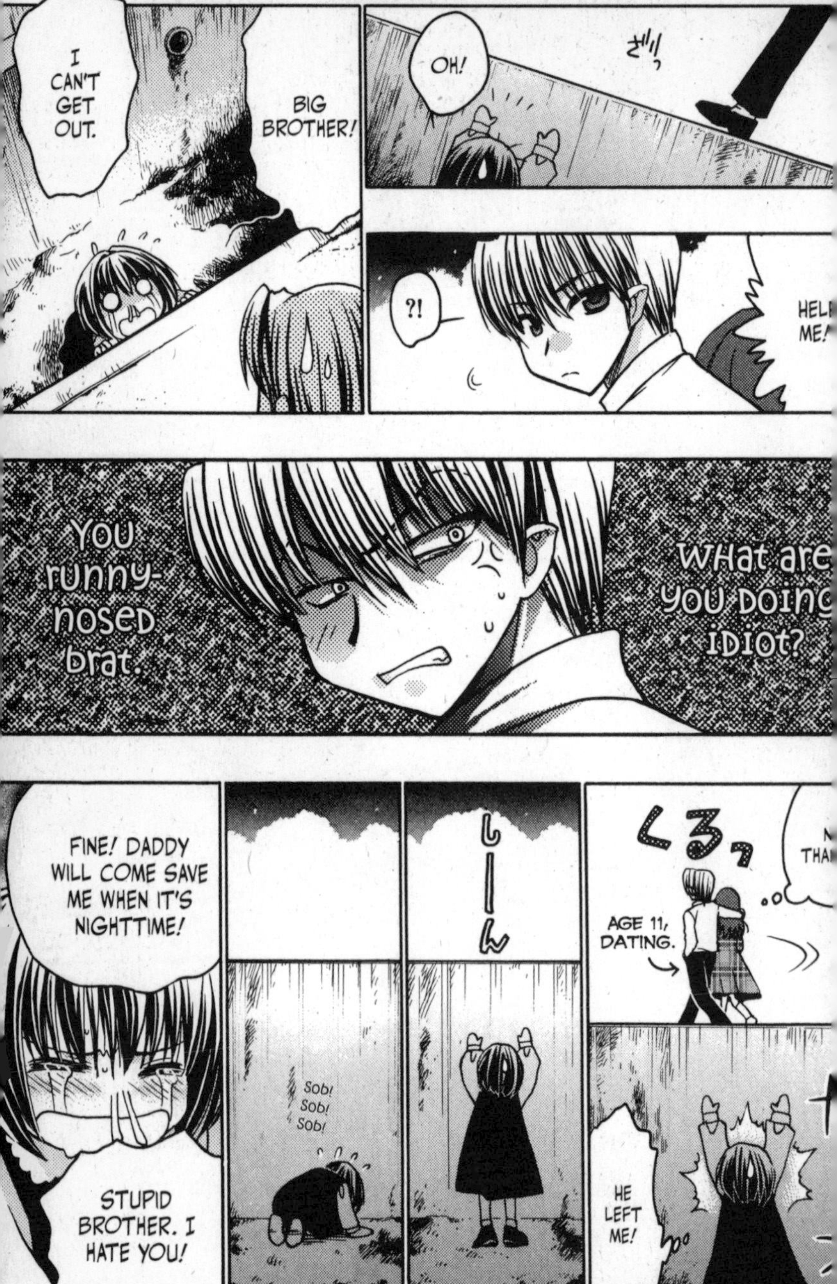
OH!
?!
HEL ME!
BIG BROTHER!
I CAN'T GET OUT.
WHAT ARE YOU DOING IDIOT?
YOU RUNNY-NOSED BRAT.
くるっ
AGE 11, DATING.
HE LEFT ME!
しーん
Sob! Sob! Sob!
FINE! DADDY WILL COME SAVE ME WHEN IT'S NIGHTTIME!
STUPID BROTHER. I HATE YOU!

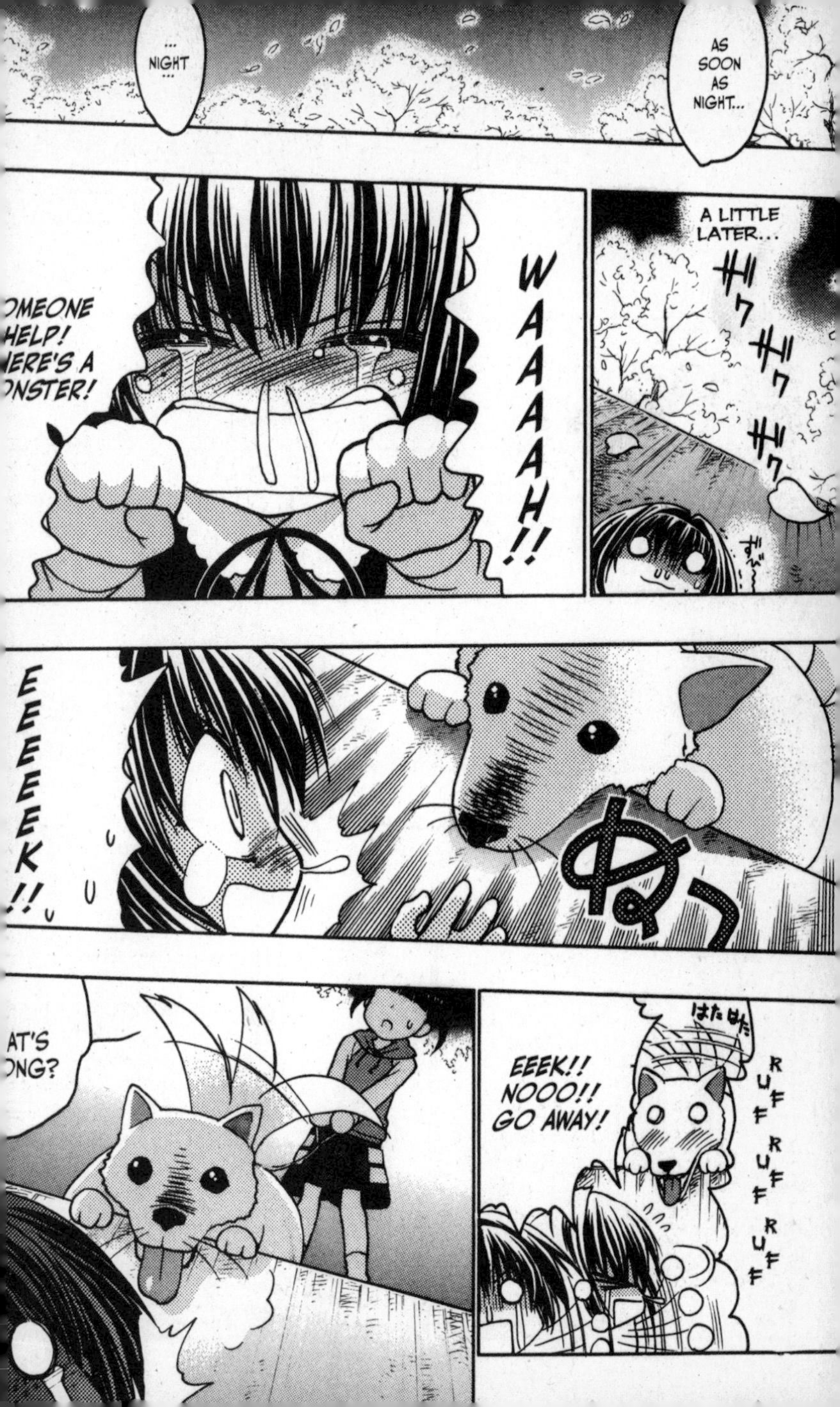
AS SOON AS NIGHT...
... NIGHT ...
A LITTLE LATER...
ギクギクギク
WAAAAAAH!!
OMEONE HELP! HERE'S A ONSTER!
ぬっ
EEEEEEK!!
はたはた
EEEK!! NOOO!! GO AWAY!
RUFF RUFF RUFF
AT'S ONG?

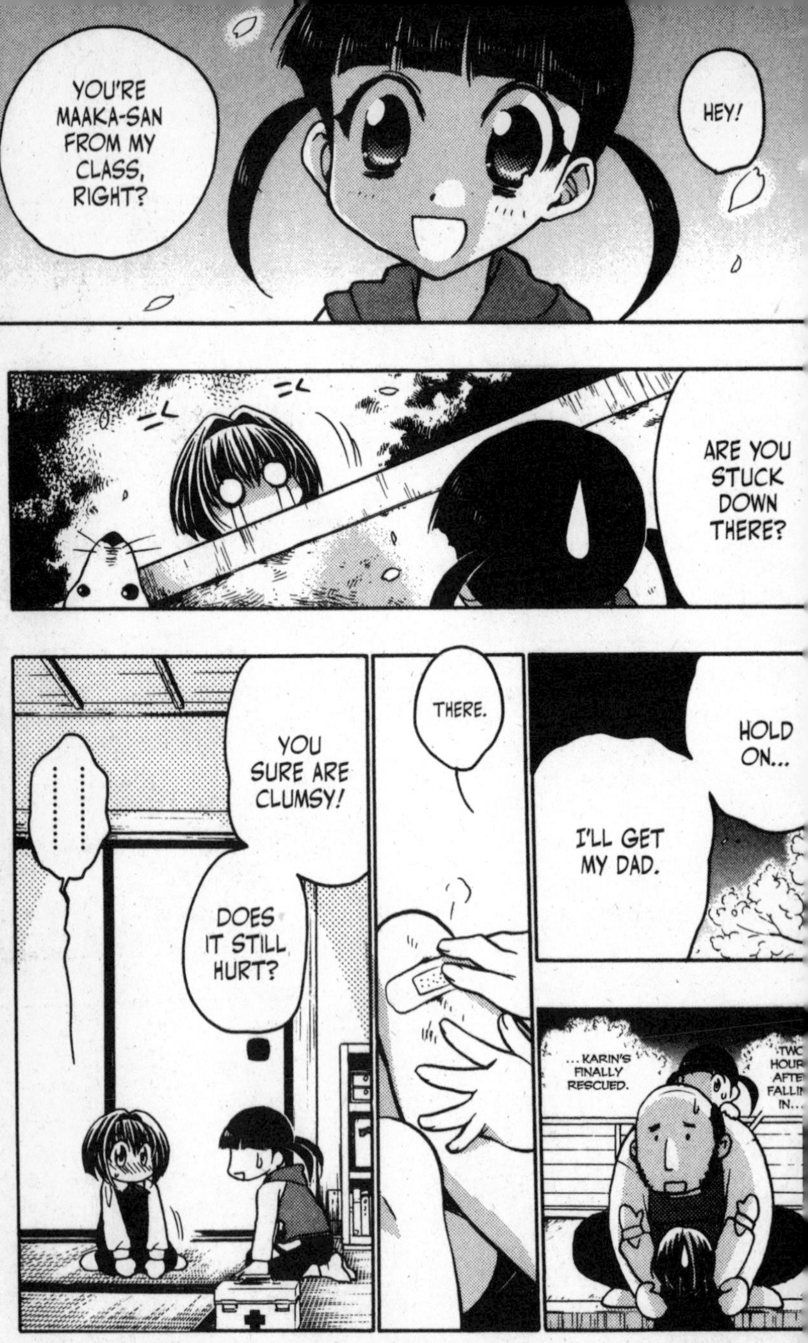

HEY!
YOU'RE MAAKA-SAN FROM MY CLASS, RIGHT?
ARE YOU STUCK DOWN THERE?
HOLD ON...
I'LL GET MY DAD.
TWO HOUR AFTE FALLIN IN...
...KARIN'S FINALLY RESCUED.
THERE.
YOU SURE ARE CLUMSY!
DOES IT STILL HURT?
......

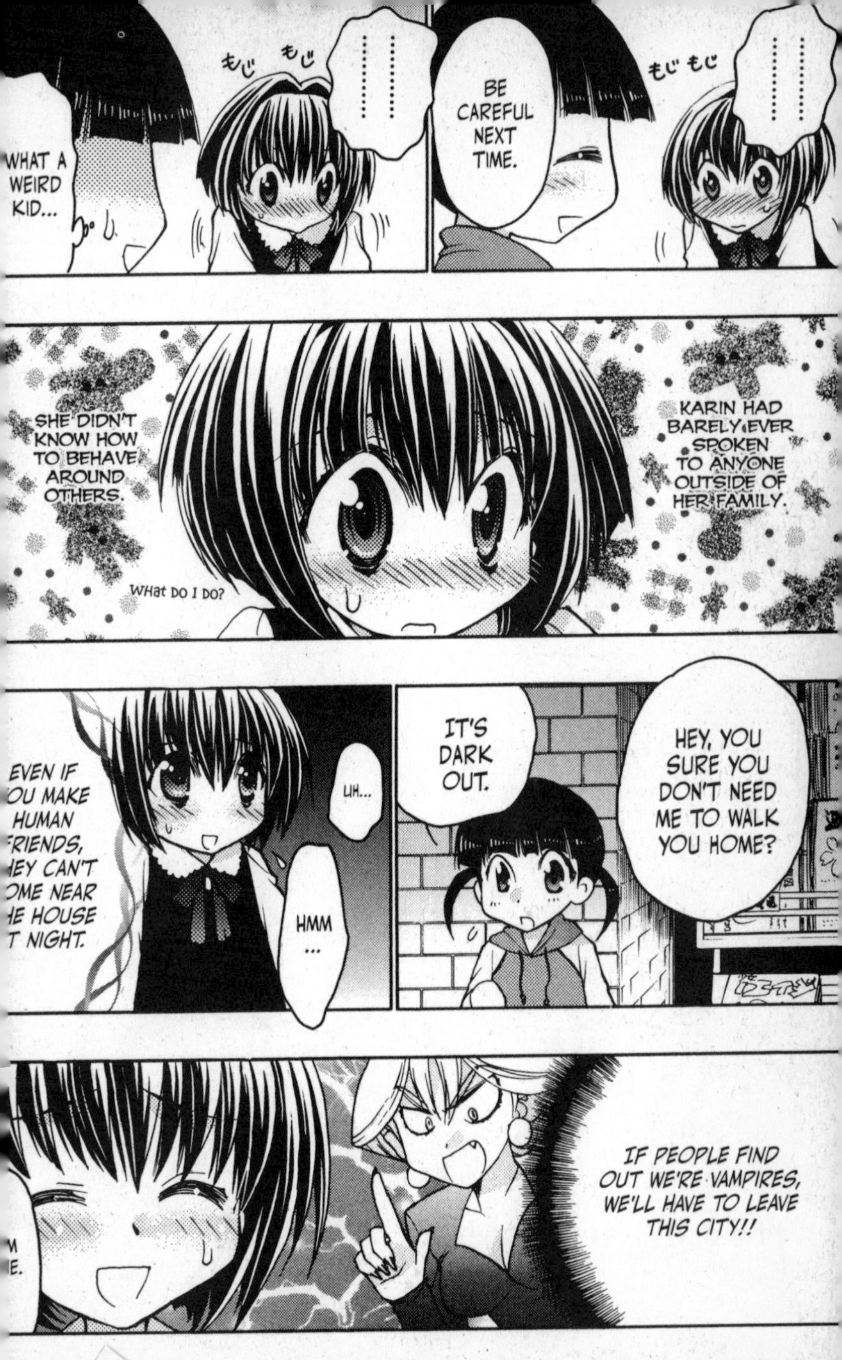
……
もじ もじ
BE CAREFUL NEXT TIME.
……
もじ もじ
WHAT A WEIRD KID...
KARIN HAD BARELY EVER SPOKEN TO ANYONE OUTSIDE OF HER FAMILY.
SHE DIDN'T KNOW HOW TO BEHAVE AROUND OTHERS.
WHAT DO I DO?
HEY, YOU SURE YOU DON'T NEED ME TO WALK YOU HOME?
IT'S DARK OUT.
UH...
HMM ...
EVEN IF OU MAKE HUMAN RIENDS, HEY CAN'T OME NEAR HE HOUSE T NIGHT.
IF PEOPLE FIND OUT WE'RE VAMPIRES, WE'LL HAVE TO LEAVE THIS CITY!!

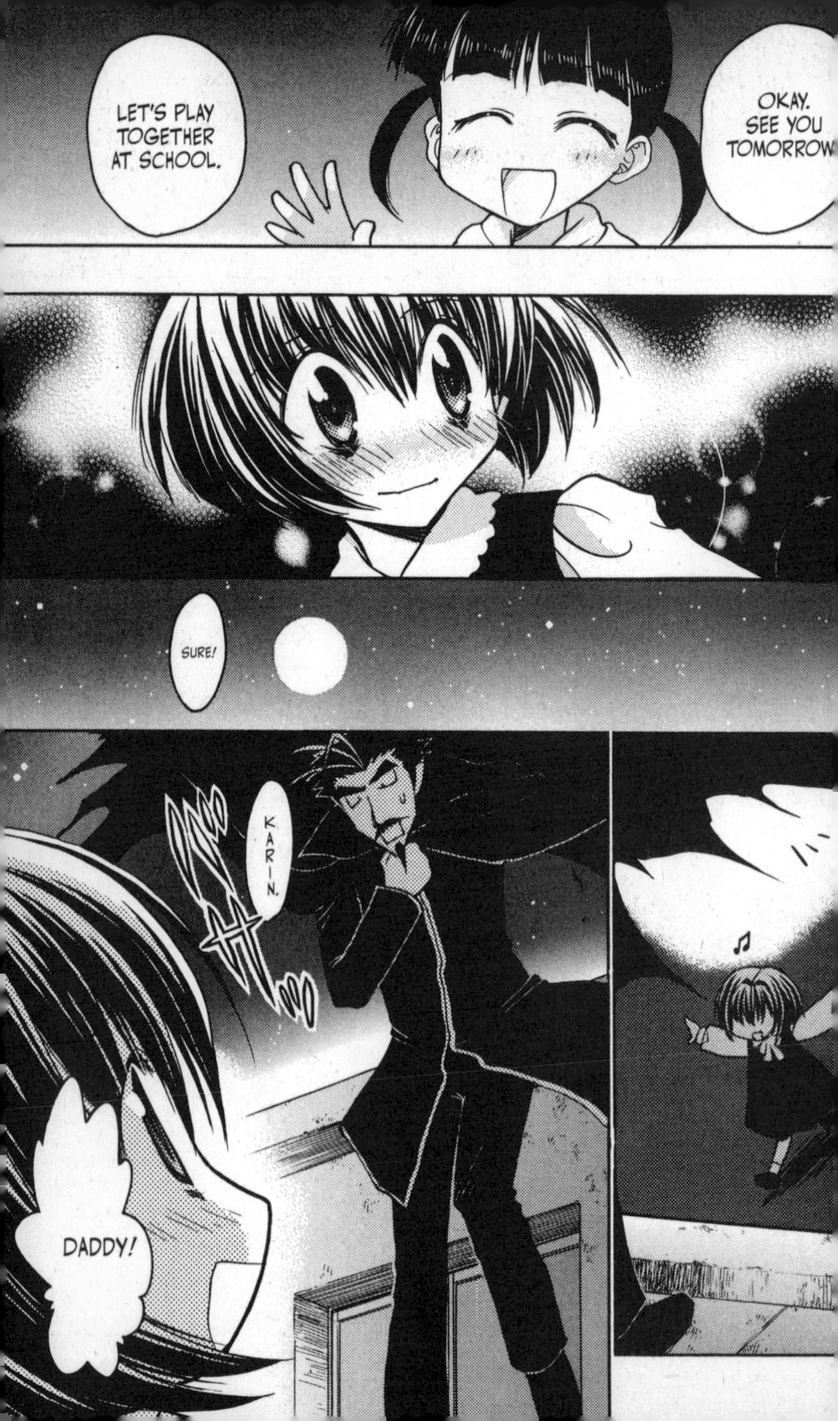
OKAY. SEE YOU TOMORROW
LET'S PLAY TOGETHER AT SCHOOL.
SURE!
KARIN.
DADDY!

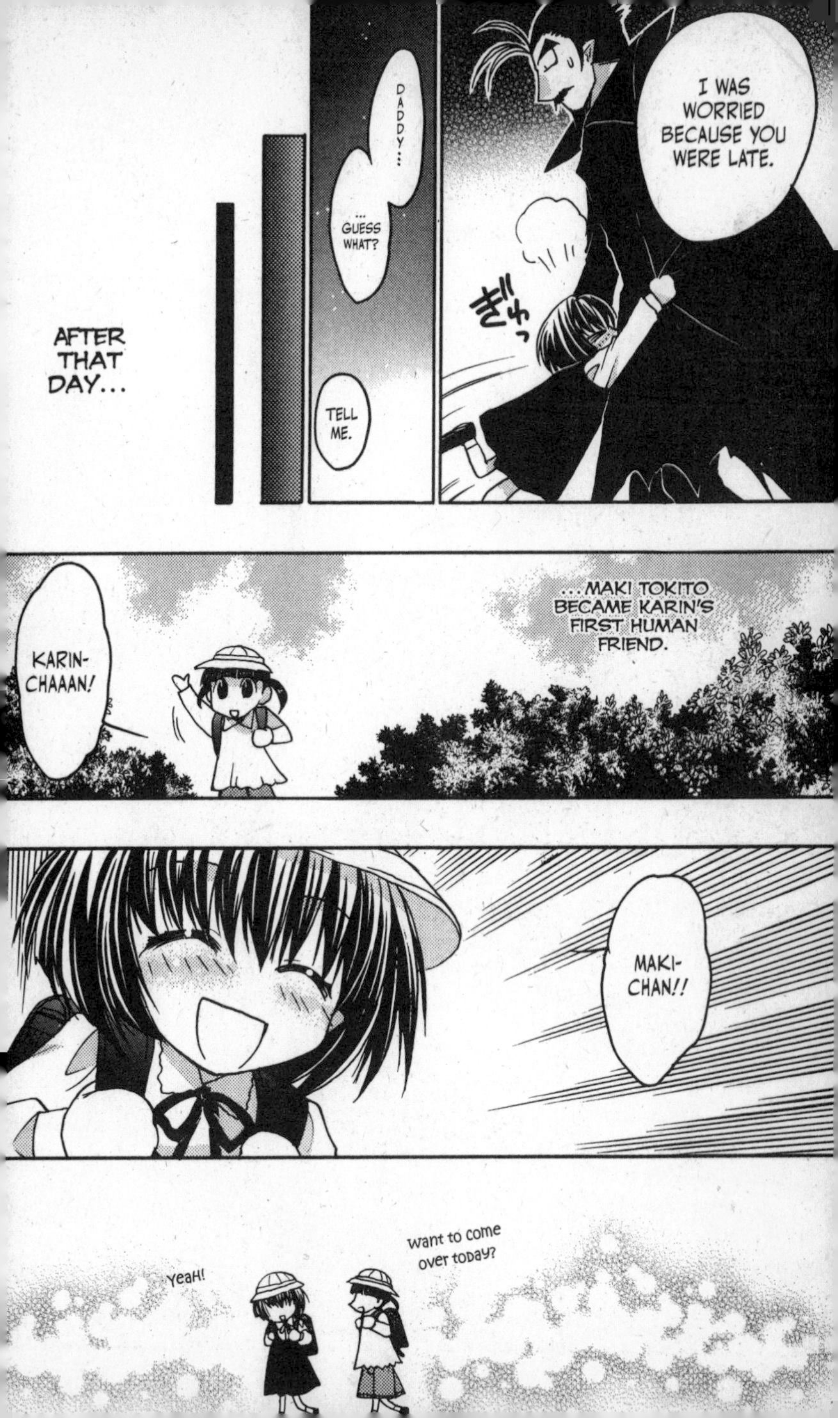
I WAS WORRIED BECAUSE YOU WERE LATE.
ぎゅっ
DADDY...
...GUESS WHAT?
TELL ME.
AFTER THAT DAY...
...MAKI TOKITO BECAME KARIN'S FIRST HUMAN FRIEND.
KARIN-CHAAAN!
MAKI-CHAN!!
Want to come over today?
YeaH!

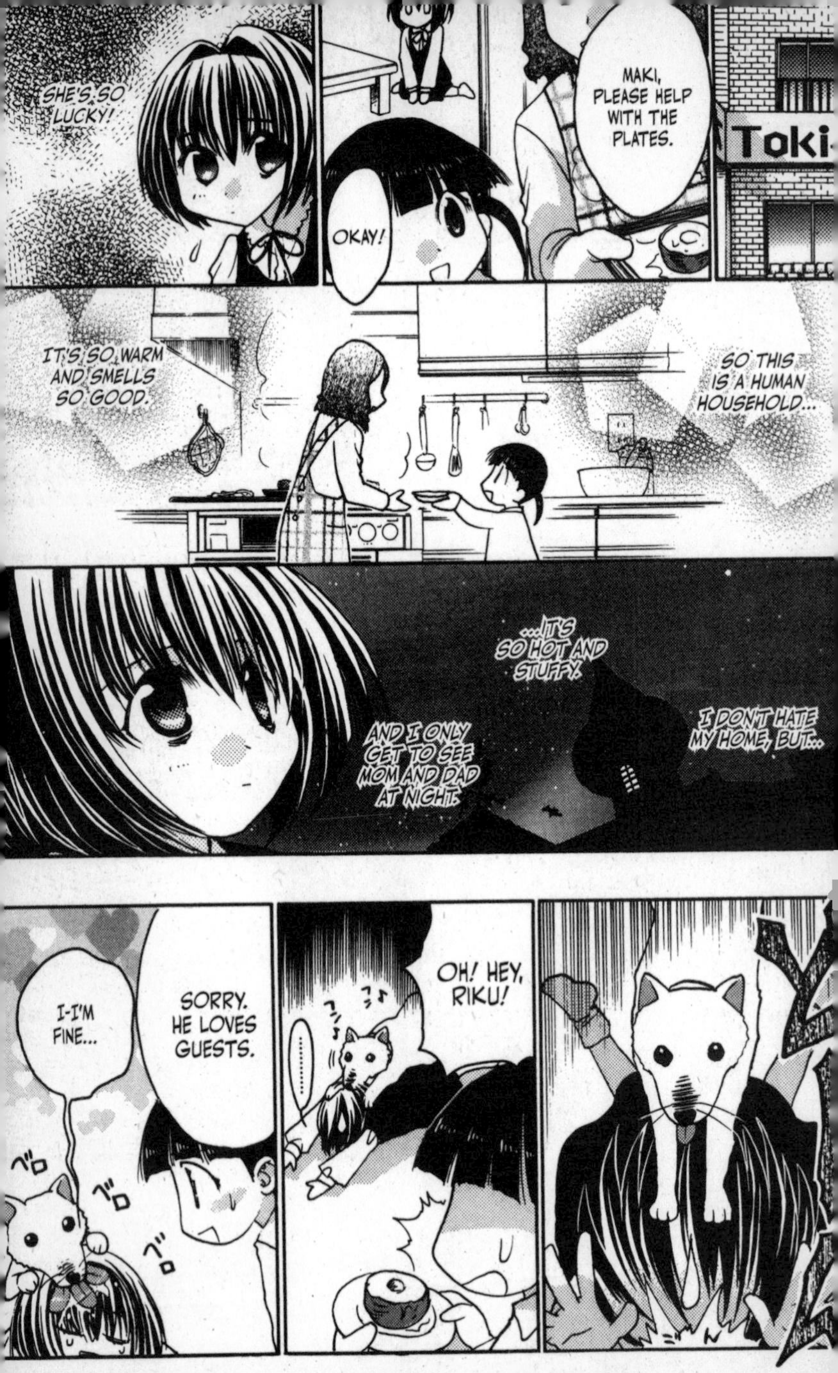
Toki
MAKI, PLEASE HELP WITH THE PLATES.
OKAY!
SHE'S SO LUCKY!
SO THIS IS A HUMAN HOUSEHOLD...
IT'S SO WARM AND SMELLS SO GOOD.
I DON'T HATE MY HOME, BUT...
...IT'S SO HOT AND STUFFY.
AND I ONLY GET TO SEE MOM AND DAD AT NIGHT.
OH! HEY, RIKU!
SORRY. HE LOVES GUESTS.
I-I'M FINE...

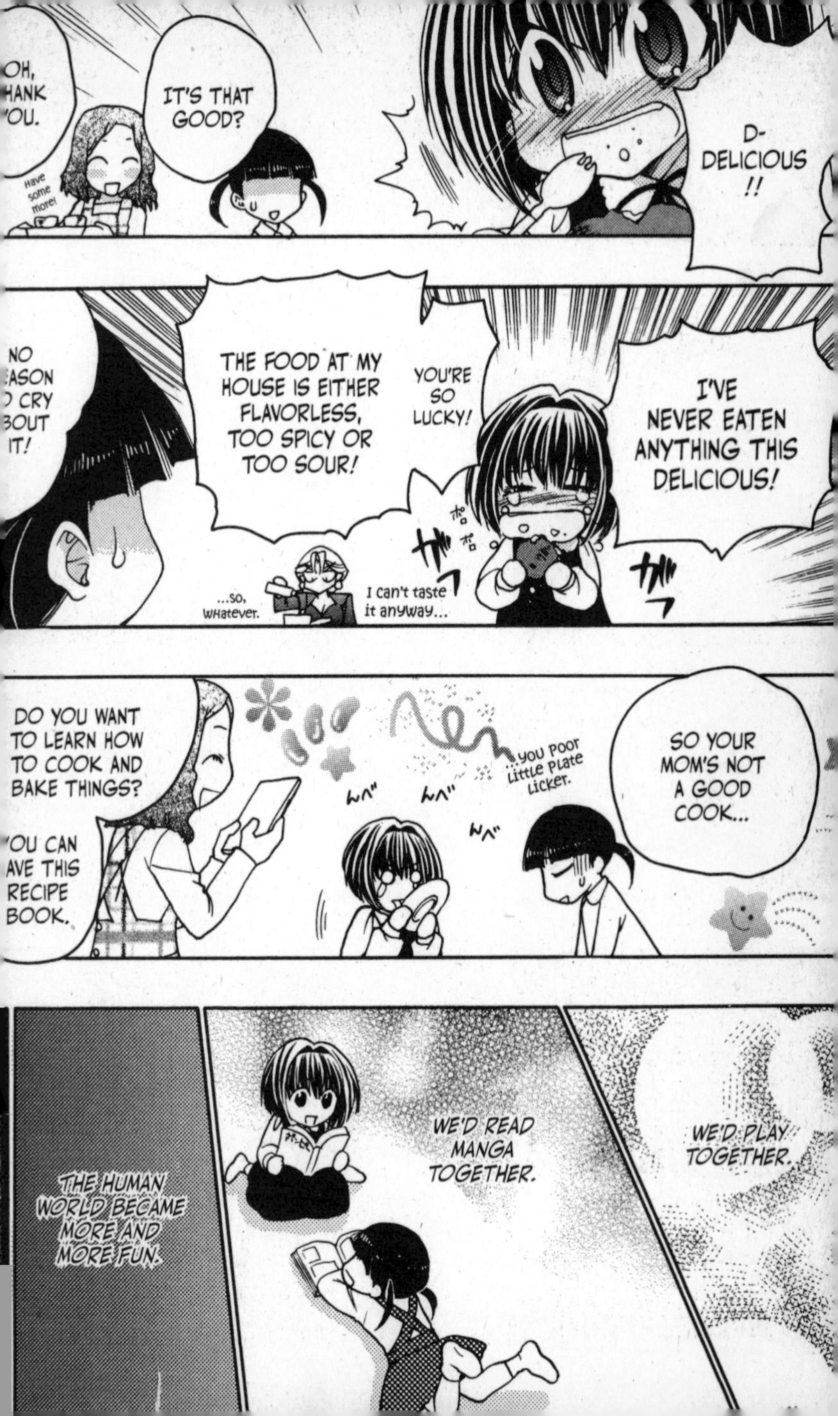
D-DELICIOUS!!
IT'S THAT GOOD?
OH, HANK OU.
Have some more!
I'VE NEVER EATEN ANYTHING THIS DELICIOUS!
YOU'RE SO LUCKY!
THE FOOD AT MY HOUSE IS EITHER FLAVORLESS, TOO SPICY OR TOO SOUR!
I can't taste it anyway...
...so, whatever.
NO EASON CRY BOUT IT!
SO YOUR MOM'S NOT A GOOD COOK...
...YOU POOR LITTLE PLATE LICKER.
DO YOU WANT TO LEARN HOW TO COOK AND BAKE THINGS?
OU CAN AVE THIS RECIPE BOOK.
WE'D PLAY TOGETHER.
WE'D READ MANGA TOGETHER.
THE HUMAN WORLD BECAME MORE AND MORE FUN.

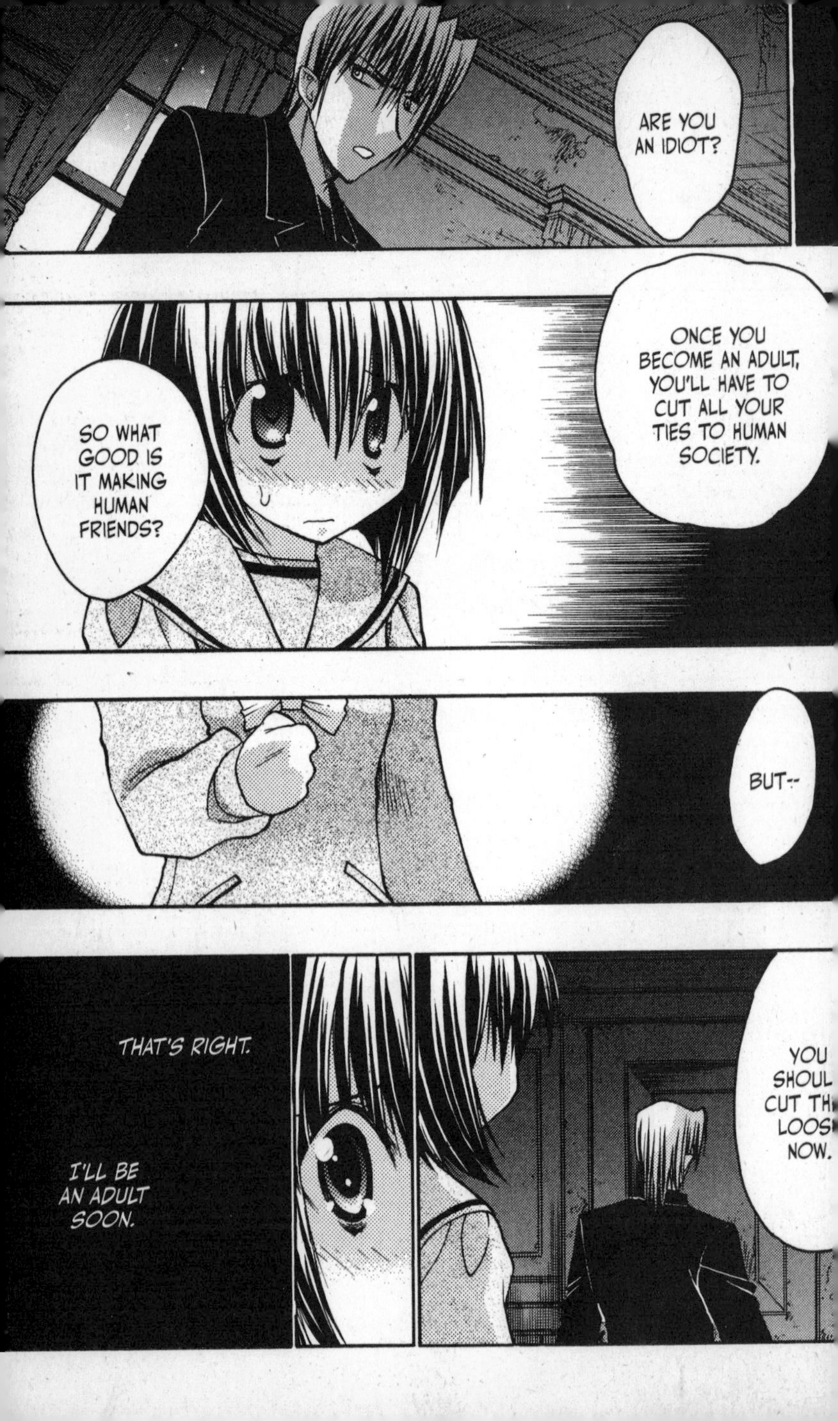

ARE YOU AN IDIOT?
ONCE YOU BECOME AN ADULT, YOU'LL HAVE TO CUT ALL YOUR TIES TO HUMAN SOCIETY.
SO WHAT GOOD IS IT MAKING HUMAN FRIENDS?
BUT--
YOU SHOUL CUT TH LOOS NOW.
THAT'S RIGHT.
I'LL BE AN ADULT SOON.

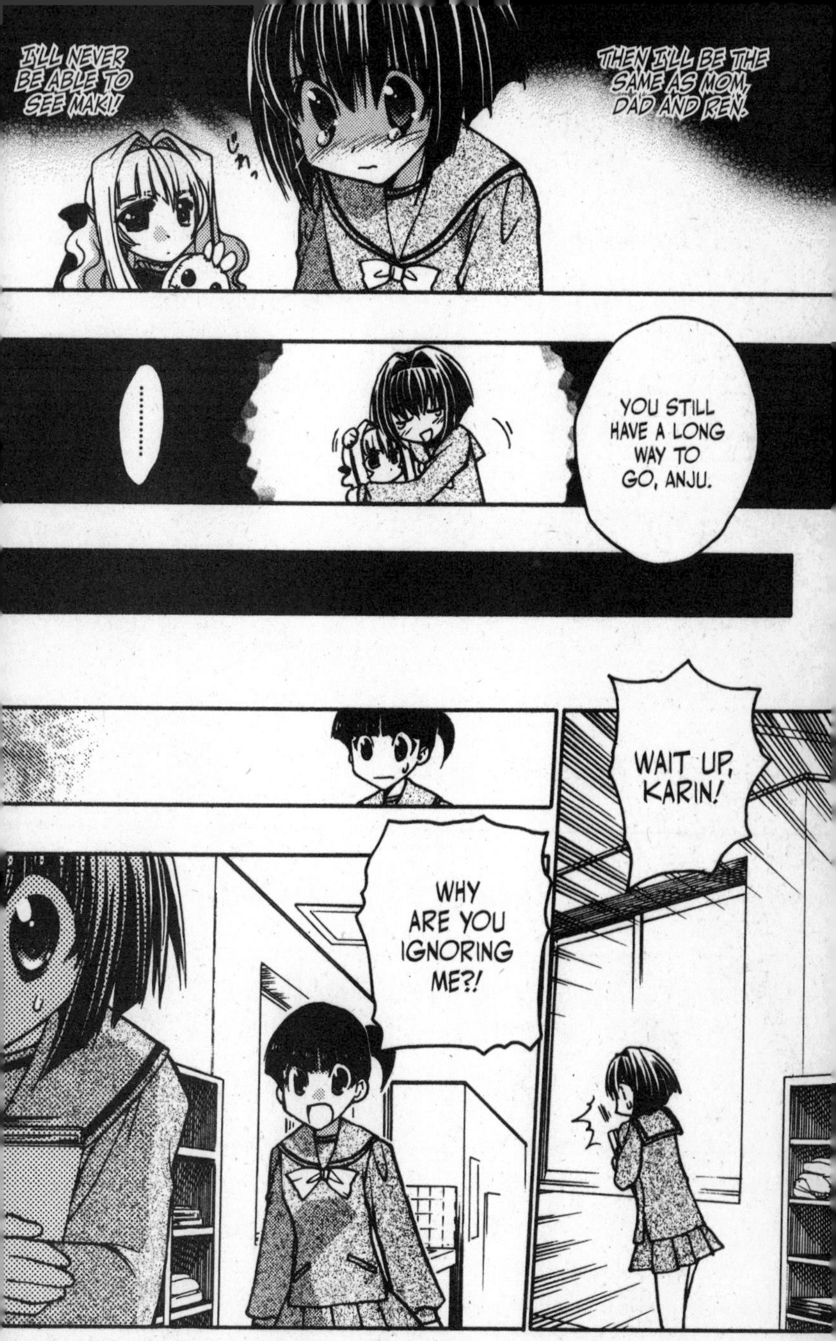
THEN I'LL BE THE SAME AS MOM, DAD AND REN.
I'LL NEVER BE ABLE TO SEE MAKI!
YOU STILL HAVE A LONG WAY TO GO, ANJU.
......
WAIT UP, KARIN!
WHY ARE YOU IGNORING ME?!

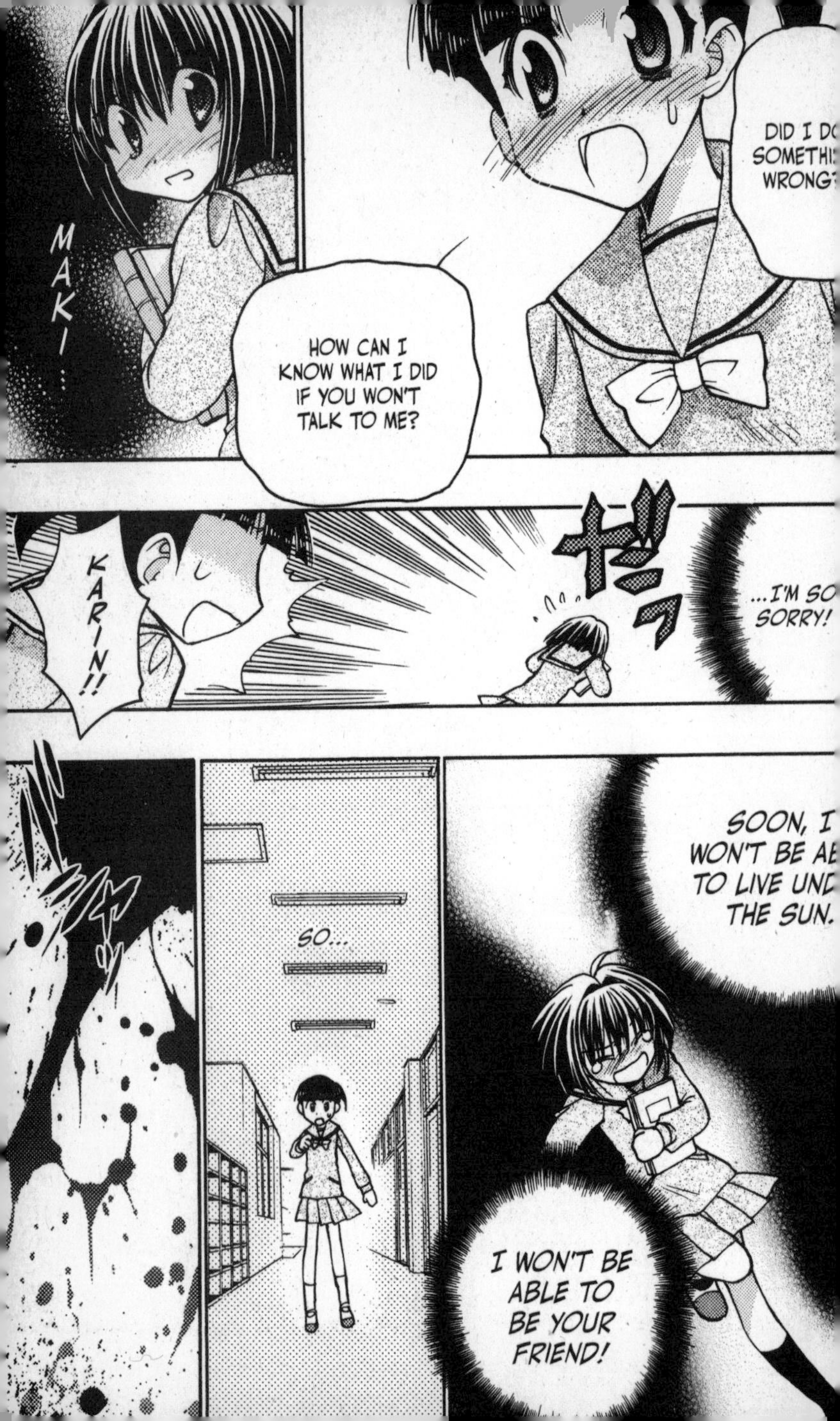

DID I DO SOMETHI WRONG?
HOW CAN I KNOW WHAT I DID IF YOU WON'T TALK TO ME?
MAKI...
ダッ
...I'M SO SORRY!
KARIN!!
SOON, I WON'T BE AB TO LIVE UND THE SUN.
I WON'T BE ABLE TO BE YOUR FRIEND!
SO...

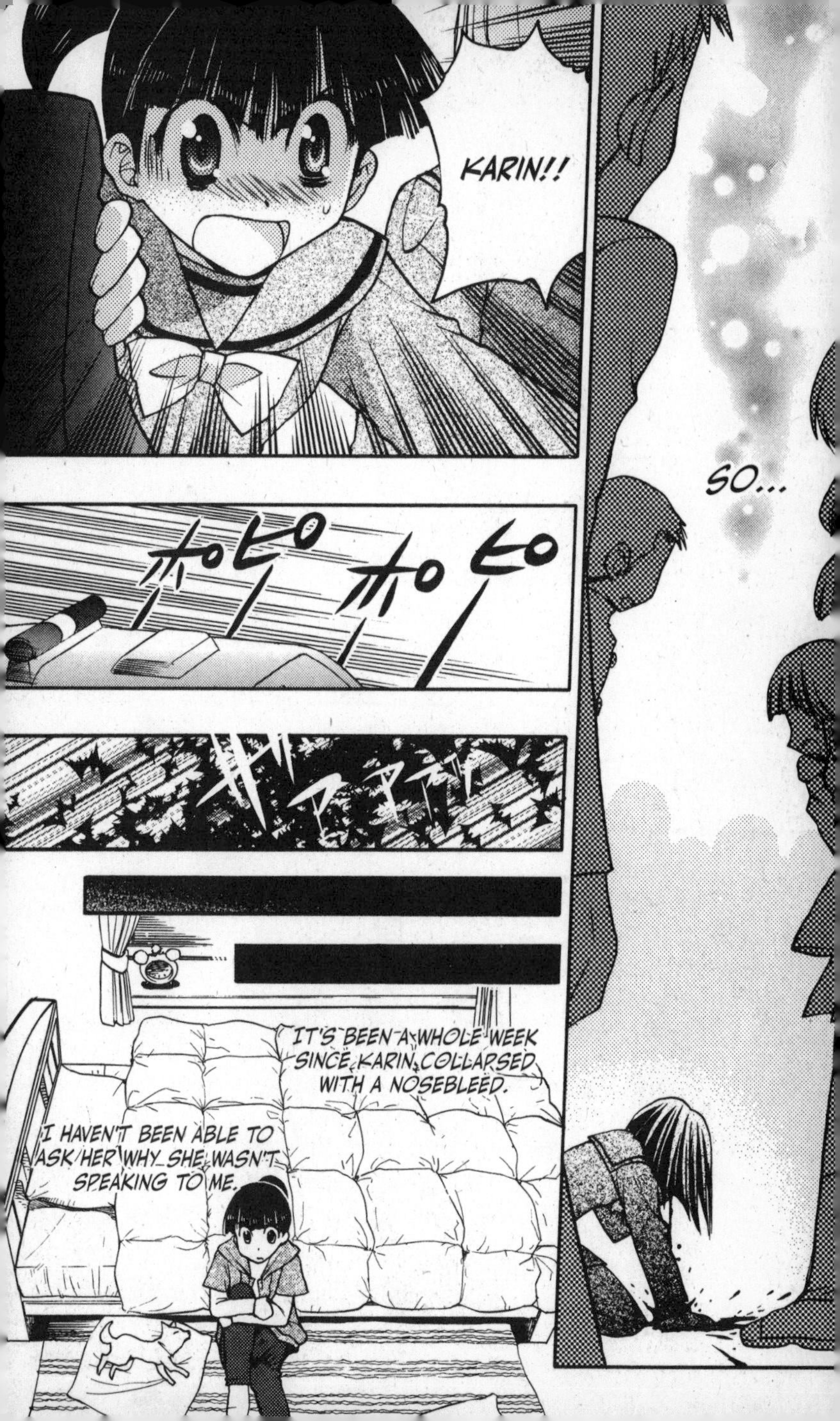
SO...
KARIN!!
[redacted]
[redacted]
IT'S BEEN A WHOLE WEEK SINCE KARIN COLLAPSED WITH A NOSEBLEED.
I HAVEN'T BEEN ABLE TO ASK HER WHY SHE WASN'T SPEAKING TO ME.

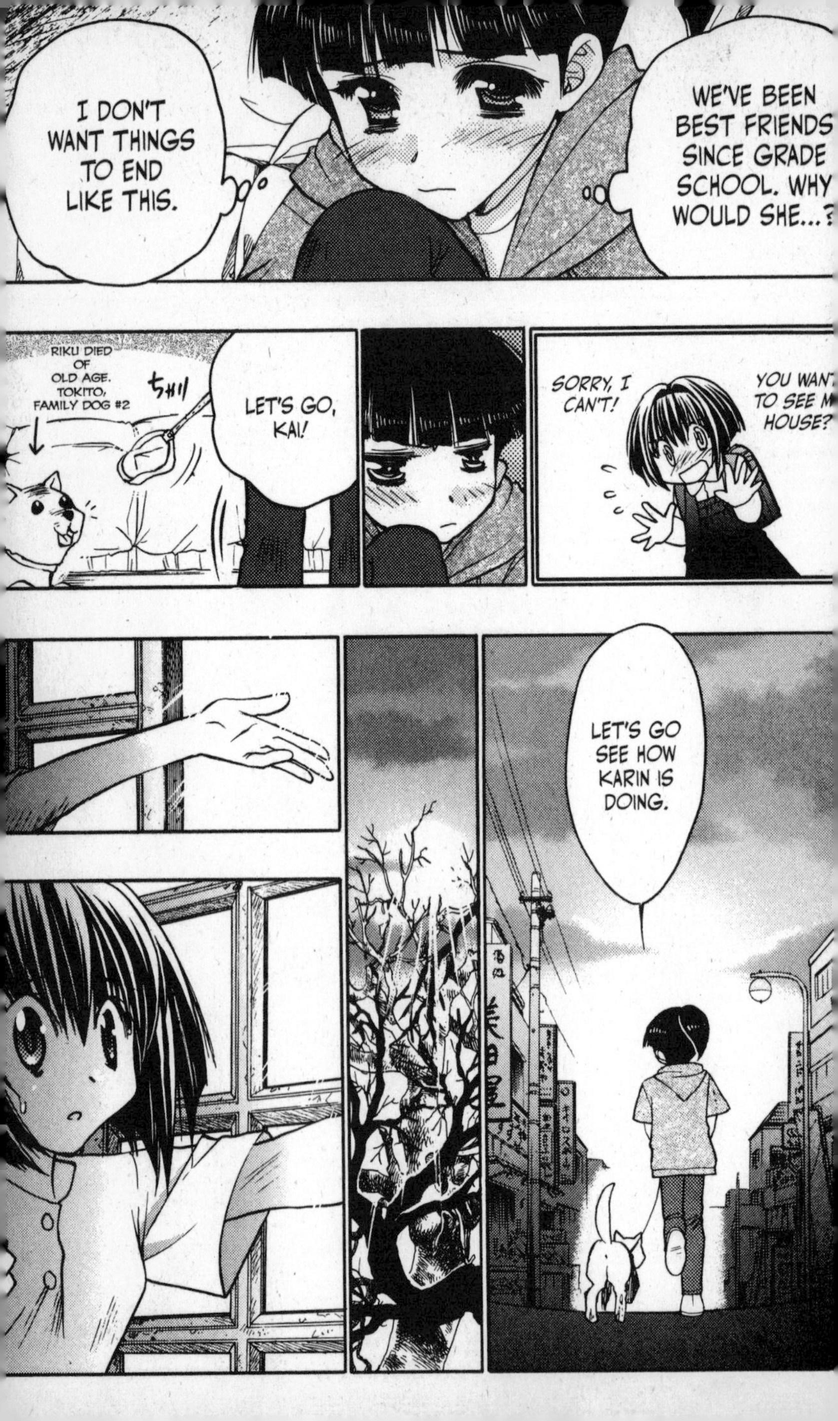
WE'VE BEEN BEST FRIENDS SINCE GRADE SCHOOL. WHY WOULD SHE...?
I DON'T WANT THINGS TO END LIKE THIS.
YOU WAN TO SEE M HOUSE?
SORRY, I CAN'T!
LET'S GO, KAI!
RIKU DIED OF OLD AGE. TOKITO, FAMILY DOG #2
LET'S GO SEE HOW KARIN IS DOING.

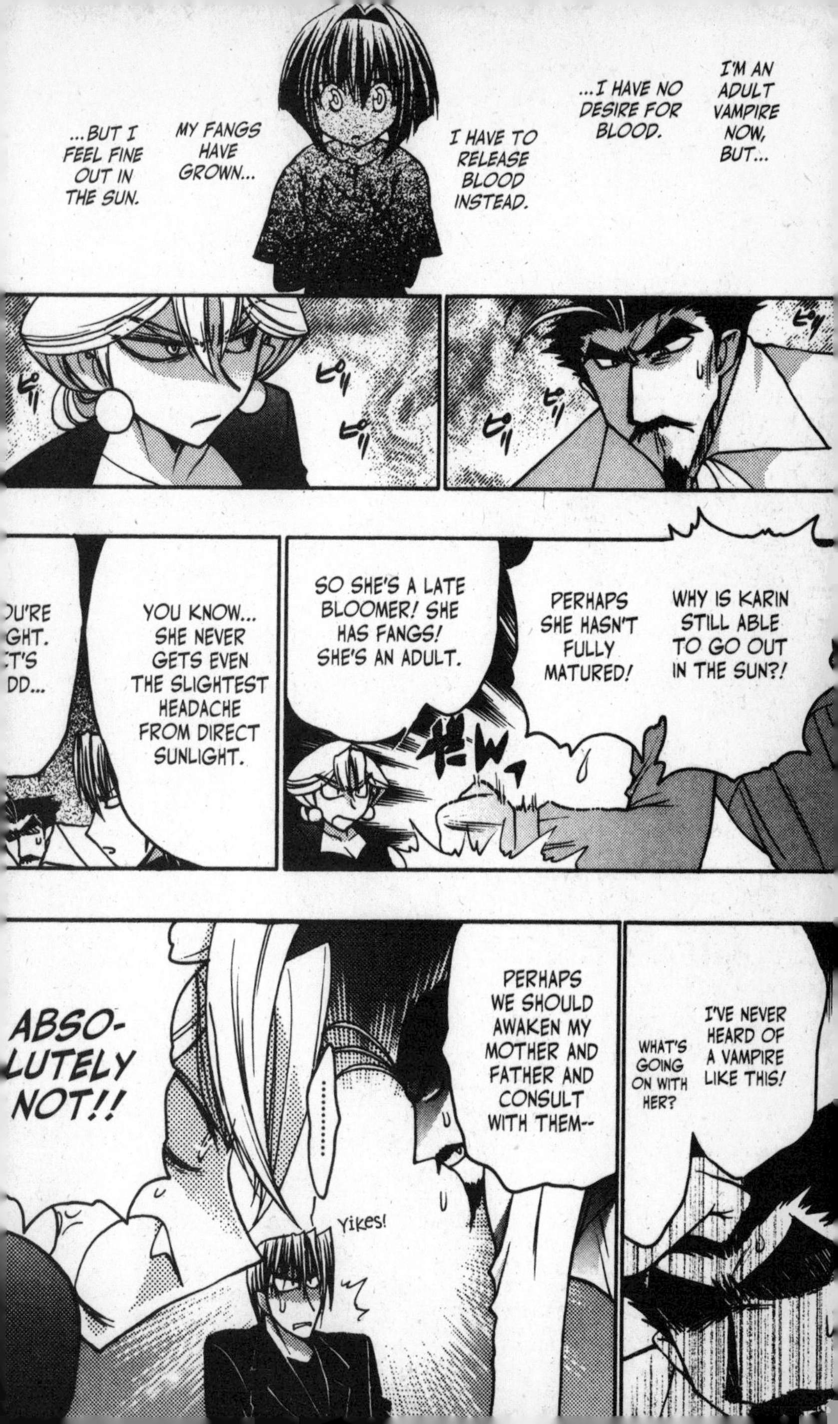
I'M AN ADULT VAMPIRE NOW, BUT...
...I HAVE NO DESIRE FOR BLOOD.
I HAVE TO RELEASE BLOOD INSTEAD.
MY FANGS HAVE GROWN...
...BUT I FEEL FINE OUT IN THE SUN.
WHY IS KARIN STILL ABLE TO GO OUT IN THE SUN?!
PERHAPS SHE HASN'T FULLY MATURED!
SO SHE'S A LATE BLOOMER! SHE HAS FANGS! SHE'S AN ADULT.
YOU KNOW... SHE NEVER GETS EVEN THE SLIGHTEST HEADACHE FROM DIRECT SUNLIGHT.
I'VE NEVER HEARD OF A VAMPIRE LIKE THIS!
WHAT'S GOING ON WITH HER?
PERHAPS WE SHOULD AWAKEN MY MOTHER AND FATHER AND CONSULT WITH THEM--
ABSO-LUTELY NOT!!
Yikes!

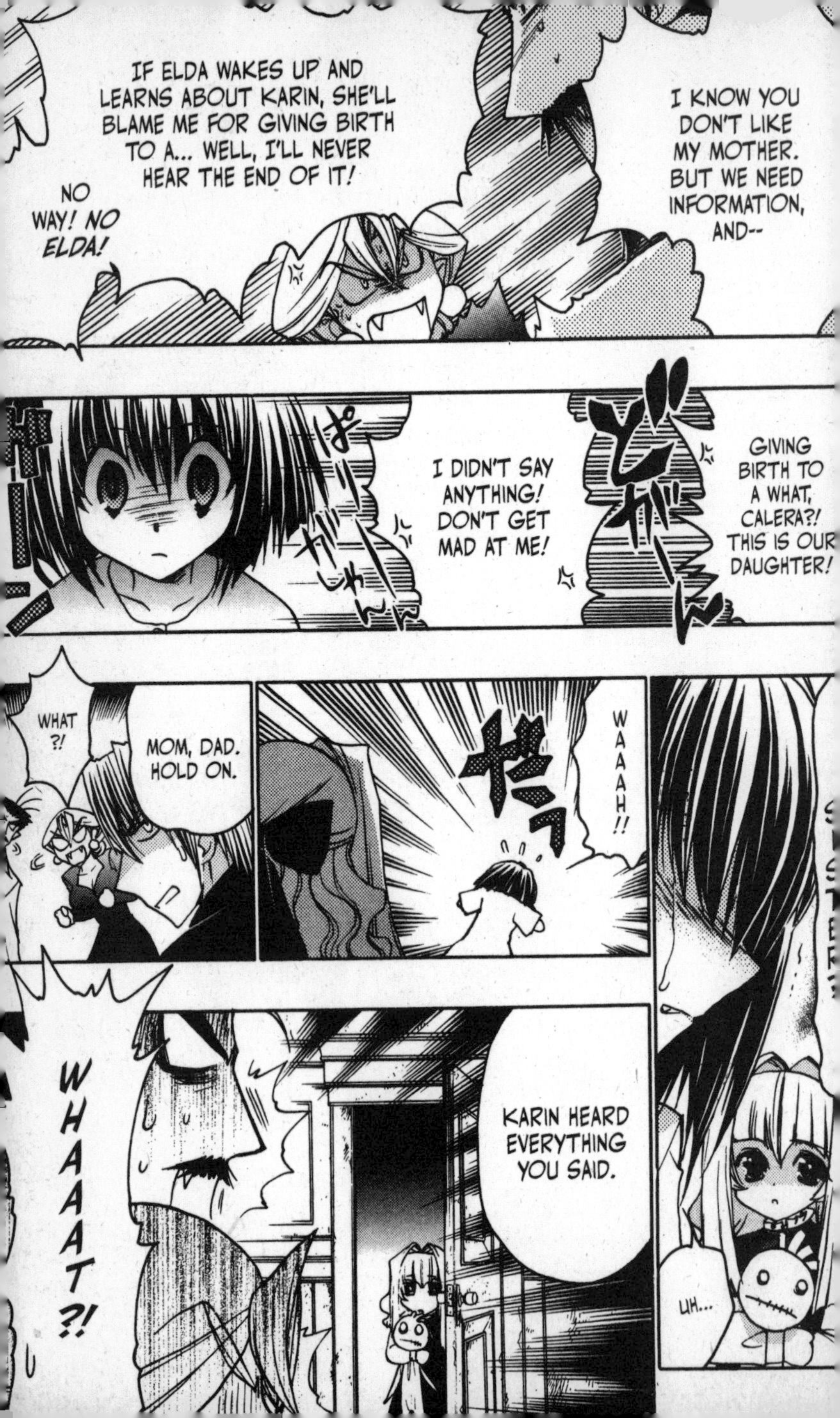
I KNOW YOU DON'T LIKE MY MOTHER. BUT WE NEED INFORMATION, AND--
IF ELDA WAKES UP AND LEARNS ABOUT KARIN, SHE'LL BLAME ME FOR GIVING BIRTH TO A... WELL, I'LL NEVER HEAR THE END OF IT!
NO WAY! NO ELDA!
GIVING BIRTH TO A WHAT, CALERA?! THIS IS OUR DAUGHTER!
I DIDN'T SAY ANYTHING! DON'T GET MAD AT ME!
UH...
WAAAAH!!
MOM, DAD. HOLD ON.
WHAT?!
KARIN HEARD EVERYTHING YOU SAID.
WHAAAAT?!

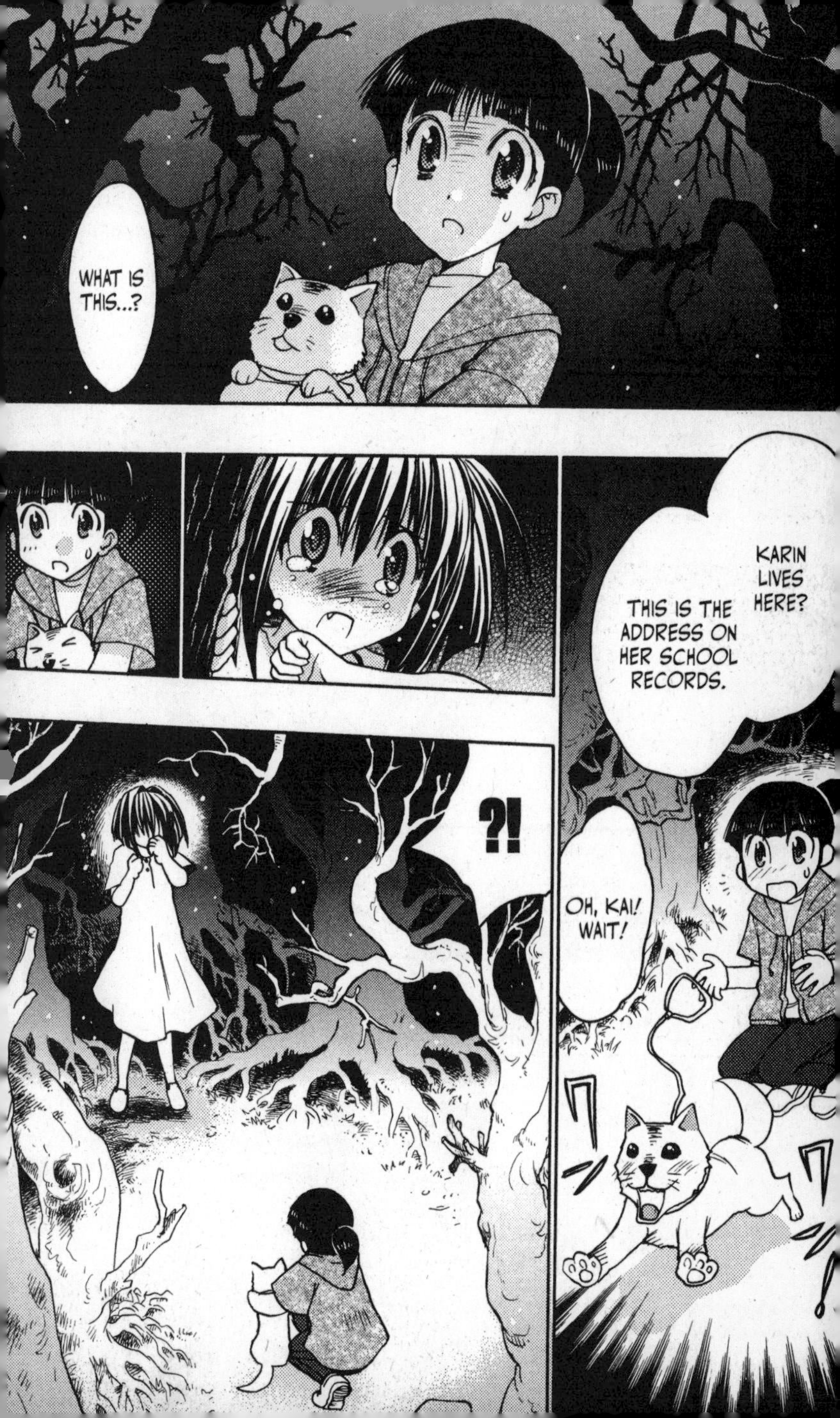
WHAT IS THIS...?
KARIN LIVES HERE?
THIS IS THE ADDRESS ON HER SCHOOL RECORDS.
OH, KAI! WAIT!
?!

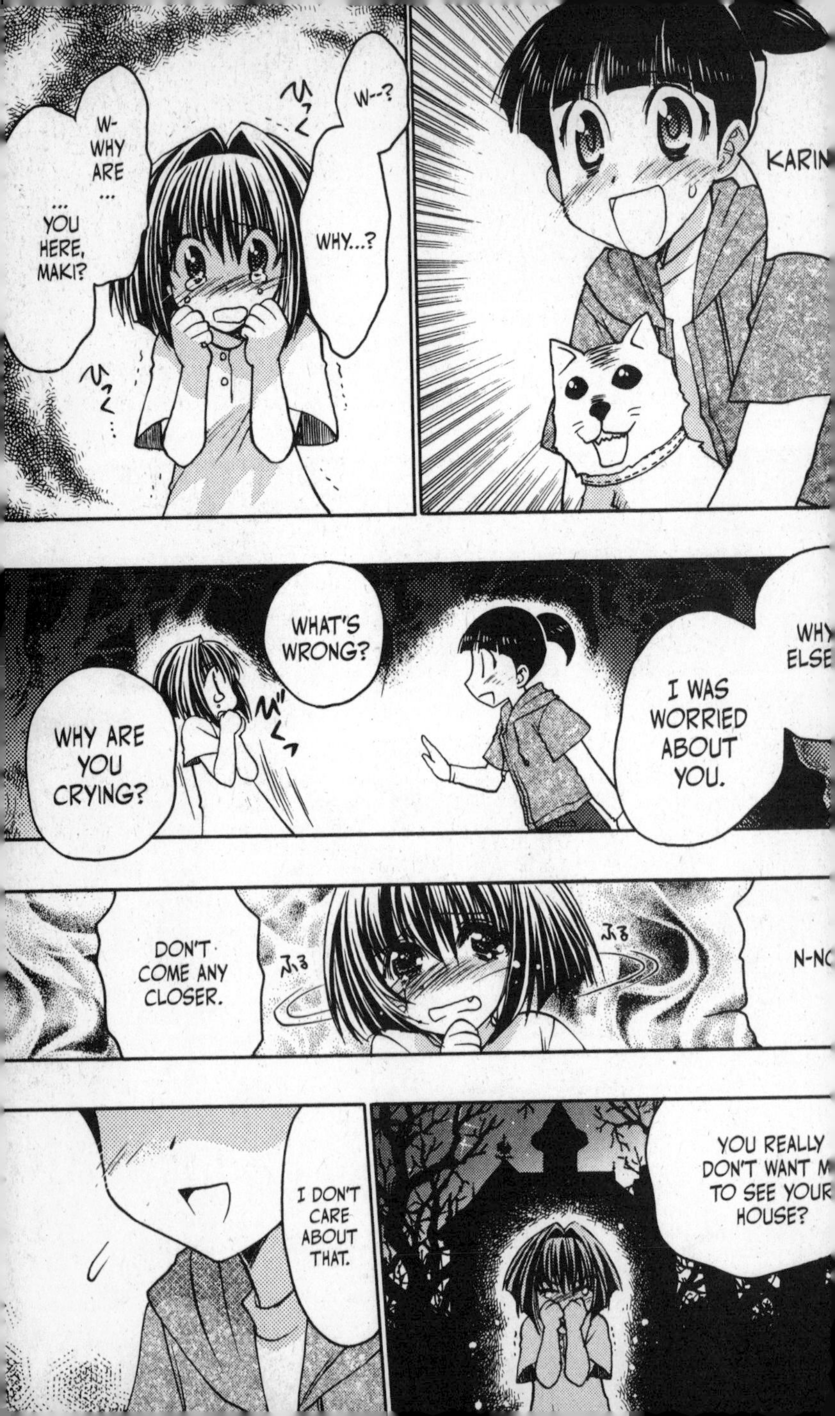
KARIN
W--?
WHY...?
ひっく
W- WHY ARE ... ... YOU HERE, MAKI?
ひっく…
WHY ELSE
I WAS WORRIED ABOUT YOU.
WHAT'S WRONG?
びくっ
WHY ARE YOU CRYING?
N-N
ふる
ふる
DON'T COME ANY CLOSER.
YOU REALLY DON'T WANT M TO SEE YOUR HOUSE?
I DON'T CARE ABOUT THAT.

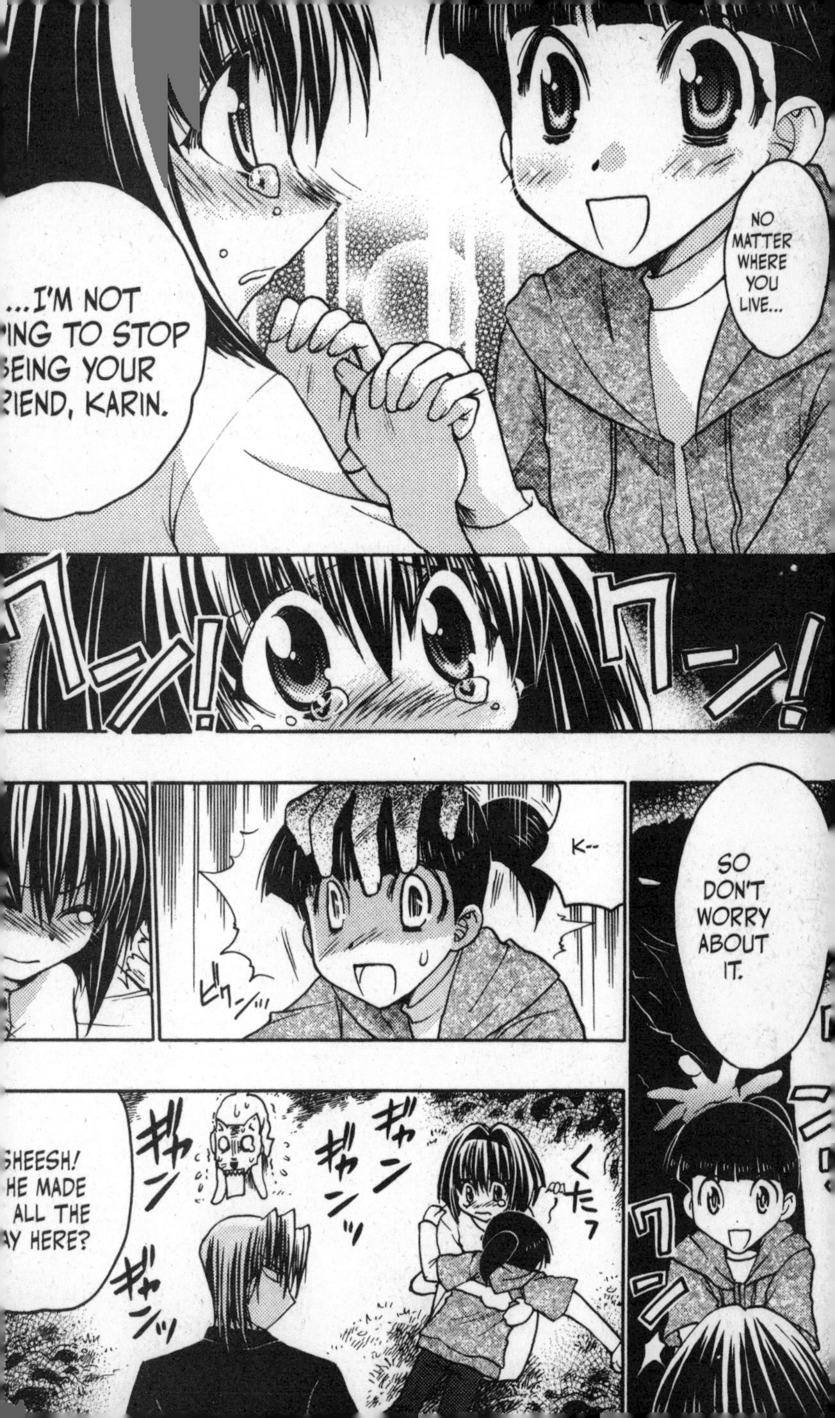
NO MATTER WHERE YOU LIVE...
...I'M NOT ING TO STOP EING YOUR IEND, KARIN.
SO DON'T WORRY ABOUT IT.
K--
ギャン
ギャン
ギャンッ
ギャンッ
SHEESH! HE MADE ALL THE AY HERE?

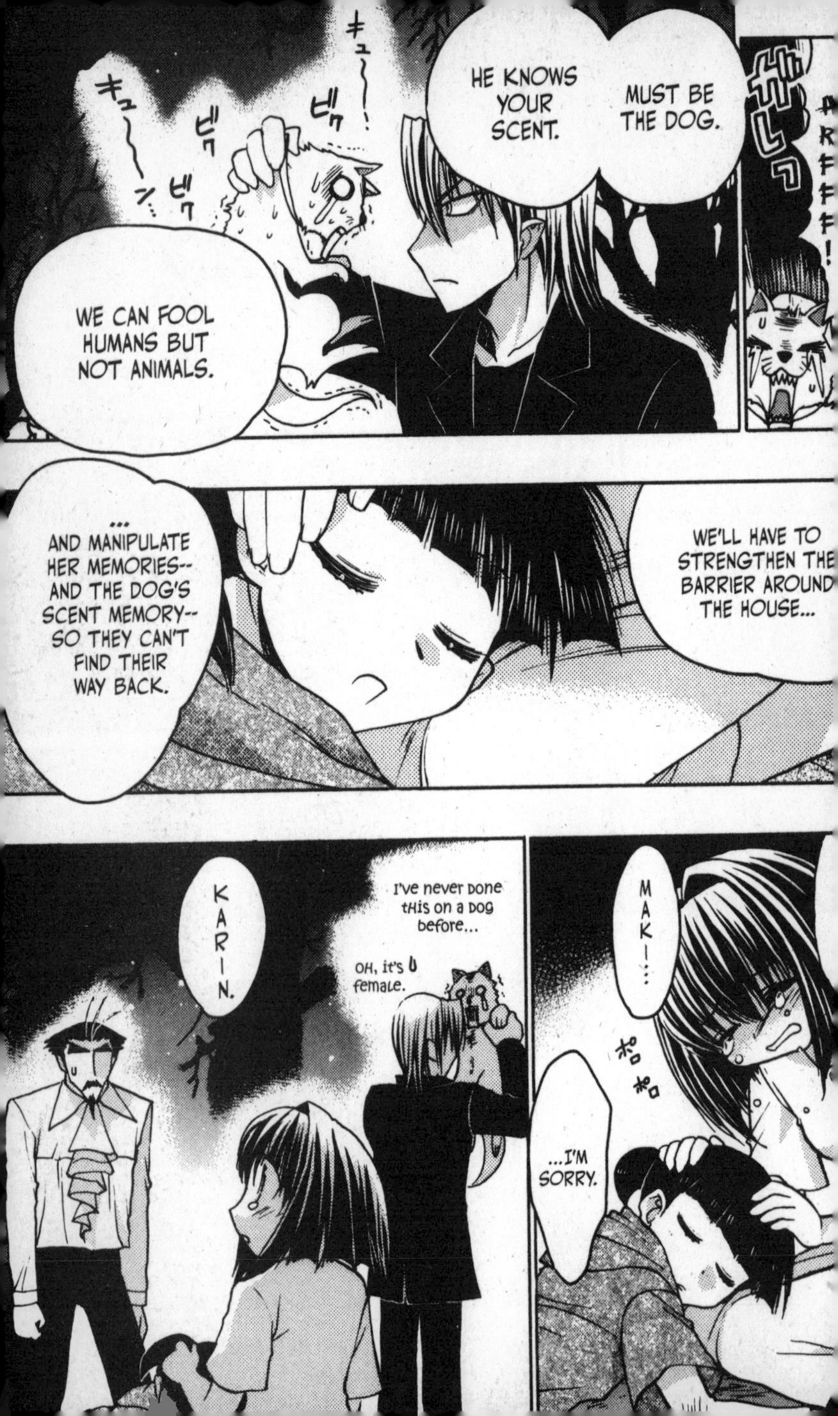
ARFFFF!
MUST BE THE DOG.
HE KNOWS YOUR SCENT.
WE CAN FOOL HUMANS BUT NOT ANIMALS.
WE'LL HAVE TO STRENGTHEN THE BARRIER AROUND THE HOUSE...
... AND MANIPULATE HER MEMORIES-- AND THE DOG'S SCENT MEMORY-- SO THEY CAN'T FIND THEIR WAY BACK.
MAKI...
...I'M SORRY.
I've never done this on a dog before...
Oh, it's female.
KARIN.

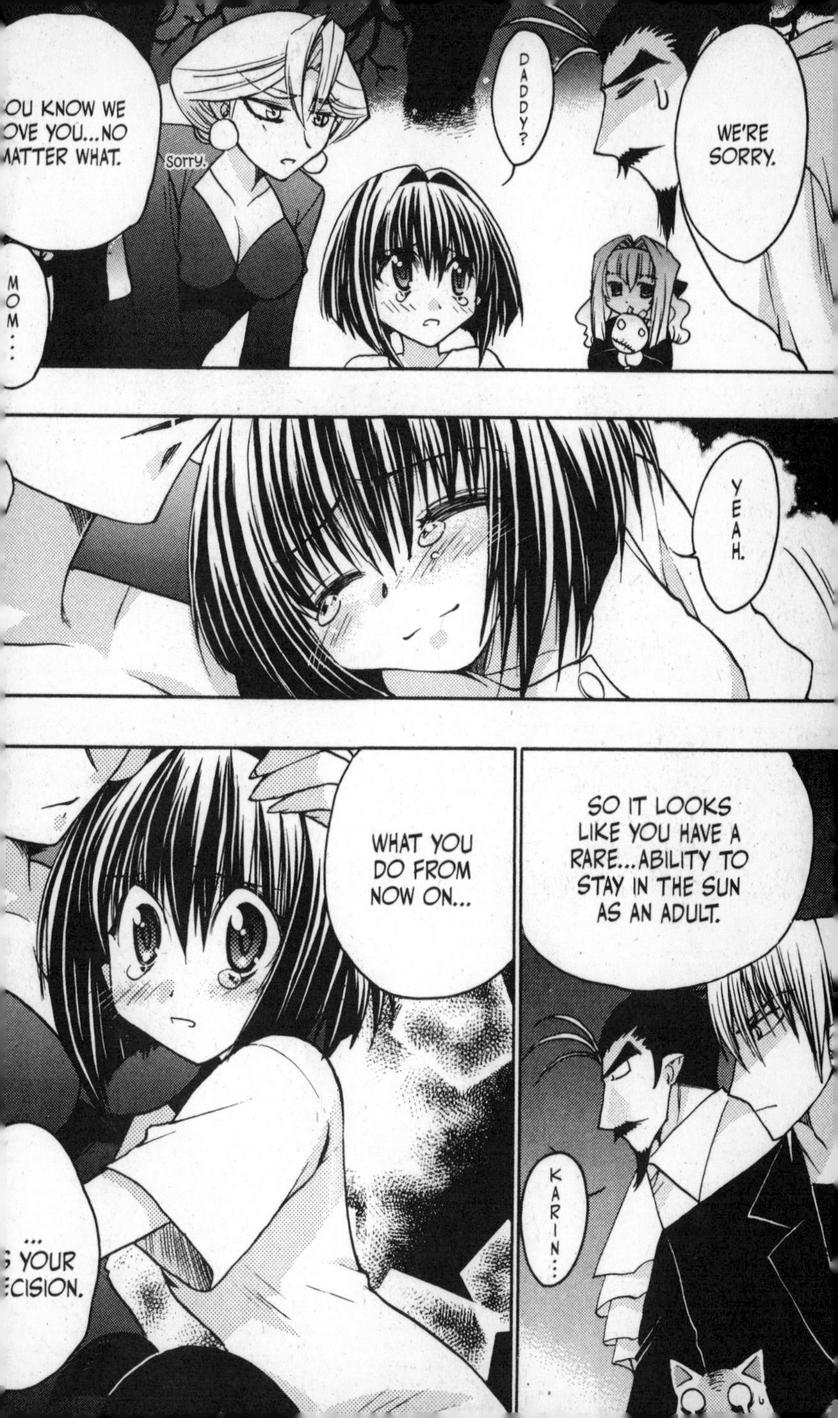
WE'RE SORRY.
DADDY?
OU KNOW WE OVE YOU...NO ATTER WHAT.
Sorry.
MOM...
YEAH.
SO IT LOOKS LIKE YOU HAVE A RARE...ABILITY TO STAY IN THE SUN AS AN ADULT.
KARIN...
WHAT YOU DO FROM NOW ON...
... YOUR ECISION.

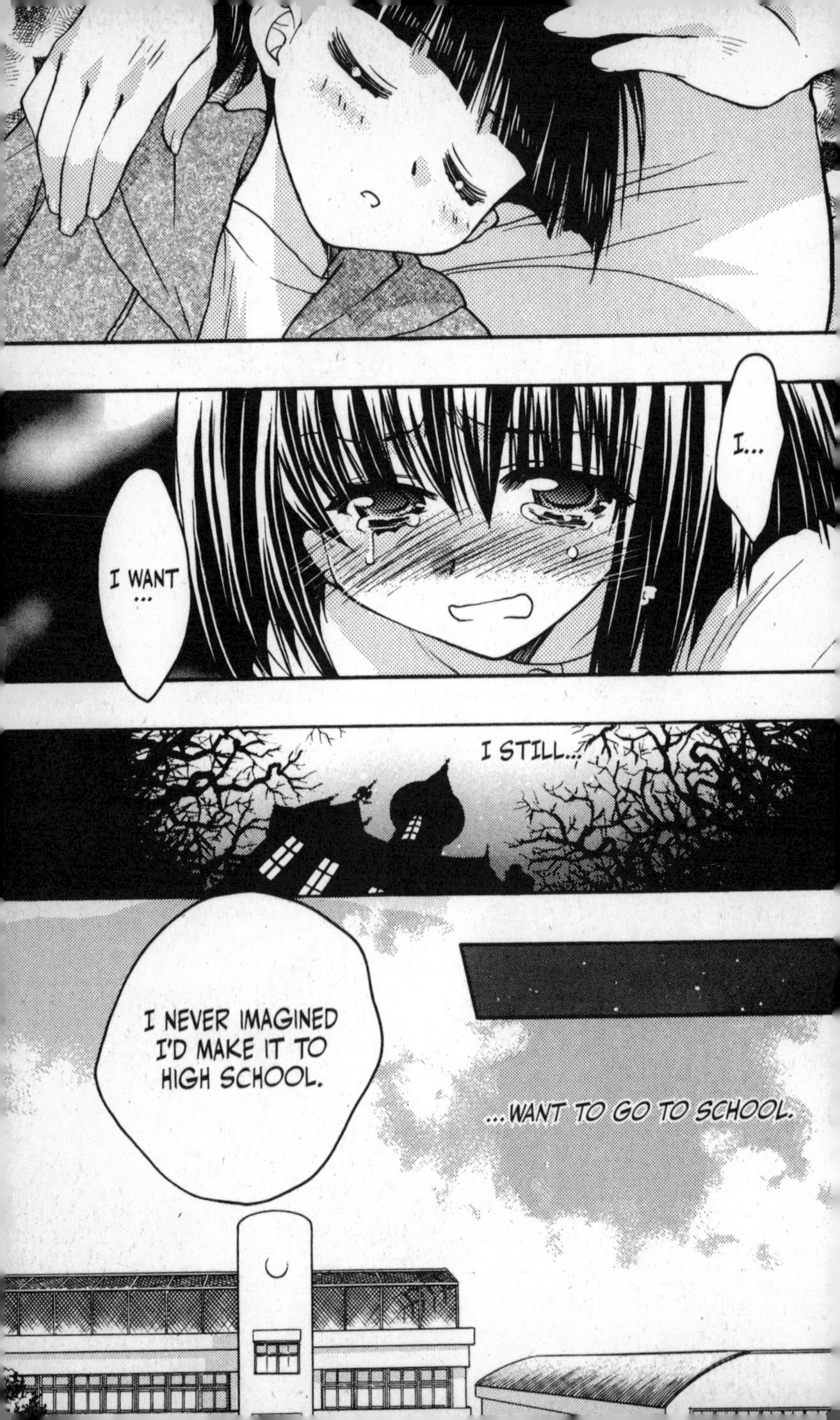
I...
I WANT ...
I STILL...
I NEVER IMAGINED I'D MAKE IT TO HIGH SCHOOL.
...WANT TO GO TO SCHOOL.

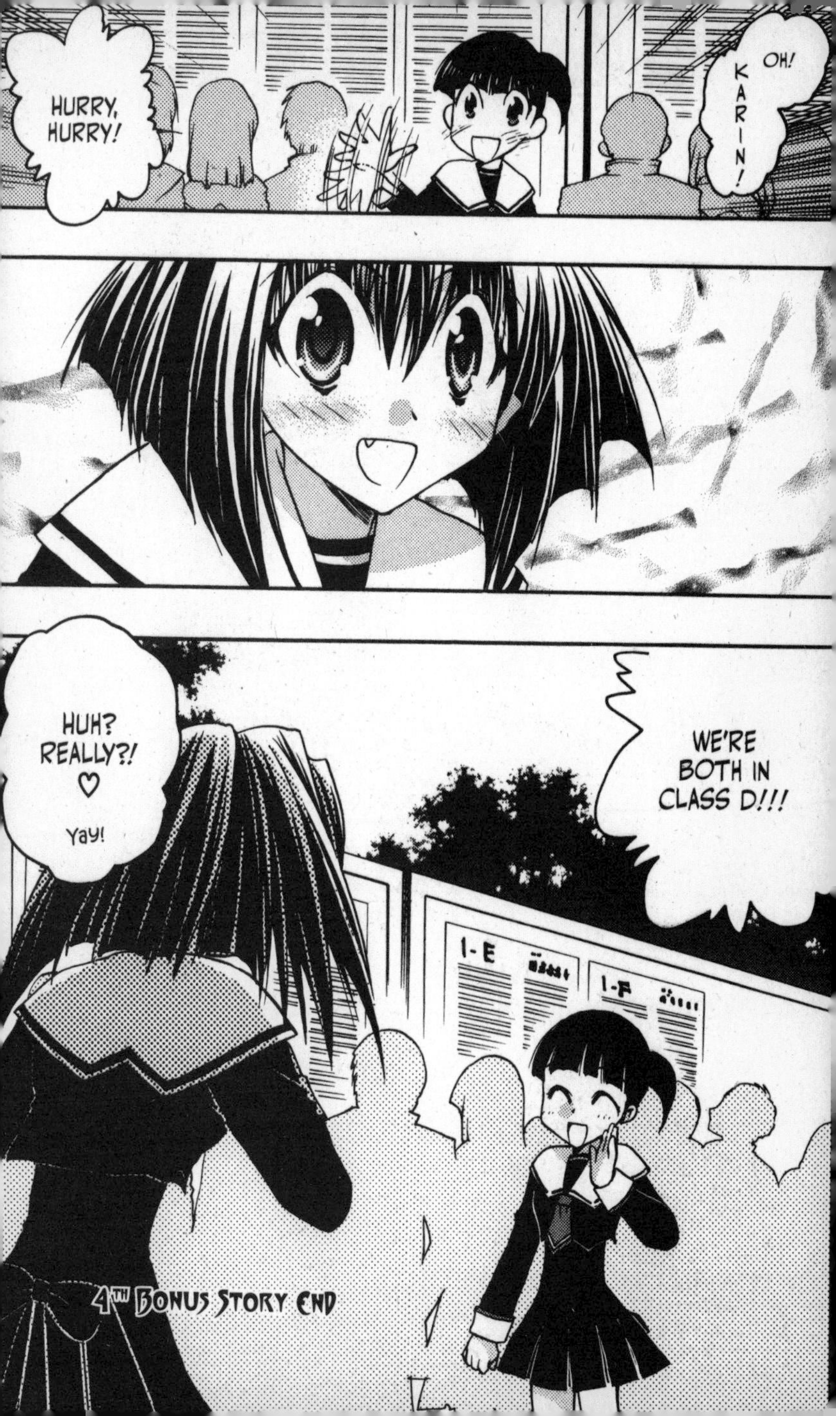
OH! KARIN!
HURRY, HURRY!
WE'RE BOTH IN CLASS D!!!
HUH? REALLY?! ♡
Yay!
1-F
1-E
4TH BONUS STORY END

Bonus

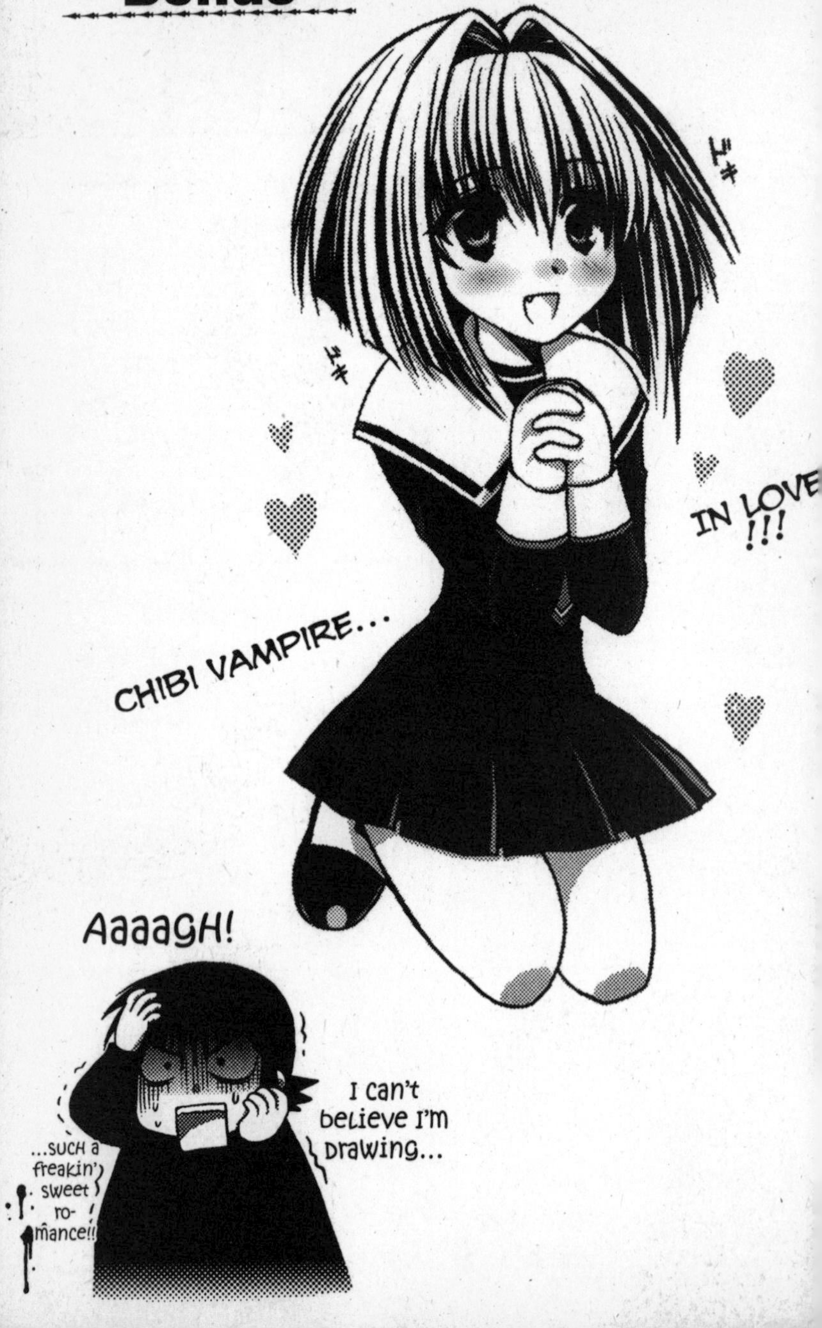
CHIBI VAMPIRE...
IN LOVE !!!
AaaagH!
I can't believe I'm Drawing...
...such a freakin' sweet ro-mance!!

The End of the First Arc

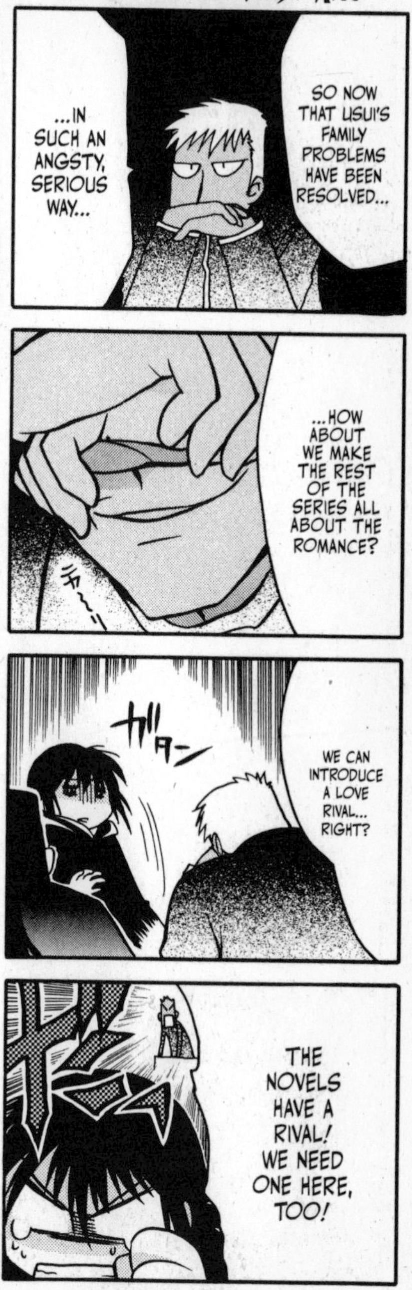
SO NOW THAT USUI'S FAMILY PROBLEMS HAVE BEEN RESOLVED...
...IN SUCH AN ANGSTY, SERIOUS WAY...
...HOW ABOUT WE MAKE THE REST OF THE SERIES ALL ABOUT THE ROMANCE?
WE CAN INTRODUCE A LOVE RIVAL... RIGHT?
THE NOVELS HAVE A RIVAL! WE NEED ONE HERE, TOO!

My Busy Year

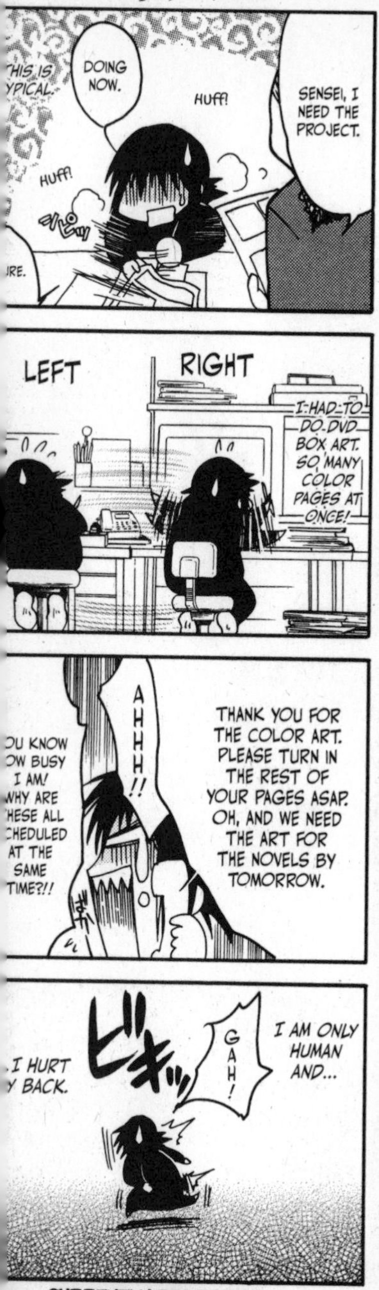
SENSEI, I NEED THE PROJECT.
HUFF!
DOING NOW.
THIS IS
YPICAL.
HUFF!
RE.
I HAD TO DO DVD BOX ART. SO MANY COLOR PAGES AT ONCE!
RIGHT
LEFT
THANK YOU FOR THE COLOR ART. PLEASE TURN IN THE REST OF YOUR PAGES ASAP. OH, AND WE NEED THE ART FOR THE NOVELS BY TOMORROW.
AHHHH!!
OU KNOW OW BUSY I AM! WHY ARE HESE ALL CHEDULED AT THE SAME TIME?!!
I AM ONLY HUMAN AND...
GAH!
ビキッ
I HURT Y BACK.

CURRENTLY RECOVERING...

OUT OF CONTROL

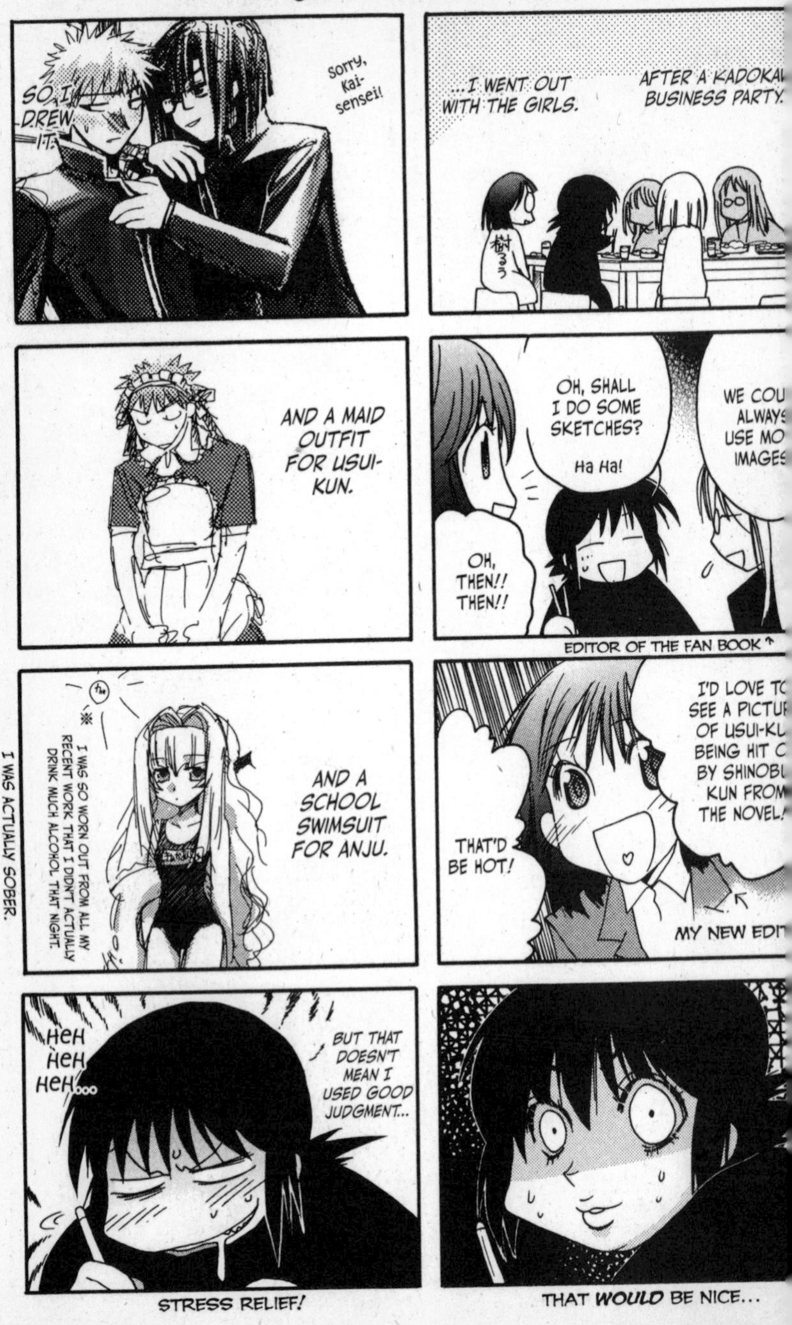
AFTER A KADOKAW BUSINESS PARTY.
...I WENT OUT WITH THE GIRLS.
樹るう
Sorry, Kai-sensei!
SO, I DREW IT.
WE COU ALWAYS USE MO IMAGES
OH, SHALL I DO SOME SKETCHES?
Ha Ha!
OH, THEN!! THEN!!
EDITOR OF THE FAN BOOK ↑
AND A MAID OUTFIT FOR USUI-KUN.
I'D LOVE TO SEE A PICTUR OF USUI-KU BEING HIT C BY SHINOBU KUN FROM THE NOVEL!
THAT'D BE HOT!
MY NEW EDIT
AND A SCHOOL SWIMSUIT FOR ANJU.
※ I WAS SO WORN OUT FROM ALL MY RECENT WORK THAT I DIDN'T ACTUALLY DRINK MUCH ALCOHOL THAT NIGHT.
I WAS ACTUALLY SOBER.
THAT *WOULD* BE NICE...
BUT THAT DOESN'T MEAN I USED GOOD JUDGMENT...
HEH HEH HEH...
STRESS RELIEF!

Just a Doodle

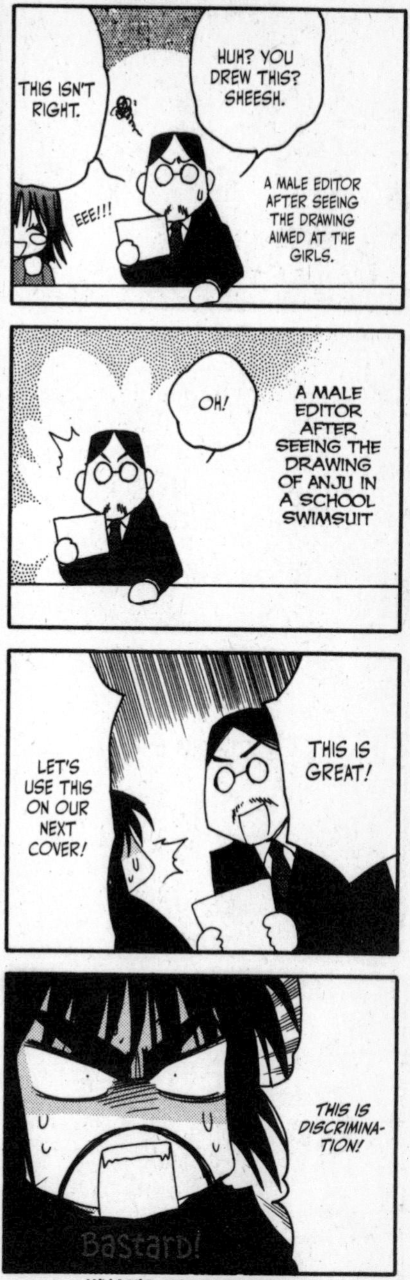

HUH? YOU DREW THIS? SHEESH.
THIS ISN'T RIGHT.
A MALE EDITOR AFTER SEEING THE DRAWING AIMED AT THE GIRLS.
EEE!!!
OH!
A MALE EDITOR AFTER SEEING THE DRAWING OF ANJU IN A SCHOOL SWIMSUIT
THIS IS GREAT!
LET'S USE THIS ON OUR NEXT COVER!
THIS IS DISCRIMINATION!
Bastard!

WHAT'S THE DIFFERENCE?

Just Had to Draw Karin

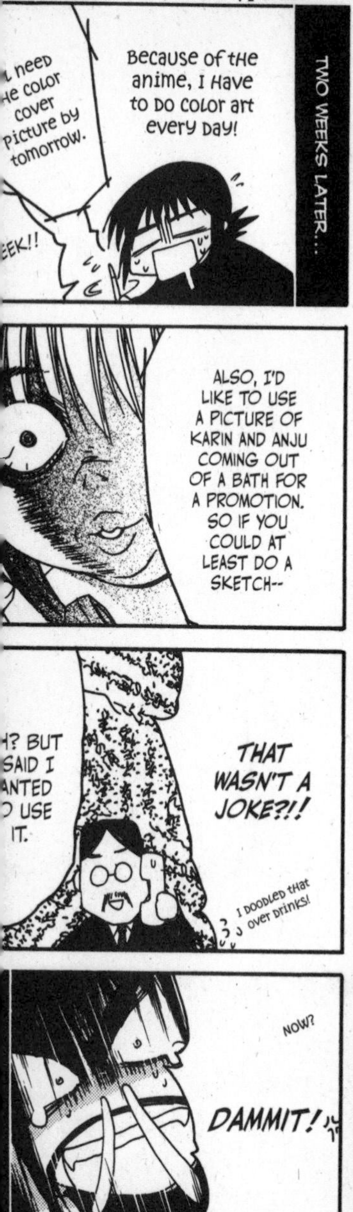

TWO WEEKS LATER...
Because of the anime, I have to do color art every day!
u need he color cover picture by tomorrow.
EEK!!
ALSO, I'D LIKE TO USE A PICTURE OF KARIN AND ANJU COMING OUT OF A BATH FOR A PROMOTION. SO IF YOU COULD AT LEAST DO A SKETCH--
THAT WASN'T A JOKE?!!
H? BUT SAID I ANTED O USE IT.
I DOODLED that over Drinks!
NOW?
DAMMIT!

LOVERS ON FILM

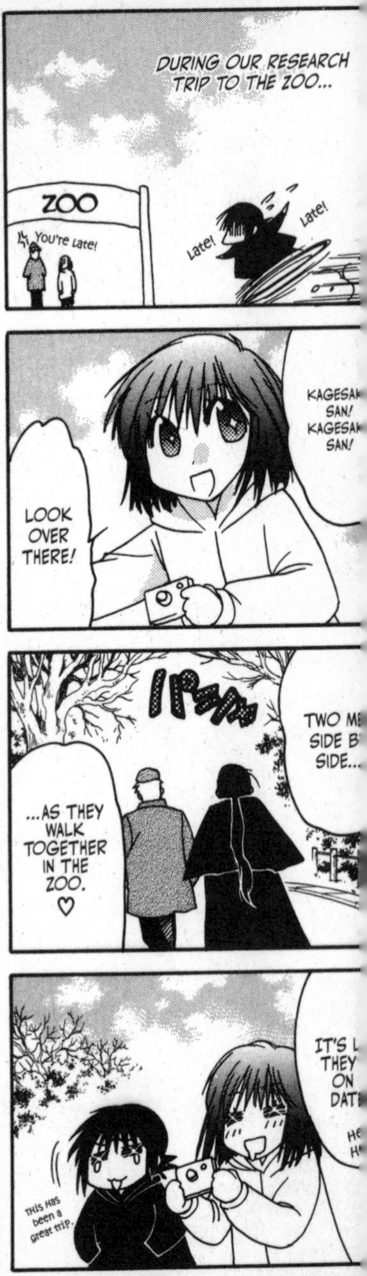
DURING OUR RESEARCH TRIP TO THE ZOO...
ZOO
You're Late!
Late!
Late!
KAGESAK SAN! KAGESAK SAN!
LOOK OVER THERE!
TWO ME SIDE B SIDE...
...AS THEY WALK TOGETHER IN THE ZOO. ♡
IT'S L THEY ON DAT
He H
This Has been a great trip.

AND NOW BACK TO THE STORY...

AFTER THE 4TH BONUS STORY

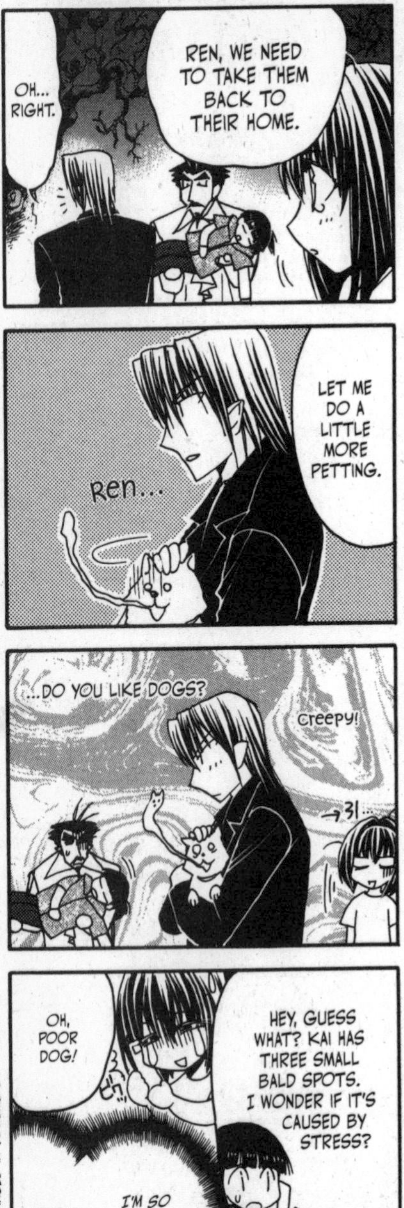
REN, WE NEED TO TAKE THEM BACK TO THEIR HOME.
OH... RIGHT.
LET ME DO A LITTLE MORE PETTING.
Ren...
Creepy!
...DO YOU LIKE DOGS?
HEY, GUESS WHAT? KAI HAS THREE SMALL BALD SPOTS. I WONDER IF IT'S CAUSED BY STRESS?
OH, POOR DOG!
I'M SO SORRY, KAI!
FORGIVE ME!

VAMPIRES DON'T USUALLY GET TO TOUCH DOGS!

CONTINUED IN VOLUME 9

IN OUR NEXT VOLUME...

chibi Vampire
TOKYOPOP
9
Created By:
Yuna Kagesaki

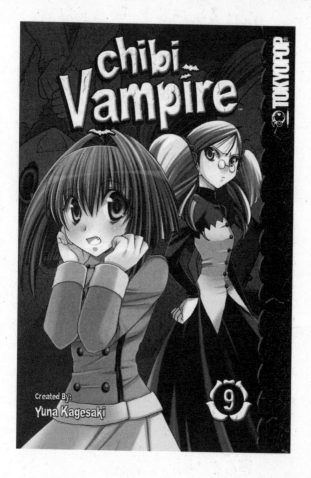

ANJU HAS SHOWN UP AT THE ZOO, AGAINST KARIN'S WISHES, TO KEEP AN EYE ON THE CLUMSY COUPLE. WHEN KENTA NOTICES ANJU, HE GRABS KARIN AND TAKES HER ON THE FERRIS WHEEL. THERE, HE TELLS HER HOW HE REALLY EELS, BUT WILL THE TRUTH DESTROY THEIR RELATIONSHIP? MEANWHILE, THE NEW GIRL IN TOWN, YURIYA, BEGINS SNOOPING AROUND IN SEARCH OF VAMPIRES. WHY IS SHE TRYING TO UNCOVER THE SECRET OF KARIN'S IDENTITY, AND WHAT SECRETS OF HER OWN DOES SHE HAVE?

NAUGHTY FUN AT THE PARK

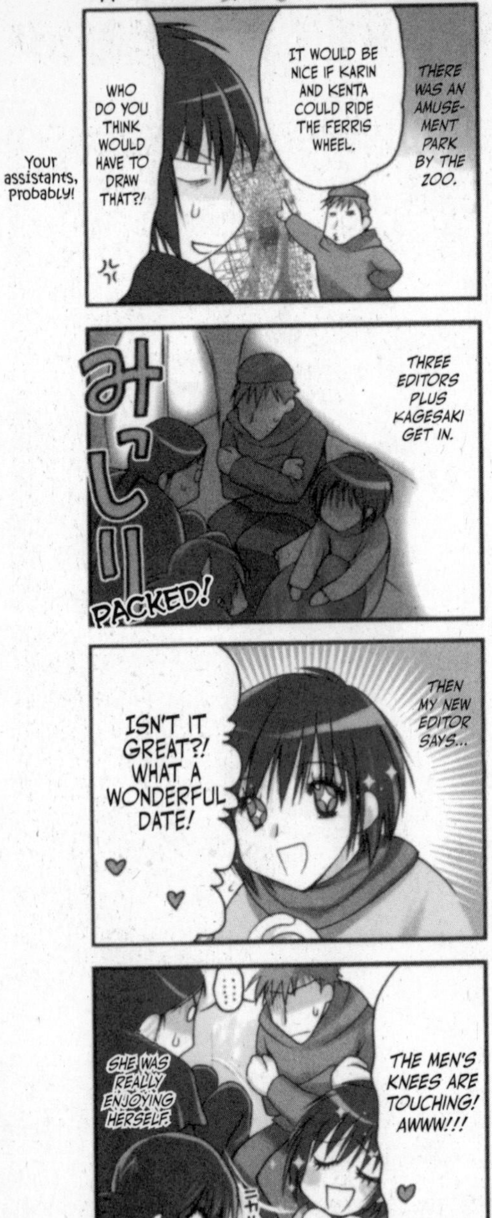
THERE WAS AN AMUSEMENT PARK BY THE ZOO.
IT WOULD BE NICE IF KARIN AND KENTA COULD RIDE THE FERRIS WHEEL.
WHO DO YOU THINK WOULD HAVE TO DRAW THAT?!
Your assistants, probably!
THREE EDITORS PLUS KAGESAKI GET IN.
みっしり
PACKED!
THEN MY NEW EDITOR SAYS...
ISN'T IT GREAT?! WHAT A WONDERFUL DATE!
THE MEN'S KNEES ARE TOUCHING! AWWW!!!
SHE WAS REALLY ENJOYING HERSELF.

I GOT A LOT OF INSPIRATION THAT DAY.

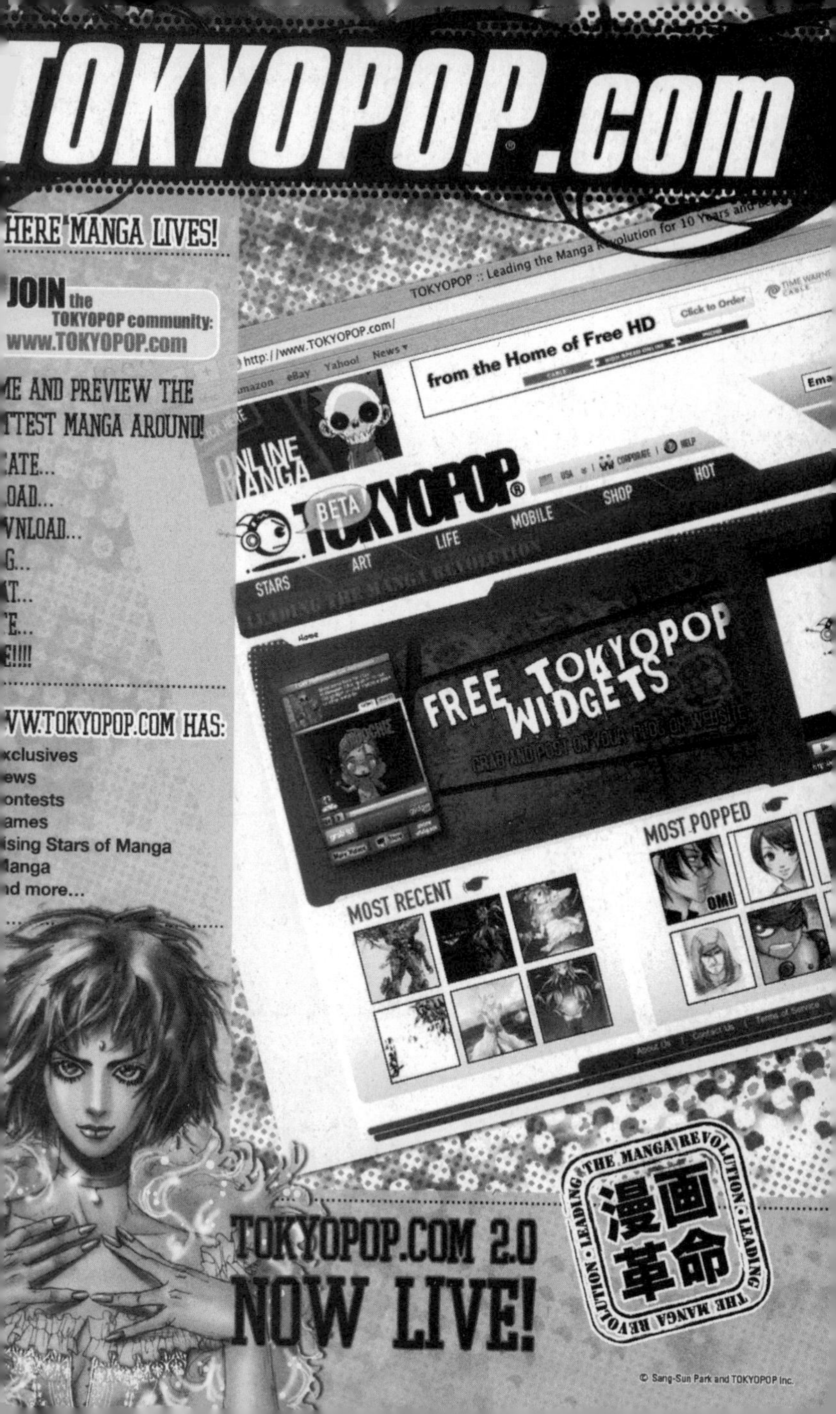

TOKYOPOP.com
HERE MANGA LIVES!
JOIN the TOKYOPOP community:
www.TOKYOPOP.com
IE AND PREVIEW THE
TTEST MANGA AROUND!
:ATE...
OAD...
VNLOAD...
G...
T...
E...
E!!!!
VW.TOKYOPOP.COM HAS:
xclusives
ews
ontests
ames
ising Stars of Manga
Ianga
nd more...
TOKYOPOP :: Leading the Manga Revolution for 10 Years and Beyond
http://www.TOKYOPOP.com/
from the Home of Free HD
Click to Order
ONLINE MANGA
TOKYOPOP
BETA
STARS
ART
LIFE
MOBILE
SHOP
HOT
FREE TOKYOPOP WIDGETS
MOST POPPED
MOST RECENT
TOKYOPOP.COM 2.0
NOW LIVE!
THE MANGA REVOLUTION
LEADING
漫画
革命
© Sang-Sun Park and TOKYOPOP Inc.

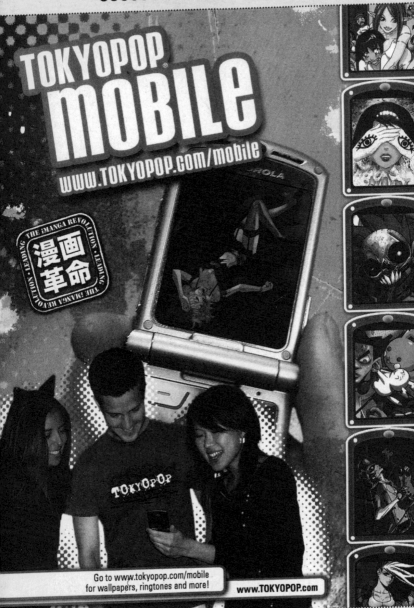

Fruits Basket™
sticker collection
stickers, pinups, and temporary tattoos!!

Fruits Basket
sticker collection
Natsuki Takaya
Includes pinups, stickers, and temporary tattoos!

EAUTIFY YOUR URROUNDINGS -AND YOURSELF!— VITH GORGEOUS ART ROM *FRUITS BASKET*!

Sample Page   Pinup Sample Page   Temp. Tattoo Sample Page

Winner of the American Anime Award for Best Manga

is limited edition art book includes:

- inup art of all your favorite *Fruits Basket* characters
- ickers
- mporary Tattoos

FOR MORE INFORMATION VISIT: WWW.TOKYOPOP.COM

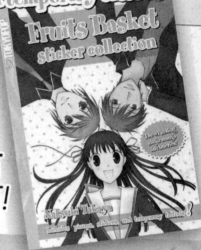

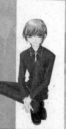

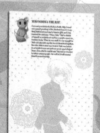

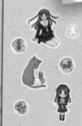

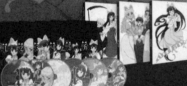
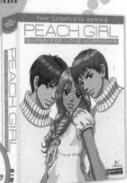
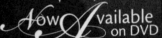

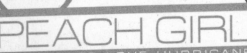

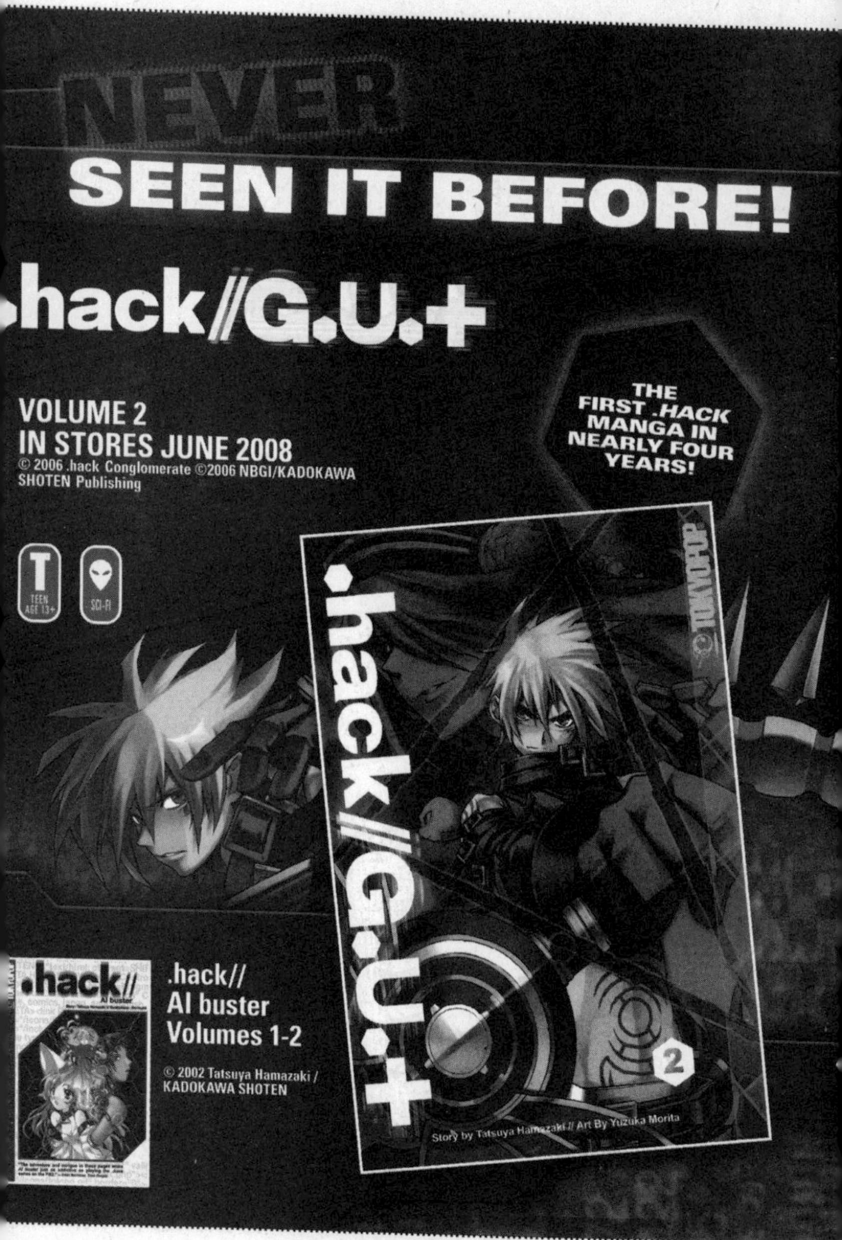
NEVER
SEEN IT BEFORE!
.hack//G.U.+
VOLUME 2
IN STORES JUNE 2008
© 2006 .hack Conglomerate ©2006 NBGI/KADOKAWA SHOTEN Publishing
THE FIRST .HACK MANGA IN NEARLY FOUR YEARS!
T
TEEN AGE 13+
SCI-FI
.hack//G.U.+
2
Story by Tatsuya Hamazaki // Art By Yuzuka Morita
TOKYOPOP
.hack//
AI buster
.hack//
AI buster
Volumes 1-2
© 2002 Tatsuya Hamazaki / KADOKAWA SHOTEN

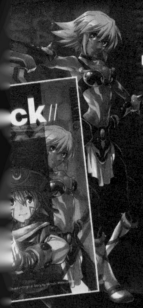
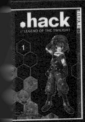
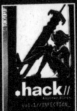

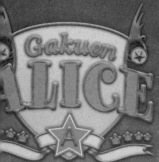
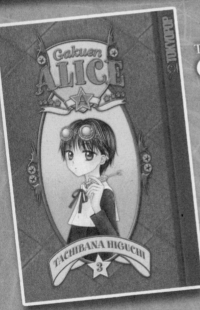

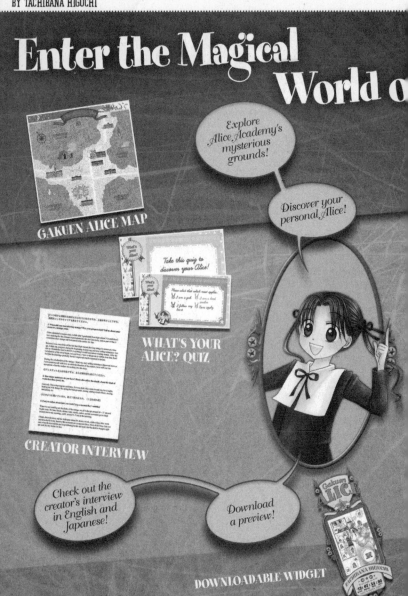

STOP!

This is the back of the book.
You wouldn't want to spoil a great ending!

P9-EEF-840

This book is printed "manga-style," in the authentic Japanese right-to-left format. Since none of the artwork has been flipped or altered, readers get to experience the story just as the creator intended. You've been asking for it, so TOKYOPOP® delivered: authentic, hot-off-the-press, and far more fun!

DIRECTIONS

If this is your first time reading manga-style, here's a quick guide to help you understand how it works.

It's easy... just start in the top right panel and follow the numbers. Have fun, and look for more 100% authentic manga from TOKYOPOP®!

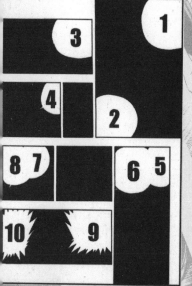

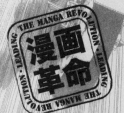